THE TROUBLE WITH WITCHES

A WICKED WITCHES OF THE MIDWEST MYSTERY BOOK NINE

AMANDA M. LEE

WINCHESTERSHAW PUBLICATIONS

Copyright © 2016 by Amanda M. Lee

All rights reserved.

No part of this book may be reproduced in any form or by any electronic or mechanical means, including information storage and retrieval systems, without written permission from the author, except for the use of brief quotations in a book review.

❦ Created with Vellum

PROLOGUE

"So ... I guess that's it, huh?"

Edith's expression was hard to read as she stared at me, her ethereal form flickering as she mimed gripping her hands together. She was a ghost, so the hand-wringing bit had to be a holdover from when she was alive.

"That's it," I confirmed, bobbing my head. I'd just told her who killed her decades ago. I'd also shared why she died, and discussed the nature of her horrible actions and how a lot of it was karma, even though no one deserved to die in the manner Edith did so many years earlier. "It's over and done."

"I see." Edith made a clucking sound as she shifted her eyes to the window. We stood – she hovered – in my office at The Whistler, Hemlock Cove's only newspaper, and even though we were alone, I knew my boyfriend, Landon Michaels, waited for me in the parking lot. He had offered to accompany me when I talked to Edith, but I knew it was something I had to do on my own.

"He's dead, Edith," I added, referring to the man who killed her. "He's gone. There's nothing left for you here."

The simple statement seemed to jolt Edith and she jerked her eyes back to me. "Nothing left for me?"

I squared my shoulders, reminding myself that I came here with a purpose and I intended to follow through no matter what. It was time for Edith to leave. "You stayed behind because you wanted to know who killed you," I reminded her. "You know that now. You know who killed you and why. You can be free and move on now."

Instead of being grateful for the words, Edith was furious. "Move on to where?" she sputtered. "This is the only life I've ever known. Where do you expect me to go?"

"Onward," I replied matter-of-factly. "I don't know what's on the other side, but it has to be better than how you've been since your death. This isn't a life. This isn't even a half-life. It's no life. There's more for you on the other side."

"How do you know that?"

That was a good question. "I have faith."

"You just said that I got a bad case of karma when I died ... and that's why I died ... but now you're saying there's something better out there for me? Which is it? You can't have it both ways."

"What you did when you were a teenager was reprehensible," I said, referring to her verbal torture of a girl she grew up with. "You did terrible things and you were paid back for them by dying. You've paid your dues, albeit in an extremely harsh and final way. You'll go to a better place."

"I don't think I can afford to believe that," Edith said.

She looked pitiable, but I couldn't muster much sympathy for her. I'd put up with a lot from her over the years – being one of the only people in a small town who can see and communicate with ghosts has certain drawbacks – but I was done feeling sorry for her.

"I don't want to play this game any longer, Edith," I said, looking away from her eyes. "I don't understand why you did what you did, and I think it would be better for everyone if you move on."

"And what if I don't?" Edith wasn't one to go quietly into the afterlife. I'd been expecting this.

"Then I'm going to have Aunt Tillie cast a spell so you're banned from the newspaper office," I replied. "We can put up wards so spirits aren't allowed inside. You'll essentially be free to wander wherever you want ... but not here."

I knew that came off as particularly harsh, but I also knew Edith had no interest in hanging out anywhere but The Whistler. I wanted her to move on because seeing her made me angry ... and disappointed ... and tired. I didn't want to be any of those things.

"But ... this is my home," Edith protested.

"A home is for the living," I argued. "You died a long time ago. It's time to let go of the past and move on to the future."

"I'm dead!" Edith barked. "I have no future."

"You have no future among the living, that's true," I said. "You do have a future on the other side, though."

"How can you possibly know that?"

"Because everyone is meant to move on," I said, adopting a pragmatic tone. "The people who remain behind do so by accident. They're anchored to this realm by horror, indecision and confusion. You're not afflicted with any of those things. It's time to embrace your fate."

For a moment I thought she would argue further with me, but her anger was too fierce. "Fine," Edith snapped. "I'm ready to move on. Are you happy? I'll leave you to your happy life and never darken your doorstep again!"

Edith was always dramatic, so I should've known that she would make this parting as painful as possible.

"Have a good afterlife," I said, refusing to give in and coddle her. "I hope you find what you're looking for on the other side."

It took another five minutes of ranting and raving from Edith, but eventually she dissipated and disappeared. I searched my heart for regret once she was gone, but found only relief.

I found Landon leaning against his Explorer in the parking lot, his arms crossed over his chest.

"All done?" Landon asked, brushing my blond hair from my face.

I nodded. "She's gone."

"How did she take it?"

"Pretty much as I expected she would."

"That bad, huh?" Landon looked exhausted. We'd had a long day. I'd almost been killed – for the second time in less than a week – and we both needed some rest and relaxation. I sank into him as he slipped his arms around me and pressed a kiss to my cheek. "I bet I know what will make you feel better."

I couldn't hide my smile. "Oh yeah? What?"

"I think we should get BLTs from the diner and eat them in a hot bath."

I giggled at his serious expression. "I thought you wanted dinner at the inn. They're going to have cake … and cookies … and all kinds of good food. I know you love bacon, but a BLT isn't going to bolster us for very long."

Landon tilted his head to the side, considering. "You have a point," he conceded. "Okay, new plan. We're going to eat dinner at the inn and then pretend we have terrible headaches the second we're done shoveling food into our mouths. Then we'll take a bath."

"I can live with that."

Landon kept me in his arms as he rocked back and forth, his lips pressed to the side of my face. "You did the right thing telling her to go, Bay. She couldn't stay. It was time for her to move on."

"I know." I took a moment to gather my thoughts and then pulled back my head and smiled. "Just think, though. This will be the first time I've been without a ghost hanging around in … years."

"Fun times," Landon enthused, poking my ribs. "We should throw a party."

"With bacon?"

"You know it." Landon smacked a hot kiss against my mouth before releasing me. "Let's go home, sweetie. I think we could both use a good night's sleep and a full day shut away from the rest of the world."

He didn't have to tell me twice. Unfortunately for us, rest and relaxation looked to be out of the question when a familiar face popped into view. The figure was short and compact, bright eyes glancing around as I hopped back to avoid inadvertently stepping through the new ghost.

"What is it?" Landon asked, instantly alert.

"There you are," Viola said, shaking her head. "I knew if anyone could see me it would be you."

My mouth dropped open as I stared at the woman – rather what was left of the woman. Only a few days earlier I'd been present at her death – which was bloody and enough to cause me to briefly go into shock – and now here she was in ghost form.

"I know who killed you," I blurted out.

"I know who killed me, too," Viola replied, unruffled. "I don't care about that."

"But ... you need to pass on," I pressed. "You shouldn't be here."

Viola didn't seem bothered by my tone – or my eagerness to get rid of her, for that matter. She merely glanced around with new ghost eyes and grinned. "I always wanted to haunt people. This is going to be neat," she said. "I think we should start with Margaret Little."

I felt helpless as I shifted my eyes to Landon, my shoulders sagging. "It's starting again."

Landon didn't look surprised or disturbed. "You're a special woman, sweetie. I think it's always going to happen."

Was that supposed to make me feel better? "But ... ."

"He's quite the hottie, isn't he?" Viola asked, looking Landon up and down. "How does he look naked?"

"I'm not answering that," I snapped, my cheeks coloring.

"That good, huh? I figured as much." Viola was all smiles as she scanned Hemlock Cove. "I'm betting there are a lot of people who look good naked in this town. I think I'm going to like haunting this place. Let the games begin."

ONE

SEVERAL WEEKS LATER

*S*ummer is almost gone.

That's all I could think about as I walked the dirt pathway between the Dandridge's parking lot and the remodeled façade of the old lighthouse that stretched majestically into the sky. The sun and humidity were still high, but I could almost feel autumn knocking on the door … and then summer will be gone and winter in northwestern Lower Michigan would be right around the corner.

I love spring, summer and fall. Michigan winters can be brutal, though. The days become shorter and the temperatures fall to inhumane levels. It's a punishing four months when all you want to do is cuddle in front of a fire and read a good book.

"What are you thinking about?" My cousin Thistle, her short-cropped hair a vibrant shade of aquamarine today, fixed me with a curious look as I walked beside her. I was so lost in thought I forgot I wasn't alone.

"It's almost fall," I replied, seeing no reason to lie. "It's almost time to pick pumpkins and bob for apples."

Thistle shot me an incredulous look, her eyes flashing. "When have you ever bobbed for apples?"

"I … ." Huh, that was a really good question. Our Great-Aunt Tillie told us that bobbing for apples was the germ equivalent of having unprotected sex with a ship full of sailors on shore leave. She made the declaration when we were young – I think I was eight – so I had no idea what that meant. Suffice it to say that we didn't bob for apples, though. Even though we didn't fully grasp her words, no one wanted to risk whatever depressing outcome she threatened.

"You know what I mean," I said finally, shoving a strand of my blond hair behind an ear as I focused on the lighthouse.

Sam Cornell, my cousin Clove's boyfriend, did a masterful job when he renovated it. Now they lived in the building together and were preparing for Hemlock Cove's busiest tourist season. They planned to turn the building and a new tanker ship Sam purchased into haunted destinations, and it was the latter we were here to get a gander at today.

You see, Hemlock Cove is all about tourism. From September to the end of November, our small town is so busy with tourists and fall color tour enthusiasts that we barely get any time off. Hemlock Cove rebranded itself as a tourism mecca several years ago when the small manufacturing base the town did have evaporated. It worked out well, and the town thrives as a fake paranormal destination.

Hemlock Cove was supposed to be full of witches and ghosts. The thing is, we're really witches. Yeah, you read that correctly. We're real witches pretending to be regular humans pretending to be fake witches. Did you keep up with that? I barely did either. Don't feel bad about it.

My name is Bay Winchester and I'm a witch. I'm also a reporter, daughter, cousin, niece and girlfriend. My life is full of work and family, and that's the way I like it. Er, well, I don't always like the family part. I love them – don't get me wrong – but they're a lot of work. Actually, they're not just work. They're what happens when you have a deadline looming for months and you leave three months of tasks to be completed in one day. No, that's not an exaggeration.

"I actually don't know what you mean," Thistle said, reminding me again that I wasn't alone.

My mind kept wandering. I couldn't explain it. I felt ... anxious. I had no idea why. Life was going well for me these days. My cousin Clove moved out of the guesthouse I shared with Thistle on our mothers' property – my mother and her two sisters, Marnie and Twila, run an inn on the site of the old family homestead – and she was happy and in love. That meant Thistle and I were at war for supremacy in the guesthouse, but that was hardly cause for concern. We were at war at least once a week, and Thistle was contemplating moving in with her boyfriend Marcus, so I might have the guesthouse to myself at some point. And, as for me, my FBI agent boyfriend Landon had spent the morning sending me flirty texts. I expected him to arrive later in the afternoon to spend the weekend. He technically lives in Traverse City, but finds as many excuses as possible to be with me in Hemlock Cove during the week. I looked forward to seeing him after two nights apart and yet ... something felt off.

"I can't even remember what we were talking about," I admitted, scratching my cheek as I locked gazes with Thistle. "Sorry. I guess I'm excited to see Sam's tanker."

Thistle was dubious as she looked me up and down. "You're excited to see Sam's tanker? Why?"

That was an excellent question. I had no idea why I was excited to see the tanker. I didn't dislike the idea of the tanker, mind you. Clove was so excited to decorate it – Thistle, too, for that matter – that I couldn't help but join in their enthusiasm. Seeing the tanker for the first time wasn't what had me so edgy, though.

"I don't know what's wrong," I said, staring at the huge bay window at the front of the Dandridge. "I feel uneasy."

Thistle and I fight like warring pop stars who think we'll be relevant forever, but when something serious throws off our equilibrium we always join forces. She looked concerned now.

"What's wrong?" Thistle asked. "Do you feel sick? Do you see a ghost? You're not pregnant, are you?"

I made a face apparently so comical Thistle couldn't stop herself from cracking a smile. "I'm not pregnant," I said. "I'm not sick either. I don't know how to explain what I'm feeling. It's ... difficult ... to put a name to."

"Try," Thistle suggested. "Although, I think it would be funny if you ended up pregnant. You would have to hear that whole 'giving away the milk for free' speech that Aunt Tillie whips out whenever she wants to distract the family from watching whatever she is doing. She makes everyone stare at us while she gets away with murder."

Thistle's eyes darkened at the thought and I had to bite the inside of my cheek to keep from laughing. Thistle and Aunt Tillie fight on a normal day. The past two weeks had been anything but normal. They'd been going at each other like crazy. They'd been fighting … and threatening curses … and pretty much annoying each other every chance they got. It was distracting, to say the least.

"Well, I'm not pregnant," I said. "Don't even think about spreading that rumor. I can only take so much."

"Oh, now that I know how much it's going to bother you, I'm totally going to spread that rumor," Thistle teased. The corners of her mouth tipped up in a smile but her eyes were serious when they latched onto mine. "You need to tell me what's wrong. You look kind of pale. Are you sure you're not getting sick?"

"I'm sure I'm not getting sick," I replied. "I simply feel uneasy. I don't know how to explain it."

"Do you think it's a premonition?"

Winchester witches all have special abilities. No one boasts legitimate premonitions, but that didn't mean it was out of the realm of possibility. I was fairly certain that wasn't happening, though. "I don't know what it is," I said. "I just feel off."

"You need to be more specific," Thistle challenged. "Do you feel off physically or mentally? If you're feeling off mentally I'm totally going to use it to my advantage and steal Clove's old room for my pottery wheel. Heck, if you're feeling off physically I'm going to do that. You've been warned."

I narrowed my eyes to dangerous blue slits. Ever since Clove moved out of the guesthouse Thistle and I had been locked in a battle of wills for control of the third room. I wanted to make it an office, and she was determined to make it a crafts room. It sat empty because both of us refused to give in. We are Winchesters, which means we're stubborn, so there is a decent possibility that room will sit empty forever.

"Don't push me," I said, wagging a finger as I focused on the back door of the Dandridge. "I'm not mentally or physically sick. I'm just ... worried."

Thistle cocked her head to the side as she regarded me, her expression grave. "Do you think something bad is about to happen?"

I saw no reason to lie to her. "Yes."

"Well, great," Thistle intoned, wrinkling her nose. "It's been quiet for two weeks. I guess we're due for a bout of trouble, huh?" She didn't look particularly perturbed at the prospect.

"I guess so," I conceded, forcing a wan smile. "No matter what it is, I don't think it's happening today, though. Let's get Clove and see this tanker we've heard so much about."

"That sounds like a plan."

"WHAT DO YOU THINK?" Clove was nervous. She chewed on her lower lip and stared at the Yeti Inferno. No, I'm not making it up. Whoever owned the 1970s tanker before Sam purchased it christened her the Yeti Inferno. I kind of liked it. Because Clove is afraid of Bigfoot, she balked when she heard it. That, of course, caused Thistle to tease her mercilessly for weeks.

"I think it looks pretty cool," I said. We stood on the dock behind the Dandridge and stared at Clove's new project. "It has a lot of personality."

In truth, the tanker wasn't nearly as bad off as I initially envisioned. It wasn't an overly large ship and it had been used for decades to ferry heating oil through the Great Lakes. The former owner retired her when she became more work than it was worth to keep up with the repairs. Sam didn't want to sail the tanker, though. He wanted to dock her and turn her into a haunted attraction. He got the tanker on the cheap and he'd already had a structural engineer examine her. The ship was sound and it had a lot of potential. If he wanted to make money

AMANDA M. LEE

off of it this year, though, we only had about six weeks to get it in shape.

"I think it's neat," Thistle said, her eyes gleaming. She's usually so snarky and sarcastic I forgot she's excitable when a new project looms. Sam said she could help decorate the tanker; she's an artist at heart so she jumped at the chance. "Let's check it out."

"Okay." Clove seemed relieved that we didn't dismiss the tanker outright.

We had to climb an iron ladder to make it onto the main deck, and because none of us are exactly known for our physical prowess we were breathing heavily when we hit the bow.

"You need to figure out an easier way to get people on board," Thistle said, resting her hands on her knees and wheezing. "That's not going to work for kids and older people."

"Sam is building a ramp," Clove said. "In fact, that's where he is now. He's meeting with the builder because we want to get that finished as soon as possible."

"I can see that," I said, working overtime to pretend I wasn't fatigued. "That's simply too much work for a normal person to deal with. Thankfully I'm a super witch, so it wasn't unbearably difficult for me."

Thistle snorted. "Super witch? You're sucking wind."

"So are you."

"I'm only resting like this because I don't want you to feel bad about what poor shape you're in," Thistle shot back.

"Hey, we're all in bad shape," I said. "In fact … I think we should start jogging or something. We need to build muscles and stuff, and get in good workout habits before we hit thirty. It's all downhill after that. Just ask our mothers."

"You have a point," Thistle conceded. "That doesn't mean I want to work out, though. Aunt Tillie said that being mean is a form of cardio. That's my plan. I'm just going to be mean to everyone."

"I think you're well on your way to mastering that," I said, smiling sweetly.

"Me, too," Clove grumbled, her long dark hair falling forward as she stared at a rusted patch of metal on the deck. "Sam is getting someone out to fix this, too. I'm worried it's going to be more trouble than it's worth to fix this thing up."

"I wouldn't worry about that," I said, kneeling. "If you need only a few cosmetic repairs this will be a real draw for people."

"I agree with Bay," Thistle said, her eyes flashing when I shot her a challenging look. She rarely agreed with me. "I agree with Bay on this," she clarified. "This tanker has a lot of potential.

"I mean ... think about it," she continued, taking on a dreamy expression as she stared at the open space at the front of the tanker. "We can do scary tableaus in every compartment. Even if we don't have time to get to everything this year for the Halloween season, we can close off some of the downstairs areas and focus on the deck and the main cabin this year."

"You can also have huge bonfires right over there," I said, pointing toward the campfire ring Sam built close to the lake. "People will love that. We can get several of those eerie fog misters to add to the ambiance. I even saw one shaped like a witch's cauldron that I kind of want to get for the guesthouse."

"I saw that, too," Thistle said, giggling. "It's purple. I love it."

"That does sound kind of cool," Clove conceded. "It's just ... daunting. There's so much work to do here."

"Well, there's no way we can do the entire tanker before Halloween this year," I said, my pragmatic side taking over. "It's impossible, so there's no sense in shooting for it. We need to decide what we can get done and then take our time doing the rest of the tanker."

"I think we should focus on the main deck and the compartments up here – it looks as if there's some storage space on the far end of the deck – and keep people out of the lower levels this year," Thistle said. "We'll be able to do some really neat stuff eventually, but we don't have time before the season hits. I can design some weird dolls and other decorations in my crafts room over the winter. By spring, we'll have so much done you'll be surprised."

I pursed my lips. It was a generous offer. Still .... "You don't have a crafts room," I reminded her.

"I will within the next week," Thistle said brightly. "Just you wait. It's going to be glorious."

"And yet it's not going to happen," I argued.

"Oh, it's going to happen."

"Do you guys always have to fight about what you're going to do with my old room?" Clove groused. "It makes me feel bad. I think you should maintain it as a shrine to me."

Thistle and I snorted in unison.

"That's not going to happen," Thistle said. "That guesthouse is small. We're going to use the space. I don't see why you're so upset, though. You live in a lighthouse with your boyfriend. You shouldn't care what we do with that room."

"It's not that," Clove protested. "It's just ... ."

I kept one ear on the conversation as I ran my hand over the metal wall outside of the main cabin. I'd heard this exact conversation so many times I'd lost count. The moment my fingertips touched the metal, though, my mind flooded with images and I felt as if my brain was overloading and the oxygen was being sucked from my lungs.

I felt my knees buckle and I had no chance of catching myself. As I plunged toward the hard deck surface, a myriad of images flitted through my mind, each one more dark and distressing than the previous one.

I didn't realize I was going to lose consciousness until the screaming started. It seemed to go with the images, yet I wasn't sure if the sound was coming from someplace else or me. I didn't get a chance to give it much consideration, because my mind couldn't handle all of the images and I slapped up barriers to keep the flood of bloody scenes out.

That's when my mind overloaded and everything tilted as image after image blurred into one another.

TWO

"*B*ay?" I could hear Clove's voice through the murky kaleidoscope of images in my head but I couldn't focus on her because my mind was too busy. All I could see was blood, and Clove's voice wasn't strong enough to drown out the screaming.

Thistle took another approach.

"Bay!" She shook me so hard I thought my head would snap off my neck.

I snapped my eyes open, the bright light of the day shoving the horrible images out as Thistle's face swam into view. "I ... ." My tongue felt thick and I couldn't make my mouth work.

"Are you okay?" Thistle looked panicked as she struggled to keep me in a sitting position.

"Are you dying?" Clove asked, her brown eyes filling with tears as she stared at me. "Are you having an aneurysm?"

"How could she possibly know that?" Thistle asked, annoyed. "If she's having an aneurysm her brain would explode and she'd never realize what was happening."

"You don't know that."

"That makes more sense than her being able to tell you she's having an aneurysm."

"I didn't realize you were a doctor," Clove said dryly. "I must've missed all of those hard years you put in at medical school."

"Oh, shut up," Thistle said. "You're such a ... kvetch."

That's what Aunt Tillie called Clove whenever things got dramatic. It seemed to fit.

"I'm not having an aneurysm," I forced out. I was happy to find that I didn't appear to be slurring my words, and the pounding in my head had receded. "I'm ... okay." That wasn't completely true, but I was feeling better.

"Have something to drink," Clove said, rummaging in her small backpack and returning with a bottle of water. "Maybe you're dehydrated. Wait ... are you pregnant? Did you pass out because you're pregnant?"

I grabbed the bottle from her, my hands shaky as I tried to remove the cap. Thistle finally untwisted it for me and I swallowed two mouthfuls before speaking again.

"I'm not pregnant," I said, knitting my eyebrows as I regarded her. "That's the second time someone said that to me today. I'm starting to think I need to go on a diet."

"Oh, no," Thistle deadpanned. "The baby bump looks good on you."

"Don't make that joke," I hissed, rubbing my forehead. "That's the last thing I need. If you even hint at that my mother will start knitting baby booties and sit on Landon until he proposes."

"Yes, but that could be fun." Thistle's tone was light but her gaze was serious. "What happened?"

"I'm not sure," I said. "I ... saw something." Actually I saw a lot of things but I couldn't put them in order and it was difficult to wrap my head around the images, let alone explain them.

"What did you see?" Clove's eyes were bright. "Ghosts?"

Most of the Winchester witches have special abilities. My mother and aunts are kitchen witches, but fully capable of whipping up potions and spells. I see and talk to ghosts – which is a royal pain in the butt – but that's not what happened this time.

"I ... no," I said, racking my brain for an explanation. "At least I don't think it was ghosts. I definitely saw something, though."

"What?" Thistle was intrigued and she leaned forward once she realized I could support my own weight. "Does this have anything to do with what you said when we were walking up the driveway?"

"I ... don't know." That wasn't a lie. It wasn't exactly the truth either. My intuition told me this was exactly what I'd been dreading. How could I possibly know that, though?

"What did she say when you were walking up the driveway?" Clove asked.

"Nothing." I massaged my forehead. "It's nothing."

"She said she felt uneasy," Thistle supplied. "She couldn't explain it. She said it was like a feeling of dread. I asked her if she was pregnant and threatened to take advantage of the situation to turn your room into a crafts area – you know, the usual stuff – but she said that wasn't it."

"I don't like this," Clove said. "Maybe we should take you to the hospital. If you are pregnant ... ."

"I'm not pregnant!" I exploded, taking them both by surprise. "Stop saying that. Good grief. Landon and I are happy, and I don't need you guys scaring him off by saying that."

"I was just joking," Thistle said, her expression rueful. "I'm not sure Clove's suggestion to go to the hospital is a bad one, though. Maybe you really do have an aneurysm or something."

"That's not what happened." In truth, a legitimate medical condition would be easier to deal with than what I witnessed when I touched the side of the tanker. "I saw something. It was too much for my brain to absorb at once, so it knocked me for a loop. I'm fine now."

Clove didn't look convinced. "What did you see?"

"Something horrible." The words were out of my mouth before I had a chance to reflect on whether or not it was wise to utter them. "It was like layers and layers of ... horror."

"I don't understand what you're saying," Thistle admitted, settling cross-legged on the deck next to me. She enjoyed messing with my brain, but when things went bad – as they often did in the Winchester household – she was the first to jump to everyone's defense. "What did you see?"

"I'm not sure how to explain it," I replied, licking my lips. "I ... it was bloody."

"Bloody?" Clove's voice hopped an octave. "What do you mean it was 'bloody?'"

"I don't know how to explain it." My patience was wearing thin. The only thing keeping me in check was the fact that I knew exploding at Clove and Thistle would make matters worse. "I touched that wall and I ... saw people running. They were screaming. There was a knife ... and a lot of blood ... and there were bodies on the deck."

Clove's hand flew to her mouth as she glanced around the deck. It was the middle of the afternoon but from the expression on her face you'd have thought we were in a *Friday the 13th* movie and she had just had sex. "Ghosts?"

"She already said she didn't see ghosts," Thistle said. "Pay attention."

"It was a legitimate question," Clove protested.

"You're being annoying," Thistle snapped. "Shut up." She focused on me. "Did you see it like a vision?"

I nodded as I stared at Clove. She was offended by Thistle's bossy nature – which she should be used to, because Thistle came out of the womb bossy – but she didn't like being bullied. Whenever something bad happened, Thistle always reverted to bullying mode.

"Do you think something bad happened on this ship?" Thistle pressed.

I shrugged. That was exactly what I thought, but I was fairly certain that admitting that to Clove was the wrong way to go. "I'm not sure what I think," I said after a beat. "Let's get off the ship, though. My stomach is a little queasy and I want my feet on solid land."

In truth, I wanted off this vessel in case I accidentally touched something and was overwhelmed by frightening images again.

"That sounds like a plan," Thistle said, gripping an arm and helping me struggle to my feet. "Then, when we get on dry land, you're going to tell me exactly what you saw. If this tanker is haunted, we could have an entirely new set of problems to deal with."

Well, crap. That's not exactly how I wanted to break the news to Clove.

"Haunted?" Clove's voice was unnaturally squeaky. "I knew this tanker was a bad idea."

Because she's the one who told Sam it was a great idea, I had my doubts. "Let's just go back to the Dandridge," I suggested. "I'm sure things aren't as bad as you think."

I was almost positive that was true.

"I THINK something really bad happened on the tanker and it could be haunted."

That probably wasn't the best way to broach the subject with Clove, but once we got back to the Dandridge and I was comfortable on the couch I started feeling bolder. She took the news better than I expected.

"I knew it!" Clove flailed her hands in the air. "It's the end of the world, isn't it?"

Thistle made an exaggerated face as she sat in the chair next to the couch. "Oh, chill out. You're such a drama queen."

"That's easy for you to say," Clove shot back. "Sam invested a lot of money in that tanker. If he just loses it ... ."

"We don't know that's the case," I cautioned, holding up my hand. Sometimes I think Thistle is mean to Clove and enjoys seeing how far she can push her. Other times I think Clove deserves to be pushed because she has a whiny quality that's completely unattractive when I'm tense. Oh, who am I kidding? It's unattractive when I'm relaxed, too.

"You just said that the tanker was haunted," Clove protested.

"I said I think it's haunted," I clarified. "I didn't see any actual ghosts."

"What did you see?" Thistle asked, her expression serious. "Was it bad?"

"It wasn't good," I replied. "It was ... dark. There were multiple images layering over one another. I saw people running and screaming. I saw a hand holding a knife."

"Was it men? Women?"

"Mostly men, but there were a few women," I said. "I don't know how to explain it. I saw a few bodies hit the deck ... and blood was seeping into the grates. The rusty grate you pointed at. That was covered in blood."

"Oh, well, great," Clove said. "Blood is eating away at the ship. It's going to sink thanks to blood. It really is the end of the world."

"Stop being such a kvetch," Thistle warned, scorching Clove with a dark look. They shared ownership of a magic shop in town and spent an inordinate amount of time together so they fought more than anyone else. "We don't know what's wrong and there's no sense freaking out before we know the whole story."

"I agree with Thistle," I offered. "It's going to be okay, Clove. Even if it is haunted ... well ... we're witches. We can cleanse the tanker of bad elements and help the ghosts pass over. It's not the end of the world."

"I also think we should take you to the clinic to have your head checked out," Thistle added.

"I don't agree with Thistle any longer," I said. "I'm fine. I was momentarily overwhelmed. I'm not going to the clinic."

Thistle and Clove exchanged a look. I knew what they were thinking but I refused to give in. "Also, I don't want you mentioning to anyone what happened," I added. "It's not going to do anyone any good, and they'll only worry if they find out I kind of passed out."

"Who is anyone?" Thistle challenged.

"Anyone outside of the three of us."

Clove balked. "But ... I can't lie to my mother. You know I can't. She always figures it out and is mean when she knows I'm keeping something from her."

"How will she figure it out?" I challenged, annoyed. "Also, how is it lying? I'm not asking you to lie. I'm asking you to not volunteer information. There's a difference."

"Not really," Clove sniffed, crossing her arms over her chest as she stared at the wall.

"While I'm not as puritan as Clove about telling the truth, I'm not exactly keen on keeping this to ourselves," Thistle hedged. "What if it happens again? What if you are sick? I think you should at least tell Landon."

Landon was the last one I wanted to tell. Er, actually that wasn't true. Mom and Aunt Tillie were the last ones I wanted to tell. Mom would hover and try to make me eat soup in bed. Aunt Tillie would call me a wimp and taunt me until I cried. Landon, though, would worry until it consumed him.

"No," I said, shaking my head. "He has enough on his plate. He's been working that gambling ring in Traverse City for two straight weeks. He's exhausted. I want him to relax this weekend."

"He would want to know," Thistle challenged. "If the same thing happened to him and he didn't tell you, there would be a lot of yelling and finger pointing. It doesn't seem right to keep him in the dark."

She had a point. Still .... "I don't want to worry him," I said. "It was a fluke thing. It won't happen again. I'm fine."

"Okay." Thistle held up her hands in mock surrender. "I won't tell him."

"Thank you." I was secretly relieved. I wasn't sure she'd go along with my plan.

"I won't tell him right now," Thistle corrected. "If something else happens, though, all bets are off. I'll tell him and not feel guilty at all."

I ground my back teeth as I regarded her. "I ... fine."

"Great," Thistle said, brightening considerably. "Now, what should we do about the tanker? I think we should conduct a little research and see what we find out about it."

"I think that's a good idea."

"What's a good idea?"

The three of us jerked our heads in the direction of the door and forced smiles as Sam walked into the room. He didn't seem surprised to see us. He had a bright smile on his face as he dropped a kiss on Clove's cheek. Apparently he hadn't been eavesdropping long because he had no idea anything was wrong.

"We were just talking about Thistle sketching out some haunted scene ideas," I lied. "Because the tanker is so big we figure that decorating only the main deck and cabin will be feasible this year."

"Yeah," Thistle said, recovering quickly. "That way we can take our time and come up with really creepy stuff for below deck. I was thinking we could do a haunted pirate room, but that will take time to plan."

"That sounds good to me," Sam said, clearly oblivious to the underlying tension flitting through the room. "As long as we make some money this season, I'm happy to give you the time to come up with something really cool. I prefer doing it right."

"We all would," I said, forcing a smile.

"Speaking of doing it right," Sam said, his eyes twinkling as he turned to Clove. "I have some huge news."

"Really?" Clove was intrigued despite herself.

"Really." Sam bobbed his head. "My parents are coming for a visit and they can't wait to meet you."

All thoughts of tanker hauntings and aneurysms obviously flew out of Clove's head as her face paled and she gripped the arm of the couch tightly. "What?"

"My parents are coming," Sam said, smiling. "They want to meet you and see the Dandridge and the tanker. They'll be here in a few days."

Clove's mouth dropped open. "I ... a few days?"

Sam nodded.

Clove hopped to her feet. "Why didn't you tell me? This place is a total mess. We have to clean everything from top to bottom."

Sam was surprised. "We do?" He glanced around. "It looks clean to me."

"It's clean for us and everyday guests," Clove explained. "It's not clean for mothers. Your mother can't see it looking like this."

Sam didn't seem motivated to join in with the cleaning even when Clove handed him a broom.

"And the kvetch is back," Thistle said, grinning as she leaned back in the chair and watched Clove melt down about the lack of cleaning supplies. "All is right with the world."

"You're kind of mean," I pointed out.

"That's also right with the world."

THREE

"There's my girl."

Landon was all smiles when he walked through the front door of the guesthouse shortly after four. He had a duffel bag in one hand and a stack of files in the other – which indicated he would have to do some work over the weekend – but I was so happy to see him I didn't care.

I gave him a big hug, giggling when he dropped the duffel bag and made growling noises into my neck as he kissed it.

Landon Michaels doesn't look like a typical FBI agent. His black hair is shoulder length, and his face is angular and handsome. He's all lean muscle and strength. There's something very masculine about him despite the long hair, which he maintains he needs in case he has to go undercover.

We met when he was undercover, and the long hair was something of a turn on. That was almost a year ago, though, and the idea of him taking off for extended periods for undercover assignments makes me sad. I know it's part of the deal – dating a law enforcement official is never easy – but when it does happen I'm sure I'll be despondent. Wait … did that sound co-dependent? Who cares, right? He's freaking hot.

"I missed you this week," I said, hugging him close. "I haven't seen you for two nights. It feels like forever."

"I was here for dinner and to spend the night Tuesday," he reminded me, pulling back so he could study my face. "I think you're just addicted to me."

"She's warm for your form," Marcus teased as he walked out of Thistle's room. He and Thistle had been dating for a few months longer than we had, and he's much more laid back than Landon. Everyone gets along, though. Er, well, everyone gets along as much as possible. Thistle and I like to fight at least three times a week. I think it keeps us looking young.

"She is warm for my form," Landon agreed, his grin impish as he smacked a loud kiss against my lips. "I missed you, too."

"Oh, great," Thistle muttered, a dour look on her face when she joined us in the living room. "Are you guys going to be all mushy for the next few hours? You know how much I hate that."

Landon regarded Thistle with a dubious look. "What don't you hate? As far as I can tell, you hate pretty much everything."

"Well, I definitely hate you today," Thistle shot back, not missing a beat. "As for what I like … well … ." She smiled at Marcus and pushed his blond hair away from his face. "I think Marcus is the only thing I like on a regular basis."

"Oh, and you accuse us of being mushy," I teased.

"You are mushy," Thistle said, flopping on the couch next to Marcus. "I find it completely embarrassing how mushy you are."

"I find it completely embarrassing how mushy you are," I shot back.

"Oh, I like it when you're both mushy," Landon said, snagging me around the waist and pulling me onto his lap as he settled in the large armchair at the edge of the room. "I think we should have a mushy weekend where we all get along and no one fights."

"I second that," Marcus said. "I like quiet weekends."

"Well, we might be okay for tonight, but it won't be a stress-free weekend," I said, working overtime to ignore the way Landon studied my profile. It felt as if he was trying to burrow into my soul.

"We have a family catastrophe to deal with for the bulk of the weekend."

"Oh, good," Landon deadpanned. "I love family catastrophes. What's wrong this time? Is Aunt Tillie selling wine again? Is she on the warpath? Should we buy a combat helmet for Mrs. Little? Actually, that might be fun. Let's buy Mrs. Little a combat helmet and lock her in a room with Aunt Tillie and see what happens."

"For the first time in I don't know how long, our catastrophe has nothing to do with Aunt Tillie," I replied. "It's Clove."

Landon's shoulders tightened. "What's wrong with Clove? She's not moving back in, is she? This place is small enough without adding her back into the mix. Although, to be fair, that would end the fights between you and Thistle about what to do with the extra room. Maybe she should move back in."

"You're extremely scattered today, huh?" I teased, running my index finger down his cheek. "Is this what happens when you spend more than one night away from me?"

"That is agony," Landon confirmed, grinning. "I thought I was getting sick this morning. It turns out I just missed my Bay."

"Oh, puke," Thistle muttered, rolling her eyes. "I cannot stand one more second of your schmaltzy verbal copulation. Why don't you guys just go in the bedroom and do it so I don't have to hear the buildup. I think we'd all appreciate that."

"I would totally appreciate it," Landon said, refusing to let Thistle rile him. "I think that sounds like a fabulous idea."

"Great," Thistle shot back. "That will give Marcus and me time to turn the extra bedroom into my crafts room. I'll pay you twenty bucks if you last more than twenty minutes."

Landon's smile tipped down into a frown. "I miss Bay every moment I'm away from her," he said. "I don't miss you, though."

"Right back at you."

"Okay, it's the beginning of the weekend," Marcus said, holding up his hands. "Let's not start it out on the wrong foot, shall we?"

"I agree," I said, shifting on Landon's lap. "There's no reason to fight ... especially because I'll make you eat dirt if you do anything to that room when I'm not looking, Thistle."

"Ooh. I'm so scared." Thistle mimed as if her hands trembled. "We both know I could take you in a fight."

"I don't think that's true, but there's no reason to test your theory without mud ... or at least Jell-O," Landon said, tightening his arms around my waist. "If you guys keep this up, I'm going to buy a roll of duct tape and cut the guesthouse down the middle. It will be like an episode of *The Brady Bunch*, and no one wants that."

"Oh, I think that sounds cute," Marcus teased, poking Thistle's side to get her to relax. "I want to be Greg if we play *The Brady Bunch*."

"No way," Landon shot back. "I'm Greg. You can be Peter."

"Why would you possibly want to be Greg?" I challenged. "He was a total geek."

"They were all geeks," Landon replied. "Don't kid yourself. Still, Greg was the coolest of the geeks, and because you're the oldest, that means you're Marcia. Greg and Marcia hooked up behind the scenes. That means I'm Greg."

"You know way too much about *The Brady Bunch*," I said.

"My mother had a thing for the show and always made me watch it," Landon explained. "Besides, you have a weird thing for *Little House on the Prairie*. At least my thing doesn't include churning butter and going blind."

"That's a great show."

"Whatever." Landon kissed my cheek. "I'm Greg."

"Well, I'm not Jan," Thistle said. "I'm not Cindy either. She had a lisp, and those curls were so annoying."

"You should be Alice," I suggested. "You can be our maid for the weekend. I think it works out for everyone."

Thistle scowled. "I hate you sometimes. I'm totally going to turn Clove's room into a crafts area and lock you out."

"I would like to see you try."

"I'm going to smack you in the mouth when I do it, too," Thistle said, smiling sweetly.

"Oh, I love being surrounded by such prim and proper ladies,"

Marcus teased, his eyes flashing. "Go back to the family catastrophe, though. What is it?"

"Yeah, I almost forgot about that," Landon said. "What's darkening the Winchester doorstep this weekend? Ghosts? Werewolves? If it's zombies I'm going to rent a hotel room for three days, because no one wants to deal with that."

I snickered. "No, it's not really a catastrophe," I said. "Er, well, it's not a catastrophe for us. It's more of a catastrophe for Clove."

"Meaning?"

"Sam's parents are coming to town," Thistle offered. "Clove was in a perfectly good mood until Sam told her. Now she's freaking out and forcing him to clean the Dandridge."

"Why is that a problem?" Landon asked, genuinely curious. "I would think Clove would be happy to meet the Cornells. They're Sam's family, after all. What could possibly go wrong?"

I arched a challenging eyebrow as I regarded him. Did he seriously not remember what happened when I met his family? "It's difficult to meet your boyfriend's parents. It's very nerve-racking."

"Why?"

"Because … ." How could I explain this to him without sounding like a big baby?

"Because there's always the chance the mother will hate you," Thistle supplied. "Heck, it's more than just a chance. Most mothers hate all of the women their sons date."

Landon snorted. "That's not true. My mother loved Bay when she met her."

He definitely remembered things differently than I did. "She didn't think I was good enough for you, and you know it. It took her almost a full week to warm up to me."

"That's not true," Landon argued. "She liked you. It's just … we were all working overtime to make sure she didn't find out about the witch stuff. Then there was the poltergeist problem. Then you fell off the horse and went missing, and I thought I was going to die because I couldn't find you."

Even when he remembered things wrong he was cute, and I

couldn't help but snuggle closer to him. "You thought you were going to die, huh?"

"I did," Landon confirmed, resting his cheek against my forehead. "My mother liked you, though."

"She didn't like me at first, and I was a nervous wreck," I pointed out. "That's neither here nor there, though. She ended up liking me, and I'm grateful for that."

"We're all grateful for that," Thistle said, making an exaggerated face. "I couldn't take the drama if she didn't like you."

"That's easy for you to say because Marcus' mother has known you since we were kids," I pointed out. Marcus grew up in Hemlock Cove before moving away when we were in high school. He moved back a year ago and immediately started flirting with Thistle. For the most part, their courtship was easy and trouble-free. "She already liked you, so you didn't have to deal with the stress of meeting a mother for the first time."

"She liked me because I'm awesome," Thistle said. "Perhaps you're not as awesome as me."

"Yes, that must be it," I said dryly, making a face as Landon chuckled.

"I don't understand why everyone is getting worked up about this," Landon said. "I wasn't nervous about meeting your mother."

"That's because you technically met her when she was wearing a track suit and we were sneaking through a cornfield," I reminded him. "Then you got shot saving Aunt Tillie and me. You were a hero before she ever really spoke to you."

"I am definitely a hero," Landon agreed, his grin impish. "Did you really worry that much about meeting my family?"

"Not your family," I clarified. "I worried that much about meeting your mother. Mothers and sons have weird relationships. If she put her foot down, she could take you away from me."

Landon's smile disappeared. "What do you mean by that?"

"I just mean that if she really hated me, you would've had no choice but to break up with me."

"That's not true," Landon countered. "I wouldn't have cared if my mother didn't like you. I was already in love with you by then, even though I hadn't admitted it to you or myself yet. There's nothing my mother could've done to break us up."

I wanted to believe that, but I wasn't sure he was telling the truth. "It doesn't matter now," I said. "We're happy and your mother likes me. Clove is going through this now, and we have to help her."

"I've decided I'm not going to help her," Thistle said. "I think I'm going to mess with her. That sounds much more fun."

I narrowed my eyes as I glared at my cousin. "That's not nice."

"Did you just meet me? When am I ever nice?"

"You can't do that, Thistle," I argued. "It's not fair to Clove. Why can't you support her and try to make this easier on her?"

"Because that sounds really boring and I don't want to do that," Thistle said. "I want to mess with Clove. That's always fun."

Thistle treated messing with Clove as an Olympic event when we were kids. "If you mess with Clove, I'm going to mess with you," I warned.

Thistle didn't appear bothered by the threat. "Bring it on."

AN HOUR later Landon and I were alone in my bedroom, my head resting on his chest as he rubbed idle circles on my back and stared at the ceiling. He took Thistle's suggestion that we spend some time alone to heart, although he seemed perfectly happy snuggling on the bed instead of engaging in something more vigorous before dinner.

"Were you really that nervous before meeting my mother?" Landon asked, shifting his eyes to me. "Seriously?"

"I seriously thought about hiding in the woods until she left."

Landon snickered as he kissed my forehead. "Women are crazy," he said. "I think you like creating drama just for the sake of it sometimes. I don't see why Clove is so worried about meeting Sam's family. She's the easiest one to get along with. She'll be fine."

I was pretty sure I'd just been insulted. "She's the easiest one to get along with?"

"You know what I mean," Landon said, edging lower on the bed and smirking when I tried to pull away. "She's sweet and everything nice. You're a little more difficult."

I doubled my efforts to escape. "Thanks a lot."

"I happen to like my women difficult," Landon said, pressing a soft kiss to my mouth and forcing me to back down from the potential fight. "I wouldn't trade you for anything."

Despite myself, the words warmed me. "Oh, yeah?"

"Yup." Landon nodded his head as he studied my face. "You seem a little pale to me, sweetie. Are you getting sick?"

The observation caught me off guard. After the news that Sam's parents were going to visit hit, I'd managed to push what happened on the tanker out of my mind. Once Landon voiced his concern, though, the images flooded back.

"I'm fine," I lied, forcing a smile. "I might be a little tired. I don't sleep very well when you're not around."

"Join the club," Landon said, rolling to his side so he could gather me close. "In fact, I could use a nap. How does that sound?"

"Do you want a real nap or a fake nap?"

"What's a fake nap?"

"It's a nap where you pretend you're falling asleep and then get a case of wandering hands."

Landon, delighted, barked out a laugh. "I thought we would take a real nap and bolster our strength. We can take a fake nap after dinner."

"Mom made blueberry pie and is grilling steaks just for you tonight," I supplied.

"Then we definitely need a nap." Landon tugged me as close as possible before getting comfortable. "I don't want you to get sick. I don't like it when you're not at a hundred percent. It makes me feel helpless."

I swallowed hard, his words causing a thick bolt of guilt to course through me. "I'm not sick. I promise."

"Okay." Landon kissed my cheek. "Let's take a nap anyway. We're going to need our strength for the fake nap later."

"I can live with that."

"I figured you were the only other person in the house up to the challenge."

FOUR

"That smells amazing."

Mom beamed at Landon as we walked across the back patio and headed toward the inn shortly before dinner. She was always happy to see him, even when he ticked her off. She's a fan of loyalty, and in her book Landon was as loyal as they come.

"It's good to see you," Mom said, smirking as Landon leaned over the grill to study the steaks. "It seems like forever since you've been here."

"I was here Tuesday."

"Yes, but you inhaled your dinner and then you and Bay disappeared to the guesthouse for the rest of the night," Mom pointed out. "I think you might've had indigestion or something."

Aunt Tillie, who sat on one of the loungers with her aviator sunglasses on, snorted. "The only thing he had was an itch in his pants."

Landon's cheeks flushed as he regarded her. He was used to Aunt Tillie's attitude and hijinks, but occasionally she caught him off guard. Apparently this was one of those times. "I didn't see you sitting there. I wasn't aware you could be that quiet."

"I'm practicing my spy skills," Aunt Tillie said, rolling her neck. "I'm going to show you how undercover work is really done."

Landon snorted. "Really?" He looked at her outfit, which consisted of pink cargo pants, purple flip-flops, a wide-brimmed green hat and a shirt that read "I'm here for the Boos," and merely shook his head. "You can't wear clothes like that when you're spying. People will see you coming from a mile away."

"So what?" Aunt Tillie was clearly in the mood to argue. "They'll take one look at me and say I stand out so I can't possibly be undercover. Then they'll dismiss me right away. When you dress down and try to look like you don't stand out, that's when everyone takes notice."

Landon opened his mouth to argue and instead ran his tongue over his teeth. "I hate to admit it, but you have a point."

"That's because I'm the best spy ever," Aunt Tillie replied. "In fact, I'm such a good spy that I could do it professionally."

Landon snorted. "Who would hire you, though? Most spies need a healthy respect for authority to move up the ladder."

"I'm going to start my own spy business," Aunt Tillie replied, blasé. "I'm going to hire Bay, Clove and Thistle to work for me."

Landon cast me a sidelong look. "Is that true? Are you going to be a spy?"

This was the first I heard about it, but I had no intention of getting on Aunt Tillie's bad side tonight. "It might be fun while you're at work during the week."

"I don't know." Landon tickled my ribs and caused me to giggle. "I don't think you'd do well under enhanced interrogation techniques."

I gasped as I slapped his hand away. "I don't think my interrogators will know my secret tickle spot."

"They'd better not," Landon said, wiggling his eyebrows.

We both jolted when a low rumble of thunder growled through the air. The sound was long and drawn out, and loud enough that the patio shook beneath our feet.

"A storm is coming," I said, glancing over my shoulder at the gathering clouds. "It will be here soon."

"The steaks are almost done," Mom said, her eyes flashing with worry as she stared at the sky. "I think we'll make it just in time."

"I love storms," Aunt Tillie said, swinging her legs over the side of the lounger. "That's another reason I'd make a great spy. I can control the weather. If someone ever catches me – and they won't, because I'm just like James Bond – I can make it storm and electrocute everyone to get away."

Landon shook his head as he regarded her. "Are you saying you caused this storm?"

"I'm saying I'm the mightiest witch in the land," Aunt Tillie replied. "Nothing happens in Hemlock Cove that I don't want to happen."

Now she was just making things up, but I had a feeling Landon already knew that.

"Well, mightiest witch, why don't you help us get the steaks inside," Landon suggested, reaching for the platter so he could help Mom. "I'm sure you want a steak, so you should want to help, too."

"You would think that, wouldn't you?" Aunt Tillie's smile was enigmatic. "I do want the steak, but I want you to serve it to me more."

Landon scowled. "You're in a mood tonight. I can already tell."

"I'm always in a mood," Aunt Tillie said. "Now you simply need to figure out who will benefit from my giving spirit."

She turned on her heel and flounced toward the door. My stomach sank as I watched her go. "She's up to something."

"She's always up to something," Landon said, holding the platter steady as Mom piled the steaks on top of it. "As long as she holds off until we're done with dinner I can put up with whatever she dishes out."

"Yeah, I'll etch that on your tombstone if you're not careful."

WOW, it is really coming down out there."

Marcus shook his blond head as he came into the dining room, rain flying everywhere as if he was a dog shaking himself. Thistle was already seated, but Annie was beside herself when he entered and she hopped up and threw her arms around his neck.

"Marcus!"

Belinda, Annie's mother, worked for my mother and aunts by helping around the inn. She was staying in the attic room with Annie until she could get on her feet financially. In truth, my entire family would welcome Belinda and Annie for as long as they wanted to stay. Everyone loved Annie, and Belinda was easy to get along with. They already felt part of the family. Belinda eventually wanted her own home, though, and no one would stand in her way when they inevitably moved. In fact, everyone was far more likely to help.

Even though he was dripping, Marcus enthusiastically returned the hug. Annie had a huge crush on him and thought he essentially walked on water. "How is my favorite girl?" Marcus asked, his eyes flashing as he stared at Annie. "Are you excited to start school in a week?"

Annie made a strange growling sound as she released Marcus and let him lower her to the floor. "No. I'm not going to school."

Belinda sighed as she helped Mom place the steak platter in the middle of the table. "Annie, we've talked about this," she chided. "You're going to school whether you like it or not."

"No, I'm not." Annie stubbornly crossed her arms over her chest. "I don't need no school."

"Obviously not," Belinda said dryly, shaking her head. "You need school. I know you're going to miss spending so much time with everyone here, but it's not as if you won't see them. Everyone will be here when you get out of school, and there's a lot to learn if you open yourself up to the opportunity."

"I don't need no stinking school," Annie said, her lower lip jutting out. "Aunt Tillie didn't go to school, and I don't have to either."

Landon furrowed his brow as he cast a look at Aunt Tillie. "Did you tell her you didn't go to school?"

"No, I told her I was smarter than everyone at the school and I should've been giving lessons," Aunt Tillie replied. "There's a difference."

"No, that's not what you said," Annie protested. "You said that you didn't need school because it's just a bunch of people making up stuff that you had to memorize and it's a complete waste of time."

Annie was young but she eavesdropped with the best of them. I had a feeling Aunt Tillie didn't say those words for her benefit. As cantankerous as she is, Aunt Tillie has Annie's best interests at heart. She always stressed the importance of school when we complained as children about going so I highly doubted she'd attempt to point Annie in another direction.

"When did I say that?" Aunt Tillie challenged.

"When you were telling Marnie why you didn't want to learn to use a new oven," Annie replied.

"Oh, well … ." Aunt Tillie looked caught. "You know how I told you to listen to everything I say and then ask me if it applies to you?"

Annie nodded.

"This is one of those times when it doesn't apply to you," Aunt Tillie explained. "You have to go to school. You'll turn out like one of those reality show personalities if you don't. You won't have any marketable skills. Do you want to be someone without marketable skills?"

Annie looked confused. "I don't know. What are marketable skills? Do you have marketable skills?"

Thistle snorted and Aunt Tillie scorched her with a dark look.

"Don't mess with me, fresh mouth," she warned Thistle. "You'll be sorry if you do. I'm talking to Annie. You're not part of this conversation."

"Yeah," I said, smirking when Thistle glared at me.

"No one is talking to you either, fresh mouth number two." Aunt Tillie licked her lips as she regarded Annie. "As for your question, I have a number of marketable skills. I make my own wine. I learned that in chemistry class. I bag my own … oregano … and I have to weigh it and stuff. I learned that in math class."

Landon scowled at mention of oregano. Aunt Tillie cultivated her own pot field, but she told Annie it was oregano. It was magically cloaked so Landon couldn't find it. I had the feeling he would burn it to the ground if he ever did.

"I also like to read," Aunt Tillie said, ignoring the faces Landon made. "You need schooling to be able to read."

"I already know how to read," Annie pointed out. "I read that fairy tale book you gave me and everything."

Landon stiffened. "Is that the book I think it is?" A few months ago, Aunt Tillie lost her temper and cursed us into the fairy tale book she wrote when we were younger. Landon didn't enjoy the experience and he'd been looking for the book so he could burn it ever since. Aunt Tillie was one step ahead of him, though, and that bothered him even more.

"I have no idea what book you're referring to," Aunt Tillie sniffed. "Now, if you don't mind, I'm trying to educate an impressionable mind. Not everything is about you."

Landon had the grace to look abashed. "By all means ... continue."

"Thank you," Aunt Tillie said primly. "Now, Annie, where were we?"

"You were saying that I don't need school," Annie answered. "I'm already smarter than everyone in the house ... er, well, except for you."

I rubbed my chin as I stared at Thistle. She looked dumbfounded. Annie was generally congenial and easy to deal with. She'd clearly been spending too much time with Aunt Tillie.

"Who told you that?" Belinda asked, confused. "You're not smarter than anyone."

"Aunt Tillie told me."

Oh. Well, that made sense. I could practically hear those words coming from Aunt Tillie's mouth. She fancied herself smarter than everyone combined. Because Annie looked up to her, of course she'd drag her along for the ride.

"Okay," Belinda said, resting her hands on her hips. "I think you and I need to have a talk in the kitchen. Grab your plate. We're going to eat alone tonight."

"No way," Annie shot back. "Marcus is here. I'm his favorite girl. He can't eat without me. Isn't that right, Marcus?"

Marcus looked caught as he locked gazes with Belinda. No matter how uncomfortable he was, he would never go against Belinda's

THE TROUBLE WITH WITCHES

wishes. "I think you should do what your mother says. I only like girls who listen to their mothers."

The rest of the table – sans the confused-looking guests, of course – snorted at his words. Thistle never did anything her mother Twila asked her to do. It was a point of pride where she was concerned.

"Oh, whatever," Annie said, flipping her hair over her shoulder as she stood. "I think you're all just trying to keep me down." Her eyes landed on Landon. "The Man always tries to keep us down. Isn't that right, Aunt Tillie?"

Aunt Tillie shifted uncomfortably on her chair. "Um ... ."

"Come on right now, Annie," Belinda ordered. She was clearly upset. "We're going to have a long talk about your attitude."

"Don't worry," Mom said. "We're going to have a long talk with the person influencing her attitude as well. We'll sort this all out."

Belinda didn't look convinced. "That would be nice."

After Annie and Belinda left the room everyone lapsed into an uncomfortable silence. The guests clearly didn't know what to think – the Winchester dinner theater was legendary – so they merely waited for us to start the second act. Thankfully, Sam swooped in to save us from saying anything stupid. Er, well, at least he saved us for the time being.

"So, my parents are coming to town Sunday," he announced. "Because you'll have some rooms opening up, I was hoping they could stay here. I would pay, of course, but I want them to meet all of you."

Marnie, Clove's mother, appeared excited by the prospect. "Your parents are coming? That sounds lovely. I'm looking forward to meeting them."

"You want them to stay here?" Clove shifted on her chair, uncomfortable. "Do you think that's a good idea with all of the ... you know ... stuff that happens?"

"I don't see why not," Sam said. "It will only be for a few days. I think it will make things easier on everyone."

"I think so, too," Thistle said, her eyes gleaming. "I can't wait to spend some time with them. I have so many stories from our childhood to relate. It's going to be amazing."

"No, I don't think that's a good idea," Clove hedged. "I ... maybe we should put them up at the Dragonfly or something."

The Dragonfly was the competing inn owned by our fathers. Even though they'd come to a meeting of the minds, there was still an edge of competition between our mothers and fathers.

"Absolutely not," Marnie snapped, scorching Clove with a harsh look. "They're staying here and that's the end of it."

"Oh, well, great," Clove murmured. "I thought things were going to be freaky but now I'm convinced I was totally wrong. Things will be just perfect now."

Marnie ignored her tone. "Things will be perfect," she agreed. "Things will be completely and totally perfect. What kind of food do they like, Sam?"

"Well, Dad will eat anything," Sam replied. "Mom is a vegetarian, though."

Mom, Marnie and Twila sucked in twin breaths. They hated vegetarians. We're a meat-and-potato kind of family.

"Well, I'm sure we can come up with some appropriate dishes," Marnie said. "I'll look through the books tonight."

"I don't trust anyone who doesn't eat meat," Aunt Tillie announced. "I love sausage."

I pressed my lips together to keep from laughing at the unintended double entendre. "That's what she said," I muttered under my breath, causing Thistle and Clove to giggle.

"Did you say something, smart mouth?" Aunt Tillie challenged.

"Nope." I pressed my lips together as Landon shot me a dubious look. "I didn't say a word. In fact, I'm going to run to the drink cart and make myself something to chase away the chill. Does anyone want anything?"

"I'm going to stick with wine," Landon answered.

"I'll take a fifth of whiskey," Thistle said.

"Coming right up."

I listened to the conversation as I left the room, smirking when I heard my mother steer the conversation toward Annie. I was almost at the cart when the lights flickered. It happened immediately after a bright flash of lightning but before the accompanying thunder roll. I glanced toward the window as the power flickered again.

This time five ghostly apparitions appeared in the window, causing my heart to pound when I locked gazes with a short man with a big beer gut. All five ghosts stared at me as I reached toward the drink cart, my fingers shaking as I fought to tear my gaze from them. It was as if I was frozen in place.

The lights flickered once more before completely going out, plunging the room into darkness.

I wanted to scream. I couldn't see anything and my mind went to a wild place where the ghosts were closing in on me as they attempted to smother the life from me. I didn't get the chance to scream, though, because one of the guests did it for me.

"It's a ghost!"

FIVE

"Bay?" I could hear Landon calling for me but I remained rooted to my spot. I was terrified to move in case I walked through one of the creepy ghosts. I didn't get a chance to study them for very long, but at least two of them appeared to have gaping wounds. Most ghosts take on a form pleasing to them. I'd come in contact with several over the years who were jerked so violently out of their lives that they looked exactly as they did in death, though, which was altogether creepy.

The room remained dark and I counted in my head. It usually took a full minute for the generator to kick on.

"Bay?" Landon's voice was closer and I pictured him feeling his way through the darkened rooms as he tried to find his way to me. I tried to speak, but no sound would come out of my mouth. Things only worsened when I thought I heard a low scraping sound in the corner of the room. Of course, that could've been my imagination working overtime.

"Bay!" Landon was more insistent now and I managed to jerk in the direction of his voice at the same moment the generator kicked on.

Of course, because we were in the middle of a storm the thunder blasted at the exact same moment, and I jumped when he reached for me.

Landon pulled me to him, smoothing my hair. He almost seemed relieved when his hands made contact with my skin. "You frightened me," he murmured into my hair. "Why didn't you answer?"

"I ... ." I wasn't sure how to answer, and when I glanced over my shoulder I found the spot dark where the ghosts stood moments before. "I'm not sure. I kind of freaked myself out." I offered him a rueful smile. "I love storms, but you know how I am about horror movies."

Landon didn't look convinced. "I do know how you are about horror movies," he said. "You like to watch them and then play pranks with Clove and Thistle. You generally don't freak out, though."

"I'm sorry." I meant it. "I just got tongue tied for a second."

Landon tipped up my chin, his expression unreadable. "You're pale again. You got some color in your cheeks after our nap but ... ."

I cut him off. "I'm fine. I'm sorry I frightened you."

"It's okay." Landon gave me another brief hug before releasing me. He grabbed a bottle of whiskey from the drink cart and held out his hand. "Come on. You look like you could use a drink."

"Some food wouldn't hurt either," I admitted. "You did promise me a busy night, after all."

"I did."

Landon kept me close as walked back toward the dining room. It was only then that I remembered the scream. "Did someone see a ghost?"

"One of the guests saw a shadow and thought it was part of the dinner theater," Landon replied, keeping his voice low. "It's okay. I mean ... it's okay if you're okay."

"It's okay then."

"I certainly hope so."

Landon waited for me to be seated before handing the bottle of whiskey to Thistle. She accepted it wordlessly, her eyes wide when locking with mine. I forced a smile for everyone's benefit even though my heartbeat hadn't returned to a normal rate.

I searched for something to fill the uncomfortable silence. "That was freaky, huh? I almost tripped into the drink cart."

"It was definitely freaky," Mom said. "I didn't realize we were supposed to get such a big storm."

"I did that," Aunt Tillie supplied. "That was my anger."

"What do you have to be angry about?" Landon asked, making a big show of putting his napkin on his lap as he tried to act as if he wasn't rattled. He had no idea what frightened me, but I knew he was worried about my reaction. He would never question me in front of guests, though. No, he would save that for later, when we were alone. "As I recall, everyone else has a reason to be angry but you."

"No one is talking to you," Aunt Tillie sniffed. "Eat your steak and shut your hole."

On a normal night her dismissive attitude might've bothered Landon. He was much more interested in me than Aunt Tillie, though. "I am definitely going to eat my steak," he said. "Then I'm going to eat my blueberry pie. Then I'm going to thank Winnie, Marnie and Twila for a wonderful meal."

Mom beamed as Landon winked in her direction. "No one can say you don't suck up with the best of them."

"Yes, well, I'm gifted in that department," Landon said, leaning back in his chair. He seemed more relaxed, if only marginally. "After that, though, I'm taking Bay back to the guesthouse. I think she needs a good night's sleep."

"I think we all need a good night's sleep," Clove said. "I'm going to be up at the crack of dawn so I can clean the lighthouse."

"What's left to clean?" Sam protested. "You scoured every inch of the lighthouse before we left."

"Oh, there's plenty left," Clove said. "I'm going to need the day off work so I can focus on my cleaning, Thistle. I hope that's okay with you. If it's not ... well ... suck it up."

"It's fine," Thistle said, her eyes never leaving me. I could lie to

Landon and put him off for a bit, but she could always see right through me. "I'll handle everything. Don't worry."

"SO, DO you want to tell me what really happened?"

Landon held it together throughout the entire meal and questioned me only when we hit the back door of The Overlook. He was a good boyfriend, kind and loving to a fault, but his FBI training refused to allow him to let things go when he sensed trouble.

"Nothing happened," I replied, rubbing my hands together when we reached the back patio. The air smelled earthy thanks to the fast-moving storm. "I just ... frightened myself."

"How?"

"I'm not sure," I hedged. "The lights flickered and I thought I saw something before they went completely out. Then I freaked out when it was dark because I couldn't decide if I really saw something."

Landon was well aware of my abilities and he accepted them without question. That didn't mean he wasn't prone to questioning me when he thought a situation warranted further investigation. "What did you see?"

"I don't think I saw anything." That was a lie, but I wasn't ready to admit the truth. I had no idea why. It wasn't as if I caused the ghosts to appear, but if I owned up to what happened earlier in the afternoon he would go into protection mode and order me to stay away from the tanker. I didn't want to do that in case I needed to return to investigate. "For a second I thought it could've been a ghost or something, but it was just the way the lights were playing with my eyes."

"Are you sure?" Landon pushed my hair away from my face and gazed into my eyes. "You know you can tell me anything, right?"

I did know that. "I'm sure. There was nothing there when the generator kicked on. I freaked out over nothing. I'm sorry I frightened you."

"I'm always frightened when your safety is in question." Landon gave me a soft kiss. "I do think you need some sleep, though. You're still white."

"Are you ready for your fake nap?" I was going for levity and it worked when Landon grinned.

"I'm ready for an entire night with you," Landon replied. "I don't care if we take a fake nap or real one. I just want us to be together."

"That sounds nice." I slipped my hand into his and we were almost off the patio when we heard voices from the other side of the railing.

"Annie, you're being ridiculous."

I recognized Belinda's voice right away. Landon and I exchanged a look before changing course. We had to check on Belinda and Annie before leaving.

"I am not." Annie was sobbing when I caught sight of her. "I saw it. I know I saw it."

"What's going on?" Landon asked, his face full of concern as he released my hand and moved toward Annie. She was pressed in tight against the side of the patio, almost as if she expected someone to come up behind her.

"She's overreacting because of the storm," Belinda explained. "I'm not quite sure what her problem is, but she didn't take it well when the lights went out. She started ... carrying on."

"Carrying on how?" I asked, my heart skipping a beat. This wasn't the first time I believed it was possible Annie saw something otherworldly. She'd seen a ghost once before. I was sure of it. If it became a regular occurrence – and I was terrified it would – her life was bound to get a whole lot more difficult. No one wanted that.

"I don't know." Belinda looked to be at her wit's end. She'd seen a few crazy things since moving in with us, but either by choice or accident she was still oblivious to the witchy secret. "She acted as if she was talking to someone who wasn't there, and then she started crying and hiding her face. Then she ran outside."

"Really?" I had no idea how to respond. If Annie had an ability – which would seem to indicate there was some witch blood in her heritage – then we would have to sit down and have a long talk with Belinda ... and it would have to be sooner rather than later.

"What did you see?" Landon asked kindly, opening his arms and smiling when Annie stepped into his embrace. Marcus was her favorite person in the world, but she'd warmed to Landon considerably since Aunt Tillie told her that he wasn't a scary person despite being "The Man." That was another instance of her mouth getting away from her.

"I saw two men," Annie replied. "They were dressed funny and they were bleeding."

"How were they dressed?" Landon asked.

"They had on funny clothes ... like jackets and ties and weird hats," Annie replied. "They had blood all over them."

"I told you that you imagined that, Annie," Belinda chided. "You didn't really see any men."

"They were there," Annie protested. "I swear it."

"Seriously, I don't know what's gotten into you," Belinda said, reaching for her daughter. Landon reluctantly relinquished her, his face stoic as he patted the top of Annie's head. "I think you're tired. You'll feel better in the morning."

Annie looked desperate when her eyes landed on me. She seemed to sense I understood her predicament. "You believe me, don't you?"

"Of course I do." The answer was automatic and I had to force myself to ignore Belinda's exasperated sigh. She wasn't magical. She'd never seen ghosts. She didn't understand the pain of having people think you were crazy or imagining things. I would never do that to Annie. "It's going to be okay. I'll look for the ghosts and see if I can get rid of them."

"You will?" Annie looked relieved. "Do you think you can really do that?"

This time the smile I shot in her direction wasn't forced. "I think I can."

Landon and I remained next to the patio and watched as Belinda led Annie into the inn. Belinda's voice was warm and caring, but she was clearly out of her element. Once the door closed, Landon turned to me.

"Do you think Annie saw what you saw?"

I wasn't sure how to answer. "I think there's a good chance she did." There was no sense going out of my way to lie to him. If this kept up, I would have to own up to everything, and I didn't want to exacerbate the problem. "It happened so fast, though."

"Bay, how can she be seeing ghosts?" Landon had come a long way when it came to accepting magic and spells, but he still didn't understand all of the intricacies of our witchy world. "Doesn't she have to be a witch to see them?"

"Not necessarily," I replied. "Sam can see ghosts, and his mother supposedly has witchy tendencies. Most men in witch families don't get the same abilities as women, though. We might never know how Annie came by her ability."

"Do you think she's really seeing ghosts?"

I searched my heart and nodded. "This is the second time she's seen something."

"I know. Why do you think that is? What are the odds of her ending up here if she really can see ghosts?"

"Maybe it was destiny."

I expected Landon to laugh at my earnest answer, but he seemed intrigued by the suggestion. "You think she was drawn to you guys for a reason, don't you? You don't believe Thistle finding her on the road that day was a fluke."

"I ... don't know what to believe."

"Well, I'd like to believe it's destiny," Landon said. "If anyone can help her, it's you."

"Why do you say that?"

"Because you're magic, sweetie," Landon replied, not missing a beat. "Everything you touch is special. If Annie is special, I don't want her suffering because of her abilities. You know exactly what she's going through, and you'll help her."

His admission warmed my heart. "Thank you."

"Oh, don't look at me that way," Landon dismissed, wagging a finger. "You act so surprised when I'm sensitive. I'm a sensitive guy."

My lips tightened as I tried to refrain from grinning. "You are a sensitive guy. In fact, I wouldn't mind going back to the guesthouse and being sensitive together."

"That sounds like a plan." Landon pulled me in for a hug as he gazed at the back of The Overlook. "You know you're going to have to explain things to Belinda once you get a handle on the fact that Annie is seeing ghosts, right?"

I nodded. "I need to talk to my mother and aunts before that. We'll probably have to do it together."

"You need to talk to Thistle, too," Landon said. "She's extremely tight with Annie. I hate to admit it, but having Aunt Tillie in on the decision-making process isn't a bad idea either. I know she's told Annie some weird things – and something definitely needs to be done about that kid's attitude before she gets out of control – but Aunt Tillie will die to protect her."

"We'd all die to protect her. You would, too."

"Yes, but I'm out of my element," Landon said. "I'm extremely sympathetic to Annie's plight, but there's nothing I can do to make the situation better. All I can do is help you when you try."

My heart rolled at his admission. Landon is a fixer, so he always wants to make things better. It takes a strong man to admit he can't fix something and to stand back and let others try. "You're a good guy."

Landon's grin was impish as he stared down at me. "I am. As a good guy, I think I deserve a reward."

"What did you have in mind?"

"I'm so glad you asked," Landon said, grabbing my hand. "I'm going to lay out my entire plan during the walk home."

Oh, well, that sounded entertaining. "Lead the way."

SIX

"Good morning."

I woke to find Landon staring at me, the morning sunshine filtering through the window and glinting off his angular features as he rubbed his thumb against my shoulder and my cheek rested on his chest.

"Morning," I murmured, taking a moment to bask in his warmth before stretching.

Landon smiled as he watched me, waiting until I was done groaning before pulling me back to him. He clearly wasn't in a hurry to get up this morning. "How did you sleep?" he asked.

"I slept hard. How did you sleep?"

"I slept okay."

His answer seemed evasive. "Did something happen I don't know about?" I moved to prop myself up on my elbow but Landon was keen to keep me close.

"You were up once last night," Landon said, his voice even as he stared at me. "You had a nightmare or something. Do you remember that?"

I racked my brain as I stared at him. I vaguely recalled waking up in the middle of the night. His voice had been soothing as he rubbed my back and sent me back to sleep. Luckily the next set of dreams had been much happier. There was something about bacon and skinny-dipping.

"I ...."

Landon's face was placid as he watched me. "What did you dream about?"

I honestly couldn't remember, but for some reason I felt guilty when I told him as much.

"You went back to sleep right away, but you were making little whimpering noises when you woke," Landon said, stroking the back of my head. "I wondered if you dreamed about Annie's ghosts."

He was giving me far too much credit. I was dreaming about my ghosts, the ones I was so reluctant to tell him about because I didn't want him to worry, and now he was worrying anyway.

"It's okay, Landon," I said, tracing the outline of his abdominal muscles. "I'm fine. It was just a dream."

"Yes, well, I prefer you to have happy dreams," Landon said. "I want to be the leading man of your dreams, but I'll take a good dream with someone else over whatever upset you last night any day of the week."

"That's kind of sweet."

"That's how I roll." Landon mustered a mischievous smile. "I love you, Bay. I want you to always be happy."

"I'm feeling pretty happy now."

Landon pressed a soft kiss to my mouth. "I'll bet I can make you happier."

I had a feeling he was right. "Did I tell you about the dream I had after I went back to sleep? That one I definitely remember."

"Oh, yeah?" Landon looked intrigued. "What happened?"

"Well, we were at the lake and you planned a picnic," I started. "Then for some unknown reason we were naked and swimming. Oh, and there was bacon."

Landon's eyes lit up. "Now that sounds like a dream."

"Do you want to make it come true?"

"You want to go down to the lake?" Landon was understandably dubious. "I'm willing to do it, mind you, but you forget that I know how lazy you are in the morning."

"Well, maybe not the lake," I conceded. "We do have a bathtub, though."

"What about the bacon?"

Now it was my turn to grin. "I was saving it for a surprise, but some lady on Etsy makes bacon-scented shower gel. It arrived yesterday."

Landon barked out a laugh, delighted. "Did you buy that for me?"

"Who else?"

"That sounds like a plan," Landon said, giving me another kiss before rolling out from beneath the covers and extending his hand as he stood next to the bed. "Come on. I'm going to make you smell like bacon. That's the way to start the day out right."

"I'm coming," I said, taking a moment to stretch my legs on the other side of the bed before padding toward the door. "If you like the smell I'll stock up on the shower gel. I'm guessing that I'll never smell like coconuts or pears ever again."

"Something tells me I'll like it," Landon said, his eyebrows knitting as he watched me attempt to open the door. For some reason, the handle wouldn't turn. "Is something wrong?"

"The door is locked," I replied, pressing the button to unlock it. "I don't remember locking it, though."

"We sometimes do it out of habit," Landon said. "I might've accidentally locked it during the middle of the night."

I twisted the handle, expecting the door to pop open, but it remained locked. "I ... don't understand." I rolled my neck until it cracked. "Why won't this open?"

"Here. Let me try." Landon pressed one hand to my hip and used the other to mess with the door. He tried three times to open it and failed each time. "Okay, that is really weird." He rubbed his chin as he stared at the door. "I'm not a construction person or anything, but I think we need a screwdriver to take that handle off."

"It's just so weird," I complained, jiggling the handle and letting my frustration take over at my fruitless attempts. "It was working fine last night."

"I think we should take this as a sign," Landon said. "The door won't open, so the universe clearly doesn't want us to leave the bedroom. Let's spend the day in bed."

He was a predictable creature – which I truly loved – but I was legitimately starving because I had eaten very little of my dinner the night before. "I want breakfast!"

"We can nourish ourselves with love," Landon suggested, his eyes twinkling as he sat at the end of the bed.

"I thought you wanted a bacon shower?"

Landon shrugged. "I do want a bacon shower. But I'm just as happy crawling back under the covers and smelling regular you this morning."

That was sort of a weird thing to say. "What do I smell like?"

"I have no idea," Landon replied. "You smell like Bay. I like it."

"As sweet as that is – and you definitely deserve a reward – I'm really hungry." As if on cue, my stomach growled. "I didn't eat my entire dinner last night because my stomach was kind of unsettled after I flipped myself out in the library."

Landon's expression momentarily darkened. "I forgot about that. You nibbled on your steak and then pushed the rest of your food around your plate to give the illusion you were eating."

Oh, he caught that. I wasn't sure. He's an FBI agent, so I guess I should've seen that coming. "Well, I'm starving now," I said, hoping to avoid an in-depth discussion about last evening's eating habits. "I need food, and the only thing in here to eat is the gum at the bottom of my purse."

"I'm happy living off love," Landon said. He didn't appear to be in a hurry to help me open the door.

"They're making bacon and omelets with bacon inside of them for breakfast up at the inn this morning," I offered.

Landon's eyes lit up and he redoubled his efforts to open the door. "You had me at bacon, sweetie."

After two failed attempts, I heard snickering on the other side of the wooden door and grabbed Landon's wrist to still him.

"Thistle?"

"No comprende." The voice definitely belonged to Thistle, but she was trying to disguise it as she laughed at us from the hallway.

"What do you think you're doing?" I asked, anger coursing through me.

"I don't think I'm doing anything," Thistle said, dropping the accent. "I know I'm putting my crafts room together today. And, since it's a Saturday, that means you don't have to go to work. I figured you and Landon would like a ... forced vacation ... so to speak."

"A forced vacation?" Landon shifted his eyes to me. "That doesn't sound so bad."

"You're missing out on the bacon," I reminded him.

"I love you more than bacon."

He was cute and sweet this morning, but I was starting to feel claustrophobic, which was ridiculous because my bedroom was the largest in the guesthouse. "I will make you pay if you don't open this door, Thistle," I threatened. "I'll declare war if you're not careful."

I couldn't see Thistle's face but she didn't sound frightened on the other side of the obstruction. "I look forward to a lively day of curses. As for now, I'm ahead. It's one to nothing."

I was incredulous as I glanced at Landon. "I'm going to kill her."

"I'm actually fine with it," Landon said, flopping on the mattress. "If we had bacon, we could live here forever."

We definitely needed to talk about his priorities.

"GET UP."

I paced the small area between the end of my bed and the door and glared at Landon as he flipped through a magazine on my bed.

"You need to calm down, sweetie," Landon chided, never moving his eyes from the article he was reading. "You're making yourself crazy, and it's not good for you. Thistle will let us out eventually."

THE TROUBLE WITH WITCHES

Did he start smoking crack when I wasn't looking? "I want to be let out now."

"Uh-huh."

"Are you even listening to me?" I strode to his side of the bed and snatched the magazine from him, tossing it against the wall as my frustration bubbled up. "We're trapped!"

"We're hardly trapped," Landon said, his eyes widening as he stared at me. I caught a glimpse of my reflection in the mirror a few seconds before I took the magazine from him and I didn't blame him for thinking I was off my broomstick. I looked a little crazy with my hair standing on end. I couldn't stop dragging my hand through it. Instead of smoothing it, my actions were having the opposite effect.

"We are trapped," I countered, instinctively knowing I sounded irrational, but unable to stop myself. "We can't get out of this room. She's going to let us die here."

"Okay, you're being a real Winchester this morning I see," Landon said, opening his arms and motioning for me to come to him. "Let me rub your back. That will calm you down."

I was never one to turn down an offered massage, but there was no way I could sit still for that. "Landon ... we're going to starve to death."

"We're not going to starve to death," Landon argued. "We've been locked in here for ten minutes. You're hardly dying."

That's not how it felt. "I ... ."

"Come here." Landon motioned for me to join him again and I reluctantly did because I was at a loss for anything better to do. "Rest your head on my chest."

I followed Landon's instructions and sighed when he began rubbing my back. His hands were gentle but insistent as he methodically attacked the kinks in my stiff muscles.

"It's okay, sweetie," Landon murmured, kissing my cheek as he tried to soothe me. "I had no idea you were claustrophobic, though."

"I'm not claustrophobic."

"You certainly don't like being locked in this room," Landon pointed out. "You were fine when you thought you could leave at any moment. The second you realized you couldn't it was as if someone threw a switch."

"I don't like feeling cooped up," I admitted.

"This is a big bedroom. You're not cooped up. Nothing bad is going to happen here. Er, well, I might play bad cop to your naughty speeder if you're feeling bored, but that's hardly the end of the world."

I snorted and shook my head. Even when I found him aggravating he always knew how to make me feel better. "I just don't like being locked up."

"Why?"

"Because ... ." I was at a loss as to how to explain my fear. "Because I got locked in the basement once when I was a kid – Thistle did that, too – and I thought the furnace was going to eat me. I was small ... and I cried ... and I turned into a real baby."

"I think that's normal," Landon said. "I was afraid of my basement when I was a kid."

"Yes, but you didn't cry and have nightmares for weeks," I pointed out. "I honestly thought I would never get out of the basement, and I woke up screaming several times until my mother charmed a dreamcatcher and put it over my bed."

"That sounds like night terrors," Landon mused, his eyes traveling to the dreamcatcher hanging on the corner post of my bed. "Is that the dreamcatcher?"

I nodded. "It's supposed to ward off nightmares."

"It didn't work last night."

He had a point. "It probably needs to be recharged," I said. "Every few months I need to cast a spell on it to keep it working. I guess I forgot recently because ... well ... I rarely have bad dreams when you're around."

"Oh, well, that's ridiculously cute," Landon said, snuggling closer. "You should definitely recharge that thing, though. I don't like it when you cry in your sleep."

I shifted my chin so I could stare at his profile. "I'm sure it was just a fluke, Landon. I didn't mean to wake you up. I won't do it again."

Landon stroked the back of my head as he locked gazes with me. "I don't care about that," he said. "I care about you getting the rest you need. I don't like it when you're unhappy."

"Two weeks ago Aunt Tillie cursed me to smell and taste like bacon and I was extremely upset," I reminded him. "You didn't mind that."

Landon cracked a smile. "That was different. You were unhappy for only five minutes, and then I made you very happy."

He wasn't wrong. "I don't remember what I dreamed about last night. I'll recharge the dreamcatcher later, though. I'm sorry I woke you."

"I wouldn't ever want anyone else to wake me," Landon said. "Don't apologize for waking me. I don't mind. I would prefer happy dreams, but that's not something we can always control."

I rested my head on the spot above his heart and took solace in the simple sound of it beating against my ear. We rested like that for five minutes before my claustrophobic angst returned. "Landon, I need to get out of this room."

"Five more minutes."

That sounded like torture given the circumstances. "I have to go to the bathroom ... and I'm starving."

"Three more minutes."

"There's bacon at the inn, Landon," I reminded him. "My mother will keep you in bacon for the rest of your life if you get me out of this room."

Landon heaved a sigh, but he was smiling when he glanced at me. "You had me at bacon."

"I know."

"You owe me a vigorous snuggle session later."

I couldn't help but laugh. "You're the only guy I know who owns up to liking to snuggle."

"I'm a man of many interests."

"You can say that again."

Landon smacked a loud kiss against my lips before sliding out from beneath me and striding toward the door. I followed him, genuinely curious as to how he was going to get us out, and then frowned when I heard the unmistakable sounds of Thistle and Marcus moving something big in the other room. I could hear them whispering to each other.

"I'm going to make her eat a mountain of dirt," I threatened.

Landon's eyes gleamed as he stared at me, and then I watched with utter delight as he removed the pins in the hinges and lifted the door away from the frame. I squeezed his arm in thanks as I stepped into the living room – sucking in a huge breath of freedom before narrowing my eyes and focusing on Thistle.

Thistle's face drained of color when she saw me, and she almost dropped her end of the big chest she carried with Marcus. "How did you get out?"

"My boyfriend is the smartest man in the world."

"Thank you, Bay," Landon said. "That was very sweet … and accurate."

I ignored him and scorched Thistle with a dark look. "You're going to be sorry you ever messed with me."

Instead of backing down like a normal person, Thistle merely smiled. "Bring it on."

SEVEN

Thistle wisely disappeared from the guesthouse before I could wrap my hands around her neck. Landon dragged me into the shower while Marcus pulled Thistle into her bedroom, and by the time we exited the bathroom they were gone.

That didn't mean I was ready to let things go.

"I'm going to make her smell like rotten cabbage and car farts for an entire week," I grumbled, entering the family living quarters at the back of the inn. "She'll wish she never met me."

"That sounds delightful," Landon said, pulling up short when he caught sight of Aunt Tillie on the couch watching a morning news show. "How is the world today?"

"Mildly entertaining." Aunt Tillie didn't even bother glancing at us. She wore floral leggings and an oversized black shirt with a glittery sugar skull on it. She'd been expanding her wardrobe of late – she loved online shopping – and she was taking some interesting risks. "One of those rappers got arrested for shooting someone."

"That's hardly news," Landon said. "What else is going on?"

"There's no peace in the Middle East."

I pursed my lips to keep from laughing. "Does that upset you?"

"I think they should send me over there," Aunt Tillie replied, finally dragging her eyes from the television. "I could settle their problems in five minutes flat."

"Oh, yeah? How would you do that?"

"Wine, pot and porn. That always helps when things are tense."

"Well, at least you have a plan," Landon said. "I think that's a marvelous idea. You should be a peace mediator. That's definitely your calling."

"I could totally do it for a living," Aunt Tillie said, focusing on me. "Thistle snuck in here fifteen minutes ago. She looked worried. What did she do to you?"

"How do you know she did anything to me?"

"Because she said you were going to make her eat dirt, and she was trying to think of ways to torture you," Aunt Tillie answered. "She wanted to know if I had any ideas."

I narrowed my eyes. "What did you tell her?" I didn't know if Aunt Tillie could be a peace mediator professionally – I seriously doubted it – but she could certainly make a living torturing people. She was a master at that.

"I told her I wasn't getting involved," Aunt Tillie said. "I'm much too mature for petty bickering."

Landon made a derisive sound in the back of his throat. "Since when?"

"Since always," Aunt Tillie replied, not missing a beat. "I'm a peace mediator, after all."

"Yes, well, I guess I must've missed that entry on your resume." Landon lifted his nose in the air and inhaled. "Is that bacon I smell?"

"Don't worry, glutton," Aunt Tillie said. "They're in there cooking up a storm. They're cooking an entire pig just for you."

"Well, my day is starting out well," Landon said. "Thistle locked me in the bedroom with my favorite person, and now there's an endless supply of bacon. What could be better?"

"Thistle locked you in your bedroom?" Aunt Tillie looked intrigued.

"Yes, she cast a spell on the lock," I said. "Landon took out the pins in the hinges, though, and then Thistle ran like the coward that she is."

"And this is all because you guys can't agree what to do with Clove's bedroom?"

I nodded.

"Okay, I've decided to take your side," Aunt Tillie said after considering her options for a few moments. "It's your lucky day, Bay. Your Aunt Tillie is here and she's going to help you pay back Thistle."

Now I was intrigued. "What do you have in mind?"

"I'm not sure yet," Aunt Tillie said. "I haven't eaten yet today. I need food to fuel my brain. Then I'll be a lean, mean revenge machine."

"Oh, well, there's a terrifying thought," Landon said, shaking his head. He squeezed my hand as he tugged me toward the kitchen. "Let's eat before you start your revenge planning. We have the entire day ahead of us to plot Thistle's downfall."

He had a point. "Okay, but I expect you to help, too."

"I can't wait."

"I think that sounds like a plan," Aunt Tillie said, padding behind us as we headed toward the kitchen. "The three of us together will be unstoppable. In fact, we should start our own company. We'll call in Revenge Inc. People will drive from miles around to pay for our services."

"I ... that's an idea," I hedged.

"It's a great idea," Aunt Tillie enthused. "What do you think, copper?"

Landon sighed as he held open the door for us. "I think it's going to be a long day."

I was pretty sure he was right.

"WHAT ARE YOU DOING IN HERE?" Landon found me in the library two hours later. After a leisurely breakfast, I left him to discuss the fate of the Detroit Lions this upcoming football season with a guest and wandered into the library. I was looking for a specific book on Great Lakes maritime shipping and lost track of time when I found an entire section dedicated to the topic.

I was comfortable on the couch, a big book spread across my lap, when Landon joined me.

"Sorry," I said, jerking up my head. "I didn't mean to abandon you for so long."

"That's okay," Landon said, settling next to me. "I'm an adult. I can entertain myself."

"I thought I was your favorite form of weekend entertainment," I teased, grinning when Landon slid closer so he could study the book.

"You're definitely my favorite form of entertainment – whether it's the middle of the week or the weekend," Landon said. "You never need to put qualifiers in there. I missed you when you didn't come back. What are you looking at?"

"It's a book on ships of the Great Lakes."

"And why do you care about that?"

I shrugged as I bit the inside of my cheek. I still hadn't told him about my experience from the previous afternoon. At first I told myself that I was protecting him because I didn't want him to worry. That was mostly true. He didn't understand paranormal happenings, so they made him nervous. Now that I'd hidden it from him, though, I felt guilty. I knew I should've told him right away, but it was too late now. He wouldn't take the admission well. He hated it when I kept important things from him, and he would consider me passing out important.

"Sam got his tanker yesterday," I explained. "We scouted it out."

"Okay."

"It's called the Yeti Inferno now – which is kind of funny given Clove's fear of monsters – but it used to be called the Gray Harker."

"How did you figure out that?"

"There's a website where you can track boat names," I said, gesturing toward my phone. "It wasn't hard."

"I keep forgetting that you're an intrepid reporter," Landon teased, running his finger over a page in the book. "Why are you so interested in this?"

I decided to split the difference on a lie and bring Landon closer to the truth without telling him everything. "Because one of the ghosts I thought I saw in here last night was wearing a captain's hat."

Landon's eyebrows flew up his forehead. "You didn't tell me that."

"I didn't remember it until we were eating breakfast. I couldn't really volunteer that in front of the guests," I said.

"So you think the ghosts have something to do with Sam's new tanker? The Yeti Inferno is a great name for a band, by the way. I'm not sure it fits a ship."

"Clove has been talking about renaming it the Bubbling Cauldron, so that name probably won't stick."

"I think they should name it the Flaming Broomstick," Landon suggested. "I think that sounds funnier."

"You and Sam can talk about that later," I said, turning my attention back to the book. "I think they'll be working on it for weeks."

"Uh-huh." Landon rubbed the back of my neck as he watched me read. "Sweetie, do you want to tell me why you're so fixated on this?"

His cop instincts were kicking into overdrive. I couldn't blame him for being suspicious. "I thought I saw something last night, but it was over so quickly I couldn't be sure. Then I felt like a real ninny because I overreacted and freaked myself out."

"I don't think that makes you a ninny. I think that makes you human."

"I still feel like an idiot," I said. "I honestly think one of the ghosts was wearing a captain's hat."

"But how did you tie that to Sam's tanker?"

I shrugged. "How else? That's the new component. I'm not sure it has anything to do with the ghosts, but we did visit it earlier in the day. It can't hurt to look up the tanker's history."

"That's a legitimate point," Landon said, licking his lips as he studied the page. "Have you found anything?"

"Actually I have," I replied. "Right before you came in I found this." I shifted the book from my lap to Landon's and tapped the page. "This says the Gray Harker made regular trips through the Great Lakes – mostly on Lake Michigan – before 1989."

"What happened in 1989?"

"The tanker vanished."

"You mean it sank?"

"No, I mean it vanished."

"Well, lots of ships have sunk in the Great Lakes."

"I said it vanished," I insisted. "But that's not the weird part."

"Okay, I give. What's the weird part?"

"It was missing for three months and then it reappeared."

"Where did the crew say they were?"

"That's just it. The crew wasn't on the tanker. They were never heard from again."

"So ... wait ... you're saying the tanker disappeared for three months and the crew disappeared – forever?" Landon tapped his lip. "How many men are we talking about here?"

"Twenty."

"How is that possible?"

"I have no idea," I answered, turning my palms up. "No one ever found any bodies. All of the life rafts were accounted for when the vessel turned up. It's a maritime mystery."

"I've never heard of it, so it can't be much of a mystery," Landon grumbled, his expression thoughtful as he studied the page. "Do you think the ghosts were from the tanker? Were they all men?"

I nodded. "No women. As for the ghosts being from the tanker, I'm not ruling out the possibility that they came from somewhere else, but I think it makes a lot more sense to follow the obvious trail."

"And that trail leads right to Sam's tanker," Landon mused, leaning back in his chair. "I wouldn't mind seeing that tanker."

My heart rolled. I knew he would say it, but I wasn't keen on returning to the tanker after what happened yesterday. It's not as if I could avoid it, though. "I figured you might," I said, forcing a wan smile. "I thought we could check out the tanker and then have lunch in town."

"As long as I get to spend time with you, I'm fine with that," Landon said, brushing a kiss against my cheek. "I do have one question before we go, though: If the ghosts are haunting the tanker, why would they come to the inn?"

I was dreading that question, too. "Perhaps they saw us on the tanker even though we didn't see them and they followed us home."

"Is that possible?"

"It wouldn't be the first time."

"Well, I don't like the sound of that," Landon admitted. "I don't want strange ghosts following you home."

"I'm less worried about me than Annie," I said. "This could completely freak her out if they keep showing up."

"Well, I'm worried about both of you," Landon said. "I want you safe, Bay. I want Annie safe, too. I think we need to figure out this ghost situation as soon as possible."

"I totally agree with you there."

"Of course you do," Landon teased, tweaking my nose. "I'm the smartest man in the world. You would be crazy to disagree with me."

"You're modest, too," I said, giggling as he gave me a kiss. Instead of immediately separating, we sank into an embrace and took a few moments to enjoy the solitude. I had a feeling we would be in short supply of it over the next few days. That's when a familiar figure popped into view in front of us and proved just how right I was.

"Ooh, are you guys about to do it?"

The recently deceased Viola Hendricks stared at Landon and me as she crossed her arms over her chest. She'd been dead for only a month – and popping up in my life on a regular basis for a few weeks – so I was still getting used to her presence.

"We're not going to do it," I muttered, wiping my mouth as Landon made a curious face.

"I wasn't trying to get you to do it," Landon said. "I love you, but I'm not an animal."

"I wasn't talking to you," I offered, holding up my hands by way of apology. "Viola is here."

"Oh." Landon couldn't see ghosts, but he didn't seem thrilled with the knowledge that we weren't alone. "What does she want?"

That was a good question. "What do you want, Viola?"

"He doesn't have to talk about me as if I'm not here," Viola complained. "I'm a person and should be treated with respect. Heck, I'm his elder. He should be worshipping me."

That sounded nothing like Landon. "He only worships me."

Landon smirked at my half of the conversation. "And only when she's naked," he added, causing me to elbow him in the stomach. "That was a compliment, sweetie. Don't be so mean."

"I'm sorry," I said, shaking my head. "I didn't mean to hurt you."

"He's kind of a wimp, huh?" Unlike most women, Viola didn't fall at his feet whenever she saw Landon. "He's pretty, though."

"He's handsome," I corrected. "He doesn't like being called pretty."

"Then he should cut his hair," Viola said. "He would be handsome if he cut his hair."

"If he cuts his hair, I'll be heartbroken," I said, twirling strands of Landon's locks around my fingers. "Not that I'm not happy to see you, Viola, but what are you doing here?" In truth, I wasn't happy to see Viola. When The Whistler's resident ghost Edith passed over a few weeks ago – her murder finally solved after she spent decades in limbo – I thought I would be ghost free for an extended amount of time. I was very wrong. I wasn't alone for five minutes before Viola showed up. She's been making something of a nuisance of herself ever since.

"Well, if he's not going to cut it you should at least convince him to braid it," Viola said. "I think that's one of the biggest disappointments out there right now. There aren't enough man braids."

Viola was one of those people who said whatever came to her mind when she was alive. She got away with it because she was elderly and no one dared call her on it. Now that she was dead and faced no repercussions at all she had absolutely no filter.

"I will ... talk to Landon about your braid suggestion later," I said, biting my lip to keep from laughing as Landon made an annoyed face. "Why are you here again?"

"I'm bored, and the only people who can see me live in this house," Viola replied. "I thought I might mess with Tillie a little bit. I saw you first, though."

"Lucky me," I deadpanned. "I ... ." Something occurred to me and I changed course. "You're bored, huh?"

Viola nodded. "I am so bored. Haunting Hemlock Cove isn't nearly as much fun as I thought it would be."

I could see that. "Do you remember my cousin Thistle?"

"What are you doing, Bay?" Landon asked, his voice low.

"She's the one with the weird hair, right?" Viola asked.

"She is," I confirmed. "You hung out with her about a week ago."

"Oh, that's right," Viola said. "She can hear me but not see me when you're around."

"Actually, now that she's heard you she'll always be able to hear you," I offered. "Clove, too."

"Oh, well, that's good to know," Viola said. "That gives me more people to talk to."

"It does," I agreed, bobbing my head. "In fact, I think you should talk to her now. She mentioned this morning that she's feeling lonely. Her boyfriend has long hair, too, and neither one of them understand about the man braid."

Landon snorted but otherwise remained quiet.

"Okay, if you think it will help," Viola said. She didn't look thrilled or disappointed with the suggestion. "What are you going to do? I don't want you to be lonely."

"I don't want to be lonely either," I said. "Thistle is already lonely, though. She told me. In fact ... yes ... didn't you once tell me that you knit slippers for soldiers serving overseas?"

"I did."

"You also told me you got a letter from each soldier and memorized each one."

"I did that, too."

"I think Thistle would love to hear about all of those soldiers," I said. "There were like a hundred of them, right?"

"Yes." The more I talked, the more intrigued Viola seemed. "Do you really think she would want to hear about that?"

"I know she would," I said. "She loves soldiers and slippers. This is going to be the best of both worlds for her."

Viola mock saluted and smiled. "I'm on it. I'll keep your cousin from boredom."

"I knew you were the right ghost for the job." I kept my smile in place until she disappeared and then shifted my eyes to Landon. "She's gone."

"You're an evil woman, Bay Winchester." Landon said the words but his eyes were filled with mirth. "Evil!"

"I thought you liked me when I was evil."

"I like you however you are," Landon said. "I do love it when you're evil, though. I'm looking forward to playing evil nap games later – you know, kissing the princess to wake her up and stuff. We need to visit the Dandridge first."

I'd almost forgotten about that. "Well, I'll make it worth your while later."

"And that's why you're my favorite person in the world," Landon said, smacking a kiss to my lips. "Now, come on. Let's check out the tanker. The faster we do our investigating, the faster we can enjoy evil Bay's … talents."

"You are kind of a pervert. You know that, right?"

"You say that like it's a bad thing."

EIGHT

Clove opened the door to the Dandridge after our third knock, a frazzled look on her face.

"I have no time for crap," she announced. "If you're trying to get me on your side in your war against Thistle, you're fresh out. I'm not in the mood to play games."

Landon smirked as he looked Clove up and down. She was dressed in knit shorts and a T-shirt – which was unheard of because she preferred looking cute and put together – and her dark hair was pushed back from her face thanks to a bandana. She had dirt smudges on her cheek and a bottle of window cleaner in her hand.

"Hello, Mr. Clean."

Clove didn't bother cracking a smile. "You're so funny, Landon. You could be a comedian if this FBI agent thing doesn't work out."

Landon raised his eyebrows as he glanced at me. "Wow. And I thought Thistle was the mean one."

"I'm sorry," Clove offered, her shoulders stiff. "I'm just very busy. I mean ... very busy. I don't have time for nonsense. That's exactly what I told Thistle when she called."

Well, that answered that question. "What did Thistle want you to do?"

"I just told you that I don't have time for nonsense," Clove groused. "Did you hear me? Are you suddenly deaf?"

"You really are the mean one today," I shot back. "Aunt Tillie would be proud ... and want to visit so she can take notes."

Despite her grouchy demeanor, Clove brightened considerably. "Do you think?"

"Definitely," Landon said, gripping the maritime book tighter as he slipped a protective arm around my waist. "We're not here to bug you, though. We're here to bug Sam."

Clove blinked twice, surprised. "Oh ... I ... ."

"Forgot I lived here apparently," Sam supplied, his smile small but genuine when he nudged Clove out of the way with his hip. "Go back to your cleaning, honey. I'll handle our guests."

"Okay." Clove looked torn. She clearly wanted to know why we were visiting Sam, but she was in cleaning mode thanks to Sam's mother's imminent arrival. She couldn't do both at once. "I'll want to know everything you talked about later."

"I'll take notes just for you," Sam quipped, earning a scathing look. "Or ... not."

"You need to have your little meeting of the minds outside," Clove ordered, pointing toward the patio. "I've already cleaned that area, so if you mess it up you're going to answer to me."

On a normal day I might laugh at the threat. She clearly meant business today, though. "I'll guard your clean patio with my life," Sam said, his smile thin and grim.

"You do that."

Landon maintained an air of calm indifference as we shuffled toward the patio, cracking a smile only when he was sure we were out of Clove's earshot. "What's with her?"

"She's a maniac," Sam replied. "Never in my life have I seen someone so ... ."

"Crazy?" I supplied.

"I was going to say determined," Sam replied, shooting me a dark look. "Don't talk about my Clove that way. She's simply focused. She's not crazy."

"She looks a little crazy to me, but I think that's the Winchester way," Landon said, sitting in one of the chairs around the outdoor table and watching as Sam put up the umbrella. "Bay went crazy this morning, but she recovered. There's nothing to worry about. With the Winchesters it seems to be temporary insanity. I'm hopeful none of them will have to be involuntarily committed at any point. The jury is still out on Thistle, though."

"Speaking of Thistle, do you know what she wanted Clove to do to me?" I asked.

Sam shook his head. "I wasn't listening."

I narrowed my eyes. He didn't quite make eye contact. "I think you know."

"And I think I'm in a bad position, so I don't want to tell you."

"Yes, but you like me better than Thistle," I reminded him. "I was mean when you first came to town because you caught me off guard. I've been nice ever since."

"You've only started being nice since I saved your life," Sam reminded me. "You're definitely nicer than Thistle, though. As for liking you better ... well ... I'm not choosing sides."

"If you don't pick a side then you're going to get it from both of us," I warned. "Aunt Tillie taught us that."

"Speaking of frightening women," Sam grumbled. "Are you sure she shouldn't be involuntarily committed?"

"She'd only escape and mete out some truly terrible revenge if we tried," Landon answered smoothly. "I'd rather be able to wear pants to work. I don't think my boss will find it funny if I have to wear jogging pants instead of a suit to meetings."

"No, probably not," Sam conceded. "As for Thistle's plan, I honestly don't know. It has something to do with clowns, balloons and the sewer, though. Clove told Thistle she refused to mess around with the sewers again and she didn't care how much Thistle threatened her. I was kind of confused when she said 'again.'"

My heart dropped. "The Pennywise Gambit," I muttered, horrified.

Landon leaned forward, intrigued. "What is The Pennywise Gambit?"

I shook my head to dislodge a terrifying memory. "You don't want to know."

"Oh, I totally want to know," Landon said. "I'm assuming Pennywise is the clown from *It*, right? I thought you hated clowns."

"I do. Why do you think it's such an effective gambit?"

"I have no idea," Landon said. "I'm curious and terrified to hear this story. I can't stop myself from asking, though. You need to tell me."

"Let's just say that clowns aren't the only things living in sewers that have razor sharp teeth," I said. "We'll have to leave it at that. I've blocked the rest from my memory."

"Well, whatever it is, Clove was dead set against it," Sam supplied. "I thought she was going to cry for a minute when she hung up. I was almost looking forward to it because I figured she would have to stop cleaning and rest if she cried. She persevered, though."

I snickered. In truth, I hated Sam when he first came to town. Actually, I feared him. He seemed to know our secret, and he wouldn't stop following me around. Eventually we found out his mother was a solitary practitioner and he was merely curious about the infamous Winchesters. Trust still came slow. I trust him with my whole heart now, though. More importantly, I trust him with Clove's heart.

"I can head off The Pennywise Gambit," I said. "I think it might call for something big, though. I need to talk to Aunt Tillie." I reached for my phone but Landon stilled me with a hand on my knee.

"Later, sweetie," he said. "Your war with Thistle can keep for a little bit. We need answers about the tanker first. It's more important."

Sam arched an eyebrow, surprised. "The tanker? Why do you care about the tanker?"

"We were on it yesterday," I replied.

"I know that," Sam said. "I saw you right after."

Whoops. I'd almost forgotten about that. "Anyway, during the storm last night, I thought I saw something in the library."

"What?"

"Ghosts."

Sam tilted his head to the side, considering. He could see ghosts, too. His ability wasn't nearly as strong as mine, but it wasn't weak. "I knew something was going on when you came back after the generator kicked on," he said. "I thought maybe Landon did something dirty when no one was looking. You seemed distracted. I didn't realize you saw ghosts."

"At first, I wasn't sure I did either," I said. "For a second I thought I was imagining them. Then, when the power went out, I thought they were going to end up on top of me once the lights came back on, and I was terrified to move. When Landon found me, they were gone."

"You didn't see them, did you?" Sam asked, turning to Landon.

"I can't see ghosts," Landon reminded him.

"You did the night you saved Bay from the ship in the cove," Sam said. "You saw Erika's ghost that night."

That was something of a mystery – and a sore subject – because Landon remained miffed that I willingly walked into trouble and he barely managed to save me from murderers thanks to a patient ghost from the Civil War era who managed to track him down and warn him of my plight. We still didn't understand why he could see Erika and he hadn't seen a ghost since. I was of the mind that he saw her because he had no choice, but he didn't like to talk about it very often.

"Yes, well, I've never seen another ghost so that's a moot point," Landon said, refusing to engage on the subject. "Bay saw them, though, and then there was an incident with Annie."

"What happened to Annie?"

"She saw two ghosts, too," I replied. "I think she has the gift … although it doesn't feel like much of a gift sometimes."

"Oh, you're gifted," Landon said, squeezing my hand. "Bay didn't mention it last night, but this morning she remembered that one of the ghosts wore a captain's hat. Then she remembered your tanker and looked it up." He opened the book to the page we read earlier and handed it to Sam.

Sam scanned the passages for a few seconds and then glanced up. "This is about the Gray Harker."

"Yes, but the Yeti Inferno used to go under that name," I supplied. "I looked it up."

"Oh." Sam seemed surprised. "You would think they would've disclosed that at the time of sale."

"Did you ask?"

"I guess not," Sam said, licking his lips. "Now that you mention it, they're only required to disclose accidents or repairs. It's not like buying a house. The seller doesn't have to disclose tragedies."

"And we have no idea what kind of tragedy happened on the tanker," Landon said. "All we know is that it was missing for months and the crew was never heard from again."

"There can't be a happy story attached to that," Sam said. "In the grand scheme of things, though, the history of the tanker will make for a much more intriguing haunted attraction."

"Yes, that's the most important thing," Landon deadpanned.

"I'm sorry," Sam said, holding up his hands. "That was a stupid thing to say. I understand that you're worried, but ... I don't know what to do with it. I've been all over that tanker, and I've never seen a ghost."

"That doesn't mean they're not there," I pointed out. "You know as well as I do that ghosts only show themselves when they feel comfortable doing it."

"But why did they go after you?" Sam asked. "Why wouldn't they reveal themselves to me once I got the tanker back here? I'm the new owner."

"They're male ghosts," Landon said. "Perhaps they like the ladies. I know if I was stuck as a ghost, there's no one I would rather follow than Bay."

"Oh, you're so cute," I said, poking his cheek. "You're going to get smothered with love later, so there's no reason to lay it on so thick."

"I was serious."

"Well, now you're going to get doubly lucky." I shot him an affectionate smile before turning back to Sam. "As for why they appeared to me and Annie, perhaps they saw me on the tanker yesterday and were intrigued. Maybe they followed me back to the inn."

"Did you go straight to the inn?" Sam queried.

I shook my head. "No. I went to the guesthouse first."

"Have you seen them at the guesthouse?"

Hmm. He had a point. "No."

"What does that matter?" Landon asked, legitimately curious. "What are you getting at?"

"I'm merely saying that if the ghosts followed her, you would've seen them at the guesthouse," Sam said. "The ghosts might very well have been intrigued by the appearance of powerful witches on the deck. For all we know, they could sense your power. Why would they show up at the inn instead of the guesthouse, though?"

"I can't answer that because I'm not an expert on ghost behavior," Landon said. "I'm not sure how that works. We can only move forward with the information we have in front of us."

"We don't know the ghosts Bay saw were from the tanker," Sam said.

"We don't," Landon conceded. "Bay made a good point earlier – as she always does because she's my little genius – but it would be one heck of a coincidence for a new tanker to arrive in town and have an unrelated fresh ghost wearing a captain's hat."

"I agree that's a little hard to swallow," Sam said, rubbing the back of his neck. "I'm not sure what to think about it. Now I'm really glad my parents will be staying at the inn instead of out here, though. If ghosts really are anchored to the tanker ... things could get ugly."

I understood what he was saying. "Maybe you and Clove should come back to the guesthouse for a few days," I suggested. "That would keep you close to the inn where your parents are and then we wouldn't worry."

"It would also keep you from having to fight dirty with Thistle over that room," Landon added.

"That, too."

"I'll talk to Clove about it," Sam said. "I'm not sure she'll agree. She really loves living in the lighthouse. She's a big fan of the swirling lights."

"Don't sell yourself short," I said, offering him a kind smile. "She's a big fan of you, too."

Sam's smile was so earnest it almost hurt my heart. "I feel the same way about her. I don't want her to be in danger, though. What do you think we should do about the ghosts?"

"There's only one thing we can do about the ghosts," I said. "We have to hold a séance."

"Oh, crap," Landon complained. "I hate séances."

"We're absolutely not having a séance!" Clove barked, throwing open the windows on the side of the lighthouse and fixing me with a dark look. She'd obviously been eavesdropping. "You know I hate séances. They give ghosts strength and they almost never work."

"That doesn't mean we shouldn't try," I argued.

"That's exactly what it means."

"Clove, you need to be reasonable," I said, adopting a pragmatic tone. "We have to figure out what these ghosts want."

"Not today we don't," Clove snapped. "Sam's parents will be here tomorrow. Tomorrow! We are not calling ghosts to that ship and questioning them when we know it will end badly."

"How do you know it will end badly?" Sam asked, glancing over his shoulder.

"Because they always end badly," Clove said. "It's not going to happen this time. Nope. No way. No how. Nothing doing."

"But ...."

"No." Clove firmly shook her head. "N-O. No."

"We have to do something," I said. "We can't ignore the problem."

"That's where you're wrong," Clove shot back. "We ignore problems all of the time. We ignored Aunt Tillie's pot field ... and wine business ... and general troublemaking shenanigans. This will be no different. It can wait a few days."

"But what if it can't?"

"If the universe knows what's good for it, it will refrain from messing with my world for one week," Clove said. "I am meeting my boyfriend's parents for the first time. I can take only so much."

Sam seemed amused. "Okay, honey. No séance."

I wasn't happy with Sam's decision, but there wasn't much I could do about it. "Fine. No séance for now. Things might change, though."

"If things change, I'm going to kick the universe in the butt and hide in bed for a week," Clove said. "I'm not joking. This is my week. I'm in charge. Don't even think about messing with me."

I didn't know how to answer, so I kept my mouth shut. Landon was another story. His voice was low when he leaned closer.

"I think she might be scarier than Thistle."

Now that was a frightening thought.

NINE

"And there's my favorite person." Chief Terry Davenport smiled when Landon and I walked into the diner on Main Street. I headed straight for him, settling in the chair to his left without asking whether or not he wanted company. I already knew the answer.

"I'm happy to see you, too," I said, grinning.

"He was talking about me," Landon said, taking the chair across from Chief Terry and smirking. "I'm his favorite person."

"You're not even in the top five," Chief Terry shot back, although he shared a small smile with Landon. They weren't exactly fond of each other upon their first meeting but they'd grown close since then, working on multiple cases together. "She's at the top."

"That's funny, because she's at the top of my list, too," Landon said, smiling at the waitress as she approached to take our drink orders. He waited until she was gone to continue speaking. "I don't care what you say. I'm pretty sure I'm in your top five."

"I'm pretty sure you're delusional," Chief Terry said, shaking his head before turning to me. "How have you been? I haven't seen you most of the week."

"I've been busy at The Whistler," I answered. "Landon wasn't here for the bulk of the week, so I got ahead. It's always a busy time when we have a festival."

Landon snorted. "This town has more festivals than it does people," he said. "What festival is going on this week?"

"The Fall Hoedown."

"You guys have a hoedown?" Landon snickered. "I don't even know what to make of that. You know I'm not line dancing, right?"

"I didn't know you did any kind of dancing," I said. "Does that mean you'll do other types of dancing?"

"That means I'll slow dance with you and that's it," Landon replied. "Isn't a hoedown a one-night event, though? How can it be a festival?"

"This town doesn't do anything in a normal fashion," Chief Terry supplied. "The opening dance is tonight and then we hold different dances every night until next Sunday."

"There are different bands each night, too," I offered.

"That sounds like a terrific way to cause ear rot," Landon said, shifting when I tried to elbow him in the stomach. "What? I didn't say I wouldn't go to the hoedown with you. I merely said I will only dance to slow songs and only if you whisper dirty things in my ear while we're dancing."

"Don't make me thump you," Chief Terry warned, extending a finger. "You know how I feel about that flirting thing you do right in front of me. She's a child."

"She's not my child," Landon countered. "Last time I checked, she's almost thirty, too."

"I'm twenty-eight."

"You're going to be twenty-nine in a few months," Landon said. "That means you're almost thirty."

He was right. Darn it! "Don't remind me. I don't want to be depressed."

"Why would that depress you?"

I shrugged. "I don't know. Thirty seems old. When I was a kid I thought everyone over thirty was ancient."

"Yes, but you're not a kid any longer," Landon pointed out. "There's no reason to be depressed. You're still young and beautiful."

"Oh, so cute!" I gave him a quick kiss as Chief Terry scowled.

"You two make me want to puke," Chief Terry grumbled. "Seriously. I have indigestion. You give me acid reflux, Landon. Does that make you happy?"

"It doesn't make me unhappy," Landon replied. "Is anything else going on around town? If you need help with something, I'm fairly certain I could talk my boss into letting me stick close all week."

I pursed my lips as I regarded him. Landon was always looking for reasons to stay in Hemlock Cove during the week. I think the knowledge that a gang of ghosts was running around haunting people made him overly eager to remain close to me. It was kind of sweet.

"There's absolutely nothing going on," Chief Terry said. "Oh, wait, that's not true. Margaret Little says she's convinced someone has been peeping in her windows. If you want to take on that case I'd be more than willing to hand it over to you."

Landon made a face. "Why would someone peep her?"

"If you believe her it's because they want to see her naked, and the world is turning into a haven for perverts and heathens."

"Do you believe her?" I asked.

"Only a disturbed mind would want to see her naked."

Landon barked out a laugh. "That's true," he said. "I really don't want to take on that case, though. I guess I'll have to head back to Traverse City on Monday whether I like it or not."

"Why wouldn't you like it?" Chief Terry asked, oblivious as I cast Landon a sidelong look. "Traverse City is much more exciting than Hemlock Cove."

"Not even close," Landon said, squeezing my hand.

When Chief Terry realized what he was talking about he screwed up his face. "You two get sicker and sicker every time I spend time with you. It's like there are pheromones dancing around your heads."

Landon cocked an eyebrow. "Pheromones?"

"Yes, they're like sex scents," Chief Terry said. "I think only dogs and perverts can smell them."

"Arf." Landon barked, causing me to smile. "Personally, I think the best sex scent is bacon."

"You would," Chief Terry said. "You're a total pervert."

"I can live with that," Landon said, leaning back in his chair and focusing on the scene out the window. The town square bustled with activity as Hemlock Cove's usual players hurried to set up the festival. "I can't believe you're having a hoedown. I didn't know you guys did that. I thought I'd seen every festival this place had to offer."

"Almost," I said. "In a few weeks we'll be back to the Halloween Festival ... and the corn maze. Wow!" The reality hit me hard. "That will be the anniversary of when we first met."

Landon slid a sly look in my direction. "Who would've thought one person could turn my world upside down in such a short amount of time?"

"In a good or a bad way?"

"In the best way," Landon answered. "You're right, though. It's been almost a year. That is just ... odd."

"It's crazy," Chief Terry said. "You two are schmaltzy and it makes me want to smack your heads together to knock some sense into you. Still ... I guess even I won't forget the first time I saw you together."

"When was that?" I asked, racking my brain. "You weren't at the corn maze the day we met."

"I wasn't, but Landon was in my office when you barged in to ask questions about the case," Chief Terry reminded me. "Don't you remember? You were suspicious and he wouldn't stop drooling. You weren't even out the door before he started asking questions. In that exact instant, I knew he was going to be trouble."

I couldn't help but be intrigued. "What questions did he ask?"

If Landon was bothered by my curiosity, he didn't show it. He leaned back in his chair and shot me a lazy grin. "I asked if you were mentally unbalanced."

"He asked if you were single," Chief Terry corrected. "Actually, well, he asked if you were mentally unbalanced first because he thought you were nervous. Then he asked if you were single."

"And do you remember what you told me?" Landon asked.

Chief Terry pressed his lips together and nodded. "I asked you if you wanted to find out how my boot felt in your behind."

"He warned me away from you," Landon said, his eyes filled with mirth. "He wanted me to be aware that if I ever hurt you he would beat the snot out of me."

"I didn't think it would get that far, but I needed to be certain," Chief Terry said. "I can handle a lot in this world. You with a broken heart is not one of those things."

His words warmed me. He was something of a second father to me after my own disappeared for a long period when I was a kid. My father was back now, but our relationship was nowhere near as close as the one Chief Terry and I share.

"I'm glad you were looking out for me," I said. "It turns out you didn't need to, because Landon is practically perfect, but thank you anyway."

"Did you hear that?" Landon asked, his grin impish. "I'm perfect."

"And I'm going to smack that stupid smile off your face if you're not careful," Chief Terry said. "Not that I'm not happy to stroll down memory lane, but I'm kind of curious what's going on with you guys. Are things quiet at the inn?"

"Things are never quiet at the inn," Landon replied. "Never. There's always some catastrophe to avert."

"And what is this week's catastrophe?"

"Well, for starters, Sam's parents arrive tomorrow and they're staying at The Overlook," Landon supplied. "Clove has gone completely mental and is cleaning like a madwoman. I'm not joking. She's scouring everything and refuses to play with her cousins, which is making both of them sad."

Chief Terry chuckled. "That sounds about right. What else?"

"Bay and Thistle are at war over Clove's old room," Landon explained. "This morning Thistle locked us in Bay's bedroom. I was fine with it, but Bay wasn't happy. I think she might be a little claustrophobic. It's weird to find that out one year in."

"We didn't get together right after we met," I reminded him. "That took a little time."

"And a big exit from Landon," Chief Terry said.

Landon scowled. "Thanks for reminding me of that." After finding out the truth regarding our witchy ancestry, Landon took a break from the relationship to think things over. It wasn't long, and he'd been accepting ever since, but he hated being reminded about what happened.

"You're welcome," Chief Terry said, not missing a beat. "What else is going on?"

"Why do you ask?" I was suddenly suspicious. "Do you know something? Has Thistle tried to get you on her side so she can steal the extra bedroom?"

Chief Terry made a face. "I don't care about the bedroom."

"Plus, we both know he'd be on your side," Landon said, flicking my ear. "There's no reason to be paranoid. Let it go."

"I'm not paranoid."

"You're always paranoid when it comes to Thistle these days. Let it go."

"Whatever." I crossed my arms over my chest and locked gazes with Chief Terry. "Are you digging for information on something else?"

"Not particularly," Chief Terry said, rubbing his cheek. "It's just ... look over your shoulder."

"What?"

"Look over your shoulder," he prodded. "I think you'll see what I was asking about."

I did as he asked, finding the table behind us empty. I was momentarily confused and then I lifted my eyes to the window, my mouth dropping open when I caught sight of Aunt Tillie walking down the street. She was dressed in pink camouflage pants, a pink satin jacket that had lettering I couldn't read, and she was wearing a combat helmet.

"What is she doing?" Landon asked, leaning forward.

"I have no idea, but she's been down here for three days straight," Chief Terry replied. "She walks back and forth on the sidewalk. The distance spans one block. Do you know what she's walking in front of?"

It took me a moment to realize what Chief Terry was referring to. "She's messing with Mrs. Little."

"Exactly," Chief Terry said. "She paces in front of the store and stares inside. Margaret stares at her as she passes. It's like a really weird showdown, although neither side talks to the other. I can't figure out what they're doing."

"Have you asked?"

"I asked Margaret. She said Tillie is unbalanced and needs to be locked up," Chief Terry replied. "I have not asked Aunt Tillie because ... well ... she's wearing a combat helmet. I'm worried that means she's armed. If she's armed, I'll have to arrest her. It seems like more trouble than it's worth."

Landon laughed, delighted. "She is a trip, isn't she? This morning she offered to join Bay in her war against Thistle. I don't think she particularly wants to help Bay as much as she wants to irritate Thistle."

"Hey, I'll take it," I said. "Thistle is so diabolical I have a feeling I'm going to need Aunt Tillie."

"I don't want the woman on my enemies list, but I'd totally take her into battle," Chief Terry said. "As for whatever she's doing with Margaret, I have a feeling that will play itself out in due time. Neither one of them can keep up the silent treatment for much longer."

"I only hope they don't cause a scene when they decide to go at it," Bay said. "That's the last thing we need with Sam's parents coming to town. Clove is a nervous wreck."

"Clove will be fine," Chief Terry said. "She's exactly the sort of girl mothers like."

What was that supposed to mean? "Am I the type of girl mothers like?" I knew I sounded whiny and petulant, but I couldn't stop myself from asking.

"You're the kind of girl everyone likes," Chief Terry answered. "You're an angel."

"Oh, good grief," Landon groused. "You say I'm schmaltzy, but you're ten times worse."

"I don't care," Chief Terry said. "Bay has always been a good girl."

Another question nudged into the front of my brain. "Is Thistle the sort of girl mothers like?"

I could tell Chief Terry didn't want to answer but he finally relented. "I think Thistle is the sort of girl mothers fear."

"It's not just mothers," Landon said.

"No, definitely not," Chief Terry said. "Either way, I'm hopeful Tillie and Margaret will work things out away from town when their tempers finally blow.

"I just want a quiet festival week," he continued. "We haven't had one of those in almost a year. It would be a nice change of pace."

I hoped he got his wish, but I wasn't holding my breath.

TEN

"What do you think Aunt Tillie is up to?"

Landon held my hand as we walked from the diner toward the town square after finishing lunch. He seemed in good spirits – which is exactly how I like him – but also appeared to be pondering something serious.

"I have no idea," I replied. "I'm sure it isn't good, whatever it is. She has a very tempestuous relationship with Mrs. Little."

"I've noticed," Landon said dryly. "Now that they're the only two left standing from that little clique they used to be part of when they were younger, I can't help but wonder if that means they're going to be far more active when it comes to hating each other."

"I'm not sure how much more active they can get," I said. "Aunt Tillie has been out to get Mrs. Little since before I was born. You wouldn't believe the things she made us do as kids."

Landon looked amused. "Like what? I love hearing stories about your adventures with Aunt Tillie when you were younger."

"You didn't like seeing them when we were stuck in her memories a few weeks ago," I reminded him.

"That's not true," Landon countered. "I actually think that was one of the best days of my life."

I giggled. "You do not."

"I do too," Landon said. "If you take Aunt Tillie getting hurt out of the equation, I had a lot of fun that day. I got to see you as a kid. Heck, I got to see you being born. I had a great time."

The confession seemed earnest, but I couldn't help but be dubious. "You also got to see some hard stuff," I said. "I don't think either one of us liked seeing the bad memories a second time."

"I don't know." Landon shrugged. "I mean ... bad memories suck. There's no getting around that. They're still part of a certain process. You wouldn't know something is good if you didn't have something bad to compare it to. I don't mind the bad memories. They remind me how far we've come."

I slowed my forward momentum and stared at him. "You're kind of like a woman sometimes. You know that, right?"

Landon's grin was sloppy as he offered me a kiss. "I don't care how much you tease me. I feel closer to you since we spent that day together. I wouldn't trade it for anything."

Funnily enough, I wouldn't either. "Well, I think I'm going to take that as a compliment."

"Good. It was meant as one."

We lapsed into comfortable silence as we finished our walk to the festival staging area. The area buzzed with activity as the workers constructed the stage and roped off the dancing area. Merchants were setting up booths along the shopping corridor. I couldn't hide my evil sneer when my eyes landed on Thistle. Her back was to me and she seemed fixated on her booth, which gave me the advantage for this battle.

"Why do you have that terrifying look on your face?" Landon asked, following my gaze. "Oh. Are you going to make Thistle eat dirt or something? If so, if you two could get in bikinis or something first that would be great."

I scowled as I narrowed my eyes. "You're a sick man."

"That's not exactly news," Landon pointed out. "Chief Terry spent an hour telling you just that over lunch. What do you think all of that talk of puking was about?"

"The fact that he still sees me as eight, which means you're a really filthy man in his head."

"Yeah, he's going to need to let that go," Landon said. "It makes me uncomfortable when I look at him and wonder if he's imagining a hundred different ways to separate my head from my body."

"I'll protect you if it gets that far," I teased, smiling. "As for Thistle, I'm not going to make her eat dirt. I'm merely going to … visit … her."

"Yeah, I'm not new to the Winchester way of thinking," Landon said. "I can tell you're going to be mean. Normally I'd like to watch whatever you're about to do – I think mean Bay is hot – but I see Margaret Little over there and I'm kind of curious if Aunt Tillie is around."

"I guarantee she's around."

"You could come with me and solve a mystery," Landon offered. "If you stay here you'll probably pick a fight with Thistle and regret it."

"I'll stay here."

"How did I know you were going to say that?" Landon grumbled, shaking his head. "Don't do anything that'll force me to arrest you. You have an audience."

"I won't."

"Good." He gave me a kiss before we separated. "If you don't take too long I'll buy you some pumpkin ice cream from that stand over there. I've never had pumpkin ice cream, but it sounds just gross enough to be delicious … kind of like beefy macaroni in a can."

"You've got a deal."

I watched Landon move across the festival grounds with a soft smile. The second he was out of sight the smile slipped, replaced with a twisted smirk. Landon wasn't wrong about things getting ugly. The question was: How ugly?

Thistle was lost in her own little world when I approached, which allowed me to sneak up on her. I bent my head over her shoulder from behind to make sure I had her attention before speaking.

"There's my favorite cousin in the world. How are you this fine summer day?"

Thistle froze at the sound of my voice, and I could tell she was

THE TROUBLE WITH WITCHES

taking a moment to collect her thoughts before speaking. She didn't want her voice to shake or come out unnaturally high. That would be a dead giveaway she was rattled.

"It's not really summer," Thistle said. "I mean, sure, it's still technically August. We all know that fall starts the third week of August when you're in northern Lower Michigan."

I couldn't argue with that fact. That didn't mean I would forgo messing with her altogether. "That was an interesting trick you pulled this morning," I said, keeping my voice low and my smile in place so anyone passing by would think we were two cousins having a simple conversation about normal things ... like festivals. "You know I can't stand being locked in a room ever since you locked me in the basement when I was a kid. I have to think you did it on purpose."

Surprisingly, Thistle's coloring shifted from a healthy peach to a wan apricot. "I forgot about that, Bay," she said. "You're not really claustrophobic, so I tend to forget that you don't like it when you're locked in places. I didn't mean to do that to you."

"What did you mean to do?"

Thistle didn't bother lying. "Annoy you."

"Well, congratulations," I said. "You managed that without breaking a sweat."

"You know I hate sweating unless it's for a fun reason," Thistle said. "Messing with you is definitely fun, but I didn't mean to upset you this morning. If I did ... ."

"I wasn't upset," I said, cutting her off. "Why would you think I was upset? Like you said, I'm not claustrophobic."

"No, but you hate being locked in places," Thistle said. "I knew that and forgot. I didn't mean to rattle you that way."

"It's not as if I was alone," I reminded her. "Landon was with me. He liked being locked in. He thought it was fun."

"Did you tell him why you hate it?"

"No."

"Did you tell him about what happened on Sam's ship yesterday?"

I narrowed my eyes. She asked the question in an innocent

manner, but there was something about her tone that set my teeth on edge. It almost sounded like a threat. "What are you saying?"

"I asked you a simple question," Thistle said, her voice positively dripping with faux sweetness. "I wasn't saying anything bad."

I didn't believe that for a moment. "Fine. I'll forgive you for what happened this morning as long as you keep the secret about the tanker."

"I wouldn't tell anyway," Thistle said, taking a step away from me so she could turn and face me down. I no longer had the power position, which was exactly how Thistle liked things. "You know I wouldn't tell Landon what happened without your approval. I promised I wouldn't."

Despite our building war, I did know that. "That's coming back to bite me anyway," I admitted. "A bunch of ghosts showed up at the inn last night and I'm pretty sure they're from the tanker. I wasn't the only one who saw them."

"What do you mean?"

I related recent developments to Thistle, including Annie's part in the tale, and when I was done she was ticked off. "Why didn't you tell me all of this last night? We need to talk to Belinda. She can't go around accusing Annie of making up stories. That will erode Annie's self-esteem. If anyone knows that, it should be you."

"I do know that and I had every intention of talking to you about the situation," I said. "Then I woke up and couldn't get out of my bedroom."

"Oh, go ahead," Thistle intoned. "Blame me. I know you want to."

"I'm not blaming you for all of it," I said. "We both had a part in it. I'm just making sure you're aware that we need to have a talk with our mothers and Aunt Tillie. Someone is going to have to explain things to Belinda, and I think it's going to have to be done in a kind manner. Otherwise she'll think we're crazy."

"Frankly, I can't believe she doesn't already think we're crazy," Thistle said. "If I was in her position, I would've called the cops and had us locked up a long time ago."

That made two of us. Still .... "We conducted some research on the tanker this morning," I said, opting to remain focused on the important part of the conversation. "The Gray Harker, which is what the ship was called years ago, disappeared from Lake Michigan in 1989. It was missing for months and people thought it sunk."

"It obviously didn't sink," Thistle said. "What happened?"

"No one knows," I replied. "It showed up on the lake one day completely empty. The entire crew was gone."

Thistle's eyebrows shot up her forehead. "Gone? Where did they go?"

"None of them were ever seen again," I explained. "All of the lifeboats were onboard and accounted for."

"So ... what are our options?" Thistle asked, rubbing the back of her neck as she stared at her feet. "I guess pirates of some sort could've boarded the vessel and tried to rob people. They could've killed everyone or forced them overboard."

"And yet it seems likely that if that happened at least one body would've washed ashore ... or got caught in a fisherman's net ... or been sighted by another boat," I said. "I don't expect all of the bodies would've been found, but for none of them to be found? That's improbable."

"Okay, what do you think happened?"

"Something violent," I replied. "Several of the ghosts who showed up last night had gaping wounds and bloodstains."

"Gross."

"That would indicate something really terrible happened to them," I added. "I'm not sure, but my guess would be either a crew member went crazy and killed everyone or there was some sort of mutiny. With twenty crew members, you'd need a substantial amount of men to subdue them."

"That's true," Thistle said, running her tongue over her teeth as she considered the scenario. "If a bunch of people died on that ship and their souls remained behind, that means they've spent more than thirty years wandering with the ship. Why make themselves known now?"

"I don't know," I answered. "Sam said he checked out the ship multiple times before buying it and never saw anything. I didn't see ghosts when I was there yesterday."

"You saw something, though," Thistle pointed out. "Maybe all of the ghosts banded together to show you what happened to them. All of that power could've been enough to cause you to pass out."

"That's a possibility," I conceded. "Something about it doesn't feel right, though. I think the ship is a conduit or something. I think it was marked by whatever happened. It was probably so bloody that all the mental angst managed to curse the ship or something."

"Wow. That sounds very dramatic," Thistle said. "Aunt Tillie would come up with a scenario like that. Are you turning into Aunt Tillie?" She looked proud of herself for the dig, but I had a bombshell that would wipe that smile off her face.

"I don't know if I am turning into Aunt Tillie," I replied. "I do know she offered to help if I declared war on you."

Thistle narrowed her eyes. "And what did you say?"

"I said that I would love to take her up on her kind offer."

"You suck eye of newt," Thistle snapped, making a face. "If you think I'm afraid of you simply because you joined forces with that demented old lady ... well ... you've got another think coming."

"Oh, I don't think you're only afraid of Aunt Tillie," I said. "I think you're afraid of me, too."

"Dream on," Thistle snorted. "There's nothing you can do to beat me."

As if on cue, Viola picked that moment to pop into existence. Thistle couldn't see her, but it was almost worse to hear incessant talking when she couldn't see the source.

"Hello, girls," Viola sang out. "How are you today?"

"I'm wonderful," I replied, my lips twitching as I fought off a smile. "I believe Thistle is lonely and bored, though. I'll bet you know a way to entertain her."

"Do I?" Viola looked excited. "I told her about all of my soldiers and their slippers earlier like you told me, by the way."

"That was you?" Thistle looked right through Viola's ethereal body as if she wanted to strangle me. "I should've seen that coming."

"I'm a little disappointed that you didn't," I said. "Perhaps you're slipping in your old age. Hey, Viola? I'll bet you have some great stories about the hoedown, right?"

"Do I?" Viola clapped her transparent hands. "The hoedown was always my favorite festival."

"Well, Thistle is something of a historian," I said. "I'll bet you went to all thirty of the hoedowns through the years. The hoedown is one of the festivals Walkerville held before the town's name was changed, so it's been around a long time. Do you remember each one?"

"I was losing my memory when I died, but now it's back and better than ever," Viola enthused. "I would love to tell Thistle about the hoedowns."

"I think that's a grand plan," I said, taking a step away from Thistle's booth. "She's going to be setting up a long time tonight. I would hate for her to be alone."

"I'll make sure she's not," Viola said, ignoring Thistle's growl. "It will be fun, Thistle. We'll bond."

"I'll make you pay for this," Thistle said, her eyes trained on my face. "You're going to cry like a little girl ... or Landon when you take away his bacon ... by the time I'm done with you."

"I can't wait to see that," I said. "May the best witch win."

"I'm so going to make you eat dirt."

"Oh, I love dirt," Viola chirped. "Remind me to tell you about the dirt in my garden when I'm done with the hoedown stories. I'm an excellent gardener. Er, I was an excellent gardener."

"I can't wait," Thistle deadpanned. "I simply cannot wait."

ELEVEN

"What is this?"

Landon enjoyed walking around Hemlock Cove festivals, so I wasn't surprised when he suggested just that before we met up with everyone else for dinner. He laughed at the kissing booth – while also making suggestive comments – and merely rolled his eyes when he saw a photo booth that allowed guests to dress as paranormal monsters. When we got to a booth selling love potions, though, he seemed perplexed.

"They're love potions," I supplied.

"I see that," Landon said, his eyes finding mine. "I thought you told me that was a bad idea."

"I'm not making them."

"I didn't say you were," Landon said, grabbing one of the bottles so he could flip it over and read the ingredients. "I swear you told me that love potions were bad, though."

"They are," I confirmed, snagging one of the bottles and shaking it so I could look at the ingredients as they floated. "I don't think this is really a love potion, though."

"What if it is?"

I shrugged. "You can't make someone love you," I said. "You can fake the emotions, but eventually the truth comes out. Love is something that happens because of a specific set of circumstances.

"Sure, you can enhance lusty feelings," I continued. "Love is completely different, though. It's unique to the individuals involved."

Landon smirked. "Do you think people are destined to fall in love?"

It was an interesting question. Most men would shy away from deep conversations like this one – conversations that had the potential to expose feelings and insecurity – but Landon wasn't most men. He had no problem talking about love and lust. Er, he especially had no problem talking about lust.

"I don't know," I replied after a beat. "I believe there's an element of destiny in life. I believe I was destined to meet you at some point, for example. Do I believe that things would be radically different if I hadn't met you that day at the corn maze? Probably not. If I met you later – or sooner, for that matter – I think we would simply be at a different point in our journey."

"Oh, that was almost poetic, sweetie," Landon said, grinning as he slung an arm over my shoulders. "I happen to believe we were destined to meet exactly when we did."

"Really?"

Landon nodded. "You were wearing a shirt that matched your eyes that day and it was the first thing I noticed," he explained. "Don't get me wrong, I noticed your hair and smile, too. I remember being really struck by the way your eyes matched your shirt, though."

"That's kind of sweet," I said. "I can't believe you remember that."

"I remember it all, Bay," Landon said. "I also remember being worried that something would happen and I would have to break my cover because you weren't shy about arguing with criminals."

"I didn't know they were criminals at the time."

"You knew they weren't good guys."

I pressed my lips together as I considered the statement. "Actually, I didn't know that," I said. "Part of me knew you were a good guy even though I thought you needed a shower."

"Cute," Landon said, kissing my cheek as he tugged me toward the picnic table area. "I was thinking we could eat here tonight and then head back to your place early. I love your family, but I could do without a dramatic family dinner."

"What makes you think dinner will be dramatic?"

Landon made an exaggerated "well, duh" face. "I've met your family," he replied. "Every meal is dramatic."

"That's not true."

"Name one meal we've shared at the inn that didn't turn dramatic."

"I ... ." I broke off, chewing on my bottom lip. Now that he brought it up, I couldn't think of one. "Huh. Well, I think there are different levels of drama. For the most part, things have been calm for weeks."

"Which means something big is due to happen," Landon said. "That's how life works in your family."

"I think you're pinning behavior on us that really isn't fair," I countered. "We're not overly dramatic."

Landon snickered. "I guess we'll have to wait and see," he said. "I've got twenty bucks that says something happens in the next forty-eight hours to prove me right."

It was an interesting bet and I wanted to join in the competition, but something occurred to me. "Clove freaking out over Sam's parents coming to town doesn't count," I said. "That's normal drama for her. That's not family drama."

Landon worked his tongue over his bottom lip. "Okay," he said after a beat. "I can live with that stipulation."

"It's a bet." I extended my hand so we could shake on it and he eyed it for a moment, amused.

Finally Landon shook my hand and then tugged me to him. "The big kids seal it with a kiss." He planted a soft kiss on the corner of my mouth before releasing me. "This big kid is starving. What do you want for dinner?"

"They have kebabs and rice at the Middle Eastern booth," I replied, pointing. "It smells really good."

"That sounds good to me," Landon said. "When we're done with the main meal, we have to try that pumpkin ice cream. I figure it's either going to be so weird it's delicious or so wacky it's disgusting. Either way, I like trying new things."

"That's what you told me the night you tried to convince me to go skinny-dipping in the lake," I reminded him.

"I was never proved wrong on that front."

Hmm. He had a point.

"I'M PRETTY sure I'm going to die if you make me stay here."

Clove was a bundle of nerves when I approached her a few minutes later. Landon and I were overloaded with food – he wasn't joking about being starving – and we lowered our selections to the picnic table where Clove sat with Sam. She crossed her arms over her chest and jutted out her lower lip. Sam didn't seem bothered by her attitude.

"You're not going to die," Sam countered. "You need a break. You're going to kill yourself cleaning if you're not careful. No one ever died from taking off for a few hours to enjoy a festival."

"That's probably not true," I pointed out. "I'm sure someone died from attending a festival."

Sam scowled. "You know what I mean. Do you have to make things worse? She's manic or something. I've never seen her like this. I brought her here because I thought you and Thistle could make her feel better."

If history was any indication, Thistle and I were bound to make things worse. That didn't mean I wasn't open to the suggestion. "I'll try," I said, flashing a smile for Sam's benefit before focusing on Clove. "You look really pretty."

Clove offered me an exaggerated eye roll. "I have things to do," she said. "Sam's mother will see our home for the first time in exactly ... fifteen hours." She lifted her wrist and looked at it even though she wasn't wearing a watch. "I'm running out of time."

"The lighthouse is spotless," Sam argued. "The only thing you're doing is cleaning things twice – which is a complete waste of time when we could be enjoying the evening together. I've never been to this festival. I'm excited, but it's only fun if we spend our time together."

"Oh, he's so sweet, Clove," I cooed. "How can you not want to have fun with him after he said that?"

Because Clove is something of a romantic, I expected her to melt. I got the exact opposite.

"He is sweet," Clove agreed. "He's also an insensitive ass. His mother is the reason I'm freaking out! What if she doesn't like me? What if she thinks I'm a terrible housekeeper? What if ... ?" Clove broke off, something so horrible occurring to her that she couldn't find the words to voice it.

"Why is she making that face?" Sam asked, alarmed.

"She thinks the world is going to end," I supplied. "She made the same face when Thistle told her the zombie apocalypse was real and then informed her we were going to have to shoot her in the leg and leave her behind so we could make our escape."

"Why would you tell her that?" Sam asked, horrified.

"Because Thistle figured that Clove would slow us down in the zombie apocalypse."

"Why?"

"Because she's slow and prone to whining," Thistle answered, giving me a wide berth as she appeared at the edge of the table. Marcus was right behind her, and Thistle didn't appear bothered in the least to realize Sam was glaring at her. "Whiners don't survive the zombie apocalypse. If we're going to survive we're going to need a solid team."

"I think Clove could rule the zombie apocalypse," Sam argued.

"Thank you, honey," Clove said, sincere. "I would totally rule the zombie apocalypse."

"Meh, I don't think she would make it past the first week. I'm surrounding myself with survivors," Thistle said. "We already have our group planned out. Bay and I did it over chocolate martinis a couple of months ago."

Landon shifted his eyes to me. "Am I on your team?"

I bobbed my head. "You're an integral part," I replied. "You're strong and smart, and we wouldn't survive without you."

"You also have a gun and a hero complex," Thistle added. "The gun will come in handy for shooting. The hero complex will come in handy if sacrifices need to be made along the way to ensure our survival."

Landon made a disgusted face. "I'm glad you've given this so much thought."

"We spent an entire night doing it," Thistle said.

"And Clove didn't make the cut?" Sam looked almost angry, which was ridiculous given the topic. "Why wouldn't you want Clove? She's strong and loyal."

"She's also loud and whiny," Thistle said. "You've never been on a covert mission with her. She's not quiet. She has skills when it comes to deflecting law enforcement – she can muster tears out of nothing, for example – but that won't help us in the zombie apocalypse."

"Don't worry, baby," Sam said, stroking the back of Clove's head. "I want you on my team for the zombie apocalypse."

Clove beamed, her cleaning frenzy all but forgotten. "Thank you. I want you on my team, too. Thistle is mean. I don't want her on my team."

"I may be mean, but I'm a survivor," Thistle said. "You shouldn't feel bad, Clove. Hard decisions have to be made during the zombie apocalypse. I'm leaving my mother behind, too."

Landon snorted out a laugh as he opened the bag of pita bread and rested it between us so we could enjoy our hummus. "So Clove and Twila are out. Does that mean everyone else is in?"

"No way," Thistle answered, shaking her head. "We want to survive, and that's simply not possible if we make our group too big."

"Uh-huh." Landon's expression was hard to read as he shifted his eyes to me. "Who else is on your team?"

"It's the four of us and Aunt Tillie," I replied. "We considered taking Marnie or Mom, but in the end we realized we couldn't deal with disappointed stares and general bossiness in the zombie apocalypse. Oh, we're bringing Chief Terry, too."

"I can see Chief Terry, but why would you take Aunt Tillie?" Landon seemed to be enjoying the game. "She can't move very fast."

"No, but she can control the weather and set things on fire if we get trapped," Thistle supplied. "We figure that's more important than speed."

"Well, I'm glad you've spent so much time on this," Landon said. "Others might think you were wasting your time when you could've been doing something productive, but I'm all for planning an apocalypse. That way we won't be caught off guard."

"That's what I said." I giggled as Landon squeezed my hand before opening the container of tabbouleh. "We're totally on the same wavelength."

"Well, except Bay has a martyr complex, while Landon has a hero complex," Thistle said, flashing an evil smirk when I tried to scorch her with a glare.

"I'm still coming after you," I reminded her.

"I'm looking forward to it," Thistle said, refusing to back down. "Come on, Marcus. Let's get some dinner. I'll fill you in on your role in the zombie apocalypse while we're deciding what we want."

"Isn't my role to survive?" Marcus asked as he fell into step with her.

"Among other things."

I watched them go, annoyance bubbling up. When I turned to Landon, he seemed to be expecting it. "Do you think I have a martyr complex?"

Landon didn't hesitate when he answered. "Yes."

"But ... no."

"Bay, you're willing to sacrifice yourself to save everyone even when there's no reason to make a sacrifice," Landon said. "That's a martyr complex. Don't worry about it. I'm used to it. I have a hero complex, after all."

He didn't seem bothered by Thistle's words. I, on the other hand, couldn't let it go. "I'm going to make her eat enough dirt to fill a sand pit before this is over."

"That sounds delightful," Landon said. "You can do that later. Stop worrying about her, though, and focus on me. We're having dinner and then going to bed early. We have a plan of our own. If the zombie apocalypse hits I plan to stay in bed eating bacon until they come for me."

I snorted, delighted by the visual. "I guess that's one way to go."

"It is," Landon confirmed. "We can practice tonight."

That didn't sound so bad. "I'll tell my martyr complex to meet your hero complex under the covers in two hours."

Landon grinned, the expression lighting up his already handsome face. "That sounds like a plan."

We lapsed into comfortable silence for a few moments, the only sounds coming from our mouths as we vigorously chewed the delightful food. Clove interrupted the quiet first.

"I really don't care about zombies," she said. "I do care about your mother, Sam. We should go home so I can clean. I'll be up all night at this rate."

"You're done cleaning," Sam said. "My mother is not a neat freak. She's not going to care how much you cleaned. She will notice if you have bags under your eyes."

Clove was horrified at the prospect and her fingers flew to her cheeks. "Do I have bags under my eyes?"

Sam realized his mistake when it was too late. "I … ."

"Oh, no!" Clove hopped to her feet and scurried in the direction of the bathroom.

Sam heaved out a sigh before following. I couldn't hear what he said as he trudged after Clove, but I swear I heard "crazy," "lucky I love her" and "I'm going to drink myself to sleep tonight" before he disappeared around a corner.

I turned to Landon. "Would you want me on your team for the zombie apocalypse?"

"You and only you," Landon answered. "I already told you that we're going to bed with bacon and waiting for them to come to us. I wasn't exaggerating."

"We'll die that way, though."

"Yes, but at least we'll be together." Landon thoughtfully chewed and swallowed before continuing. "We'll probably need chocolate cake, too."

"Well, at least you've thought it out," I teased. "I ... ."

I didn't get a chance to continue because the unmistakable sound of someone screaming filled the air. Landon and I jumped to our feet in unison, turning in the direction of the display booths.

I could see smoke rising from one of the back booths and found myself moving before uttering a word.

"And here comes the drama," Landon said. "You're going to owe me twenty bucks before we go to bed tonight."

"I'll bake you a cake instead."

"Even better."

TWELVE

Landon has longer legs, so I struggled to keep up as he raced through the crowd. By the time we hit the end of the row of booths, the smoke was thick and I could make out flames as a black column snaked into the sky.

"What happened?" Landon asked, pushing two small children back so they wouldn't get too close to the flames.

"I don't know," a woman replied – I think it was Jennifer Calendar. "It was quiet and the next thing we knew it was on fire."

"Okay," Landon barked out. "Someone call the fire department."

"There's a hose over here," Marcus called out, grabbing the end of the hose and hurrying forward. "We can put it out ourselves."

Landon controlled the crowd while Marcus sprayed water. In an effort to help, Thistle and I took faux antique buckets from one of the rustic store booths and scooped water from the fountain. Despite our best efforts, it took ten minutes to put out the fire. The fire department didn't show up until five minutes after that.

My cheeks were black with soot and I couldn't stop coughing when Landon moved to my side.

"Are you okay?" He looked concerned.

"I'm fine. I just inhaled too much smoke."

"Then come over here and rest a second," Landon said, guiding me toward a bench and tugging Thistle to make sure she accompanied us. He made us both sit and studied our faces through glassy eyes as the fire department poked at embers and made sure the fire was really out. "Does it generally take that long for the fire department to get here?"

I shrugged. "We don't have many fires." I broke off and coughed into my hand, causing Landon to rub my back as he wiped a smudge of soot from his cheek. "I guess I never really thought about it."

"Well, I'm going to talk to Chief Terry about that," Landon said, glancing over his shoulder when he heard approaching footsteps. Marcus, his face grimy, hurried to Thistle when he saw us sitting. "She's okay. They got too close to the fire with the buckets. I think they got the smoke worse than we did."

"You should've stayed back," Marcus said. "You could've been hurt."

Thistle made an incredulous face. "It was a small booth, not a house," she pointed out. "We weren't inside. There was no danger of the roof falling. We're fine."

"We're totally fine," I agreed. "This is why we're going to survive the zombie apocalypse when others will fall behind and get eaten."

"I heard that," Clove groused, moving closer to me. She looked mildly concerned, but also irritated. "I've decided I'll sacrifice both of you in the zombie apocalypse, and laugh when you get eaten and I escape."

"Oh, whatever." Thistle rolled her eyes. "We all know I'll win the zombie apocalypse."

"I don't think there's such a thing as winning when you have an apocalypse," Landon said, shaking his head. "This could be the dumbest conversation we've ever had."

"Oh, not even close," I shot back. "Two weeks ago we spent an entire night arguing about the best James Bond. You said it was Sean Connery. Marcus maintains it was Pierce Brosnan."

"That wasn't a dumb conversation," Landon argued. "That was a lively debate."

"I don't even like James Bond movies."

THE TROUBLE WITH WITCHES

"Yes, well, I'm going to have to leave you behind in the zombie apocalypse because your taste in movies sucks," Landon teased, giving me a quick kiss before straightening. "Where the heck is Chief Terry? I thought he would be here by now."

"There he is," Clove said, pointing toward the corner of the destroyed booth. "He doesn't look happy."

"I don't blame him," Landon said, moving to leave but then thinking better of it and swiveling. "Do you want to stay with me or go home with Thistle? I might be a little bit."

That was a tough choice. "I want to stay with you."

Landon smiled and extended his hand.

"I also don't want to give Thistle too much time alone in the guesthouse. I think she's going to steal our extra room," I added.

Landon scowled as he stared at Thistle. "I thought you were going to move in with Marcus?"

"I am," Thistle replied. "I can't do it until all of the construction is done, though, and that won't happen for several months."

"So why can't you wait and do your crafts room under Marcus' roof when the construction is done?"

"Because then I won't have beaten Bay," Thistle replied. "I want to win."

"I think that's essentially the Winchester motto," Landon said. "Frankly, I don't care who wins right now. I want you to promise you're not going to do anything to that guesthouse tonight, though. I don't want Bay complaining the entire night."

Thistle chewed her lip and tilted her head to the side. "Okay," she agreed. "I'm only doing it because I'm tired, though. Plus ... I need a shower. I'm filthy and smell bad."

"We all smell bad," Landon said. "Thank you, though." He shook his hand again and I took it, relieved I wouldn't have to make a tough choice when I really wanted to find out how the fire started.

"Speaking of smelling bad, I have to get back to the lighthouse," Clove announced. "Your mother is coming tomorrow, Sam, and I want our place to smell like fresh lemons."

Sam's expression was hard to read. "What if I want it to smell like lavender?"

"Get used to disappointment."

Sam heaved a sigh. "Lemons it is," he said. "I guess we're not going to have a relaxing night."

"We never were," Clove said. "I was simply going to refuse to let you go to sleep until you did everything I wanted."

Sam smiled. "That sounds vaguely dirty."

"I wanted you to clean the toilet," Clove said, not missing a beat.

"That sounds vaguely depressing," Sam complained, although he fell into step with her. "Can we at least kiss a few times or something?"

Clove shot him a winning smile. "I'm going to let you see me naked."

"That sounds promising."

"Yeah." Clove bobbed her head. "Since we smell like a campfire we'll have to strip outside before going inside to clean."

"That sounds really annoying," Sam muttered. "You're going to be the death of me. You know that, right?"

"Stop being dramatic," Clove chided. "When I think someone is being dramatic, you know there's something wrong."

I pursed my lips to keep from laughing as Landon squeezed my hand. "Let's talk to Chief Terry," I suggested. "I want to know how this happened. It seems ... odd."

"It definitely seems odd," Landon agreed. "Come on. I'm still hopeful we can get our ice cream tonight ... and I might even buy you some popcorn."

Well, there were worse ways to spend an evening.

"DO YOU KNOW WHAT HAPPENED?"

Chief Terry jerked his head in our direction and frowned when he saw how dirty I was. "What happened to you?" he asked, running his finger down my cheek. "How close were you to the fire?"

"We weren't close at all when it happened," I replied. "We were eating dinner at the picnic tables. We heard someone scream and saw smoke, so we ran in this direction."

"We put out the fire ourselves," Landon explained. "Marcus found a hose, and Bay and Thistle used buckets, although I'm not exactly happy with how close they got to the fire. It took us a little bit of effort, but we put it out."

"Where was the fire department?"

"That's exactly what I was going to ask you," Landon said. "It took them fifteen minutes to get here. The entire town square could've caught fire if it had been windier."

"I suppose we should be thankful that it was just the one booth," Chief Terry said, rubbing the back of his neck. "The department here is made up of volunteers. Sometimes it takes them a little while to group together."

Landon wrinkled his nose. "That doesn't sound very safe."

"What do you want me to do?" Chief Terry challenged, obviously taking Landon's words as a personal affront. "The town is small and the tax base is limited. We're not a big city. We can't afford a full-time fire department."

"I'm sorry," Landon said, holding up his hands in a placating manner. "I wasn't attacking you. I was merely stating that it doesn't sound safe."

"It's not safe," Chief Terry agreed, exhaling heavily. "I've been bothered by the fire department situation for a long time. I don't know what to do about it, though."

"Well, we're okay for now," I pointed out. "We don't have a lot of fires – which is good – and this should fill our quota for the month. There's no reason to argue." I didn't like it when Chief Terry and Landon snapped at one another. Good-natured ribbing was one thing, anger was another. For some reason, I always sought Chief Terry's approval, and I didn't want him to dislike my boyfriend. Wow! That sounded a little pathetic, huh?

"Calm down," Landon said, rubbing the back of my neck. "We're not arguing. We're having a discussion."

"That's what men do," Chief Terry said, offering me a wink. "I'm sorry I snapped at you. I was in the middle of Marnie's cream pie when I got the call about the fire. I didn't get to finish."

My mouth dropped open at his words, and Landon snorted at the unintended double entendre.

"Nice," Landon said. "And here I thought you'd choose Winnie if it came down to it."

It took Chief Terry a moment to realize what Landon was saying. "Banana cream pie!" he barked. "I was eating Marnie's pie, not her ... oh, you're such a pig." He cuffed the back of Landon's head and made a face. "Why does your mind always go to the gutter?"

Landon shrugged, the tension from earlier completely dissipating. "I think it's my super power. Hey, Bay, there you go. When the zombie apocalypse comes we will survive thanks to my dirty mind."

"That sounds like a plan," I said, weariness momentarily overcoming me. "I think that's better than the bacon-and-cake plan."

"Am I missing something?" Chief Terry asked, confused.

"You probably don't want to know," I said.

"You definitely don't want to know," Landon added. "What have you got on the fire so far?"

"Just that it was Kelly Sheffield's booth," Chief Terry answered. "She wasn't present when it started. She'd closed up to take a break. She was over by the pie tent – don't say anything filthy – when it started. One of my officers is bringing her here now."

"It went up quick," Landon said. "I have no idea what would cause it. Bay and I were in here earlier and all she had was love potions. I don't think those are flammable."

"I should hope not," Chief Terry said.

I kept one ear on their conversation as I shuffled over to the burnt shell that used to be the shopping booth. Nothing survived the fire. There were potions strewn in every direction and broken glass littering the ground. Even though it was a mess, I knew the Hemlock Cove Festival Committee would have things looking like new by tomorrow morning. Because we are a town that relies upon tourism, the committee knows how to cover up a crisis.

"Do we think it was an accident?" Landon asked, shifting his attention as a tall woman with dark hair cut through the crowd. It was Kelly Sheffield – I knew her from high school.

"Of course it was an accident," Kelly said, making a face as she looked Landon up and down. "Who are you?"

"This is Landon Michaels," Chief Terry replied. "He's an FBI agent out of the Traverse City office."

Kelly's eyebrows rose. "The FBI? Why would they be here for a booth fire? I'm going to need a copy of the report, by the way. I have to file a claim with my insurance company. I lost all of the potions."

"I understand," Chief Terry said. "Agent Michaels was already in town. He just happened to be here."

"Why?" Kelly wasn't overtly checking out Landon, yet I could tell she liked what she saw.

"He was staying with me," I said, dusting my hands off on my jeans as I rose from the wreckage.

Kelly narrowed her eyes as we locked gazes. We might've gone to high school together, but that didn't mean we were friends. In fact, we were sort of enemies. Lila Stevens was my biggest enemy, but Kelly was one of Lila's best friends, and they made it their mission to shower misery on me all through middle and high school.

"You're with Bay?" Kelly made a derisive sound in the back of her throat. "How terrible for you."

Landon kept his face impassive, but I didn't miss the annoyance lurking in the depths of his eyes. "Mrs. Sheffield, do you have any reason to believe anyone would target you to burn down your booth?"

"Ms. Sheffield," Kelly corrected, gracing him with a flirtatious smile. "I'm not married."

"I can see why," Landon said dryly. "Do you have any reason to believe someone did this on purpose?"

"Absolutely not," Kelly said. "I'm sure it was some sort of accident. There was a lantern hanging between my booth and the one right next door. I'm sure it probably fell into my booth or something. I mean ... why would someone burn down a booth? It makes no sense."

"Maybe it's because you're hawking rose water and oregano and calling it a love potion," I suggested.

"No one is talking to you, Bay," Kelly snapped, narrowing her eyes.

"Actually I would like to hear what she has to say," Landon countered.

"Me too," Chief Terry chimed in. He looked irked with Kelly's attitude. "She runs the newspaper, after all. She's often one step ahead of us on investigations."

"Well, perhaps that's because she's a loser and has nothing else better to do," Kelly said, tossing a challenging look in my direction. "As for my potions ... well ... they're the real deal."

"They're common household items," I corrected. "They're props, not the real deal. Has anyone approached you wanting a real love spell and expressed disappointment when it didn't work?"

Kelly narrowed her eyes to dangerous green slits. "My potions are real and they always work. Of course no one approached me over a faulty potion. It's been a normal day."

Landon's eyes were thoughtful when they locked with mine. I could tell he was curious about Kelly's demeanor, but he wouldn't question me until later. "Okay," he said after a beat. "Thank you for your time. I'll make sure you get a copy of the report so you can file it with your insurance company."

"You can drop it off yourself if you want," Kelly offered, her expression triumphant when she met my irritated gaze.

"Oh, that doesn't sound fun at all," Landon said, extending his hand so I could take it. "I'm sure Chief Terry has an officer who can deliver it. I have more important things to do."

Kelly was incredulous. "Her?"

"There's also bacon and cake," Landon said. "She's the main draw, though. Now, come on, sweetie. I believe I promised you ice cream."

That sounded like the perfect end to a long day.

THIRTEEN

"Do you want to tell me about your friend?"

Landon refrained from asking me about my interaction with Kelly until we returned to the guesthouse. It was dark inside, indicating Thistle and Marcus had already retired for the night, so I kept my voice low as we moved toward my bedroom.

"There's not much to tell," I said, shrugging out of my hoodie and hanging it over one of the chairs at the edge of the room before kicking off my shoes. "Kelly and Lila were friends. We didn't really spend any quality time together."

Landon was well aware of my history with Lila Stevens. He met her before she was arrested for complicity to theft, and then he got a chance to see a younger version of her up close and personal when we spent time trapped in Aunt Tillie's memories a few weeks earlier. He hated Lila on principle, which was only one of the reasons I loved him. He's the most loyal person I know.

"I kind of figured that out on my own," Landon said, tugging his shirt over his head before unbuttoning his jeans. "Was she mean to you?"

"Define mean."

"Bay, this will go a lot faster if you just tell me," Landon prodded. "I already know something happened. I'm assuming she was mean to you."

"Most of the kids were mean to me," I replied. "They thought I wandered around talking to myself when I was really talking to ghosts. It wasn't easy, but I survived. Kelly doesn't mean anything to me, and she was nowhere near as bad as Lila."

Landon pursed his lips as he regarded me. "I don't like people being mean to my Bay. I'll be mean to her when I see her next."

"Do you anticipate that being soon?"

Landon shrugged. "I have trouble believing that fire started by accident."

"Fires don't generally fall under the purview of the FBI."

"Oh, baby, I can make anything fall under the purview of the FBI," Landon teased. "If it keeps me in town an extra few days, I am more than willing to become an arson investigator."

"I guess I can live with that."

"Good," Landon said, jerking the covers back on the bed and pointing to the mattress. "Now climb in. I want to show you something else that falls under the purview of the FBI. I think you'll be impressed."

Something told me he was right, and I couldn't stop giggling as he chased me into the bed.

"Prepare to be amazed," Landon said. "I'm an excellent investigator."

"You could totally do it for a living," I agreed.

"You've got that right."

I WAS in a good mood when we made our way to The Overlook the next morning for breakfast. I slept hard, and when I woke I was refreshed and rejuvenated. Landon glanced at his phone a few times as we walked, but didn't say anything. I wasn't keen on prying until he did it a fourth time, and then I couldn't help myself.

"What's going on? Has something bad happened?"

"What?" Landon was caught off guard as he held open the back door so I could enter. "No, sweetie. Nothing is wrong. Er, well, I guess something is wrong. Chief Terry called in a state fire inspector last night. Apparently accelerants were used on the booth. I'm not exactly surprised by that."

I lifted my eyebrows. He might not have been surprised, but I was. "That means someone purposely burned it down."

Landon nodded. "That's exactly how it looks."

"But ... why would someone burn down a festival booth?" I asked. "Seriously, that was all fake stuff. There couldn't have been more than a hundred dollars in merchandise ruined. The festival committee owns the booth, so that money doesn't come out of Kelly's pocket."

"I have no idea why someone would purposely burn it down," Landon said. "Chief Terry is coming out for breakfast, so we can ask questions then. I'm not sure he has more information than what he has already shared, though."

I cocked my head to the side as I considered the statement, stopping in my tracks when I caught sight of Aunt Tillie sitting in front of the television. She was watching a morning news roundtable discussion and was dressed in a terrifying set of leggings. Seriously, those things should come with an age limit.

"Where did you get those?" I asked, confused.

"What are those?" Landon interjected, narrowing his eyes. "They look like giant pool balls."

"I'll have you know those are planets," Aunt Tillie said, making a face. "It's the solar system."

Landon leaned his head to the side and stared at the leggings. "Oh," he said, realization dawning. "Now I see it. Earth kind of disappeared beneath ... it kind of disappeared somewhere in there."

I knew exactly where he thought Earth disappeared to but decided to keep the observation to myself. "Did you hear there was a fire at the festival last night?"

"I did," Aunt Tillie confirmed, bobbing her head. "I heard that Kelly Charlatan's booth burned down. I'm guessing that was karma."

"And lighter fluid. Her name is Sheffield, by the way."

Aunt Tillie stilled. "Someone purposely burned it down?"

"That's what it looks like."

"It's still karma," Aunt Tillie said, shaking her head. "As for the name, I think Charlatan fits her better. She always was a nasty piece of work. I think she got away with a lot of things because I was always so focused on Lila."

"Landon met her last night and didn't like her either," I supplied. "She flirted with him."

"He's too smart to fall for that," Aunt Tillie said.

"Oh, I think that's the nicest thing you ever said to me," Landon said. "You must be in a good mood today."

"Of course I'm in a good mood," Aunt Tillie said. "I'm ruler of the universe. See." She shifted her position and pointed so Landon had no choice but to look at her crotch – which is where Venus was strategically located – and he immediately looked away.

"Oh, holy planets," Landon whispered, staring at the ceiling. "I think I might be scarred for life."

I pressed my lips together to keep from laughing and Aunt Tillie adopted a suspicious look.

"What did he just say?" Aunt Tillie was clearly spoiling for a fight.

"He said he's starving and wants his bacon," I replied, pushing him toward the door. "Is everyone else here?"

Aunt Tillie didn't look convinced, but she nodded anyway. "Yeah, they're all in the dining room. Clove is in a mood."

"Sam's parents arrive today," I said. "She's a nervous wreck."

"I don't see why," Aunt Tillie said. "Clove is a catch. Sam's parents should feel lucky she's dating him."

"Now that's the nicest thing you've ever said," I pointed out, grinning. "It seems as if you're in a mood today, too. You're in a good mood, though."

"Don't get used to it," Aunt Tillie said breezily. "I think the power of ruling the universe is going to my head."

"And now the sight of the universe is going to cause mine to explode," Landon said, pressing his hand to the small of my back. "You need to save me from the visual."

"I'm on it."

I led Landon through the kitchen and into the dining room. The food was already on the table. Mom looked annoyed.

"You're late."

I returned her scowl with one of my own. "Like two seconds," I said. "We were talking to Aunt Tillie."

"Oh." Mom didn't apologize, but she marginally relaxed. "Where is Aunt Tillie?"

"She's boldly going where no one has gone before," Landon replied dryly, shaking his head to dislodge the memory of the leggings. "Trust me. You probably want her to stay in the kitchen."

"Why is that?" Mom was understandably suspicious. Aunt Tillie was always up to something, and her wardrobe was generally one of the easiest things to deal with. "She's been disappearing during the afternoons for four days now. Is she doing something illegal?"

"Technically I could probably arrest her for public lewdness if she leaves the house, but she's not directly doing anything illegal," Landon replied. "She is doing something that could end the world, though. At least my world. Yeah, she could definitely end my world."

"What is he babbling about?" Mom asked, annoyed again.

"Aunt Tillie bought new leggings."

Mom frowned. "Leggings? I told her that leggings weren't appropriate for anyone over the age of thirty."

"She probably took that as a challenge," Thistle offered from the far end of the table. She sat between Marcus and Clove – the latter of whom looked remarkably pale – and she seemed to be enjoying herself as she waved a forkful of corned beef hash under Clove's nose. "Are you really going to puke, Clove? If so, I think you should make a big show of it."

"Leave her alone," Marnie barked, her gaze falling on her daughter. "She's nervous about meeting Sam's parents. She can't help herself. There's no reason to be ... well ... you."

"Yes, now that should be the new family motto," Landon teased. "There's no reason to be Thistle."

"No one asked you," Thistle shot back, making a face.

"Oh, good," Chief Terry said, strolling into the room and taking a seat next to Landon. "I was worried I was going to miss the morning snark."

"There's no chance of that happening," I said, moving my eyes to a morose-looking Annie as she sat between Marcus and Belinda. She looked positively miserable. "What's wrong with you, Annie? You seem sad."

"Did you see Aunt Tillie's leggings, too?" Landon asked.

Annie tossed eye daggers in Landon's direction. "Those are a sophisticated clothing item. You should be so lucky to wear them."

"Uh-huh." Landon didn't look convinced. "Did Aunt Tillie tell you to say that?"

"She said that they were special pants and she didn't care what anyone said about them," Annie explained, crossing her arms over her chest. "She also said they were going to make people mad, and that made her more powerful and they were sophisticated. I don't know what that word means, but it must be something good."

Thistle snorted into her juice as Mom frowned.

"Now I'm really afraid to see these pants," Mom muttered.

"You should be," Landon said. "I'm scarred for life."

"At least you didn't see Uranus, because she was sitting," I offered.

Instead of smiling, Landon scorched me with a murderous look. "Now I'm definitely going to have nightmares."

"Don't say I never gave you anything." I patted his leg under the table and turned my attention to Annie. "What's wrong? If it's not the pants, it must be something else. Are you worried about starting school?"

"I already told you people I'm not going to school," Annie snapped, taking everyone by surprise with her vehemence. Thankfully, all of the guests had already left and only family and friends were grouped around the table this morning. "I don't need school. I hate school!"

"We've talked about this," Belinda said, keeping her voice low. "You're going to school."

"If you're worried about school, I think I have a fix for you," Thistle offered. "How would you like it if Marcus and I dropped you off a few times a week? That's about the time I have to head in to open the store."

Annie may have been angry, but the idea of Marcus taking her to school obviously held some appeal. "Fine," she conceded. "I'll consider going to school. I'm not promising, though."

"I thought you could stop by the stable after school as long as the weather holds, too," Marcus said. "I know you want to learn to ride a horse. I thought I would give you some private lessons."

I couldn't help but smirk as Annie's eyes widened.

"Really?" Annie acted as if he announced he was going to buy her a pony. "I ... well ... that sounds cool."

"You have to go to school, though," Marcus said. "Those are the rules."

Annie heaved a dramatic sigh. She would make a marvelous teenager one day. "Fine. I'll go to school."

Marcus winked at her. "Good. I don't like my women stupid."

I opened my mouth to say something snarky about Thistle but I thought better of it when she shot me a slit-eyed glare. I automatically changed course. "Does that make you feel better, Annie? Are you in a better mood now?"

"Not really," Annie replied, taking me by surprise. "I'll never be in a better mood again if the ghosts don't leave me alone."

I stilled, my shoulders stiffening. "What do you mean?"

Annie didn't immediately answer, so Belinda did it for her. "She won't stop talking about ghosts," Belinda supplied. "I think it's just an elaborate ruse to get out of going to school."

"It is not," Annie protested, indignant. "Now that I know I get to spend time with Marcus, I want to go to school. The ghosts don't have anything to do with Marcus."

"What ghosts?" Mom asked, legitimately confused. "Where did you see ghosts?"

"She saw them the other night when the power went out," I explained.

"I told her she imagined it, but she won't listen to me," Belinda said. "People don't see ghosts, Annie. That's stuff you see in movies."

Mom shot me a worried look. All family sniping fell by the wayside. Belinda might not have realized that ghosts were real. The Winchester witches knew better.

I tried to keep my voice neutral as I flashed a warm smile for Annie's benefit. "Have you seen the ghosts since the other night?"

Annie nodded. "They keep following me around. They're talking to me."

I glanced around the room but I couldn't catch a glimpse of anyone but the living. "Do you see them now?"

Annie shook her head. "They're hiding."

"Why are they hiding?"

Annie shrugged. "I don't know. They said they only liked me and that there were bad people here. They said I had to keep them a secret, but ... I don't like them. They frighten me."

I didn't blame her. "How many times have you seen them?"

"A lot," Annie answered. "They were in my bedroom all night."

"She has such an active imagination," Belinda said, offering a nervous laugh. I could tell she was worried she would have to take Annie to a professional if the ghost talk kept up. The reality was much worse. Annie wasn't crazy. She was gifted. Unfortunately, the gift landing on her shoulders was something of a curse. "I don't know what to do with her sometimes."

"You could believe me," Annie offered, making a face. "I'm telling the truth!"

"I don't think you're a liar, Annie," Belinda protested. "I think you have a very vivid imagination. I was the same way when I was your age."

Something occurred to me. "Did you see ghosts, too?" Perhaps Belinda had an ability and didn't realize it. If she was raised outside of a witchy family, she might not have understood what was happening.

"I never saw ghosts," Belinda said. "I had invisible friends. I always thought I saw fairies, too. They turned out to be butterflies, but that's the magic of childhood."

I couldn't help but be a little disappointed. "Oh." I glanced at Landon. He looked as troubled as me. "Well, I'm sure everything will work out." My heart rolled as Annie rubbed her cheek. I realized I missed the dark circles under her eyes on first inspection. Could the ghosts really be keeping her awake at night? "We'll make sure we figure out a way to keep the ghosts out of the house. I promise."

Now I just had to make sure I could keep that promise.

FOURTEEN

"Bay, what are you going to do about Annie?"

Landon and I sat on the back patio enjoying the pleasant morning weather after breakfast. I could tell he was as bothered by Annie's outburst as I was.

"I don't know," I admitted, leaning back in my chair and stretching my legs out in front of me. "What do you think I should do?"

"I don't know how to answer that, sweetie," Landon replied. "You're the magical one."

"Or the cursed one."

Landon rubbed the back of his neck as he stared at me. "Do you really think you're cursed?"

"I … ." I wasn't sure how to answer. I didn't want to sound like the main attraction at a pity party sideshow.

"Do you?" Landon prodded. "From where I stand, you're amazing. I know it was hard for you growing up with your ability, but you're an adult now. I don't think you're cursed. Could you snag me if you were cursed?"

I didn't want to laugh because it was a serious situation, but I couldn't help myself. "I guess not," I conceded. "Living in Hemlock

Cove allows me to run into some of the people who tortured me when I was younger. I guess I'm just feeling sorry for myself."

"It's okay to feel sorry for yourself," Landon said. "I wish you would smack around your enemies instead of beating yourself up, though. I think it would be healthier. I'm not the boss, so how you deal with it is up to you."

"You're not the boss?"

"That's what I said."

"Huh, I seem to remember you saying differently last night."

Landon's cheeks colored as he chuckled. "I stand corrected. I'm rarely the boss. I only want you to be happy."

"Do you think I'm unhappy?"

"I think something is bothering you and you don't want to tell me about it," Landon answered. "You've been ... distracted ... all weekend."

My mind briefly traveled back to the incident on the tanker. I could hardly argue with him given what happened. "I'm not distracted," I countered. "I'm ... worried."

"About Annie?"

I nodded. "If she's really seeing ghosts and they're telling her not to speak about them to others ... well ... that's not a good thing."

"I can't see ghosts, but I figured that out myself," Landon said, grabbing my hand and resting it against his heart. "You know I have to leave tomorrow morning, right?"

I nodded. "You leave every Monday morning."

"Not if I can help it."

That was true. Whenever he got a chance to spend more time in Hemlock Cove he took it. Sometimes he volunteered for assignments in neighboring towns even though they were boring. The distance between his home and mine was starting to wear on him.

"I thought you were going to try to turn the arson into something worth your time," I reminded him. "What happened to that?"

"I emailed my boss and told him about the fire, but it turns out that I'm not nearly as convincing as I thought I was," Landon said. "My boss doesn't happen to believe a festival booth fire – even though it appears to be arson – is worth my time. I have to go."

"You're working on that big gambling case," I said. "That could be big for your career. How is that going?"

"It's fine," Landon said. "It's boring work."

"It's too bad you couldn't do the boring work from here."

"I agree," Landon said. "It seems the nights I have to stay away from you are becoming more and more difficult. I blame you."

I barked out a laugh. "You blame me?"

"You're irresistible," Landon said, grinning as he leaned forward. "I do blame you, though. Before I met you I was focused on my career. Now I find I want to focus on you."

"You're very cute," I said. "But you have a job to do. I would never get in the way of that."

"I don't care about you getting in the way," Landon said. "I care about being away. I'm going to have a talk with my boss. I'm hopeful we'll be able to figure out a way for me to move here full time."

My heart rolled at the admission as hope coursed through me. "Really?"

Landon nodded. "I don't want you to get too worked up, though," he cautioned. "It's not going to happen overnight. There are some rules we're going to have to get around and I still have several months left on my lease."

"Still ... I mean, you would probably be happier here," I said, working overtime to keep my expression neutral. "I want what's best for you."

"Very smooth," Landon teased, grabbing me around the waist and pulling me from my chair so I was sitting on his lap. "Would you like it if we lived together?"

Was he joking? "I think I could live with that," I hedged. "How would that work, though? Would we get an apartment?"

Landon shrugged. "I haven't gotten that far," he admitted. "I'm warning you right now that things won't happen overnight. It's going to take a few months to work everything out."

THE TROUBLE WITH WITCHES

"Still, that's something to look forward to," I mused. I did the math in my head. "Maybe we can be together full time by Christmas."

"That's the plan," Landon said. "This is kind of our first Christmas together."

"We knew each other last Christmas."

"We did, but we were a little hot and cold at the beginning and we didn't get really hot until after Christmas," Landon reminded me. "I don't think that counts. I'm looking forward to a full Christmas with you this year."

The remnants of summer beat down against my skin, yet all I wanted to do was hop in moon boots and make snow angels. "I'm looking forward to it, too."

"Good." Landon gave me a soft kiss. "As for Annie, I trust your judgment. You'll make the right call when it's time. I don't think you should wait too long, though. The longer Belinda lives in the dark, the more likely Annie is to be upset. You need to remember how things were for you at that age and then ask yourself how much worse they would've been if your mother didn't believe you."

His words had a chilling effect on our happy moment. "I know. I'm going to do something. I'm just not sure how to approach it."

"You also need to figure out what the ghosts want," Landon added. "I'm not an expert, but something fishy seems to be going on here ... and I'm not just saying that because you're convinced that the ghosts came from the tanker."

"I'm going to conduct some research," I promised. "I'm going to start the second you leave tomorrow. I don't want to ruin our day."

"That sounds like a plan." Landon pressed a soft kiss to my cheek.

"I also don't want to miss the chance to watch Clove melt down," I added. "I should probably find my phone so I can film it."

Landon heartily chuckled as he shook his head. "That sounds mean, but knock yourself out. I have a feeling it's going to be a long day for everyone."

LANDON and I lost track of time on the patio, aggressive cuddling –

okay, and a little kissing and other stuff – making for a fun morning. That all changed when I heard someone clear her throat behind us.

"And this is my cousin Bay and her boyfriend," Clove gritted out, forcing a smile for the middle-aged couple to her left. "Apparently they forgot we were having visitors today."

If looks could kill I'd be scheduled for a mortuary visit in about thirty seconds. Something told me Clove was about to throw her weight in Thistle's direction when it came time to battle it out for the room.

"Hi," I said, stumbling in my haste as I tried to get to my feet. Landon caught me before I could pitch forward and make things worse – if that was even possible – and I extended my hand. "It's so nice to meet you."

"This is Maggie and Richard Cornell," Clove said. "Sam's parents."

Maggie shook my hand and I didn't miss the hint of amusement that flitted across her features. She obviously recognized Clove's tone for what it was, although she didn't seem bothered by what she caught Landon and me doing. "It's nice to meet you, Bay," she said. "I've heard so much about you. Both of you."

Maggie's smile was pleasant when it landed on Landon, and she shook his hand as well. After exchanging greetings with Richard, we lapsed into uncomfortable silence for a moment. Landon smartly jumped in to save us.

"How was your trip?"

"It wasn't too bad," Richard replied. "It was about four hours, but we stopped a few times to stretch our legs."

"That's good," Landon said. "Sam said you live on the west side of the state, right?"

"We actually live closer to Ann Arbor," Maggie supplied. "We used to live on the west side when Sam was younger, but we moved a few years ago."

"Oh, well, Ann Arbor is a great town," Landon said. "I've worked a few cases there."

"That's right. Sam said you're an FBI agent," Richard said. "That must be an exciting job."

THE TROUBLE WITH WITCHES

Landon shrugged. "It has its moments."

"What are you working on now?" Maggie asked. "Besides Bay, I mean."

Landon had the grace to look embarrassed as Clove scorched us with a dark look. Sam seemed merely amused.

"I'm not sure Landon is allowed to talk about his cases, Mom," Sam said. "He's generally here every weekend visiting Bay and then he comes once or twice during the week for dinner."

"And where is your office?" Richard asked. He seemed intrigued by Landon and his line of work more than anything else. "Is it close by?"

"It's in Traverse City," Landon answered. "It's only an hour away, but I have to maintain an apartment there – for now, at least – so I don't get to spend as much time here as I'd like."

"That's too bad," Maggie said. "It must be hard on Bay for you to be away so often. Plus, well, it's a dangerous job. That must wreak havoc on her nerves."

"I don't think it's easy for her, but she seems to find more trouble than I do," Landon quipped. I could tell he regretted his words when Clove glared at him. If she were capable of shooting fire out of her eyes, Landon would smell like lunch right now. My cousin clearly wasn't settling into her role as hostess very well. "What I mean to say is that it's not easy but we make it work. Things will settle down eventually. I'm almost sure of it."

"That's good," Richard said, shifting his eyes from Landon to the expansive backyard. "This is an amazing setup here. How much property do you own?"

"It's quite a bit," I answered, my eyes refusing to leave Clove as she shuffled from one foot to the other, wringing her hands. She was so pale and nervous I feared she would pass out. "It's a large parcel of land."

"And there's a guesthouse, right?" Maggie asked. "I believe Sam said that's where Clove used to live before she settled in with him."

"Yes, I still live there with our other cousin," I replied. "It's a nice place. You can come see it whenever you want."

"I just might do that," Maggie said. She seemed friendly. She shared her coloring with Sam, although her dark hair was shot through with gray, and she seemed genuinely happy to be here. I couldn't help but worry that Clove's manic reaction to everything would somehow turn her off, even though she appeared genuinely amiable.

"You guys are here all week, right?" I asked, grasping at straws to keep the conversation going. "We're having a festival downtown. You should check it out."

"That sounds lovely," Maggie said. "Sam told us about the festivals. We're looking forward to seeing the lighthouse and his new tanker, too. I understand you're all helping him decorate it."

I took the opportunity to praise Clove since she apparently wasn't capable of forming words right now. "Clove is doing most of the work – just like she did with the Dandridge – but I'm happy to help," I said. "I'm not the craftiest person. That title belongs to Thistle. She's a total witch, but she's amazing with a paint brush."

The last part of the sentence escaped before I had a chance to think better about the intelligence associated with uttering it. The look on Clove's face made me realize I'd said the worst thing possible. Instead of being taken aback by my words, though, Maggie chuckled.

"Yes, I heard that you, Clove and Thistle are more like sisters than cousins," Maggie said. "I have two sisters myself. I know how that goes."

Every time the woman opened her mouth I liked her more and more. She was definitely more warm and giving than Landon's mother when I first met her. "We're extremely loyal, but like to mess with one another."

"They definitely like to mess with one another," Landon confirmed. "It's just part of the joy of visiting the Winchesters. You'll get used to it very quickly."

"I'm looking forward to it," Maggie said. "This inn is absolutely gorgeous. I ... ." She broke off, her eyes traveling to a spot over my left shoulder.

For a moment I worried she'd seen a ghost – or perhaps several ghosts from Sam's tanker, for that matter – and I was trying to think of an appropriate way to explain what was happening. Thankfully for us it wasn't ghosts that caught her attention. It was Aunt Tillie and her gentleman caller.

"Is that Kenneth?" Landon asked, following my gaze.

Kenneth and Aunt Tillie dated – er, well, kind of – for several months before she broke his heart. A few weeks ago she found that she was jealous and wanted him back. They kind of flirted with reconciliation before Aunt Tillie got distracted by harvest season in her pot field. I hadn't seen Kenneth for almost two weeks, but his presence was enough to make me smile.

"That's him," I replied. "It looks like they're having a good time."

I had no idea what Aunt Tillie and Kenneth were up to, but Aunt Tillie remained in her leggings and she had on a combat helmet and carried a golf club. Kenneth held a chainsaw and had a whistle perched between his lips. If I didn't know better I would think they were hunting. I had no idea what they expected to catch with that weird assortment of items, though.

"Oh, that's your great-aunt?" Maggie looked excited. "I can't wait to meet her. Sam has told me oodles about her."

I shifted my gaze to Sam and found him smiling, although the signs of tension in the corners of his eyes were obvious. "Yes, she's a great woman," I said. "I think you're going to love her."

"What is she doing?" Clove asked. She looked worried. "Why do you think they have a chainsaw?"

"Whatever it is, it can't be good," Landon said. He watched them for a full twenty seconds before turning to me. "Who wants cookies?"

Richard looked dubious about our reaction. "Shouldn't you find out why she's walking through the woods with a golf club and chainsaw?"

"I only worry if she's got a shovel," Landon replied. "That means she's hiding a body." He was going for levity but Maggie and Richard obviously didn't realize he was joking. "I ... definitely need a cookie."

I patted his arm. "Me too. Let's eat."

What? If you think I'm following Aunt Tillie into the woods when she has a chainsaw, you obviously don't know me at all.

FIFTEEN

I wasn't keen on returning to the festival on Landon's last night in town, but Clove was firm when she informed Thistle and me that we were not only expected to attend but be delightful conversationalists as well.

It seemed as if she was asking a lot given what was going on in our world, but we promised to be on our best behavior. Then we pulled each other's hair and threatened war when she wasn't looking. What? That's the Winchester way.

I linked my fingers with Landon's as we followed Maggie, Richard, Sam and Clove toward the festival. Marcus and Thistle were to our right, and I kept darting suspicious looks in their direction, which was starting to irritate Landon.

"Ignore her," Landon ordered. "She's just trying to get under your skin. She doesn't even care about that room. She's going to move in with Marcus in a few months. There's no way she's actually going to move a pottery wheel – which is ridiculously heavy, mind you – twice if she doesn't have to."

He had a point. Still … . "Did you just meet Thistle?" I challenged. "She'll do anything to irritate people. That's her superpower."

Landon smirked. "Superpower?"

"Everyone has a superpower," I explained. "Thistle's is making people cry."

"Ah." Landon released my hand and slipped his arm around my waist. "What's my superpower?"

"You're the handsomest man in the land."

"I guess I can live with that," Landon said, puffing out his chest. "What's your superpower?"

"I'm dating the handsomest man in the land."

Despite the jocularity, Landon's smile turned earnest. "I think your superpower is that you're the strongest person I know."

"That, too."

"You're also loyal," Landon said. "What's Aunt Tillie's superpower?"

I tilted my head to the side, considering. "I think it's that she's even worse than Thistle."

Landon barked out a laugh, delighted. "I can see that," he said, pressing a kiss to my forehead. "I know this isn't what you wanted to do tonight, but I think it's nice that you're going out of your way for Clove."

"She's acting a little crazy."

"She's acting a lot crazy," Landon corrected. "I think that's a girl thing. For some reason you all become deranged lunatics when you meet your boyfriend's mother. It must be one of those things that happen when girls get their periods. I can think of no other explanation."

Now it was my turn to laugh. "You're a funny guy, Landon Michaels."

"I do my best," Landon said, his eyes twinkling. "I figure we can follow Clove around for an hour and let her know we're on board for her evening and then sneak out when she's not looking."

"That doesn't seem very nice."

"Probably not," Landon conceded. "I'm not interested in being nice tonight, though. I'm interested in being naughty."

That was a very good point. "You'll also be long gone when Clove exacts her revenge on me," I mused. "You're smart, funny and handsome. You really are the entire package."

"And don't you forget it," Landon teased, smacking a loud kiss against my lips. He groaned when a familiar presence moved in at his side. He recognized the leggings before he moved his face away from mine. "Why can't you put on pants?"

Aunt Tillie didn't seem bothered by Landon's attitude. "I'm wearing pants. If I wasn't, my butt would be hanging out."

"And no one wants to see that."

"I do," Kenneth volunteered, raising his hand. His smile was so wide it almost engulfed his entire face. Apparently he was having a good time now that he'd reconciled with Aunt Tillie. "I'm a big fan of the leggings, though."

"That's because I'm master of the universe and everyone should bow down to me," Aunt Tillie said. "Speaking of bowing down, what's Clove's deal? I tried to say something to her when she walked past and she pretended she didn't know me."

Hmm. How should I answer that question?

"She's with Sam's parents," Landon explained, giving me time to gather my thoughts. "She's nervous and antsy. She's also a little annoying, if you want to know the truth. Maggie and Richard seem like perfectly nice people. She's overreacting."

"That's what she does," Aunt Tillie said, rolling her eyes. "That's her superpower."

I pressed my lips together to keep from laughing. "I told you we all have a superpower."

"Yes, mine is making the world a better place for humanity," Aunt Tillie said. "That's why I'm here."

"I wondered," I said, working overtime to keep from staring at the leggings. They were silky and shifted into unfortunate locations when Aunt Tillie moved around too much. "You should wear real pants."

"These are real pants," Aunt Tillie shot back. "I bought them on the Internet. The women wearing them were standing in front of trees and on beaches, which means they're for outdoor wearing. They're pants. Shut it."

"I stand corrected," I said, holding up my hands. "Speaking of outdoors, we saw you and Kenneth leaving The Overlook a few hours ago. You had a golf club and Kenneth had a chainsaw and a whistle."

"That wasn't us." The lie rolled smoothly off Aunt Tillie's tongue.

"It was you," I argued. "I know what you look like."

"You must've been mistaken," Aunt Tillie challenged. "It wasn't me."

"Like I could possibly mistake those leggings for anything other than your ... kind of ... pants," I said. "Where were you going?"

"It wasn't me," Aunt Tillie replied, her tone sharp. "Stop accusing me of things I didn't do. It's hurtful and mean."

That was rich coming from her. "But ... ."

"Let it go," Landon instructed. "She's obviously not going to own up to whatever she's doing. I'm sure we'll hear about it eventually."

They were sage words, but I wouldn't be me if I could let things go that easily. "Does this have something to do with Mrs. Little? Chief Terry says you've been following her around for days."

"Terry has a big mouth," Aunt Tillie said. "If he's not careful, he's going to have a big boot in his behind to match it."

"That wasn't really an explanation or denial," I pointed out.

"Oh, you're right." Aunt Tillie squared her shoulders. "That wasn't me either."

She's so full of crap sometimes I worry she'll overflow and kill us all when the sewer that is her mouth finally exceeds its capacity. "But ... ."

"Bay, I'll buy you an elephant ear if you drop this," Landon offered. "It's supposed to be a nice day and I want to spend it with you, not ... trekking through the universe."

He had a point. I heaved out a sigh and held my hands palms up. "Okay," I said after a beat. "If you get arrested, though, I'm not bailing you out."

"I have no intention of getting arrested," Aunt Tillie said. "I'm smarter than all of the cops in town combined. That goes for 'The Man' here, as well."

Landon scowled. "You're delightful. Has anyone ever told you that?"

Aunt Tillie ignored the question. "Besides that, it wasn't me," she said. "I already told you that. Why are you so suspicious?"

"I have no idea," I deadpanned. She's the most suspicious and paranoid person I know. "It must be some fluke of my genetics."

"Well, get over it," Aunt Tillie said, patting me on the arm. "Enjoy the festival. Fawn over your boyfriend. Have a good day."

"I second that," Landon said.

"Oh, and if you hear a loud noise and Margaret Little screaming, just ignore that," Aunt Tillie said. "It has nothing to do with me because I'm innocent, and I'm not going to be responsible for that either."

And there it was. "Maybe we should go home now," I suggested, focusing on Landon.

"Let's get some junk food first and see how we feel after that."

He honestly has a one-track mind where his stomach is involved.

FOR SOME REASON, as the afternoon wore on I couldn't ignore the fact that my inner danger alarm began pinging. It seemed ridiculous, but I found myself glancing over my shoulder at every turn and I couldn't stop myself from staring into shadows. I don't know what I expected – ghosts or old high school enemies – but I couldn't relax no matter how hard I tried.

Landon noticed my hyper-vigilance but he didn't comment. He was probably saving that for later when we were alone. I couldn't wait. Oh, wait, I could. Thankfully, Clove managed to sneak away from Maggie and Richard at the exact moment I was about to make a fool of myself and admit my worry.

"She hates me."

I shifted my eyes to Clove and looked around. "Who? Did you finally see Aunt Tillie's leggings? She's not wearing them because she hates you. She's wearing them because she hates me."

Landon chuckled. "I think she's wearing them because she hates me."

"Not Aunt Tillie," Clove snapped. She was in no mood for games, verbal or otherwise, and I could tell her patience was wearing thin. "I'm talking about Maggie. She hates me."

Even though Landon and I didn't visit every booth with Clove and Sam's parents, we kept an eye on them throughout the afternoon. Maggie seemed to be engaged in the conversation and eager to talk to Clove. Richard was a typical man and focused on the food above all else. He was always friendly when talking to Clove, though.

"You're crazy," I said, shaking my head. "Maggie likes you. She's been talking to you nonstop."

"I know," Clove said. "That means she hates me. Have you seen the way she looks at me?"

Landon moved up behind me and slipped his arm around my waist as he rested his chin on my shoulder. "She looks at you as if you're a little doll," he said. "You're tiny. People think you're adorable."

"She does not," Clove scoffed. "She looks at me as if I'm not good enough for Sam. Admit it. I know you've seen it. You've been watching us for hours. That's creepy, by the way."

"The only thing that's creepy is your insistence on making this fail," I shot back. "She likes you, Clove. That woman is the friendliest person I've ever met. She's ... amazing."

"I don't like to take sides, but I agree with Bay," Landon said. "Maggie likes you. I think she likes everyone. She was even nice to Mrs. Little when you showed her the porcelain unicorns. That shows true strength of character, because anyone else would've laughed ... or run away screaming."

"Oh, whatever," Clove snapped. "You always take Bay's side."

"That's because her side is always cutest," Landon teased, rubbing his cheek against mine. I could tell he was ready to depart the festival and spend some time alone. It wasn't even about romance. He wanted us to have a few moments to ourselves. Solitude was in short supply when the Winchester witches were around. "As for the rest, I stand by it. She likes you. You're acting nuts, though, and if you keep it up you're going to turn that woman off and make her hate you. It will end up a self-fulfilling prophecy."

Clove's mouth dropped open. "That's the meanest thing you've ever said to me."

"Which part?" Landon asked, not missing a beat. "Are you talking about when I said you were nuts or when I suggested Maggie will eventually turn against you? To be fair, I'm not sure she'll ever turn against you. That is seriously the nicest woman I've ever met."

"All of it," Clove snapped. "She hates me. Why won't you admit it?"

I couldn't take much more of this. "She doesn't hate you, but I'm beginning to really dislike you," I said. "You need to calm down. You're a bundle of nerves. It isn't healthy."

Instead of firing back an insult, Clove's eyes filled with tears. "I know I'm making things worse," she sniffled. "I don't know what to do, though."

My heart went out to her. Not long ago I was in the same position. Of course, Thistle and Clove didn't do anything to help me when I was freaking out. They made fun of me instead. But I was a bigger person. I was willing to make things better. Oh, crap. That's probably that martyr thing Landon mentioned earlier.

"You need to have a drink and take a breath," I said, resting my hand on her shoulder. "That's the only way things will calm down. If you keep acting the way you're acting, you're going to pass out or something."

"Do you really think I should have a drink? Will that work?"

"Have ten of them and find out," Landon said, pulling me away from Clove. "As for us, we're leaving."

"You can't," Clove protested. "What if I need you, Bay?"

"I need Bay," Landon said. "We're tired and we need a nap."

Clove narrowed her eyes. "Aunt Tillie is right. You're a filthy pervert."

"Aunt Tillie is wearing leggings that show off every crack and crevice – and some of them look like they're struggling to come back after an earthquake," Landon said. "If she's my opposition, I'm more than happy to take on the competition."

"I'm going to tell her you said that," Clove warned, extending a finger. "She's going to be angry."

"Well, at least we know her chainsaw is already out of the house," Landon said, grabbing my hand. "You'll have Bay for backup the rest of the week. She's mine for the rest of the day."

Clove let loose with a long-suffering sigh. "Fine. If something bad happens, I'm totally blaming you."

"I can live with that."

Landon held my hand as we walked toward the parking lot. He seemed lost in thought. My agitation – which dissipated while talking to Clove – was back in full force as I scanned the trees to my right.

"What are you thinking?" Landon asked, forcing my gaze to him. "You seem tense. Are you worried about Clove? If you don't want to leave … ."

"It's not Clove," I said. "I just … can't shake the feeling that someone is watching us."

Landon ceased his forward momentum and glanced around. His eyes were keen as he scanned the open area. Finally he gave up and focused on me. "I don't think anyone is watching us."

"Maybe ghosts are watching us." I was surprised when the words slipped out of my mouth.

"Do you see any ghosts?"

I shook my head.

"Then how do you know ghosts are watching you?"

"I don't know anything," I replied. "I feel it. I can't explain it."

"Do you want to know what I think?"

I couldn't decide. "Not if you think I'm crazy like Clove."

Landon grinned. "I think you want me to stay and you can't help yourself from feeling antsy," he said. "I have a feeling I'm going to feel ghosts watching me before I leave tomorrow morning, too. That's why we should spend some time together now."

"Okay," I said. I wanted to believe him, but I couldn't shake my worry. "You're going to have to massage my back to make me feel better, though."

"Done." Landon leaned over and gave me a kiss, only pulling away when the telltale sounds of a chainsaw assailed his ears. The distinctive noise came from the festival.

My heart sank when I heard it. "What do you think she's doing?"

"Who cares?" Landon asked, grabbing my hand. "You have enough food to allow us to be hermits when we get back to the guesthouse, right?"

I nodded, surprised. "Are you really going to ignore what she's doing?"

"Something tells me it's not bad enough to keep me in town," Landon said. "That means I'm going to ignore it."

That didn't sound like him at all. "What if it's illegal?"

"Then it's Chief Terry's problem."

That didn't sound like him either. "Do you really miss me that much when you're gone?"

Landon's smile was impish. "I really miss you twice as much as that when I'm gone."

The admission was enough to shove my misgivings and worry out of my mind – er, well, at least for tonight. "Let's go," I said, holding out my hand. "I have macaroni and cheese, and popcorn back at the guesthouse."

"Now that's the way to a man's heart, sweetie."

SIXTEEN

I woke to someone bouncing on the bed.

"Not again, Landon," I croaked. "I need coffee first."

I jerked a pillow over my head and kept my eyes shut. The bouncing finally stopped and it took me a moment to remember what day it was – and the fact that Landon usually took great pains not to wake me when he slipped out early on Monday mornings.

He should already be gone.

I jerked the pillow away from my face and wrenched open an eye, glaring at Aunt Tillie when I saw her kneeling on my bed and staring. "Oh, what fresh hell is this?" I muttered, taking a moment to study her outfit. She was wearing leggings again. The fresh pair sported a pattern of zombies. She'd either bought stock in a legging company or was purposely doing this to drive people crazy. My money was on the latter, but Aunt Tillie is so unpredictable it could honestly be the former.

"You're a real grouch in the morning," Aunt Tillie said, making a face. "You know that, right?"

"I think I'm an absolute delight in the morning," I corrected. "I think you're the one who broke into my bedroom and ... ." My eyes drifted to Landon's empty pillow and landed on the small grouping of Hershey's Kisses nestled there. "You brought me candy? Oh, man! What did you do? If you need money or manipulation to keep yourself out of jail, I'm going to sit back and watch with a camera instead."

"Ha, ha, smart mouth," Aunt Tillie snapped, wrinkling her nose. "I didn't buy you candy. Your boyfriend left it for you. I'm just eating it."

I narrowed my eyes as I propped up my body on my elbow and regarded the candy. I couldn't help but smile. "He left me candy?" I felt like such a girl when my cheeks burned. The gesture was unbelievably sweet.

"Uh-uh." Aunt Tillie didn't look nearly as thrilled about the candy as I felt. "He left you a note, too."

"Where?" I didn't see a note.

Aunt Tillie waved a small card in front of my face. I didn't even see her holding it until now.

"I read it," Aunt Tillie volunteered. "It's extremely boring. He's a total moron when it comes to writing love notes."

I snatched the card from her and flipped it open. The message was simple and to the point: I love you. I found the note incredibly stimulating for my heart. Sadly, I found Aunt Tillie's presence incredibly stimulating for my irritation.

"Oh, look at that schmaltzy face," Aunt Tillie groused. "You actually like that card. You're thinking Landon is romantic ... and loving ... and hot because he somehow manages to keep long hair and look like a rock star while working for the government. You make me want to puke."

I scowled and slapped away Aunt Tillie's hand when she reached over to steal one of my candy pieces. "You make me want to kick you in the butt," I shot back. "That's my candy. If you're going to puke, I don't want you eating my candy."

"Oh, whatever," Aunt Tillie said, rolling her eyes. "You're just as much of a kvetch as Clove sometimes. You know that, right?"

She made it sound like an insult, but it felt more like a compliment. "What are you doing here?" I challenged. "I heard your chainsaw when we were leaving. I didn't hear any fallout, so I'm

THE TROUBLE WITH WITCHES

guessing you didn't kill anyone when you did ... whatever it is you did."

"You're imagining things," Aunt Tillie said. "I didn't have a chainsaw and I didn't do anything. I was on a date last night."

Despite my agitation, I couldn't help but grin. "You *were* on a date last night, weren't you? I didn't realize you and Kenneth were a couple again. Are you in love?"

Instead of answering, Aunt Tillie smacked me across the face. The blow sounded worse than it felt, but she clearly had my attention.

"Hey!" I cupped my cheek and widened my eyes. "What was that for?"

"You're being stupid ... and I can't abide stupid."

"You're in my bedroom," I reminded her, tossing off the covers and sliding out of bed. Thankfully I remembered to throw a T-shirt on before falling asleep the previous evening. "If you're not here to talk, why are you here?"

"I didn't say I wasn't here to talk," Aunt Tillie clarified. "I said you're being stupid. There's a difference."

I heaved a sigh as I studied her. "You make me tired. You know that, right?"

"You've been spending too much time with Landon," Aunt Tillie said. "He says things like that. You're a young woman in your prime. You should be getting ready for your sexual peak as you go into your thirties. You shouldn't be tired."

I was mortified by the "sexual peak" comment, yet that wouldn't stop me from expanding on it. "I thought women hit their sexual peak in their forties."

"I'm still in my sexual peak, so I can't verify that," Aunt Tillie said. "Some women defy scientific categorization. I happen to be one of them."

She happened to be ... something. I pursed my lips as I stared at her. This conversation had been going on for what felt like forever and she still hadn't told me why she was here. "What do you want?"

Aunt Tillie pasted an innocent look on her face. "Can't I just want to spend time with my favorite great-niece?"

Now I was definitely suspicious. "Since when am I your favorite great-niece?"

"Always."

"Oh, well, that's kind of sweet," I said. "I still know you want something."

"I'm not sweet," Aunt Tillie said. "You have absolutely no competition. That's the problem. Clove can't be my favorite because she's a kvetch, and Thistle can't be my favorite because ... well ... she's Thistle."

I could see that. "And why are you here again?"

"Oh, right." Aunt Tillie swung her legging-clad legs off the bed and stole another piece of candy before standing. "We need to have a serious discussion about Annie because she can see ghosts. You have to shower first because you smell like sex and 'The Man,' though. I won't be able to concentrate if you don't shower."

I scorched her with a look. "I really dislike you sometimes. You know that, don't you?"

Aunt Tillie didn't appear particularly perturbed by the admission. "I'll meet you in the living room in twenty minutes. Don't take too long in the shower crying about how much you miss Landon. I have a feeling you'll be seeing him much sooner than you think."

I watched her flounce out of my bedroom, my heart constricting. "What was that supposed to mean?"

BY THE TIME I was done showering and drying my hair I'd managed to calm myself, but only marginally. Aunt Tillie had apparently shifted her attention from me to Thistle during my absence. She stood next to the counter drinking coffee and poking Thistle in the cheek when I emerged from the bathroom.

"What are you doing?" I asked.

"I once heard that if you poke a bear enough times it will bite you," Aunt Tillie replied. "I'm testing that theory."

"I'm going to test my foot in your butt if you're not careful, old lady," Thistle threatened, jerking her cheek away. "Why are you even here? You don't come down here unless you want something. Just for the record, whatever you want, I'm not giving it to you."

"Someone didn't get a good night's sleep last night," Aunt Tillie said. "That makes you crabby, Thistle. You should get on a schedule. Bay is crabby in the morning, but she makes you look like the devil to her angel."

"Oh, that's very sweet," I said, shuffling toward the counter. "I'm confused about why you're here, too. You said something about Annie."

Despite how grumpy she is in the morning, Thistle lifted her head and stared at me. "What's wrong with Annie?"

There are times I think Thistle is the meanest person in the world – like when she's trying to steal the extra room for her pottery wheel. There are other times I know that's all a cover because she's actually a giving and caring person. Her concern for Annie always highlights that part of her personality.

"Annie has been seeing ghosts," I answered, pouring myself a mug of coffee and offering Marcus a wan smile as he strode out of Thistle's room. He'd obviously heard at least part of the conversation. "She's terrified, and Belinda doesn't believe she's seeing anything, which only compounds the problem."

"Annie is seeing ghosts?" Marcus' lips twisted. "But ... how can you be sure?"

"Because I saw them at least once, too," I replied, opting for honesty. "The night the power went out, I saw several ghosts watching me in the library. They didn't look normal – I think they might be bordering on that crossover threshold for poltergeists or something – and I kind of froze in place.

"That's where Landon found me. I wasn't sure what to tell him, but I'm almost positive the ghosts came from the Yeti Inferno," I continued. "That has to explain what happened to me the other day."

"I knew there was more than you let on," Thistle barked, extending a finger as she glared at me. "I knew it!"

"Yes, you're wise and lovely," I deadpanned, rolling my eyes. "Is that really important now?"

"It's important because Annie is being haunted," Thistle snapped, catching me off guard with her vehemence. "Annie is a little girl. She doesn't deserve this. If you'd told the truth that day ... ."

"What?" Aunt Tillie challenged, narrowing her eyes. "How would Bay telling the truth about whatever happened – and we'll get back to that in a second because I'm ticked off no one told me – manage to save Annie from what she's going through? We still don't know what we're dealing with or why the spirits seem attracted to Annie."

Thistle balked. "We could've exorcised them or something right away."

Aunt Tillie snorted. "We're witches, not priests. You need to watch fewer movies and focus on real world issues."

That was rich coming from her, but because she was on my side I decided to let it slide. "Besides, I didn't realize we were dealing with ghosts," I pointed out. "I didn't see ghosts on the tanker that day. I saw ... something else."

If Aunt Tillie was intrigued before, she was practically salivating now. "Okay, I have to know what you saw."

"I don't know how to explain it," I admitted, running a hand through my freshly cleaned hair. "We were on the tanker and Thistle was talking about ideas for what we could get done before Halloween. I touched one of the metal walls and ... it was as if I was transported somewhere else."

"Where?" Aunt Tillie pressed. "I've always wanted to go to New Orleans and learn about voodoo. Did you go to New Orleans?"

I love the woman, but there are times I want to smack her. "No. I was transported in time or something. It was as if I was seeing someone's nightmare, only I think it was a terrible memory because it probably really happened.

"I heard screaming ... and there were a lot of men yelling ... and then I saw a knife and blood," I continued. "Landon and I did a little research on the tanker and we found out that it had a twenty-person crew go missing in 1989. That had to be what I saw."

"What did Landon say when you told him about the vision?" Thistle asked.

I averted my eyes. "I kind of left that portion out," I admitted. "I told him that I saw a captain's hat on one of the ghosts – which is totally true – and that I had a feeling it had something to do with Sam's tanker."

"So you lied," Thistle mused.

I balked. "I didn't lie. I just … I don't want him to worry. It's not as if he can fix this problem, and his boss will never let him work from Hemlock Cove this week because his girlfriend sees ghosts."

"He would still want to know," Marcus pointed out. "He loves you. If you're in danger … ."

"I'm not in danger," I said, cutting him off. "I'm not the one seeing the ghosts. In fact, I haven't seen the ghosts since that first night. Annie has, though. I've heard her talking to Belinda."

"I wonder why they're fixated on Annie," Thistle said, rubbing the back of her neck. "That can't be good."

"They're probably focused on her because she's young and has a brighter aura," Aunt Tillie said. She looked lost in thought. "I had an inkling she had some witch in her. I didn't think it would come on this strong and fast, though."

"Is that why you like her?" I asked.

"I like her because she doesn't give me crap when I suggest something," Aunt Tillie replied. "She's a good girl."

Aunt Tillie always manages to take me by surprise. Every time I write her off as a menace or general nuisance, she does something caring that knocks back my opinion. "She is a good girl," I agreed. "Belinda doesn't believe her, though. That's going to really hurt Annie if we're not careful."

"You should know," Aunt Tillie said, her expression thoughtful as she watched me. "We're going to have to tell Belinda something. She needs to know that Annie is gifted and that she can't ignore what Annie is saying just because she can't see it."

"Oh, that's going to be an awesome conversation," Thistle drawled. "Hey, Belinda? Do you know all of those times we disappear into the woods at night and come back sloshed? Well, we're witches. Not only do we dance naked out there, we call to the four corners and cast spells, too.

"We also curse people and Bay can see ghosts," she continued. "Oh, what? You don't believe us? Well, it gets worse. Your daughter can see ghosts, too. No, wait! Don't run screaming out of the house and never let us see Annie again."

If Clove is an optimist, Thistle definitely carries the family pessimist gene.

"That was lovely," I said. "I know you're upset, but we're not going to do that."

"Certainly not," Aunt Tillie agreed. "You're not giving Belinda enough credit. I'm pretty sure she knows something is going on. As for Annie, we have to do what's right for her. It won't be easy or simple, but being a witch never is."

"What do you suggest?" Thistle asked. She was annoyed with Aunt Tillie – as she always was – but she was determined to help Annie.

"Well, for starters, I want to check out that tanker," Aunt Tillie said. "If we can shut these ghosts down at the source we might be able to buy ourselves some time before telling Belinda what's going on.

"If Bay is right and these aren't normal ghosts, we'll have to have a very uncomfortable conversation with Belinda," she continued. "We can spare one morning to look at that tanker and make a plan."

"What about Sam and his parents?" I asked. "I think they're supposed to be spending the day out at the Dandridge. How will we explain what we're doing?"

"We'll lie," Aunt Tillie replied simply. "Don't worry about that. Leave the explanations to me."

Thistle and I exchanged a dubious look.

"Oh, good," Thistle said dryly. "I haven't been in jail for at least a year. I figured it was about time to break that streak."

"No one needs your lip, smart mouth," Aunt Tillie snapped, cuffing Thistle. "I have everything under control. Trust me."

And there they were, the most terrifying words in the English language being uttered by Aunt Tillie as if she didn't have a care in the world. It was enough to strike fear in the hearts of all mortals.

It was definitely going to be a long day.

SEVENTEEN

"This is ... ridiculous."

Thistle complains on a normal day, so making her hike through the woods with Aunt Tillie as we tried to hide our movement from others was essentially asking too much from her fragile patience.

We parked on the side of the road that leads to the Dandridge, trying to camouflage the car as much as possible in case Sam and Clove caught sight of it and got suspicious. Maggie and Richard were already at the lighthouse – they left right after breakfast – and because Clove was already melting down we didn't want to add to the problem.

Our concern for leaving Annie alone spurred Marcus to volunteer to take her to the stable with him for the day. Belinda was surprised by the offer, but Annie was so glum she readily agreed. Even if the ghosts approached Annie while she was with Marcus, we knew he would somehow find a way to keep her safe. He also planned to film her reaction should she start talking to invisible people so we could see it after the fact.

"Stop your bellyaching," Aunt Tillie ordered, making a face as she traipsed through the heavy underbrush. She was in her eighties but remained spry. I was fairly impressed at how easily she navigated the wooded expanse. "If I can hike to the tanker, so can you."

"What are we going to do if the Cornells are at the tanker when we get there?" I asked.

"We're going to lie." Aunt Tillie's response was short and to the point.

"But how?" Thistle pressed. "What will we say we're doing?"

"I haven't decided yet, but I'm gifted so I'll make up a story on the spot," Aunt Tillie said. "There's no reason to work yourselves up. Everything will be fine. Trust me."

Thistle and I exchanged a dubious look.

"It's not that we don't trust you," I hedged. "I'm worried what will happen if we're caught doing something goofy. Clove is living on the edge right now."

"Clove is a pain in the butt," Aunt Tillie said. "She's always been a pain in the butt and she'll always be a pain in the butt. She's a whiner. She's going to find a reason to melt down no matter what we do. I figure we're doing her a favor and actually giving her something to complain about."

"You would think that," Thistle challenged. "You're a terrible person when you want to be."

"I'm going to ignore that because you're still waking up," Aunt Tillie said, stepping over a fallen tree branch and causing the light to hit her leggings at an odd angle. They were so shiny they almost caused a glare. "You're a crabby person, Thistle. You need to learn that being crabby won't get you anywhere in life."

That was rich coming from her. "You're a crabby person," I pointed out. "It seems to have worked for you."

"I'm temperamental," Aunt Tillie corrected. "There's a big difference. I can be temperamental because I'm eccentric. People happen to love eccentric individuals. That means I can do whatever I want and get away with it."

I opened my mouth to argue and then snapped it shut. She had a point. "Can I ask you something?"

"No." Aunt Tillie tilted her head to the side when the lake popped into view. It was still early enough in the morning that the sun wouldn't bake us, but it was going to be a scorcher by the end of the day. The humidity wasn't helping.

"You don't even know what I was going to ask," I protested.

"I can tell by your tone that it will annoy me," Aunt Tillie said. "You always ask annoying questions. You've done it since you were a kid."

"Ha, ha," Thistle teased, smirking when I burned her with a hot look. "Aunt Tillie is right. You've always asked annoying questions. It made me want to punch you when we were younger."

"I wouldn't get so high and mighty, mouth," Aunt Tillie warned. "Bay's questions were much easier to deal with than your sarcasm."

"Ha, ha," I said, my nostrils flaring as I glared at Thistle. "How does that make you feel?"

"Like I want to punch you," Thistle replied, not missing a beat. "I've wanted to punch you all week. You're the reason that Viola won't stop talking to me. That's definitely worth a punch."

I bit the inside of my cheek to keep from laughing as we cut to our right and headed toward the tanker. "I have no idea what you're talking about."

"Oh, you're such a terrible liar," Aunt Tillie chided, shaking her head. "I taught you to lie better than that. Put some effort into it."

Aunt Tillie is the only person who encourages people to lie better when talking to her. "I'll take a class or something."

"I could give you a master class if I wasn't so busy," Aunt Tillie said, frowning as we circled the tanker and stood on the dock in front of her. Her eyes landed on the ancient ladder on the side of the vessel. "Huh. Is that the only way up?"

I'd forgotten about the difficulty we had climbing onto the ship the other day. "Sam is going to put an entry ramp up, but for now ... ."

"Maybe you should stay here," Thistle suggested, her expression mischievous as she stared at Aunt Tillie. "You are old, after all. You probably can't climb that ladder. We understand."

Aunt Tillie narrowed her eyes. There was nothing she loved more than a challenge. "Keep it up, mouth," she said, reaching for the ladder. "I'll show you old."

Thistle smirked. "I'll catch you if you fall. Don't worry."

"You'll catch my foot in your behind if you don't shut up," Aunt Tillie snapped. "Let's do this."

"PULL!"

"Push!"

Somehow Aunt Tillie lost the bulk of her strength during the climb, but she refused to turn around. Ten minutes after we started our ascent, Thistle had to conduct a dangerous maneuver and climb over Aunt Tillie so she could be ahead of her and I could follow. That allowed us to buffer her between us. Now that we were at the top, however, we had another problem.

"Push, Bay!" Thistle barked, jerking on Aunt Tillie's arm as she tried to pull her over the gunwale. "I can't do everything myself."

"I am pushing," I growled, shifting my hands so I had a better grip on Aunt Tillie's hips. The legging material was slippery. "She's like a fish and keeps wriggling around."

"That's because my underwear are riding up," Aunt Tillie snapped. "Can't you two do a simple thing ... like push me onto the boat?"

"It's technically not a boat," I groused, shoving her as hard as I could and taking Thistle by surprise as she tried to keep hold of Aunt Tillie as she toppled over the edge and onto the deck. They both disappeared from view and I heard a loud thump as Thistle landed. "Are you okay?"

I climbed the final three rungs of the ladder and glanced over. Thistle was on the deck, Aunt Tillie resting safely on top of her, and she looked ticked.

"I'm going to kill you later," Thistle muttered, her face red from exertion. "I'm going to make you cry and kill you. Landon will be attending your funeral by the end of the week."

"Oh, stop being such a baby," I said, swinging my leg over the edge of the tanker and helping Aunt Tillie to her feet once I was stable. "Aunt Tillie barely weighs anything."

"That's easy for you to say," Thistle snapped. "She didn't land on you. She's as heavy as a hibernating bear."

"I think she's more like a really large porcupine," I countered.

"You're both on my list," Aunt Tillie growled, shaking her head as she glanced around. "Huh. This is kind of cool, huh?"

It wasn't the reaction I was expecting. "You like the tanker?"

"I always thought I would make a fabulous boat captain," Aunt Tillie explained. "This isn't a boat but it's somehow better. I could totally be a captain, don't you think?"

"Yes," I answered automatically. "You could do it professionally."

"I hear that." Aunt Tillie screwed up her face in concentration as she studied the deck area. "Do you feel that?"

"I'm still trying to wipe the feeling of your leggings out of my head," I replied.

"Yeah, what's the deal with you and the leggings?" Thistle asked. "Are you trying to irritate our mothers or the people in town?"

"I never limit my irritation factor to one group," Aunt Tillie replied. "I'm not trying to irritate anyone, though. I simply like the leggings."

I didn't believe that for a second. I heard Aunt Tillie grunting when the fabric slid into uncomfortable places as we hoisted her up. "Why really?"

"Because your mother told me that I needed to start dressing appropriately for my age and I told her to stuff it," Aunt Tillie said. "I told her I would wear whatever I wanted and … well … then I saw these when I was shopping online. I thought they would be perfect for proving my point."

"Ah." That made perfect sense. "What did she say when she saw them?"

"She hasn't commented on them yet, but I can tell she hates them," Aunt Tillie replied. "She's trying to keep her mouth shut instead of admitting she hates them. She knows I'll win if she says something, and everyone in this family hates losing."

"I hear that," Thistle teased, her eyes twinkling. "How long do you think it will be until she cracks?"

THE TROUBLE WITH WITCHES

"Not long." Aunt Tillie's grin was evil. "I have three more pairs. Each set is designed to make her more and more uncomfortable. I don't think she'll make it to the last day, but I guess we'll have to wait and see."

"You have a sadistic streak," I told her. "You know that, right?"

"It keeps me young," Aunt Tillie said, wiping her hands on her leggings. "So ... where should we start?"

I shrugged. "I'm not even sure what we're doing except trying to find ghosts."

"You said you saw visions," Aunt Tillie pointed out. "That sounds like an echo to me."

Did she just explain something? "What's an echo?" I asked, legitimately curious.

"When something terrible happens in a place, negative energy is expelled all at once from multiple sources," Aunt Tillie explained. "If there's enough energy, it latches on to a location. A lot of people mistake echoes for hauntings."

"Annie is seeing ghosts, though," Thistle pointed out. "Bay saw them, too. That means this is a haunting."

"I think it's far more likely that it's both," Aunt Tillie said. "Something truly terrible happened here. As much as I like this thing, I can smell the fear and terror from decades ago."

"You can?" Holy crap. That's weird, right?

"Can't you?" Aunt Tillie challenged, arching an eyebrow. "You're the most sensitive one, Bay. I would've assumed you could feel what's lurking here."

I bit my lip as I considered her words. "I ... don't know what I feel. When we were getting ready to visit the tanker that first day, I felt a sense of dread I couldn't explain."

"I forgot about that," Thistle admitted, her eyes keen as they bore into me. "You told me that and I made fun of you."

"Yes, well, that's your way," Aunt Tillie said, patting Thistle's arm. "You could do it professionally."

Thistle made a face as she jerked her arm away from Aunt Tillie. "You're a mean old lady. You know that, don't you?"

"I know you're going to grow up to be just like me, so I enjoy when you insult me," Aunt Tillie said. "Keep it up."

Thistle's mouth dropped open as she locked gazes with me. "This is going to be the worst day ever. I can already tell. I hope you're happy."

I wasn't exactly unhappy, but we had bigger issues than Thistle's temper. "Just look around," I suggested. "If something is here, maybe we'll luck out and figure out what it is before we have to share a very difficult discussion with Belinda."

"That discussion is going to happen no matter what," Aunt Tillie said. "All we're hopefully doing today is buying ourselves some time."

"I can live with that."

I separated from Aunt Tillie and Thistle as I shuffled across the deck. By tacit agreement, everyone opted to stay above deck instead of venturing below. If we had to walk into the darkness beneath the ship's deck, I was worried we would never come out again.

I was lost in thought, worry about Annie's wellbeing overwhelming me, when I trailed my fingertips across the railing and got knocked back by a flash. It was so powerful it actually jerked my shoulders in the opposite direction and caused me to gasp.

The images flooding my mind were violent and terrible. I could see the men ... they were running. Other men came over the side of the tanker. They used the ladder we'd just climbed. They had weapons ... and evil black auras. I had no idea how I knew that, but I did.

In my head, I knew I was still on the deck and the bright sunshine was beating down on me. In my heart, I travelled to another time.

I got so lost.

"BAY!"

Thistle screeched in my face when I returned to the present. I opened my mouth to respond, but Aunt Tillie smacked me across the face before I could.

"What was that for?" I sputtered, rubbing my cheek. That was the second time she slapped me today and it was getting old quickly.

"You went someplace else," Thistle replied, her expression reflecting worry. "We've been trying to snap you out of it for ten minutes."

"Oh, you're such an exaggerator," Aunt Tillie said. "It was like forty-five seconds."

"Well, it felt longer," Thistle said, crossing her arms over her chest. "What did you see?"

I tried to organize the memories into a coherent timeline but struggled with the overload of images. "Someone boarded the tanker after dark," I answered. "There was a lot of screaming and crying ... and there was a lot of blood."

"So someone murdered the crew?" Thistle asked, surprised. "But why? Weren't these tankers used to transport oil most of the time? Is oil worth killing for?"

"It depends how desperate the murderers were and what this tanker was really hauling," Aunt Tillie replied, her expression thoughtful. "Did anyone see you in the memory? Did they try talking to you?"

"No." I shook my head. "I was an observer, nothing more."

"What does that mean?" Thistle was getting increasingly shrill. She didn't like it when she couldn't control things. "What's happening here?"

"I'm not sure," Aunt Tillie admitted. "It sounds like an echo and haunting, but ... I honestly don't know."

"Then what good are you?" Thistle blinked back tears as she rubbed her cheek.

"Listen, mouth, I'm doing the best that I can," Aunt Tillie snapped. "I know you're worried about Bay and Annie, but we have to take this one step at a time. There's only so much we can do without more information."

"I'm sorry," Thistle said, taking me by surprise with her grim countenance. "I didn't mean to blame you. It's just ... Annie is so little."

"And you feel responsible for her because you found her on the road that day and you love her," Aunt Tillie said. "I get it. I love her, too. We'll figure it out."

Thistle mutely nodded as Aunt Tillie focused on me.

"As for you, Bay, I don't think you should return to this tanker until we have a better feel for what's happening," Aunt Tillie said. "You're susceptible to whatever this is. I felt evil when I was walking around, but it almost overwhelmed you. That's because you're a more powerful conduit."

That almost sounded like a compliment. "So what do we do?"

Aunt Tillie shrugged. "Research ... I guess."

"Then what?"

"We do what we always do," Aunt Tillie said. "We wing it."

That sounded like a terrible way to go. I opened my mouth to argue, but something high in the tree line caught my attention and I shifted my eyes in the direction of town. It took me a moment to realize I was staring at smoke – and there was a lot of it.

"Holy crap!"

Thistle and Aunt Tillie followed my gaze, dumbfounded.

"Something is on fire in town," Thistle said. "Omigod! What if it's the store?"

"We have to get there," I said, pushing myself to my feet and heading toward the ladder. "It could be anything. We need to see what's going on."

"Let's go," Aunt Tillie said, biting her lip as she stared over the side of the tanker and glared at the ladder. "So which one of you is carrying me down?"

Thistle was beside herself. "Son of a ... !"

EIGHTEEN

My shoulders and back hurt by the time we got Aunt Tillie to the bottom of the ladder. She, however, was in a great mood. She kept yelling "giddyap" while Thistle and I struggled with our descent. You wouldn't think a tiny woman would weigh so much, but apparently evil is heavy.

After hitting the ground we were forced to hike through the woods again, so by the time we made it back to the car and into town the smoke had turned white – which meant the fire was out. We parked in front of Thistle and Clove's store and walked toward the crowd about a block down. The fire truck was parked in front of Mrs. Little's porcelain unicorn store, and when we closed the distance I realized that's what caught fire.

"Oh, it's my lucky day," Aunt Tillie said, clapping her hands. "Karma has paid a visit in the form of fire."

"Shh." I shot her a dirty look. "Don't say things like that. People can hear you."

"I don't care," Aunt Tillie said. "I never say anything I don't mean."

I didn't believe that for a second. All of the Winchesters were blessed with leaky mouths and Aunt Tillie's was the leakiest of all. "You regretted telling Annie that Landon was bad because he was 'The

Man' and you told her she should always trust him when I pointed out how dangerous that was."

Aunt Tillie cocked her head to the side. "I meant that," she said. "I just didn't mean for Annie to take it so seriously. I haven't been around children for a long time – you girls don't count because you're old and only act immature – and I forgot how impressionable young minds are."

There was a lot of truth in that statement. "You still regretted it."

"Don't make me curse you so your tongue falls out," Aunt Tillie warned. "I can be pushed only so far."

That was a sobering thought. I moved toward Chief Terry when I saw him, his face grave as he stared at the front of the store. He was deep in conversation with a man I didn't recognize, but as I got closer I managed to read the writing on his shirt. He was a state fire inspector.

"What's going on?" I asked, drawing Chief Terry's attention.

"The Unicorn Emporium caught fire," Chief Terry replied. "We're not sure how yet, but I can smell gasoline. You know what that means."

I did. "Arson."

"It's the second fire in three days," Chief Terry said. "I think we have a firebug."

That couldn't be good. "Was anyone inside? Was anybody hurt?"

Chief Terry opened his mouth to answer. He knew what I was really asking. Was Mrs. Little dead? It was a horrible thought and I knew I should feel bad about the prospect, but she was a terrible woman who did downright obnoxious things. No one deserves to die. Of course, Thistle was under the impression evil never dies so she was probably fine.

Chief Terry never got a chance to respond because that's when Mrs. Little rounded the corner. She looked frazzled – her gray hair standing on end and her shirt and slacks filthy – but her eyes were murderous when they landed on Aunt Tillie.

"You!"

Aunt Tillie didn't look bothered by Mrs. Little's screech. "You," she shot back.

"You did this," Mrs. Little bellowed as she pushed her way through the crowd. "I know it was you. You're evil!"

"It takes evil to recognize evil," Aunt Tillie said. "You should know, because you're the most evil of them all."

"Aunt Tillie, you should probably be nice to her," I warned, my voice low. "She's been through a trauma."

"Did you just meet me?" Aunt Tillie was positively apoplectic. "I don't care about her store ... or her stupid unicorns ... or that hairy mole on her lip she keeps telling people is a beauty mark. She's evil. This is karma."

Crap! Why do I ever bring Aunt Tillie to town? She always makes things worse.

"That is a beauty mark," Mrs. Little screeched, fingering the ugly protuberance on her lip.

"You have to be pretty to have a beauty mark," Aunt Tillie said. "You look like an elephant's hemorrhoid after it's been inflamed for three days and someone decided to pop it like a zit."

My mouth dropped open as Thistle barked out a delighted laugh.

"I'm going to kill you," Mrs. Little seethed, jerking forward.

Chief Terry grabbed her before she could attack, which was probably a good thing for her. Aunt Tillie is old but she's strong. She's also sadistic when she gets involved in a fight. "Don't even think about it," Chief Terry warned.

"She did this!" Mrs. Little exploded, her face red with effort. "You know she did this. I want her arrested right now!"

"I want her arrested, too," Aunt Tillie announced. "She's a blight on humanity. I want her tried for war crimes."

Chief Terry tapped his foot as he scowled. "What war?"

"This war," Aunt Tillie snapped. "This war has been raging for more than sixty years. I want her hanged. No, wait! I want her put in front of a firing squad. I've got a gun and I'll help. Heck, I've got six guns. They're hidden around the property so Winnie doesn't find them, but I can be back in five minutes."

"Knock it off," Chief Terry warned, extending a finger. "You're not helping matters."

"I didn't know that's what I was supposed to be doing," Aunt Tillie said. "In that case ... um ... has anyone ever built a homemade electric chair? That could be fun."

"I'm going to throw a party when you're locked up for burning my store," Mrs. Little said. "It's going to be a huge party. Everyone is going to dance and tell Tillie stories. They'll all start with, 'Remember that crazy lady who used to curse people and cast spells?' I can't wait!"

"Oh, yeah? I'm going to dance on your grave," Aunt Tillie said. "I'm going to line dance ... and then twerk just because I know it will really annoy you. I'm going to be naked when I do it, too."

The crowd appeared to be enjoying the fight, but I heard several people gasp when that visual pushed its way to the forefront of their brains.

"That's enough!" Chief Terry bellowed, catching everyone by surprise. "I want both of you in my office right now!"

For a moment I thought Aunt Tillie was going to argue. Instead she squared her shoulders and narrowed her eyes. "Everyone is on my list!"

THISTLE AND I stood in the middle of Chief Terry's office, making sure to keep Mrs. Little and Aunt Tillie separated as he sat at his desk and glared at us. His gaze seemed directed at me, which was hardly fair because I didn't cause this ruckus.

"I ... ."

"Be quiet, Bay," Chief Terry admonished. "You're not part of this."

His words hurt my feelings. Chief Terry must've realized it, because he shot me an apologetic look.

"I'm sorry," Chief Terry said. "That was unnecessary and unfair. It's just ... I feel old. I feel like I'm a hundred years old and somehow I'm being punished by angry old women."

"Who are you calling old?" Aunt Tillie challenged. "I'm in my prime. Heck, I'm middle-aged. You have to be old to be called old."

Chief Terry furrowed his brow. "You be quiet, too."

Thistle and I exchanged an amused look as Chief Terry shifted his eyes to Mrs. Little. "Now, let's talk about your store." His voice was soft and deadly. "What do you think happened?"

"I think that Tillie ... ."

Chief Terry waved his hand to cut off Mrs. Little. "I want to know exactly what happened in the store and we'll go from there. I want to know what you saw. I made a mistake just now when I asked you what you thought. That's not what I want to hear. I want to know what you saw."

"I didn't see anything," Mrs. Little said. "I was in the back room going through a new delivery box and I heard glass break. I didn't understand what was happening because I have that bell over the door and that alerts me if someone enters. The store was empty."

"I had no idea the gates of Hell had bells," Aunt Tillie intoned.

Chief Terry ignored her. "Then what happened?"

"I raced out front," Mrs. Little replied. "I thought maybe a shelf fell, but the window was broken and there was a huge flame. I smelled gasoline ... or maybe it was lighter fluid. They both smell the same to me."

"That sounds like a Molotov cocktail," Thistle said. "Why would someone firebomb a unicorn store?"

"Why don't you ask your aunt?" Mrs. Little suggested.

"We're asking you," Chief Terry said. "What did you see out the window? Did you look in either direction?"

"I was too frightened," Mrs. Little answered. "I wanted to put out the fire, but it was too big. I ran out the back door instead, and someone on the street called for help. That's all I know."

"Thank you." Chief Terry rubbed the back of his neck as he stared at his desk. "The state boys are going to run some tests, but I could smell gasoline inside the store. There's moderate damage, so you need to get your insurance people on the phone."

"I already called them," Mrs. Little said. "I'm not an idiot."

Aunt Tillie opened her mouth to argue the point, but I shook my head to quiet her.

"You can let some of them go," I whispered.

"Hardly."

"She's the one who started the fire," Mrs. Little said. "We all know it. You know it. I know it. Bay and Thistle know it. I want her arrested and charged."

"On what evidence?" Chief Terry challenged.

"She doesn't have an alibi."

Chief Terry shifted his eyes to Aunt Tillie. "We don't know that," he said after a beat. "Do you have an alibi?" He looked terrified to utter the question. If Aunt Tillie didn't have an alibi he might have to arrest her, and if that happened my mother would cut him off from dinners until the situation was resolved. No one – least of all him – wanted that.

"I want a lawyer," Aunt Tillie announced, crossing her arms over her chest. "I want a good one, too, because I'm going to sue everyone in this town for being war criminals."

Chief Terry heaved a sigh. "I take that to mean you don't have an alibi."

"That's not true," I argued. "She was with Thistle and me."

"And where were you?"

I wasn't keen on answering, but saw no reason to lie. "We were on Sam's tanker."

"Why?"

"Because ... ." I couldn't use ghosts as part of Aunt Tillie's alibi. That wouldn't go over well.

"Because I'm helping him decorate it and Aunt Tillie wanted to play pirate," Thistle supplied.

Chief Terry didn't look convinced. "Why really?"

"She was bored and wanted to show off her new leggings," I answered.

"Yes, those are truly ... something to behold," Chief Terry said. I didn't miss the fact that he kept his eyes above waist level so he didn't accidentally see any of Aunt Tillie's naughty bits highlighted by the leggings. "How long was she with you?"

"She woke me this morning by bouncing on the bed," I answered.

"Then we all had coffee in the guesthouse before going up to the inn for breakfast. After that we left immediately for the tanker. We were together the entire time."

"Can you corroborate that, Thistle?"

Thistle slid a sidelong look in Aunt Tillie's direction, her mind clearly working overtime. I could tell she wanted to mess with our mischievous great-aunt but the stakes were too dire. "We were all together," Thistle confirmed. "Aunt Tillie couldn't have done it because she was with us the entire time."

"Well, they're obviously lying," Mrs. Little sputtered. "You know they're lying. Tillie has been out to get me for decades."

"While I don't doubt that, I see no reason for Tillie to try to burn down your store," Chief Terry said. "What's her motivation? If she burns it down then she can't make fun of you for selling porcelain unicorns."

"Those are collectibles!"

"Ugly collectibles," Aunt Tillie muttered.

"It doesn't matter," Chief Terry said. "She has no motive. This is the second fire we've had in three days. Why would she burn down the booth at the festival?"

"Because ... ." Mrs. Little licked her lips as she racked her brain. "Oh, because they were selling love potions and that puts Kelly Sheridan in direct competition with Hypnotic. Kelly is behind on her bills, and she's really been amping up production. I'm sure that drives Tillie crazy."

Thistle snorted. "Hardly. Those potions are rose water and oregano."

"And not the good kind of oregano," Aunt Tillie said, referencing her pot field. She often lied and called it oregano when people asked.

"Don't go there," Chief Terry warned, shaking his head. "As far as I can tell, Tillie has no motive other than your longstanding feud. That generally takes the form of snide remarks and the occasional slap – or whatever it is Tillie is doing when she parades in front of your store and does her little dance. It's never involved fire and accelerants."

161

Mrs. Little refused to back down. "There's a first time for everything."

"Well, we'll keep Tillie on the possible suspect list, but we're going to look elsewhere," Chief Terry said. "If that's all ... ."

"That's not even close to all," Mrs. Little seethed, turning on her heel. "I'm going to make all of you pay."

"I'm looking forward to that," Aunt Tillie called to her back. "We've already had to pay because that lip mole haunts us."

Chief Terry waited until he heard the door slam. "Why were you really on the tanker?"

He knew us too well. He recognized the lie about Aunt Tillie wanting to play pirate.

"Because we think the tanker might be haunted and wanted Aunt Tillie to look around," Thistle replied, matter of factly. Chief Terry knew about our witchy ways, but liked to pretend otherwise. "Something bad happened on Sam's tanker in 1989, and the ghosts are still hanging around."

"I didn't hear that," Chief Terry said, shaking his head. "She was really with you, though, right? You're not making that up, are you?"

"She was really with us," I said. "I'll have bruises on my shoulders tomorrow to prove it, because we had to carry her down a ladder."

"And she weighs a ton," Thistle added. "I didn't realize pure evil made a difference on the scale."

Aunt Tillie narrowed her eyes to dangerous slits. "You're on my list."

Thistle ignored her. "She couldn't have done it," she said. "Whoever is doing this, it isn't Aunt Tillie."

"That's what I'm afraid of," Chief Terry said. "We have an arsonist on the loose, and whoever it is seems to be getting bolder. Do you know what that means?"

"More fires," I answered.

"We've been lucky so far. No one's been hurt," Chief Terry said. "How long do you think that lucky streak will last?"

That was a very good – and terrifying – question.

NINETEEN

I was lost in thought, pacing in front of the inn as I waited for Chief Terry to arrive for dinner shortly before seven. The fire at Mrs. Little's store bothered me, but the visions I saw on the tanker haunted me. I couldn't decide which problem I wanted to focus on, so I decided to obsess about both of them.

When a pair of headlights bounced off me and a vehicle swung into the lot I figured Chief Terry had finally arrived. That meant I could focus on the fire, which at least gave me direction. However, the figure I saw moving up the driveway didn't look like Chief Terry. He was slimmer, long hair sweeping broad shoulders in the limited light. I recognized him right away.

"Landon?"

"Hey, sweetie." Landon's grin was lopsided as he opened his arms for a hug.

I readily threw my arms around his neck and gave him a kiss, backing up only when I got my fill of the embrace. "What are you doing here?"

"Oh, I feel so loved," Landon teased, rubbing his thumb over my cheek. "Maybe I missed you."

"You left just this morning."

"Maybe I'm a pathetic sap," Landon suggested, his eyes unreadable as they scanned my face. "What's wrong?"

I don't know how he does it, but he always seems to know when something is bothering me, even when I try to hide it. "I ... there was another fire today." It wasn't the most auspicious of greetings, but I figured the fire was a safer topic.

"I know," Landon said, pushing a strand of hair behind my ear. "Chief Terry called. They're putting together a small arson task force. Two fires in such a small area is cause for concern."

Hope gathered in my chest as something occurred to me. "Is that why you're here?"

Landon nodded. "I'm the head of the task force. But because the task force consists of Chief Terry, Noah and me, that's not saying much. I'll take it because it means I get to stay here with you, though."

That was both good and bad news. The idea of Landon being close always makes me feel warm and fuzzy. The notion of his dumbass partner – and I use that term in the loosest possible sense – being around while all of this was going on was disheartening.

Agent Noah Glenn was a gung-ho recent recruit with a lot of enthusiasm and a bad attitude. Several weeks ago he suspected Aunt Tillie of being a murderer and wanted her arrested. That fizzled – and the real culprit was dead – but my dislike remained. Aunt Tillie had an alibi for today's fire, but if Noah fixated on her again ... well ... things were about to get uncomfortable.

"Noah?"

Landon smiled at my disgusted expression. "He's staying at your father's inn, so you don't have to worry," he said. "He wasn't thrilled about coming back to Hemlock Cove either – trust me – so he had to be persuaded. Fires in a small town like this can get out of hand quickly."

I was intrigued despite myself. "What do you mean?"

"I mean that two fires in a few days is quite the escalation for whoever is doing this," Landon replied, opting not to gloss over the severity of the situation. "We need to be vigilant, because the next fire could really hurt someone."

"Oh." I ran my tongue over my teeth as Landon rubbed my back. "Mrs. Little accused Aunt Tillie of setting the fire."

"I know." Landon didn't seem bothered by the accusation. "I talked to Chief Terry before heading over. He said you and Thistle supplied Aunt Tillie with an alibi."

"She was really with us," I protested, moving to pull away.

"I believe you," Landon said, refusing to let me increase the distance between us. "I don't believe Aunt Tillie would set a fire in the middle of the day anyway. She'd be far happier setting a mental fire and torturing Mrs. Little with the constant sight of her leggings than burning out her store. It's okay."

"I ... ."

"What's wrong, Bay?" Landon asked, his expression serious as he stared into my eyes. "Why were you out here?"

"I wanted to talk to Chief Terry," I admitted. "I wanted to make sure he didn't suspect Aunt Tillie."

"Chief Terry is on his way, and he doesn't suspect Aunt Tillie," Landon said. "Bay, whoever is doing this could be a deranged individual. It could be someone who is legitimately mentally unbalanced. We simply don't know."

"What do your statistics tell you?" Landon had specifics on every sort of crime imaginable. He enjoys researching them as much as he loves bacon for breakfast. Er, well, maybe not quite. It was close, though.

"My statistics tell me that it's a man and he's probably in his twenties, thirties or forties," Landon said. "I don't like to focus on statistics to the detriment of everything else."

"Are you here for the whole week?" The idea settled me. I had no idea why I wanted Landon close. The feeling of dread was back, though, and it plagued me from the moment we left the tanker. Something bad was going to happen.

"I'm going to be here until we catch whoever is doing this," Landon cautioned. His smile was mischievous. "Somehow I expect I'll be able to stretch out the paperwork to last through the week."

I giggled as he poked my ribs and rested my head against his shoulder. "I'm glad you're back."

"I'm always glad to be back."

We lapsed into comfortable silence for a moment and then I remembered something. "Thank you for the note and candy. It was really sweet."

"Did you think of me when you were eating the candy?"

I answered without thinking. "Aunt Tillie stole the candy. She read the note before I got a chance to. She woke me up by jumping on the bed and stealing my treat."

Landon stilled. "Why was Aunt Tillie in your bedroom so early?" He's naturally suspicious by nature – it's a product of his work – but I realized my mistake when it was too late to take it back.

"She ... ."

"Bay?" Landon pulled his head back and locked gazes with me. "What is Aunt Tillie up to?"

Oh, well, that was a loaded question. "She wanted to see the tanker," I said. It wasn't a lie. "She thinks whatever Annie is seeing is coming from there. That was our goal for the day. We were going to help Annie. Then we saw the smoke and ... it didn't really happen."

"Oh." Landon openly relaxed as he cupped the back of my head. "Well, we'll figure out how to keep Annie safe and happy while I'm here, too. I'll multitask."

It was a sweet offer, but I wasn't sure what he could do. "Just as long as you're here and Aunt Tillie isn't a legitimate suspect, I'm happy."

"I'm happy, too," Landon said, pressing a soft kiss to my mouth. "I jumped at the chance to take the case. I told my boss it was because I hadn't investigated an arson case in years. He didn't believe me."

Now it was my turn to smirk. "Does he think you're a fool for love?"

"He thinks I'm a fool for you," Landon corrected. "He made a few jokes and imitated the crack of a whip, but he was happy to let me go."

I widened my eyes. "Does he really think you're whipped? That doesn't seem fair."

"Oh, don't do that," Landon chided. "We all know I'm whipped. Pretending otherwise doesn't make me feel more manly."

I chewed on my bottom lip as I regarded him, conflicted. "Would it help if I told you that whipped men are hot?"

Landon flashed me a genuine smile. "It helps that we're together," he said. "As for the rest, I don't care what other people think."

That was a refreshing outlook and I smacked a scorching kiss against his mouth before pulling back. "I'll make sure you get two desserts for such a stellar answer."

"And that's exactly why I don't care what anyone thinks," Landon said. "Bring on the pot roast and cake."

"How did you know we were having pot roast?"

"I have a magic nose."

"You have a magic everything," I said, tugging him toward the house. "I'll make sure you're full and happy before we head to the guesthouse for the night, though. It's the least I can do."

"I think it's going to be a great week, sweetie," Landon teased. "The food is only part of it."

"I'M NOT SITTING THERE," Annie snapped, her head swishing back and forth as she fought Belinda's efforts. "I want to sit next to Marcus."

It was a Monday, so the dining room was mostly empty of guests at The Overlook – which I couldn't have been more thankful for given Annie's mood. Worry over her continued meltdowns caused a hard pit of anger to form in my stomach. Belinda looked to be at her wit's end.

"Annie, there's no reason for you to act like this," Belinda snapped. "You're supposed to be a big girl. Big girls don't act like this."

Belinda's words didn't have their intended effect. "I don't care," Annie seethed, furious. "I want to sit by Marcus. I don't want to sit by you. I hate you sometimes!"

The words were like a fist to the face for Belinda, and I didn't miss the way her eyes rapidly opened and closed as she blinked back tears.

I felt sympathy for both of them. Belinda was hurt because she thought Annie was acting out for no reason and being purposely hurtful. Annie was hurt because she was seeing things she didn't understand and was terrified. I didn't know what to do to help her. Thankfully, Aunt Tillie stepped in and solved the problem.

"Why don't you sit by me, Annie?" Aunt Tillie asked, flashing a smile. "I would enjoy that."

Instead of jumping at the chance to spend time with her favorite elderly witch, Annie made a face. "I don't want to sit next to you," Annie shot back. "I want to sit next to Marcus. Are you all deaf? Can you hear what I'm saying? I want to sit next to Marcus!"

Marcus' eyes widened and he took everyone by surprise when he grabbed Annie's shoulders and forced her to meet his even gaze. "Don't talk to your mother like that," he admonished, his voice low. "She's trying to help you. You're being rude."

"But … ." Annie broke off, her lower lip quivering. "I want to sit next to you."

"You can sit next to me," Marcus said. "I would love to sit next to you. But I don't like your attitude. Your mother loves you and doesn't deserve to be treated this way."

Annie's expression was conflicted as she stared into Marcus' somber eyes for a moment. Then she shifted her sheepish gaze to her mother. "I'm sorry."

Belinda looked relieved but not entirely placated by the apology. "I'm sorry, too," she said after a beat. "You can sit next to Marcus for dinner, but then you're going to bed early. Do you understand?"

"But that's not fair," Annie protested. "I don't want to go to bed early. I'm not tired."

"Well, you're going to bed early," Belinda said. "I think you're overwrought. I think sleep is exactly what you need to make you feel better."

"I think I need you to shut up to make me feel better," Annie exploded, causing everyone to suck in a breath.

Landon shifted his eyes to me, his expression unreadable. Annie was generally a sweet girl who always capitulated to her mother.

THE TROUBLE WITH WITCHES

Whatever was happening with the ghosts was getting out of hand quickly.

"What's going on here?" Chief Terry asked, strolling into the room. He looked confused when he saw everyone standing around the table. "Nothing happened to the roast, did it? I've been thinking about roast all day."

"The roast is fine," Mom answered stiffly. "It's Annie. She's ... having a bad day."

"Is that so?" Chief Terry's eyes twinkled as he stared at Annie. He clearly didn't understand the gravity of the situation. "I'll bet some pot roast will make you feel better."

"And I'll bet you're a real jerk if you think that," Annie retorted, scathing disdain practically dripping off her tongue. "You're a real jerk no matter what, though, aren't you?"

Belinda's mouth dropped open as dumbfounded disbelief washed over her. "That's it!" she exploded, reaching for Annie's waist. "You're going to bed without supper. You ... you ... that was horrible!"

"You're horrible," Annie screeched, violently shaking her head as she tried to escape her mother's grip. "You're all horrible and I hate you all!"

"Annie, stop this," Marcus said. He tried to help Belinda rein in Annie, but she was fighting the effort so completely that he looked worried about sticking his hands into the mix in case he inadvertently hurt her. "Why are you acting like this? This isn't like you."

As if on cue, Annie snapped her head up and squared her shoulders. Hatred flitted through the depths of her eyes. "This is me," she said. "This is the new me. I ... they're here."

The way she said it was eerie, as if we were stuck in *Poltergeist* and the television was about to eat us. Marcus appeared vexed by her words but I was instantly alert as I scanned the room. I knew exactly what she was referring to and I had no intention of letting anything terrible happen.

"Where are they?" I asked, moving my gaze from corner to corner. "Where, Annie?"

"Where's what?" Belinda asked, confused.

AMANDA M. LEE

"What is going on?" Chief Terry asked.

"Do you see anything?" Landon asked, keeping his voice low.

"No." Even as I said the word something manifested in the corner of the living room. The man was short and portly. He couldn't have been taller than me, which wasn't saying much because the women in my family are short. He was as round as he was tall and he had a wiry gray beard. He wore a captain's hat and blue pants, and his gaze initially landed on Annie before moving to me.

"Bay?" Landon sounded concerned but I ignored him.

"Leave her alone," I said, taking a step forward. "She's a little girl."

The ghost didn't respond.

"Do you see him?" Annie looked so hopeful it almost ripped out my heart.

"I see him," I said, bobbing my head. "You're not imagining things. I promise."

"What do you see?" Belinda asked, frustrated. "Don't play games with her. That's not good for anyone."

"No one is playing games," Aunt Tillie said. "There's something in this room."

"What?" Chief Terry asked, annoyed. "Is it another poltergeist? If so, I'm leaving. I'm taking the cake and roast with me when I go, but I'm leaving."

"It's something else," Landon said. He looked helpless as I took another step away from him. He couldn't see the enemy and had no idea what to do. "Bay, be careful."

"Leave her alone," I repeated, locking gazes with the ethereal captain. "She's a child. She can't help you. If you need help ... ."

The captain didn't respond with words. Instead he floated in Annie's direction, his hand outstretched. I didn't miss the terror as it flitted across Annie's face and I reacted instinctively. I shoved Marcus out of the way and stepped in front of Annie, absorbing the spirit's malevolence before it could wash over her.

That's when I heard it ... the screaming.

That's when I saw it ... the endless blood.

That's when I felt it ... the terror and resignation.

And that's when my knees buckled and my mind flooded with images and sounds I never want to see or hear again.

At the back of my mind, I registered the fact that Landon caught me before I could hit the ground. The last thing I heard before the blackness came was the sound of his anguished voice.

"Bay!"

TWENTY

"Bay?"

Landon shook me back to awareness, and when I finally managed to focus I found his eyes swimming with tears.

"Hi."

"Don't 'hi' me," Landon said, pulling me close. "You scared the crap out of me."

"What just happened?" Chief Terry asked. He knelt next to Landon and his features were ashen. "Did I miss something?"

"She expelled a ghost before it could touch Annie."

I jerked my head to the right and found Maggie Cornell studying me with a thoughtful expression. When did she get here? "I ... ."

"It's okay," Maggie said hurriedly, flashing a smile. "I know about you guys. There's no reason to hide."

"I didn't tell her," Sam said, frowning when Aunt Tillie glared at him. "You guys are famous in certain circles. I've kept everything I know to myself."

"I can vouch for that," Maggie said, patting my arm kindly. "I've been grilling him and he refuses to say anything. It's very disappointing for a mother."

"You saw the ghost?" Aunt Tillie asked, her expression curious. "I thought Sam said that wasn't your gift."

"I can't see ghosts, but I can see auras," Maggie explained.

"I saw the ghost," Sam volunteered. "It was wearing a captain's hat. I ... huh. Do you think it came from the tanker? It had to be the stuff you were talking about the other day, right?"

I pursed my lips as I stared at the ceiling, my back resting against Landon's knees as he bolstered me from behind. "I think that's a very good guess."

"I think I want some answers," Landon said. "What just happened?"

"The ghosts are interested in Annie," I explained, licking my lips as I glanced toward the spot where Annie stood moments before. "Where is she?"

"Belinda took her upstairs when you passed out," Thistle answered. For once she didn't have a snarky response. She looked stricken. "She didn't understand what was happening and thought everyone was acting odd."

"She can't understand what's happening," Aunt Tillie clarified. "It's surreal to her and she doesn't know what to think. We need to explain things ... although I'm not sure how open she'll be when that happens."

"She's a good person," Thistle protested. "She'll understand."

"She's a great person," Aunt Tillie said, bobbing her head. "This is still a world she can't fathom. We'll have to do our best when it's time. For now, Annie is safe upstairs."

"Safe?" I challenged. "She's not safe. The ghosts are interested in her. They've completely lost interest in me. It's my fault."

"What do you mean by that?" Landon asked, suspicious. "When were the ghosts interested in you?"

Uh-oh. The time for hiding that little tidbit was clearly over. "I ... saw something ... the day we visited the tanker for the first time," I admitted. "That's why I wanted to conduct research on it."

"Okay." Landon remained calm even though it looked as if the effort strained him. "What did you see?"

"A bunch of flashes."

"Like?"

"Like scenes from the past," I replied. "I'm not sure how to explain it. I think someone boarded the Gray Harker after dark and ... massacred ... the crew. It's hard for me to put what I saw into words because it's a jumbled mess of visions ... and screams ... and blood."

"Whatever it was caused her to pass out that first day, too," Clove supplied. "We were worried, but then we found out that Maggie and Richard were coming to visit right away and I kind of forgot about it."

"Well, that's just great," Landon said, his agitation coming out to play. "That's ... freaking awesome!"

Thistle ignored his sarcasm. "I didn't forget," she said. "We've been trying to figure out what's going on for days. It's not easy to do that when we have guests, an arsonist and whatever Aunt Tillie's latest scheme is barreling down on us. We're doing our best."

"I'm not questioning your distraction level or dedication to helping Annie," Landon said. "I want to know why no one told me about this."

"I ... ." I broke off, biting my lip.

"She didn't want to worry you," Clove supplied. I knew she was trying to help, but the way Landon clenched his jaw told me she was doing exactly the opposite. "She loves you, Landon. You never want the person you love to worry."

"Yes, well, good job on that," Landon said, pushing me to a sitting position and slipping out from beneath me. I missed his warmth the second he put distance between us, although Thistle grabbed my arm to make sure I didn't fall back. "I'm not worried at all."

"Okay, calm down," Chief Terry admonished, lifting his hand. "I need to be caught up on things here ... and I would prefer doing it over pot roast."

"Oh, the pot roast!" Marnie, Mom and Twila wiped the worried looks off their faces and hurried back in the direction of the kitchen. They wanted to be updated on recent events, too, but serving a burnt meal was somehow more abhorrent than my swoon.

"What did you feel?" Thistle asked, her pointed gaze burning into me. "Could you feel the ghost going inside of you?"

"Not really," I answered. "It was more that I felt anger and panic and could see people screaming and yelling as they ran across the deck of the tanker. Something really terrible happened there."

"Which is going to make it a hot ticket when it finally opens," Sam said, rubbing his hands together. He had the grace to look abashed when his mother scorched him with a dark look. "That's after we help the ghosts move on and Annie and Bay are safe, of course."

"What I don't get is why Sam hasn't seen any ghosts," Clove said, her expression thoughtful as she rolled her neck. "He can see ghosts, too, and the ones on the tanker haven't approached him at all. They were interested in Bay that first day, but you never saw anything, did you, honey?"

Sam shook his head. "I never saw a thing," he said. "I sensed something. It was kind of cold ... and dark. The best way to describe it is to say I felt a sense of dread."

"That's what I felt, too," I admitted, my eyes drifting to Landon. He refused to look at me, instead staring at the wall as he his hands rested on his hips. "I couldn't figure out why I felt that way, and it left me feeling unsettled."

"Well, I guess we know now," Landon said. "The first day you visited the tanker was the night the power went out here, right?"

I nodded.

"What did you really see that night, Bay?"

I swallowed hard. I didn't like his tone. "I saw ghosts in the library," I answered. "I think there were six of them. They were staring at me. I already told you that."

"No, you said you thought you saw something and then later linked it to the tanker," Landon said. "You already knew at that point that the ghosts came from the tanker, so that was a lie."

I pursed my lips. "I ... ."

"Okay, let's not get dramatic," Chief Terry said. "I can't pretend to understand what Bay saw or did, but I'm guessing it was somewhat heroic, because she saved Annie. Speaking of Annie, I've never seen her that angry or mean. Are the ghosts doing something to her?"

"I think they're showing her images and visions," I answered, swallowing the painful lump in my throat. Landon's anger made me want to cry. "It's frightening and she doesn't know what to do with what they're showing her. She doesn't mean to be such a pain."

"I think the ghosts must've followed Bay home from the tanker that day," Thistle said. "We were at the tanker this afternoon and Bay saw something again."

"Did you pass out?" Landon's eyes were on fire.

I shook my head. "I just saw flashes."

"I'm pretty sure it was an echo," Aunt Tillie explained. "I don't know how else to explain it. Whatever happened on the tanker was terrible enough to leave an impression decades after the event. That means the ghosts will be particularly hard to get rid of."

"Oh, well, that sounds lovely," Landon intoned, shaking his head. "I just … ." He broke off and pressed the heel of his hand to his forehead. He seemed lost and hurt. I couldn't blame him.

"Landon … ."

"Not now, Bay," Landon said, his voice low.

"But … ."

"No." Landon shook his head. "I'm so angry with you right now I know I'll say something terrible that I'll regret if we talk about this before I have a chance to process. I am not going to yell at you given what just happened."

"Because she's a hero," Clove said solemnly. "She's a big hero, and you shouldn't be angry with her, because you can't fight with heroes."

Landon's shoulders were stiff but I didn't miss the way his lips quirked when he turned to Clove. "I love how you guys fight constantly but back each other up when something bad happens," he said. "It makes me laugh."

"You don't look like you're laughing now," Thistle pointed out. "I don't know about anyone else, but I think we'd all feel better if you laughed. I know Bay would."

Landon finally turned his full attention to me. "I'm not in the mood to laugh."

"Are you in the mood to eat?" Chief Terry asked, turning his gaze to the swinging door as my mother and aunts barreled through it, their arms laden with serving dishes. "There's no problem too big that pot roast can't make it better."

Landon shrugged. "I could eat."

Well, that was at least something. He didn't storm out and he was sitting through dinner. That's good, right? Yeah, I'm not so sure either.

DINNER WAS A SOMBER AFFAIR. Landon sat in his regular spot, but he didn't so much as utter a word to me and I was relegated to talking to Maggie, who seemed thrilled by what happened rather than worried. I could tell her reaction annoyed Landon further, but there wasn't much I could do about that, so I pretended I was unbothered and happy to discuss ghosts even as Landon stewed next to me.

After eating two huge slices of cake and promising to come up with a plan of action to help Annie the next morning, Landon and I left through the back door. I was ready for a fight ... and maybe even some groveling ... but the sight of Aunt Tillie hurrying back toward the inn with her arms full of herbs was enough to give me pause.

"What are you doing?" I asked, confused.

"That had better not be pot," Landon said, his voice flat. "I'll arrest you if it is."

"It's not pot," Aunt Tillie scoffed, her eyes thoughtful as they bounced between us. "I'm casting a ritual spell with your mothers to block spirits from the house. We're doing it before bed. That should keep Annie safe – er, well, at least somewhat safer."

"That's a good idea," I said, rubbing the back of my neck as weariness overcame me. "Do you need help?"

"No, you need rest," Aunt Tillie said. "We've got this."

"Great," Landon said woodenly. "Let's go, Bay."

I fell into step next to him, resigned to the fact that we were going to have a long night. Aunt Tillie didn't let us go quietly, however.

"Landon, you need to let her off the hook," Aunt Tillie said, taking me by surprise with her serious expression. "You're being a butthead."

Landon stilled. I could practically feel the anger radiating off of him. "Why should I let it go?" he challenged, glaring at Aunt Tillie.

"She could've been hurt. I don't know what happened, but I felt the serious nature of it. She could've died in my arms. I don't know how I know that, but I do."

"But she didn't," Aunt Tillie said pragmatically. "She's alive and she protected Annie. What else would you have her do?"

"Not get hurt." Landon's answer was so simple it caused my heart to roll.

"You go to your job every day knowing that you could get hurt," Aunt Tillie pointed out. "You would've done the same thing to protect Annie if you could. Don't bother denying it."

"I ... ." Landon's jaw worked, but he couldn't find the appropriate words, so instead he simply scowled.

"You're a good man, Landon," Aunt Tillie said. "You're 'The Man' and I hate you on general principle, but you're still a good man and you love Bay. You can't control everything. She's just as much of a hero as you are. You merely take different roads to the same destination. You should be proud of her, not angry."

"That's a nice sentiment and thought," Landon said. "I'm always proud of her." The simple declaration was enough to make hope surge through my chest. "But I won't survive if something happens to her. I need her to use her head. I need her to tell me the truth when this stuff pops up.

"I don't want to change her," he continued. "Heck, I don't want to change any of you. Well, I might change you a little, but for the most part I'd leave you exactly as you are, too. I don't like secrets.

"Now, I understand why she didn't tell me everything that was going on when we first met, because you had to keep yourselves safe," he said. "Now, though, I think I've been pretty good about all of this. I don't pretend to understand, but I don't fight what you're doing and I always try to help."

"You've been great," I interjected. "That's not why I kept it to myself."

"Then why did you?" Landon asked. He looked hurt and upset. "Why not tell me that first night?"

"Because I didn't want to ruin the weekend," I admitted. "I wanted us to have a good time together, and if you thought that something bad was going on you would've insisted on fixing it right away and we wouldn't have had enough time together.

"I feel as if I'm always living on a timetable because you're mostly here on the weekends," I continued. "I didn't want to ruin the weekend and I also didn't want to tell you because I knew you would worry. You would've killed yourself figuring out a way to be close and still do your job. That's not fair to you."

Landon's expression softened, which relieved some of the tension building in the pit of my stomach. "None of this is fair to you," he said, cupping the back of my head. "I'm sorry you feel as if we're living on a timetable. I'm going to figure it out. I promise."

"That's not what I meant," I protested. "I'm not trying to force you to do something to make me happy."

"See, that's the problem, Bay," Landon said. "All I want to do is make you happy. I don't like living on a timetable either. Until I can fix things, though, you need to have faith in me.

"I don't want to worry about you, but not knowing what you're up to is worse," he continued. "I love you so much, sweetie, but you can't shut me out of stuff like this. It makes things too hard, and I don't want to spend every weekend wondering what you're not telling me."

The reality of his words washed over me. I wasn't being fair to him even though he worked overtime to be fair to me. "I ... ."

"That sounds like a good idea," Aunt Tillie said, gripping the herbs closer to her chest. I'd almost forgotten she was there. "I think everything will work out if you two stop being idiots."

"That's not what I said," Landon admonished.

"Huh, and yet that's what I heard," Aunt Tillie said, an evil grin spreading across her face. "Do you want to know what I think?"

Landon and I shook our heads in unison.

"Not even remotely," Landon answered.

"I'm going to tell you anyway," Aunt Tillie shot back. "I think you two like the drama. This entire family likes drama, so Bay being dramatic doesn't surprise me. You're 'The Man,' so you're naturally dramatic, too."

"Thank you," Landon said dryly.

Aunt Tillie ignored his tone. "You like a little drama here and there because it keeps things fresh and exciting," she said. "That's how Calvin and I lived our lives, too. Before he died, we loved the drama. It made making up much more exciting and ... vigorous."

It took me a moment to realize what she was insinuating. "Oh, you're so gross."

"And so are the two of you," Aunt Tillie said. "Your biggest problem is that you get in your own way. Knock it off. Landon wants to know when something is going on and you want to tell him, Bay. Stop trying to protect each other at every turn. Follow your natural instincts. That's what good people do ... and you're both good people, so your instincts won't lead you astray."

Landon smirked. "You're smarter than you look sometimes. You know that, right?"

Aunt Tillie shrugged. "I'm a genius. You two are morons."

"And ... we're done," Landon said, rolling his eyes as he slipped his arm around my waist. It was the first time he'd touched me in almost two hours and it was such a relief I wanted to cry. "I'll consider what you said and get back to you tomorrow morning over breakfast."

Aunt Tillie grinned. "I'll be the one eating your bacon."

"And only a stupid woman would say that," Landon said, tugging me close. "We'll see you tomorrow."

"I can't wait ... and I'm still eating your bacon."

TWENTY-ONE

I woke to find Landon curled around me, his chest pressed to my back as he spooned close. We didn't have a deep talk upon returning to the guesthouse – even though that's how I imagined our night going during the walk. Instead we took a long bath and went right to sleep.

I was refreshed and energetic in the face of the new morning. That lasted exactly thirty seconds ... until Landon opened his mouth.

"We need to talk."

I groaned and buried my face in the pillow. "I knew it!"

I heard Landon chuckling behind me as he drew me closer. "I said we need to talk, not argue."

That sounded better, but only marginally. "What do you want to talk about?"

"Seriously?"

"Landon, I'm sorry I didn't tell you," I said, opting for honesty. "I knew it was a mistake even when I was doing it."

"Then why did you do it?"

"For all the reasons I said," I answered. "I can't stand it when you're worried. You get this pinched look on your face – like you're really constipated or something – and my heart hurts."

"I'm going to let the constipation remark go, but only because you seem to think you're funny and I don't want to dissuade the laughter this morning," Landon said, rolling me onto my back so he could stare into my eyes. "As for the rest ... ."

I hated the conflict clouding his eyes. "I really am sorry," I offered. "I knew it was wrong, but then it was too late. I knew if I told you after the fact that you would have a meltdown. I hate when that happens."

"That makes two of us," Landon said, poking my ribs before resting his head against my chest. I ran my fingers through his hair as he pressed the palm of his hand to my stomach. "Bay, I love you. We need to communicate better."

"I thought we were communicating better."

"We've been communicating a lot better, but you still have a penchant for covering things up," Landon said. "I think part of it is that you want to protect me. I think another part of it is that you hate explaining witch stuff, because you think I don't get it."

He wasn't wrong. "The other part of it is that you can't help me with some of this stuff and I don't like it when you feel helpless," I said. "That seems somehow ... selfish."

"It's not selfish for you to tell me what's going on," Landon countered. "I'm not always going to understand it. I'm not always going to be able to help. I am always going to love you, though. I don't have to understand everything. You don't understand everything in my world."

"I definitely don't understand why you brought Agent Asshat back to town with you," I said, digging my fingers into his sore neck and causing him to groan. "Why did Noah come with you?"

"I think it's my boss's idea of a joke," Landon replied. "He knew I volunteered to handle the arsonist as a way to be close to you. Noah has been irritating him, so it seemed like a great idea to punish Noah by sending him to Hemlock Cove at the same time he was messing with me."

"This could be a problem," I said. "How are we supposed to fight ghosts with Noah hanging around?"

"Noah won't be hanging around," Landon clarified. "He's going to be investigating the arson case. Chief Terry is coming for breakfast at the inn, by the way, and I need to talk to him before we meet up with Noah later. Don't let me forget."

"I won't." I kissed his forehead. He always woke up looking effortlessly handsome, the stubble along his jawline giving him a dangerous edge. I, on the other hand, look as if I slept in a wind tunnel most mornings. "Even if he's focused on the arson, Mrs. Little is going to keep pointing her finger at Aunt Tillie. He'll end up out here. We both know it."

"I'll warn him about that," Landon said. "I'll make sure he knows that Aunt Tillie has been cleared."

"That puts you in the unenviable position of having to make excuses for me and my family again," I said. "Noah will think you're protecting us. That's what you do."

Landon's eyes were serious when he shifted them in my direction. "Bay, I will do whatever it takes to keep you safe and happy. As for Noah, he's not a threat. He's an idiot."

"Wrong," I corrected. "He's an FBI agent who has his nose out of joint because his theory on what happened a few weeks ago turned out to be ludicrous. Then he got captured by the bad guy and saved by other people. He's not going to take that well."

Landon pressed his lips together and tilted his head to the side, considering. "I never considered it that way," he admitted. "I didn't think about the fact that he was saved by two women."

"He was saved by you," I clarified. "Aunt Tillie and I merely bought him time with our mouths."

"Yes, but that's still a form of saving him," Landon said. "I'm going to make fun of him about that when I see him in a few hours."

"Landon!"

"Bay!" Landon mocked my tone as he growled and tugged me closer. "Don't worry about Noah. He's the least of our problems."

"What's the most important problem?" I was legitimately curious.

"I'm starving, ghosts are after you and Annie, we have an arsonist in town, Sam's mother seems really curious about the witch stuff,

Clove is kind of frazzled and that sucks because she's the steadiest of your little trio, Annie is behaving like the world's biggest brat, you and Thistle are fighting over the guesthouse even though she's going to move in a few months, Clove is pouting about you fighting over the guesthouse and did I mention I'm starving?"

I couldn't help but laugh at his hangdog expression. "That's because you didn't eat your dinner last night," I reminded him. "You pushed it around your plate and ate cake. Cake is not enough to sustain you."

"Love sustains me," Landon teased, kissing the tip of my nose. "As for the food, I couldn't make myself eat. My stomach was upset."

"Because I lied?"

"Because you fell into my arms – and not in a good way," Landon replied. "I don't like the idea of you getting hurt. It bothers me."

"It bothers me to think about you getting hurt, too," I said. "You got shot for me not long after we met. You haven't forgotten that, have you?"

"Nope." Landon shook his head. "I plan to remind you of that for the rest of our lives. Whenever I do, you'll give me a massage and strip naked."

I snorted as Landon rolled us so I was situated on top of him, giggling as he tickled me. "Stop. That hurts."

"Life hurts, Bay," Landon said, sobering. "You need to trust me with the truth even when you think it's going to upset me. I would rather be upset by the truth than blindsided by a lie. Do you understand?"

I solemnly nodded. "I'm sorry."

"I know you are," Landon said, kissing the corner of my mouth. "The fight is over, though. I'm done arguing."

"It wasn't much of a fight."

"That's because I'm a lover, not a fighter," Landon teased. "Now ... give me a kiss."

I arched a challenging eyebrow. "Just a kiss?"

"For starters," Landon replied. "We have an hour before breakfast. Let's see where the morning takes us.'

That sounded like the perfect way to start the day.

"OH, YOU two look happy and in love again," Aunt Tillie said as we entered the dining room an hour later, a Mardi Gras mask – complete with feathers and sequins – perched on her face as she sat in her usual spot at the head of the table. "It makes me want to puke."

"Join the club," Chief Terry teased, smirking when Landon shot him a dirty look. "I always want to puke when I see them together."

"Really?" Mom raised her eyebrows as she stared at us. "I always want to plan a wedding when I see them. Isn't it funny how everyone sees something different when they look at Landon and Bay?"

My cheeks colored at her words and when I risked a glance at Landon I found him smiling. "It's not funny," I muttered. "Aren't you embarrassed?"

Landon shook his head. "There's bacon, Bay. I don't get embarrassed when there's bacon."

"But ... she's trying to shame you," I pointed out.

"She's not trying to shame me," Landon countered. "She's trying to figure out what my intentions are regarding her daughter. For the record, my intentions are good. I'll tell you before I propose just to make sure you're ready, Winnie."

Mom beamed at him. "That was a very good answer, Landon."

"I'm not new," Landon said. "I know exactly what you want to hear."

"Speaking of what I want to hear, what are we going to do about Annie?" Mom asked, sobering. "We cannot let Belinda operate in the dark like this. It isn't fair to her or Annie."

"Where is Belinda?" Landon asked, glancing over his shoulder. "Should we be talking about her when she might be able to overhear us?"

"She took Annie to the doctor," Mom replied, causing my heart to flop. "Don't worry, Bay. She didn't take her because of what happened last night. Annie needs a checkup before school starts. She is going to ask the doctor about Annie's mood swings, though."

"We have to do something," I said, shifting my eyes to Aunt Tillie. "We can't let this go on."

"I know that, Bay," Aunt Tillie said. "I'm not new either." She winked at Landon in a saucy manner. Given the mask, it was unsettling. "I have everything under control."

"I'm not in the mood for an argument – which is why I'm not asking about that mask – but how do you have things under control?" Landon challenged. "I don't think you have anything under control given what I saw last night."

"Don't make me put you on my list," Aunt Tillie warned, staring at her reflection in the back of her spoon. "We've warded the house, so Annie is safe here. I think the ghosts followed Bay because they were initially drawn to her light – she has a bright aura – but when they saw Annie they focused on her instead. No one has a brighter aura than a child."

Landon turned to me with a dubious expression on his face. "Did she just explain something?"

"She explained that the ghosts are fixated on Annie because of me," I supplied. "This is my fault."

"That's not what I said, drama queen," Aunt Tillie snapped.

"It's not your fault," Landon said. "If I'm agreeing with Aunt Tillie, you have to know that you're being ridiculous. You can't blame yourself for this."

"There's no one else to blame."

"Perhaps that's because there's no one to blame," Landon argued. "You didn't do this. There's no way you could've stopped it from happening. Sam didn't do this. There's no way he could've realized what was on that tanker. Try as I might, I can't think of a way to blame Aunt Tillie – which must be some sort of record."

I giggled despite myself. "What are we going to do?"

"We're going to do everything we've already been doing," Landon replied. "We're going to keep an eye on Annie and protect her. We're going to figure out what happened on the tanker. Hopefully that will allow you to put the spirits to rest ... or whatever it is you do with ghosts."

"Help them move on."

"Yeah, that," Landon said. "We'll take it one step at a time and go from there."

"That sounds very pragmatic," Aunt Tillie said, bobbing her head. She looked as if she was going to take flight thanks to the feathers on the mask. They really were distracting.

"What about the arsonist?" Chief Terry asked, sipping his coffee. "We can't forget about that."

"I'm not forgetting about that," Landon said. "That's the primary reason I'm here, after all. We essentially have two cases with no tie to one another. That hardly ever happens in Hemlock Cove.

"Still, we need to figure out the ghost angle to help Annie and the firebug angle to help everyone else," he continued. "Whoever is setting these fires is bold. He's doing it in the middle of the day when there are a lot of potential witnesses around."

"You said arsonists are usually men," I said. "Why is that?"

"Because men like to burn things," Thistle answered. "They're all 'fire good, tree ugly.' Women are more 'tree pretty, fire bad.' It's the age-old battle of the sexes."

Landon poured two glasses of tomato juice and handed one to me. Before we started dating, he hated tomato juice. I wasn't sure if he started drinking it because I enjoy it or as a show of solidarity, but now he had it every morning we ate together.

"Sadly, Thistle isn't wrong," Landon said. "Men get off on fire in a way women don't. There's a psychology behind it. The odds of our arsonist being a woman are slim."

"So how will you catch him?" Thistle asked.

Landon shrugged. "I have no idea."

"Well, while you're focusing on the arsonist, I'll put all of my efforts into figuring out what happened on the Gray Harker," I said. "We need to solve the old mystery before we can force the ghosts to do what we want and leave the ship."

"Oh, that sounds fun," Maggie enthused. "I would love to help."

I opened my mouth to answer – searching my mind for a way to let her down gently because I didn't want to put her in danger – but Landon did it for me.

"You can conduct research, and that would be a great deal of help," Landon said. "As for you going off on your own to investigate this, Bay, that's not going to happen. You're sticking with me today."

What did he just say? "But you said we have two problems with no ties," I reminded him. "One of those problems is mine and the other one is yours."

"And we're a couple and I'm not comfortable letting you out of my sight after what happened yesterday," Landon said. "We have two separate problems, but we're investigating both together."

"But ... how will that work?"

"I haven't figured that part out yet," Landon admitted, reaching for a slice of bacon when Mom slid the serving platter toward the middle of the table. "We'll figure it out, though. I promise."

I wasn't convinced. "You're kind of bossy."

"You can boss me around all you want while we're investigating," Landon said. "I'm fine with that. I even find it a turn-on."

Chief Terry cuffed the back of his head. "That's not the proper way to speak to a lady."

"Yeah," I teased, smirking. Somehow the knowledge that Landon wanted to keep me close made me feel better while simultaneously annoying me. That's love, right? "I'm sure we can figure out how to solve both of our problems if we put our heads together."

"That was my thought exactly," Landon said, shoving a slice of bacon in my mouth as he gave me a kiss on the cheek. He momentarily focused on Aunt Tillie as I chewed my bacon. "Okay, I have to ask, what's the deal with the mask?"

"I'm undercover," Aunt Tillie replied simply. "I'm on the case ... just like you two."

"Uh-huh." Landon shook his head. "Whatever floats your broomstick."

Aunt Tillie smiled widely. "I knew you'd see things my way."

"Goddess, help us," Thistle muttered.

She could say that again. The entire world was topsy-turvy these days.

TWENTY-TWO

"Be careful, Bay," Landon ordered, pressing his hand to the small of my back as we surveyed the ruined display room in Mrs. Little's shop. "Don't trip and hurt yourself."

Chief Terry and Agent Glenn were with us, although I was doing my best to pretend I didn't see the younger agent. What? I don't like him. "This is terrible," I said, shaking my head. "It's going to take her months to get this place back up and running."

"That's not necessarily true," Noah said, puffing out his chest as he readied himself to impart some insightful truth nugget. "The structure is sound. All of the drywall will have to go … and the floor will have to be replaced … but other than inventory, the damage isn't terrible."

I narrowed my eyes. I hate it when people talk down to me. "And how long will that take?"

"I would guess about eight weeks."

"So two months," I said, rolling my eyes. "I'm pretty sure that's exactly what I just said."

"Calm down, tiger," Landon teased, smirking as Noah frowned. "You're smarter than him. Everyone knows it. There's no sense in proving it when two members of your fan club are already here."

"That's right," Chief Terry said, kneeling next to one of the corner displays. "I never doubted for a second that you were smarter than Agent Glenn."

Even though I was irritated, I couldn't help but smile. "Thank you both," I said, shooting a victorious look in Noah's direction. "I'm glad you appreciate my input."

"I always appreciate your input," Landon said. "Just don't fall down and get hurt. I have plans for you later."

"Don't make me smack the crap out of you," Chief Terry warned, extending a finger. "You know I don't like that."

"That's exactly why I do it," Landon said, his grin cheeky. "What did the fire inspector say?"

"He said it was a simple accelerant," Chief Terry answered after a beat. "It was common lighter fluid and it was put in a plastic bottle. There's nothing to track with either purchase because both can be found at any gas station in the area."

"That's a bummer," I said, leaning over so I could collect the head of a broken unicorn. "So someone tossed a Molotov cocktail through the front window in the middle of the day and took off without anyone noticing. How does that happen?"

Chief Terry shrugged. "That's a good question," he said. "I'm not sure how it is that no one saw what happened. Whoever did it obviously waited until the street was clear."

"THAT'S STILL gutsy on Main Street during a festival," I pointed out. "Granted, this isn't one of our biggest festivals, but there are still plenty of tourists in town. The inn was at full capacity Friday and Saturday."

"Yes, but The Overlook is always at full capacity," Chief Terry said. "Your penchant for dinner theater has spread throughout the state. People want to stay at the inn because they've heard the food is the best in the area and the dinner theater can't be matched.

"I was at a new technology symposium in Traverse City about three weeks ago and I met a sergeant from a sheriff's department in the Detroit area, and when I mentioned where I lived he immediately asked me about the crazy women who perform a different skit at every meal," he continued. "I knew it was you before he mentioned the inn named after a hotel in a Stephen King book."

"Yeah, why did your mother name the inn that?" Noah asked. He appeared genuinely curious. "Did they want people to fear being murdered in their beds?"

"Actually they didn't name The Overlook after *The Shining*," I replied. Answering Noah's question was grating but I figured I should be civil for Landon's sake. "They named it The Overlook because of the bluff on the other side of the property. It overlooks the town."

Noah wasn't convinced. "They had to have known about *The Shining*."

"I honestly don't think they did. That's not their type of entertainment. They're much more interested in Martha Stewart and home improvement shows."

"And what about your great-aunt?" Noah pressed. "She's almost a character right out of the book."

I wanted to be affronted on Aunt Tillie's behalf, but she loved that movie and book, and I was fairly certain she would take that as a compliment – especially if she could take an ax to his head. "She didn't have anything to do with naming the inn," I explained. "She owns the property, but it will go to my mother and aunts in equal portions when she dies."

"So will they sell it when that happens?" Noah asked. I couldn't tell if he was simply manufacturing conversation or really wanted to know. "I would bet that property in this area would go for a lot these days given the tourist base. She'll probably die in the next year or two, right? It might be worth even more then."

My heart skipped a beat at his callous words. "Aunt Tillie will be around a lot longer than a year or two."

"Of course she will," Landon said, stepping between us. It was as if he sensed trouble was about to manifest. "Don't say things like that to her, Agent Glenn."

"I wasn't trying to upset her," Noah protested, holding up his hands in a placating manner. "It was a simple question. That woman is old."

"Yes, well, evil never dies," I shot back, annoyed.

"Knock it off, Noah," Landon ordered, taking me by surprise when he rested his arm on my shoulder. He generally went out of his way to be professional when we were together on a case and others were present. Of course, Chief Terry didn't care about our relationship, and Landon got off on irritating Noah. "Stop trying to rattle her. I don't like it."

"I'm not trying to rattle her," Noah argued. "I was trying to make conversation. I don't understand why she's here anyway."

"She's here because I want her here, and she knows the store better than we do," Landon said, the lie seamlessly rolling off of his tongue. "I've never been in this store other than one time when I first came to town. Bay will notice anything that's out of place."

"Isn't that Chief Terry's job?" Noah challenged.

"Do I look like the porcelain unicorn type?" Chief Terry asked. "Bay has been in here recently. She agreed to help us. There's no reason for you to get your panties in a bunch. She's not bucking for your job."

Now it was Noah's turn to be offended. "I don't wear panties, so that is an offensive comment."

"No more offensive than you trying to unnerve Bay with talk of her great-aunt dying," Landon said. "Aunt Tillie is in her eighties but she's young at heart. Besides that, Bay is right. Evil never dies."

"And that woman is completely evil," Noah muttered under his breath. If he thought we didn't hear him, he was sadly mistaken. I was fairly certain he wanted me to hear him. He liked pushing my buttons.

"I'll tell her you said that," I said calmly. "I'm sure it will earn you a prominent place on her list."

"I have no idea what that means," Noah said, blasé.

"You will," Landon said, urging me toward the far side of the store. "Now, keep looking around. We need clues. We have to be missing something. Find it."

"**I THINK** IT FEELS LIKE A TEENAGER."

Suspicion had been niggling the back of my brain for the past four hours, so when we finally took a break from searching the store and questioning downtown shopkeepers I gave voice to what I was feeling.

Landon, a glass of iced tea in his hand, slid me a sidelong look as we sat next to each other in the diner. It would've felt like a cozy meal if it wasn't for Chief Terry and Noah sitting across from us. Actually, to be fair, I would've been fine with Chief Terry being present. Noah is a tool, though.

"Why do you say that?" Landon asked.

I shrugged. "It's just a feeling I get," I replied. "I mean ... who goes after porcelain unicorns? You said yourself that the accelerant was simple lighter fluid. If we had a real firebug, wouldn't whoever was doing it get more joy out of going fancy?"

"I guess that's true in theory," Landon said, rubbing his chin. "Arson is different from other crimes, though, Bay."

"How?"

"He means that the psychology is different," Noah supplied. "The kind of person who likes to start a fire is very different from the sort of person who shoplifts ... or even commits murder. We've both studied this extensively, so you shouldn't feel bad if you don't understand what's going on."

I furrowed my brow as I glared at him. "I don't feel bad. Wait ... did you just call me stupid?"

Noah balked. "Of course not," he said. "I merely stated that you couldn't be expected to understand the ins and outs of an arsonist's mind. You work for a weekly newspaper, after all."

Okay, this time I was certain he was insulting me. "You listen here ...."

"Okay, that's enough of that," Chief Terry said, grabbing my hand when I tried to reach around him and tug on Noah's hair. I had no idea what would happen if I got a hold of him, but I really didn't care. "Bay, keep your hands to yourself."

"How can you take his side?" I was incensed.

"I'm not taking his side," Chief Terry said. "Agent Glenn, stop poking Ms. Winchester. I understand you're trying to see how far you can push her – and possibly Landon by extension given what happened last time you were here – but I'm going to put up with only so much."

"I am not poking her," Noah said, crossing his arms over his chest.

"You're definitely not poking her," Landon agreed. "I'll kick your ass if you try."

"Stop being a pervert," Chief Terry chided, shaking his head. "Why do you always have to go there?"

Landon shrugged, unbothered. "I have limited space in my mind," he explained. "I have room for Bay and our case. Everything else gets muddled."

"You're so sick I can't stand it," Chief Terry groaned. "She's still a little girl. That's how I see her."

"Yes, but she's not my little girl," Landon said. "She's my ... sweetie."

"Oh, you're very charming today," I said. "I think you're going to be rewarded later."

"I know I am." Landon leaned forward to give me a kiss. I didn't miss the hateful expression that flashed across Noah's face. It was brief, but obvious. If Landon thought all of the hard feelings regarding Noah's failure in Hemlock Cove a few weeks ago were forgotten, he had another think coming.

"She's my little girl," Chief Terry said, slipping his hand between Landon and me and smacking Landon's lips with his fingertips. "She'll always be my little girl."

The admission warmed my heart. He was always giving and wonderful where I was concerned, going out of his way to spend time with me when I was younger. When I was upset, he'd listen to my complaints. When I was happy, he'd encourage me to keep being happy. He wasn't my father, but he was my biggest male role model.

"Thank you." My voice was small when I uttered the words, but Chief Terry offered me a wink to let me know he'd heard them.

"Oh, now I'm going to puke," Landon said, slipping his arm over my shoulders. He enjoyed teasing Chief Terry, but I knew he didn't mean it. He was often fascinated by our relationship. "Go back to what you said about it being a teenager, Bay. Why do you think that?"

"Because I feel as if something is off here," I answered, unsure how to explain. "The emotions tied to the deed somehow feel young to me."

"Yes, but we don't solve crimes with intuition," Noah pointed out. "Only idiots do that."

"I use my intuition on every case," Landon corrected, his gaze steely. "Stop insulting her. I've had it."

"You're not my boss," Noah shot back.

"I'm your superior," Landon said. "If you have a problem with that, I'm sure you can take it up the supervisory chain. I'm fine if you want to file a formal complaint."

Landon might've been fine with it, but I wasn't. "Landon ... ."

"It's okay," Landon said, squeezing my shoulder. "Noah has been angry ever since Aunt Tillie was proven innocent. He hasn't gotten over it. Frankly, I'm sick of the drama."

"I don't want to be the cause of you getting in trouble at work," I said.

"You're not the cause of any work trouble," Landon said. "You're the cause of all my personal life happiness."

"Oh, barf," Chief Terry said, wrinkling his nose. "That was the schmaltziest thing I've ever heard."

"We're still making up for the fight last night," Landon said. "What do you want from me?"

"A little decorum would be nice."

"I agree," Noah said. "You're completely unprofessional, Landon."

If Landon was mildly irritated before, he was on the edge of a meltdown now.

"Then file your complaint," Landon prodded. "I look forward to answering it with some things of my own. That's your right as an agent, and if you feel I'm not doing my job, I think you should make our superiors aware of the situation. I can respect that.

"What I can't respect is the way you're talking down to Bay and dismissing almost everything Chief Terry says," he continued. "You're not smarter than everyone in the room. You know that, right?"

"I'm smarter than her," Noah shot back, jerking his thumb in my direction. "She thinks a kid is doing this when we know the statistics on arson. It's a man in his twenties, thirties or forties. It's always a man in that age group."

"I agree that the odds lead us to believe that's the case," Landon said, his voice low. "There would be no need for statistics if everything happened exactly one way, though. There's always an exception to every rule."

Noah was incredulous. "Does that mean you agree with her?"

I saw the pained look on Landon's face when he glanced at me.

"No," Landon replied, his cheeks flushed. "I don't happen to agree that it's a teenager. That doesn't mean I don't think she has a right to state her opinion."

"But she's wrong!"

"You don't know that," Landon snapped. "She's been right more times than I can count. I never want a teenager to be guilty, because that means they're losing a life they haven't even begun to live yet. But I learned a long time ago not to count Bay out when it comes to investigating a case. She's smart and has the best instincts of anyone I know."

Pleasure bubbled in my stomach at his words. "Thank you."

"I agree with Landon," Chief Terry said. "The odds of it being a teenager are slim. I would never bet against Bay, however. She has a feeling for these things, and she's very rarely wrong."

"Well, I have a feeling, too," Noah said. "I have a feeling I'm going to solve this and she's going to be left looking like a fool."

Aunt Tillie taught us at a young age that it was better to win than be right. If you can do both, though, you can be queen of the world. Is that misguided? Sure, but for some reason that was the lesson I latched onto now.

"I guess we'll just have to wait and see who is right, huh?" I challenged.

"I guess so."

"Ugh," Landon grimaced. "Why do I feel this is going to get worse before it gets better?"

"Because you've met the Winchesters," Chief Terry answered. "It's not just that they don't like to lose, it's that they refuse to do anything but win."

"You've got that right," I said, rolling my neck until it cracked. "Where is the waitress? I want my lunch. I've got a lot of investigating to do this afternoon so I can win."

"Yup, it's definitely going to be a long day," Landon said, lifting his finger to get the server's attention. "I'm going to need some pie, too. Pie always makes things better."

"So does winning."

TWENTY-THREE

With little forward momentum on case one, Landon and I left Noah with Chief Terry and decided to tackle case number two. Landon made up a lie about wanting to check out local stores to see if anyone remembered selling lighter fluid. Because it was still barbecue season in Michigan, that number would be huge, even in Hemlock Cove. We headed toward the Dandridge.

That's where we found Maggie, Richard, Clove and Sam poring over Sam's collection of old maritime books on the side patio.

"Did you find anything?" I asked, pouring myself a glass of iced tea from the pitcher at the center of the table and sitting in one of the comfortable Adirondack chairs. Landon did the same, settling next to me with a heavy sigh. He looked exhausted even though we'd been working only a few hours.

"We found a lot of interesting things," Clove replied. She seemed to be calmer since given a task to focus on, and I didn't miss the fact that Maggie sat next to her and they appeared to be getting along extremely well. "We even found a blog online referring to old maritime disasters with some theories about what happened to the Gray Harker."

"I'm also thinking of going back to that name because it will add to the mystique," Sam added.

Landon made a face. "Can we get rid of the ghosts before you see little dollar signs dancing in your head?"

"I'm just saying that I'm considering it," Sam sniffed. "I didn't mean to offend you."

"You didn't offend me," Landon said, holding up his free hand. "I don't like it when Bay is in danger and I literally can't see the enemy. I didn't mean to snipe at you. I'm just ... tired."

"It's only three," Clove said, glancing at her phone screen. "How can you be exhausted? You've been working only a few hours."

"Yes, but Bay and Noah have been getting along like Aunt Tillie and Mrs. Little, and it makes me tired," Landon said. "I don't mean to be such a grouch. I really don't. I'm sorry."

"It's okay," Clove said, sympathy rolling off her in waves directed at my boyfriend. "I understand what it's like to be around immature people. I grew up with Bay and Thistle."

"Hey!" I leaned forward, annoyed. "I'm not the one being a baby. That would happen to be Agent Diarrhea Mouth."

Maggie snorted. "Who are we talking about?"

"Agent Noah Glenn," Clove supplied. "We met him for the first time a few weeks ago. He arrested Aunt Tillie for murder. It's been all downhill since then."

"I can see where that would be irksome, but why are you fighting with him, Bay?" Maggie asked.

"I was arrested, too," I supplied.

"You were arrested for breaking and entering," Landon clarified. "You weren't arrested for murder."

"He still suspected us ... even when we were almost shot."

Landon leaned back in his chair and pinched the bridge of his nose. "Don't remind me. I still have nightmares."

I took pity on him and patted his knee. "I'm sorry. I forget how sensitive you are sometimes. I can call a ceasefire with Noah if you want. I don't have to compete with him to solve the fires. I know I'm better than him. Heck, you know I'm better than him. That's all I need."

Landon barked out a laugh, taking me by surprise. "Right there! Just now you reminded me of Aunt Tillie. I thought Thistle was most like her, but you have a few of her mannerisms."

"I'll bet that terrifies you," Sam said. "I know it would terrify me."

Landon shrugged. "Surprisingly, I'm fine with it. I don't care if you keep competing with Noah. I want him to lose."

"That's because he's a loser," I muttered.

"He is," Landon said, squeezing my hand. "Tell me what you found out about the Gray Harker. We're nowhere on the arson case, so we're focusing on the tanker for the rest of the afternoon."

"Well, we have official documentation about how the Gray Harker was found when it reappeared," Richard supplied. He looked to be enjoying his research. He was quiet most of the time, but he leaned forward, excitement lining his face, and fixed me with an appealing smile. "There were rumors for years about how it was found, but three years ago the Coast Guard scanned all of its files into PDFs and put them online. You just need to know where to look."

"My father is something of a maritime geek," Sam explained. "He loves stories about boats ... especially ghost stories."

"Did you develop the interest before or after you realized your son could see ghosts?" I asked.

"Before," Richard replied. "The fact that Sam can see ghosts is an added bonus."

"Okay, hit me," Landon prodded. "What did you find?"

"There are a lot of stories out there that turned out to be untrue," Richard answered. "I remember hearing one about blood being found on the deck. According to official reports, the Gray Harker was found drifting in Grand Traverse Bay. It was sighted by a pilot flying over the bay and then disappeared in the fog.

"It kind of grew to be legend for two weeks because people kept seeing it, yet no one could find and board it," he continued. "That all changed on a November day in 1989 when the Grand Traverse Marine Patrol found the boat."

"Did they board it right away?" I asked.

Richard nodded. "They checked it out from end to end that day," he replied. "No blood was found. All of the crew's belongings were in the sleeping compartments, but nothing of value was left behind."

"That could either mean that everything of value was stolen or they had nothing of value to begin with," Sam offered. "I would lean toward the former, except it was a work boat. Who would take anything of value with them on a work boat?"

"I can see that," Landon said. "So their belongings remained in the cabins and there was no blood. What about the lifeboats?"

"All attached to the ship and accounted for," Richard said.

"What happened to the tanker after that?" I asked, rubbing the back of my neck. I smiled when Landon absentmindedly reached over and started kneading out the kinks for me.

"The owner had already filed an insurance claim on the ship so it was forfeited to the state," Sam said. "It was sold at auction and the new owner changed the name. It's changed hands more times than I can count since then."

"Is that normal?"

Sam shrugged. "I think there's high turnover in freighters, tankers and other stuff, but this seems a little extreme to me. No one kept the tanker for more than two years."

"Which could mean they knew it was haunted," Landon mused. "I mean ... that's what you're saying, right?"

"I think that's a definite possibility," Sam said. "Even people who aren't as intuitive as Bay might've sensed that something was wrong with the ship. I'm betting sensitive people were plagued by nightmares."

"There are also stories in online forums about creepy things happening on the tanker," Clove said. "One person claimed that he saw a ghostly captain staring back at him from a mirror two nights in a row. Another guy claimed that one of his crewmates swore up and down that someone was running around the deck with a machete ... but he could see through him and thought it was a ghost. He jumped overboard and drowned as he was trying to get away."

"I don't give a lot of credence to online forums," Landon said. "They have forums for people who have seen Bigfoot, too."

"Yes, and Clove is on one," I teased, smirking as my cousin scorched me with a dark look. She was notoriously terrified of Bigfoot. It was a running joke in the Winchester household. "Just because it's online in a forum, that doesn't mean it's not true."

"There are so many stories about the Gray Harker – and the various other names the ship sailed under over the years – that I'm hard pressed to ignore all of the stories," Sam said. "Even if only a fraction of them are true, that means a lot of bad things happened on my tanker throughout the years."

"Which means these ghosts are really mean," Landon surmised, shaking his head. "Well, I didn't like ghosts before. I really don't like these jerkoffs – especially because they're terrorizing a small child."

"They probably don't realize they're terrorizing a small child," I said. "To them, they might simply be trying to communicate."

"Well, either way, we need to find out what happened and send them on their way," Landon said. "I don't want Annie terrorized, and I'm not thrilled with the idea of Bay putting herself at risk to protect Annie."

"No one is thrilled with that," Clove said. "Aunt Tillie is working on a way to communicate with the ghosts. She thinks she might have something soon."

Landon didn't look impressed with the announcement. "Is that a good or a bad thing?"

Clove shrugged. "I guess it depends on how you look at it," she said. "On one hand, Aunt Tillie is walking around in a Mardi Gras mask just because she wants to irritate people. On the other, she's so terrifying even ghosts live in fear of her. It's a double-edged sword."

Landon pursed his lips as he considered the statement. "You have a point," he said. "I guess I'm Team Aunt Tillie."

"Now there's something I never thought I'd hear you say," I teased.

"You and me both, sweetie."

"**DO YOU** want a bite of my hot dog?"

Landon's grin was devilish as he shoved the messy concoction he'd just finished putting together in front of the festival's hot dog stand in my face.

I rolled my eyes at the lame joke. "You obviously don't want to kiss me if you plan to eat all of those onions," I said, pointing at the hot dog, which was piled high with chili, mustard and onions.

"Oh, I'm going to kiss the crap out of you later," Landon said, taking a huge bite of the hot dog and chewing as he studied me. He waited until he swallowed to speak again. "Aren't you hungry?"

"I am," I said, nodding as I sat at the nearby picnic table and slid over so he could get comfortable beside me. "I was just thinking."

"About what?"

"About the ghosts on the ship," I replied honestly, seeing no reason to lie. "If someone came on board, how did they manage to kill everyone without at least one person getting away? What happened to all of the bodies?"

"I don't know," Landon said, using his napkin to wipe the corners of his mouth. We considered heading out to the inn with everybody else for dinner but ultimately decided that spending some time alone held more appeal. "They could've been weighted before they were tossed overboard ... or maybe they were transported in a different boat and dumped elsewhere."

"I still don't understand why no one escaped," I pressed. "Wouldn't you at least try for a lifeboat?"

"That depends on what kind of situation they were dealing with. Maybe they didn't have that option."

"But ... how?"

"I don't know, Bay," Landon said. "Maybe there were a lot of people boarding the ship and they were armed. The waters of Lake Michigan are cold even in the summer. They might not have wanted to chance it ... or they might not have been given the choice."

"Whatever happened, I know it was bad," I said. "I keep seeing flashes, and some of the ghosts have wounds. Their clothes are bloody."

"Isn't that normal?"

"Actually it's not normal," I replied. "I never saw Edith with food all over her face even though she died in her dinner. Viola had her head blown off and she looks normal. Erika was sick when she died and I didn't see any hint of that."

"You have a point," Landon mused, finishing the last bite of his hot dog. "What do you think it means?"

"That it was violent ... and terrible ... and bloody ... and really fast."

Landon's eyes were thoughtful as they locked with mine. "I know you want to solve this – and I want to solve it, too – but I don't want you making yourself sick over this. We'll figure it out."

Would we? I was beginning to have my doubts. Still, he clearly wanted to relax for a few hours without letting the real world ruin our fun. "Well, we can't do anything about it tonight," I said after a beat. "How would you feel about going to the festival?"

The corners of Landon's mouth tipped up. "We are at the festival."

"I know, but I thought you could win me a stuffed animal ... and then we could spend some time in the kissing booth ... and then I might even let you get to second base in the House of Mirrors."

Landon visibly brightened. "You had me at second base."

"Clearly," I said dryly. "That explains the onions."

Instead of responding, Landon smacked a hot kiss against my mouth. "You'll learn to live with the onions," he said. "If you eat onions, too, then we'll both stink. You won't even notice."

He had a point. "You're on."

"WHAT ARE you going to name this one?" Landon asked, staring at the stuffed octopus in my arms and shaking his head. It took him twenty minutes and thirty dollars to win the stuffed animal – which probably would've cost five bucks in a store – but he didn't give up until he claimed the animal I wanted. He was good like that.

"I was thinking of naming him Ollie," I replied, watching as

Landon handed two tickets to the woman running the door at the House of Mirrors before following him inside.

Landon snorted. "Ollie the octopus? That's original."

"I could name him Landon," I shot back. "There are times I think you have eight arms."

"That's a compliment, sweetie," Landon said, pressing his hand to the small of my back as he ushered me into the first room. It was wide and rectangular, boasting at least a hundred mirrors ... and they all made me look fat.

"Ugh. I hate it when they make me look short and fat," I said, making a face. "I like it better when they make me look tall and thin."

Landon studied his reflection in the nearest mirror. He looked to be about four feet tall with a unibrow and receding hairline. "Yeah, let's find more flattering mirrors," he said. "I don't think the onions are going to be the turnoff tonight if this keeps up."

I giggled as we moved to the next room, pulling up short when I saw the myriad of reflections looking back at me. For a few seconds I thought the room was filled with people in dated costumes. Then I realized I was looking at the ghosts from the tanker. It was as if they were locked in the mirrors and trying to get out, each extending their hands in my direction, fighting against the glass they couldn't break because they had no form.

I stilled. "Landon ... ." I wanted to warn him that we weren't alone. I wanted to yell at him to run. I wanted to demand that we escape.

I didn't get the chance.

"What the ... ?" Landon's face drained of color as he glanced from mirror to mirror, his arm instinctively slipping around my waist and tugging me close.

I was dumbfounded. "Do you see them?" My voice was barely a whisper.

"I see them," Landon said, smoothing my hair as he stared down the evil captain. He knew the ghost in the captain's chair was the one who almost knocked me out the night before. "Oh, baby. I see them."

TWENTY-FOUR

"How?" My hands shook as Landon gently pushed me to a sitting position on a picnic table bench outside of the Hall of Mirrors. He wrapped his hands around mine – his fingers warm – and forced a wan smile.

"I've always been gifted," Landon explained. "I guess your version of being gifted simply rubbed off on me."

I didn't believe that for a second. "Landon ... ."

"I don't know how it happened," Landon said, keeping his voice low as he watched people milling about the festival. His shoulders were squared and he emitted a dark vibe when anyone looked in our direction. He was clearly sending a message: Don't come over here.

"But you really saw them, right?" I pressed. "You didn't make that up, did you?"

"I saw them, Bay," Landon said. If his patience was wearing thin, he didn't show it. "I saw the guy in the captain's hat for sure. I saw at least three others, too. I focused on the captain, though. He's the one who knocked you down. I hate him."

He was so vehement I couldn't help but smile. "You can see ghosts!" I was in awe.

"I guess I can," Landon said, squeezing my hands. "It's okay."

He was strong and secure in his identity, but for the first time I saw doubt reflected in his eyes. That's when I realized he was putting on a show for me. "Are you angry?"

Landon stilled, surprised. "Why would I be angry?"

"Because you didn't see any of this before you met me," I pointed out. "Maybe you ... I don't know ... blame me or something."

"I don't blame you," Landon said. "I don't blame you for anything. This isn't your fault. You need to stop worrying about crap like that. It drives me crazy ... and I do blame you for that."

"But ... you saw them."

"I did," Landon confirmed, seemingly unbothered. I knew better, though. I could feel his agitation, although it was also tinged with excitement. "Right before it happened, do you want to know what I was thinking?"

I wordlessly nodded.

"I was thinking that I wanted to see the ghosts because I don't like you being exposed to an enemy I can't hope to fight," Landon admitted. "I'm not joking. Like thirty seconds before we walked into that room, that's what I was thinking."

"Well ... voila!" I barked out a laugh. "You got your wish and you really are magic."

"I always knew I was magic," Landon said. "Only someone magic could win your heart." He leaned forward and pressed a kiss to my forehead before resting his cheek against the spot he kissed. "It's going to be okay."

We sat like that for a full five minutes, quiet and introspective, and then Thistle showed up and blew our bonding moment to smithereens.

"What are you doing?" Thistle asked, annoyed. "Is this some new form of foreplay I haven't heard about? I'll bet you saw it on *The View* or something, didn't you?"

Landon scowled as he pulled his head back. "We were just ... bonding."

"You're so bonded I'm surprised you haven't fused together,"

Thistle said, clearly missing Landon's annoyance as she sat on the bench next to me. "Winnie commented on you missing family dinner, by the way. You're going to hear about that if Landon wants his bacon tomorrow morning."

"Well, great," Landon said, smoothing my hair. "I always love a good lecture before greasy goodness."

"We just wanted a little bit of time to ourselves," I explained. "We're going to head back to the guesthouse and go to bed early." We hadn't really talked about that, but it seemed like a good idea in light of recent developments.

"I think that's code for sex," Thistle explained to Marcus, earning an eye roll and headshake. "You guys are fiends. I'm starting to agree with Aunt Tillie on that one."

"Awesome," Landon drawled, making a face. "Well, I don't want to disappoint you, so we'll be proving you're right when we leave in a few minutes."

"You can't leave," Thistle said, her eyes thoughtful as they bounced between us. "Is something wrong?"

"Nothing is wrong," Landon answered hurriedly. I could tell he wanted time to digest what happened before announcing it to the family. I didn't blame him. "We're just ... total sex fiends and want to grope one another."

I widened my eyes. "Really?"

"Well, it's not exactly a lie," Landon said, resting his hand on my shoulder as he straightened. "What are you guys doing here? I didn't think you were going to be festival-bound tonight."

"Chief Terry was at dinner and suggested we attend the festival," Marcus explained. "He's worried someone is going to set another fire. He wants us to walk around and see if we find any suspects."

"He does?" Landon was clearly surprised. "Why didn't he tell me that?"

"He said you were already down here with Bay and figured that's what you were doing."

"Oh." Landon glanced at me, sheepish. "I guess I probably should've been doing that, huh?"

"Yes, well, that would've been more productive than eating hot dogs, winning me an octopus and dragging me into the kissing booth," I teased.

Landon barked out a laugh and the sound was reassuring. He was confused by what happened – we both were – but he seemed fine. "Well, I guess we should pair off and look around then," he said. "Is anyone else here?"

"Sam, Clove, Maggie and Richard are on their way," Marcus answered. "Maggie and Richard are really excited to be part of an arson investigation, by the way. They'll probably find a hundred different suspects."

"That doesn't sound bad to me," I said. "They have fresh eyes. They might see something we don't."

"That's a definite possibility," Marcus said.

"Aunt Tillie wanted to come," Thistle added. "She said that she would make a great arson investigator – you know, she could do it professionally – but she also didn't want to put on regular pants, and Mom insisted when she saw today's offering."

It took me a moment to realize I hadn't seen Aunt Tillie since this morning. "What do today's leggings look like?"

"They have eyeballs all over them," Thistle replied. "Like thousands of pairs of eyeballs."

"It's like her thighs are staring at you," Marcus said, involuntarily shuddering.

"I'm not worried about her thighs," Thistle said. "I'm worried about other parts. Her butt, knees and … other stuff … appears to be staring, too."

"Okay, well, that is just frightening," Landon said, horrified. "So she didn't come to town because she refused to change her pants?"

"Pretty much," Thistle said. "Winnie threatened her with great bodily harm – and a missing wine vat – if she didn't wear something that covered all of her naughty bits. Aunt Tillie was offended."

"I can see that," I said, smirking. "Well, I guess we should break up into five teams and look around then, huh?"

"Definitely," Thistle said. "Maggie and Richard are together. Sam and Clove should be here within the next five minutes. Chief Terry and Agent Glenn can do whatever it is they want to do. That leaves just the four of us."

I turned to Landon and offered him a soft smile. "Do you want to be my partner?"

Landon returned the expression. "Always."

"Oh, that's so sweet," Thistle said, wrinkling her nose as she reached between us and grabbed my hand. "I'm going to be Bay's partner, though. You can be partners with Marcus."

Landon's forehead creased. "Why would I want to be Marcus' partner?"

"Because you like to do that male bonding thing." Thistle was blasé. "You guys are friends. You'll be fine."

"But ... ." Landon darted a furtive look in my direction. "We want to stay together."

"I know you do," Thistle said, tugging harder on my arm. "I need Bay, though."

"Why?" Landon challenged.

"Because I want to know what you two are hiding, and she won't tell me until you leave the area," Thistle replied, shoving me away from Landon and toward the shopping area. "We'll see you while we're doing rounds ... and don't even think of trying to steal my partner until she's shared all of the gossip with me."

With those words, Thistle pushed me so hard I had no choice but to stumble away from Landon. How did this even happen?

"**WHAT** ARE YOU HIDING?"

Thistle isn't exactly known for her patience and she's much more intuitive than people give her credit for. That's why I wasn't surprised when she shoved me behind the ticket tent and forced me into a spot where I couldn't escape.

"I'm not hiding anything," I sputtered, slapping away Thistle's hand when she tried to press it to my forehead. "What are you doing?"

"You're pale," Thistle explained. "I thought maybe you had another incident and that's what Landon was hiding. Oh, and don't bother denying that he was hiding something. You're both terrible liars."

Because Landon worked undercover, he was actually a terrific liar. Thistle and Marcus simply caught us off guard after a troubling incident. "I ... nothing is going on."

"Knock it off, Bay," Thistle snapped. "I know something is going on. You might as well tell me."

"I ... ." I didn't want to betray Landon's trust because he was clearly struggling with what happened, but I didn't see the sense in lying to Thistle.

"What is it?" Thistle pressed. "I'm practically salivating here. This must be good."

The time to lie was over and I knew it. "Landon saw ghosts when we were in the House of Mirrors."

Thistle stilled, her face unreadable. "Ghosts?"

"We walked into one of the rooms and the mirrors were filled with ghosts," I explained. "One of them was the captain from the tanker. I'm fairly certain the others were from the tanker, too, but they were less recognizable."

"Did he see the ghosts in real life or only in the mirrors?"

The question caught me off guard. "I ... don't know," I answered after a beat. "Why does it matter?"

"Because mirrors have mystical properties," Thistle replied. "Maybe these ghosts are so powerful they can make anyone see them. It might not mean what you think it means."

What did I think it meant? Even I wasn't sure. "Landon took it better than I expected," I admitted. "He didn't seem bothered. He said he was magical and made a joke about it, although I could tell that he was kind of flustered, too."

"Do you blame him?" Thistle challenged. "He just saw ghosts for the first time."

"Second time," I corrected. "He saw Erika that night when we almost died in the cove. That's how he knew to come to us."

"I forgot about that," Thistle said, rubbing her cheek. "I always assumed he saw Erika that night because she forced the issue. We would've died without him, and somehow she made him see it. It was ... serendipity or something."

"I always thought that, too," I admitted. "Tonight, though, well ... was different."

"Don't jump to conclusions," Thistle admonished. "You don't know what happened because it could've been several different things."

"Like what?" I prodded, genuinely curious. "What else could it have been?"

Thistle held her hands palms-up and shrugged. "It could've been the mirrors. It could've been these ghosts. It could've been a mutual hallucination."

I made a face. "Do you really believe that?"

"I'm not sure what to believe," Thistle answered. "I'm not ruling out the possibility of it being the mirrors, though. These ghosts seem to be particularly strong and they're working in tandem. We've never faced off with a group of ghosts like this before."

She had a point. That hadn't occurred to me before. I licked my lips as I regarded her. "Do you think it's possible for one person to somehow ... I don't know ... shift things so an ability can be shared?"

Thistle's eyebrows rose. "Do you think that's what happened? Do you honestly think you're sharing your ability with Landon?"

"I have no idea what to think," I said. "Right before it happened Landon claimed he wished he could see the ghosts so he could help protect me."

"Well, that's it right there," Thistle said. "You're not sharing your ability. Landon is stealing it."

I pinched her arm for good measure and scorched her with a dark look. "This is not funny."

Thistle jerked her arm away and rubbed it. "It's a little funny," she said, annoyed. "That hurt, by the way."

"It was supposed to hurt," I shot back. "You're just lucky there isn't any dirt nearby because I would totally make you eat it."

"Oh, yes, you're terrifying when you threaten me like that," Thistle deadpanned. "I'm going to have nightmares about you and your terrifying pinching fingers of death."

"Will you be serious?" I challenged, annoyed. "What if ... what if ... ?"

"What if what?"

"What if I turned Landon into a witch or something?" I asked, finally giving voice to my real concern. "Is that possible?"

"I think that's highly doubtful," Thistle answered. "We both know that witches are almost always female. Even Sam, who has witch blood, isn't very powerful. As far as we know, Landon's mother was a dabbler in college, but she wasn't a born witch."

"That only bolsters my theory."

"Bay, you didn't make Landon a witch," Thistle said, snickering. "At best you made Landon so codependent he willed himself to see ghosts so he can protect you. At worst these ghosts are so powerful that they did it all on their own."

"Which do you think it is?"

Thistle shrugged, helpless. "I don't know. You'll probably have to test the theory."

"How?"

"Viola is running around," Thistle said. "She's been driving me crazy with old stories. You might want to bring her around Landon. If he sees her, then your theory about him manifesting a power is true. If he can't, that means whatever is happening is unique to the ghosts from the tanker."

"I'm honestly not sure which outcome I prefer."

"I get that," Thistle said. "If Landon can see ghosts now, you're not alone. He'll also be tortured like you when it happens. I get why you're torn."

"I ... ." Was she right? Did I want Landon to see ghosts so I wouldn't be alone? "I don't want Landon to see ghosts," I said finally. "He already deals with so much. I think this would be too much."

"I think Landon should be the one who decides how much is too much," Thistle said. "You said yourself that he wished he could see ghosts so he could help you. Let him deal with it in his own way."

"I really hope this is a case of strong ghosts and not shifting abilities," I said. "I like things how they are. You know, I'm the paranormal expert and he's the law enforcement expert. It's a nice balance."

Thistle smirked. "I think it's a nice balance, too," she said. "Don't worry. You'll figure it out."

"We should probably get back to the festival," I said, as I took a step toward the walkway. "I ... ." I broke off when something caught my attention.

Thistle followed my gaze to the box of items hidden in the corner of the small alcove. "What's that?"

I tugged off the cloth covering the box and knelt, frowning when I saw three plastic containers. I grabbed one and opened it, lifting it to my nose so I could inhale. I coughed as the pungent liquid assailed my olfactory senses and handed it to Thistle.

"What do you make of that?" I asked.

Thistle sniffed the liquid and made a face. "It smells like lighter fluid."

"Yup."

"Who would leave a box of lighter fluid in a spot where no one can find it?" Thistle asked. "I mean ... that doesn't make sense and it's definitely not safe." It took her a moment for the realization to sink in. "Oh!"

"Oh," I intoned, bobbing my head as I reached for my phone. "We need Landon."

"Let's just hope a real person is doing this and not ghosts," Thistle said, returning the cap to the bottle. "Otherwise, that will cause two unfortunate worlds to collide."

Now that was a terrifying thought.

TWENTY-FIVE

"Do you think they'll be able to find fingerprints on the canisters?"

Landon had been mostly quiet for our drive back to the guesthouse. While I enjoyed our easy camaraderie, I was also dying to hear what he thought of our discovery.

"There's always a chance," Landon said, pulling into his regular parking spot and killing the engine. "I don't know what to think about it. Why would someone hide their supplies in that location?"

"So they wouldn't risk being seen carrying it on a busy night maybe?"

"I guess that's a possibility," Landon said, rubbing his chin. "I don't know … it feels … weird."

I figured that wasn't the only thing that felt "weird" in his world right now. "Do you want to talk about what happened in the Hall of Mirrors?"

Landon shifted his contemplative eyes to me. "Not really."

"Okay." I didn't want to push him to talk before he was ready. "I told Thistle what happened, by the way. I'm sorry. I know you wanted to keep it to yourself, but she tricked it out of me."

Instead of reacting with anger, Landon smirked. "She tricked it out of you? How did she do that?"

"She's a powerful witch."

"Did she cast a spell on you?"

"No, she asked," I replied. "She did it in a mean way, though."

Landon snickered, amused. "I don't care if you tell her," he said. "I figured you would the second she insisted on you being her partner. It's okay. What did she say?"

"She said that she thought I was freaking out about nothing."

"I would agree with that," Landon said, capturing my hand and rubbing his thumb over my knuckles as he stared at the dark guesthouse. "Why are you freaking out at all? I would think this is normal in your world."

"You're not a woman. That's pretty far from normal in my world."

Landon knit his eyebrows, confused. "I'm definitely not a woman," he agreed. "That would change our relationship and there would be more fights over the body gel in the shower. There would also be more pillow fights."

I snorted. "That's such a man thing," I said. "You know women don't have pillow fights, right? That's something dreamed up by movie directors in the eighties."

Landon made an exaggerated face. "Oh, you just ruined everything for me, woman! How could you be so cruel?"

I pressed my lips together and gave him my best wide-eyed look. "I'm truly sorry."

"I suppose I'll survive," Landon said, lifting my hand so he could kiss the palm. He was putting on a good show of being fine with everything but I knew his mind was busy with the possibilities. "What did Thistle think?"

"She thought there were several explanations," I replied. "The first would probably be the best for everyone. It could be the ghosts. They're extremely powerful because there's so many of them in a small location and they've been feeding off each other's powers.

"Mirrors can sometimes serve as a portal," I continued. "You didn't

AMANDA M. LEE

see the ghosts standing there. You saw their reflections. We both did. It might be an isolated incident."

"Okay. What else could it be?"

I shrugged. "Well ... you said yourself that you wished for the ability to see ghosts right before it happened," I said. "It could be something of a self-fulfilling prophecy. Of course, you could be a genie. If so, I wish for an entire day in bed with no one to bother us."

Landon grinned as he squeezed my hand. "Yes, Master. I'll get right on that. Do you want me to dress up in one of those *I Dream of Jeannie* pink outfits when I grant your wishes?"

"That might be freaky, but I'm up for anything once."

"Good answer," Landon teased. "What was her other suggestion? You said she had a few."

"The other suggestion was mine," I clarified.

"And?"

"And I'm wondering if I somehow fed you some of my magic – er, some of my ability I guess would be more apt – without realizing it."

The admission took Landon by surprise. "Can you do that?"

"Not that I've ever heard of before, but that doesn't mean it's no possible," I answered. "I honestly don't know. Thistle suggested putting you close to Viola so we can see what happens."

"We can do that," Landon said, choosing his words carefully. "I would rather sleep on things tonight if that's all right. It's a lot to take in, and we didn't get much of a chance to deal with that before we went on the hunt for the arsonist."

There was something surreal about the way he phrased it and I couldn't help but giggle. "We don't live normal lives. You realize we're sitting in your truck talking about seeing ghosts and searching for a firebug, right? What do you think normal couples do on a midweek night?"

"I don't really care," Landon said. "You're not normal and I love you just the way you are. We're not a normal couple, and that makes me happy. As weird as things get, Bay, I love every minute I spend with you."

I could think of a few minutes when that wasn't true, but I wisely opted against ruining the moment. "I love every minute I spend with you, too."

"Good." Landon leaned over and gave me a soft kiss. "Would you care to love thirty minutes in the bathtub with me? I feel tense and would like to relax."

"You had me at bath."

"Now we only have to think of a way to add bacon to our night," Landon teased, pushing open his door. He waited at the front of his Explorer for me to join him. The night was beautiful and I lifted my head to the sky. Even though it was still summer by the calendar, the moment the sun set I could feel autumn creeping into the breeze. Fall is my favorite season, and it was almost here.

"It's almost time for the fall festivals," I mused, slipping my hand in Landon's for the walk up the pathway. "Soon everything will be pumpkins, corn mazes and ghost stories."

"I like pumpkins," Landon said. "We should buy some to carve this year."

"That sounds fun."

"I think we can avoid the corn mazes, though. I've had enough of corn mazes to last a lifetime."

"I have to cover the opening of several corn mazes for The Whistler," I reminded him. "You don't have to come, though. It's weird to think it's been almost a year since we met, isn't it?"

"I don't think it's weird," Landon countered. "This has been the best year of my life. I can't wait to repeat it."

The words warmed me. "This has been the best year of your life?"

Landon nodded, amused by the way my cheeks flushed. "Of course it has," he said. "You're a righteous pain and your family is crazy, but I've never been happier. I hope you feel the same way."

"I do," I said. "I ... ." I didn't finish what I was saying – and it was definitely going to be romantic and schmaltzy – because something caught my attention close to the bush by the front door. I narrowed my eyes as I stared, instinctively ceasing my forward momentum.

"What's wrong?" Landon asked, instantly alert. "Do you see something? Is it the ghosts?"

"I'm not sure what I saw," I said, licking my lips. "I thought I saw movement by the bush but I could've been imagining it."

"That's not likely," Landon said. "You're not prone to dramatic fits about stuff like this. Your family and dinner hour is always theatrical, but you've got your feet on the ground for the other stuff. Stay here."

Landon released my hand and moved toward the bush. I opened my mouth to call him back, but it was already too late. A small figure detached from the bush. I recognized it right away. It was too small to be a threat and too terrified to give me pause.

"Annie?"

Annie burst into tears when she saw me and raced down the front steps. She blew past Landon and threw her arms around my neck. I could do nothing but catch her.

"What's wrong?" I asked, stroking the back of her head.

"The ghosts won't leave me alone," Annie wailed, tightening her grip on me. "They want me to do something."

"What?"

"They want me to go to a boat," Annie said. "They want me to join them there. They say I can live with them forever, but I don't want that. I'm so ... afraid!"

I tugged Annie close, wrapping her legs around my waist to make it easier to hold her as I scanned the dark foliage surrounding the guesthouse. I didn't see any signs of ghosts, but that didn't mean they weren't there. It certainly didn't mean they weren't a threat.

I was surprised when Landon draped himself around Annie from the other side, sandwiching her between us. "What are you doing?"

"Protecting you the only way I know how," Landon said. "If those ghosts want to get either of you, they'll have to go through me first."

It was an incredibly sweet sentiment ... and altogether unlikely. "We have to get her back to the inn," I said, keeping my voice low. "She's not safe out in the open like this."

Landon was intense as he met my gaze. "Let's do it."

"ANNIE!"

Belinda was beside herself when she saw me carry Annie through the front door of the inn. Instead of risking a walk even though it was a nice night, Landon herded us into the Explorer and drove us to The Overlook. The lights ablaze on every floor told me that a search was underway for the youngest inn inhabitant.

"Where did you find her?" Mom asked, her face a mask of concern as she petted Annie's head.

I transferred Annie to her mother's waiting arms and sucked in a breath as Belinda rocked the girl, all the while fighting off her own tears.

"She was hiding in the bushes by the guesthouse," Landon supplied.

"Why did you sneak out, Annie?" Belinda asked. "You knew I would worry. How could you do that?"

"The ghosts told me I had to do it," Annie said, her voice thick with phlegm. "They said I had to go to them."

"Stop talking about the ghosts," Belinda snapped. "There's no such thing as ghosts!"

It was time for a very difficult conversation and I didn't give myself time to think of the best way to approach the discussion before blurting it out. "There are ghosts and Annie is being terrorized by a group of them right now."

Landon shook his head, incredulous. "It's a good thing you're not a doctor," he said. "Your bedside manner is ... terrible."

"I'm sorry," I said, locking gazes with Aunt Tillie as she shuffled into the foyer. Thistle wasn't lying about the leggings. The eyeballs were terrifying. "Belinda needs to know. We can't keep hiding this ... especially with Annie is at risk. She can't wander around the property after dark."

"I thought you cast a spell to keep the ghosts out," Landon challenged, focusing on Aunt Tillie. "Isn't that what you said?"

"I did," Aunt Tillie replied. "No spirits are getting in this house. I can promise you that."

"Annie said the ghosts are trying to entice her to the tanker," I argued. "How can they do that if they can't get inside of the house?"

"That's a good question," Aunt Tillie said, moving closer to Annie. "Where did you see the ghosts?"

"They were on the patio," Annie sniffed, wiping her snot-covered nose on her mother's shoulder as Belinda rocked her. "I saw them outside. I tried to ignore them, but they kept waving their hands and telling me to come outside. I didn't mean to do it."

Aunt Tillie and I exchanged a dubious look. "They're gutsy," I said. "I have to give them that."

"We need to widen the spell," Aunt Tillie said. "We need to cover more of the grounds."

"Can you do that?" Landon looked hopeful.

"We can, but we're going to need more supplies," Aunt Tillie answered. "I'll call Clove and tell her to bring everything she has from Hypnotic tomorrow morning."

"The spell is all well and good, but we need to be more proactive," I argued. "We need to go after the ghosts. They're strong. They're so strong that Landon saw them tonight."

Multiple sets of surprised eyes landed on Landon.

"You did?" Mom arched an eyebrow. "How is that possible?"

"He saw them in the mirror at the festival funhouse thing," I explained. "Thistle thinks that because the ghosts are extremely powerful and the mirrors act as a conduit, he was able to see them."

"That's a possibility," Aunt Tillie conceded. "It's also a possibility that he has traces of the ability in his blood. His mother was a dabbler years ago. Some of that might've stuck with him."

"I don't care why it's happening," Landon said. "Bay is worried I'm going to freak out, but I'm fine. I'm much more interested in keeping Bay and Annie safe. What Bay failed to mention about what happened in the mirrors is that the ghosts were fixated on her. They were ... beckoning. They wanted her to go to them."

They were? I searched my memory for images from the incident and realized he was right. "I didn't even notice that," I admitted. "I ... wow!"

"I noticed," Landon said. "You were too distracted by the fact that I could see them. It's okay, sweetie. I didn't want to add to your worry, so I was going to wait until tomorrow morning to discuss it."

"What are we going to do?" Annie asked, her lower lip trembling. "I don't like them. They're scary."

"We're going to fix it," I promised. "You'll be safe. That's our top priority."

"Does someone want to tell me what's going on here?" Belinda asked, finally speaking up. Her expression was unreadable as her eyes hopped from face to face. "Are you saying that Annie is really seeing ghosts?"

I nodded. "She's special."

"I know she's special," Belinda spat, cradling her daughter closer to her chest. "I've always known she's special."

Mom licked her lips as she stepped closer and drew Belinda's attention to her. "I know this is going to come as something of a shock, but ... we're witches. We have actual magic abilities. I'm sorry we didn't tell you sooner, but we need to work as a group if we're going to fix this situation."

Belinda stared from face to face.

"We don't ride around on brooms or anything," Twila supplied. "But we are witches. We were born into power."

"Speak for yourself about riding around on brooms," Aunt Tillie interjected. "I'm an excellent broom rider. I'm better than Harry Potter. I could do it professionally."

Instead of reacting with disbelief or anger, Belinda merely shook her head. "Do you think I'm stupid? I know you're witches. I've known since I met you."

My mouth dropped open. "You have?"

"Of course I have," Belinda said. "I know you saved me in the hospital. I know that you've fought off several threats in recent months. I know about all of it. What I don't understand are the ghosts. Are you telling me they're real, too?"

I wordlessly nodded.

"Well, now I'm ticked," Belinda said, pressing a kiss to Annie's forehead. "I've been calling Annie a liar for days and you all knew she was telling the truth. I'm extremely pissed off with all of you."

Shame washed over me. "I ... ."

"Don't speak right now, Bay," Belinda ordered, lifting Annie so she could carry her toward the stairs. "I need time to think. I know you're sorry, but ... this is a big deal. I called my daughter a liar. That's not fair to her."

"Don't blame Bay," Landon said. "They were all trying to figure out the best way to tell you."

"Perhaps they should've trusted me," Belinda suggested, her eyes flashing. "That would've been better for all of us. It certainly would've been better for Annie."

"I'm sorry," I offered lamely. "We thought we were doing the right thing."

"Well, it was the wrong thing," Belinda said as she ascended the stairs. "I'm keeping Annie with me for the night. We'll talk more about this in the morning. I'm assuming she's safe for the night, right?"

"She's safe," Aunt Tillie said solemnly. "I promise we'll keep her that way."

"Let's hope so," Belinda said, her tone cold. "If I lose my daughter because of this, I'll never forgive any of you."

The words stung, but I couldn't blame her. We all watched helplessly as she carried Annie to the second floor. Once she was gone, Aunt Tillie finally broke the uncomfortable silence.

"She'll be fine after a good night's sleep."

"You don't know that," I challenged. "She's upset. I would be, too."

"She'll be fine," Aunt Tillie repeated. "She's exhausted. We just explained something she didn't know existed. It's going to be okay."

"How can you know that?"

"Because I'm the most powerful witch in the Midwest," Aunt Tillie replied. "I know all and see all."

"Awesome," Landon muttered. "Do you know that those leggings are obscene?"

"I know that they're amazing, and I love making a fashion statement," Aunt Tillie countered. "As for the rest ... stuff it. Now, who wants to make me some tea and get me some cookies?"

Landon remained unruffled by her tone. "I thought you're the most powerful witch in the Midwest. Why can't you do it for yourself?"

Aunt Tillie extended a craggy finger in warning. "You're on my list."

TWENTY-SIX

I was nervous when we entered the inn for breakfast the next morning. Aunt Tillie wasn't in her usual spot in front of the television – never a good sign – and the morning news telecasters were getting off easy without her derisive comments.

Landon and I hit the kitchen. He perked up when the scent of bacon hit his nostrils. The food was already gone, though, and he looked disappointed when he realized the room was empty.

"They wouldn't have eaten without us, would they?"

I glanced at the clock on the wall. "We're right on time," I said. "I'm sure there will be plenty to eat."

"There'd better be bacon," Landon said, following me toward the swinging door that led to the dining room. "If there's no bacon, I'm going to cry."

Despite how rough our past twenty-four hours had been, I couldn't help but smile. "If there's no bacon, I'll go into town with you and buy you some at the diner."

"That sounds like a plan."

The dining room table was full of people, although the only guests were Maggie and Richard. They looked uncomfortable. Everyone silently stared at their plates. I didn't miss the morose look on Belinda's face as she sat at the end of the table with Annie. Marcus rested on the girl's other side, spreading fresh blackberry jam on Annie's toast. Nobody spoke.

Landon clearly didn't like that.

"Good morning," he announced, ushering me toward our usual chairs and flashing a charming smile. "How is everyone today?"

"No one is talking," Annie volunteered. "I think they're in a fight." She was either oblivious to what had happened the previous evening or over it. I couldn't tell which.

"Everyone will start speaking now," Landon said, reaching for the bacon platter first. "It will probably be loud talking, but you don't need to worry about that. No matter what is said, everyone here loves you and we're trying to make sure you're taken care of."

Annie widened her eyes. "Everyone is fighting about me? How come?"

"We're not fighting about you," Thistle said, flashing a smile. "We're not technically fighting at all."

"Oh, we're fighting," Belinda intoned. "I'm still really angry with all of you."

"I don't blame you for that," Thistle said, glancing to the open door frame that separated the dining room from the rest of the inn. Chief Terry smiled as he breezed inside, and Thistle relaxed when she realized he was alone. "You have every right to be angry with us. We should've told you about being witches ... and ghosts ... and magic ... before now."

"Oh, Criminy," Chief Terry groused as he sat next to me. "What did I miss?"

"We found Annie outside of the guest house last night," I explained. "She was running from the ghosts."

"And these are the ghosts from the tanker?" Chief Terry was up on the latest, but he was never comfortable when we talked about the paranormal. It was as if he couldn't wrap his mind around it. I knew he believed us, but he probably would've been a much happier man if he chose to surround himself with people who didn't wreak havoc by controlling the weather and cursing each other so their pants didn't fit.

I nodded. "They're strong ghosts, and they want Annie for ... something."

"Speaking of that, Annie, can you tell us what the ghosts have been saying to you?" Landon asked the question as if it was entirely normal and he was trying to solve a regular case. "What exactly are they trying to do?"

"I already told you," Annie replied. "They want me to go to the big boat by the lighthouse. They say I can live with them. I don't want that. I like living here."

"We like you living here," Mom said. "We'd be lost without you."

"You are planning on staying, right?" Twila asked Belinda. She appeared uncomfortable when asking the question, but that didn't stop her. "It's not safe for you to move and take Annie away right now."

"I have no intention of leaving ... at least for the time being," Belinda said stiffly. "I've been saving money so we can afford a down payment on a house eventually, but I'm nowhere near that point yet. Also, if what everyone says is true, it seems this is the safest spot for Annie right now.

"You might not think I'm trustworthy or want to share your secrets, but I believe I'm a good mother," she continued. "I wouldn't risk Annie for anything."

"No one thinks you're untrustworthy," Thistle argued. She was incredibly tight with Annie, and I could tell Belinda's words – and swirling anger – weighed heavily on her diminutive shoulders. "That's not why we didn't tell you."

"Then why didn't you tell me?" Belinda challenged. "We've been living under the same roof for months. If you weren't trying to protect yourselves, why hide something that big from me?"

"We didn't volunteer the part about us being witches right away because we didn't want to freak you out," I supplied. "You were in the hospital for almost two weeks after your accident. We were worried you'd think we were crackpots and take Annie away if you knew."

"We planned to tell you a few weeks after you moved in," Clove added. "We talked about it. When it came time, though, we never seemed to find the right moment. The more time that passed, well, the more difficult it became."

"I understand that," Belinda conceded. "It can't be easy for you, but I've known about the witch stuff since the beginning. I don't remember being unconscious or how you woke me, but I had dreams after the fact.

"My first inclination that my dreams might've actually been real came when I saw everyone dancing naked under the full moon," she continued. "I was surprised, to say the least, and I eavesdropped a bit. You talked about curses and spells while you were out there."

"Just for clarification, we don't all dance naked under the full moon," Clove explained to Maggie, her cheeks red. "That's something the older generation does. We don't participate."

"I definitely don't participate," Landon agreed, flipping his eggs on top of his corned beef hash and mashing everything together. "I do like the wine, though, and I've gotten used to seeing my girlfriend's mother's boobs. Wow. There's a sentence I never thought I'd say."

Chief Terry slapped his hand to his forehead and glared at his plate while Aunt Tillie snickered.

"You should consider yourself lucky," Aunt Tillie said. "Most men would pay money to see our boobs. We could show our boobs professionally if we wanted. Wait ... that came out wrong."

"Oh, it's too late to take it back," Thistle said. "You're a professional stripper. Deal with it."

Aunt Tillie didn't appear bothered by Thistle's tone. "I've been called worse," she said, shifting her eyes to Belinda. "We're sorry we didn't tell you, but you have to understand that we didn't do it out of malice.

"We love you and Annie and you're part of our family," she continued. "You were right about us not telling you the ghosts were real. We should've done it the second we realized what was going on. That's on us. You're wrong about the rest, though.

"Intentions count in the real world, and we've been working our asses off to keep Annie safe," she said. "We don't always do it the right way, but no one is perfect. So, if you want to be angry that we didn't own up to the ghosts being real, that's your right. If you want to be angry about the other stuff, well, grow up. No one was trying to hurt you. We don't have time for childish crap with a pack of ghosts on the loose."

My mouth dropped open. "You can't say that to her."

"I just did," Aunt Tillie shot back, unruffled. "We have big things to discuss this morning. We need to put the bad feelings behind us."

Belinda's face was unreadable as she scanned the concerned faces at the table. Finally she heaved a sigh. "Fine. I'm not angry any longer. I'm not happy, but I can't hold this against you. You were trying to do right by your family."

"Good," Aunt Tillie said, beaming as she shoved the tomato juice carafe in my direction. "Drink up, sourpuss. You're always such a downer, but I knew it would work out."

I couldn't help but be agitated by her smugness. "One of these days you're going to be wrong," I said. "I hope to be there when it happens."

"You never know, Bay," Aunt Tillie said. "Today might be your lucky day. Everyone needs to finish their breakfast, and then it's time for a strategy session. We need to take these ghosts head on ... and we need to start today."

I pursed my lips as I glanced at Landon. He didn't seem bothered by Aunt Tillie's attitude. "What do you think?"

"I think I hate it when she gets bossy," Landon replied. "She's not wrong, though. We have two problems and no solutions. Today is the day we need to find solutions."

"Okay, but if this backfires on us, I'm going to remind you of this moment."

Landon patted my knee under the table. "You're a woman, sweetie," he said. "All women do that. They can't help themselves."

I was pretty sure he meant it as an insult so I stole a slice of his bacon and made a face. "You're on my list."

"SO WHAT DO WE DO?" Belinda seemed in better spirits by the end of breakfast, but when we met in the library to discuss our options she appeared shaky.

Annie was upstairs playing hide and seek with Marcus, seemingly unbothered by the drama floating through the inn. That's one of the joys of being a kid. When you're younger, the big things in life seem somehow easier because the adults want to absorb all of the pain for you.

"We need to figure out what the spirits want," Aunt Tillie said, flopping on the couch between Landon and me and squeezing between us so we had no choice but to separate.

"What do you mean?" Belinda asked. She was behind when it came to discussing ghosts, but she was working overtime to catch up. "What do ghosts usually want?"

"It's hard to say, but a lot of ghosts don't realize they're dead. They eventually pass on when someone tells them the truth or exposes the facts of their death," I explained. "Others stick around for revenge. Once their killer is caught and some form of retribution is meted out, they're usually content to leave."

"And you see ghosts, too?" Belinda asked. "Why don't all of you see ghosts?"

"Because it's a specific gift passed down through bloodlines," Aunt Tillie answered. "I can see ghosts. Neither of my sisters could, although one of my sisters didn't share my mother's blood, so that's not surprising.

"None of my nieces have the gift," she continued. "I was hopeful it would skip the younger generation, but it didn't. I knew when Bay was really young that she could see ghosts and it would mark her for life."

"I don't understand why it's such a heavy burden," Belinda admitted. "Wouldn't it be nice to speak to ghosts?"

"Not when no one believes you and everyone thinks you're a freak because they see you talking to yourself all of the time," I supplied.

Landon shot me a sympathetic look before reaching across Aunt

Tillie's lap to touch my shoulder. Aunt Tillie slapped his hand away before he could.

"Don't get fresh," Aunt Tillie warned, causing Landon to scorch her with a look. "We don't need any foreplay today. We have real work to do."

"Soothing her isn't foreplay," Landon challenged.

"They look the same to me," Aunt Tillie said. "Bay is right. It's a hard gift. It will be easier for Annie because we'll be here to help her. We'll figure out how to do that once we get the immediate threat under control."

"If the ghosts are hanging around until someone pays for what happened to them, why not solve the mystery of their deaths?" Belinda asked. "Isn't that what will send them away?"

"In theory, yes," I confirmed. "The problem is that you don't usually run into a group of ghosts like this. The most I've ever seen together is two. This is, like, eight of them, and they've spent so much time together it's as if they've somehow combined powers."

"Yes, they're like the Justice League of spirits," Thistle deadpanned. "We're just waiting for them to suit up and beat the crap out of the living."

"That's not helping, Thistle," Mom snapped, cuffing the back of her head. "We need to figure out a way to get the ghosts out of here."

"What would happen if Sam moved the tanker?" Twila asked. "I mean ... if the boat is gone, won't the ghosts leave, too?"

"Where am I going to move the tanker?" Sam challenged. "It's not exactly built for the open lake these days. Aside from the money I'd be out – which I would gladly sacrifice to keep Annie safe, mind you – I can't simply dump the boat in the middle of the lake."

"And selling it will take weeks or months," Chief Terry mused, rubbing his chin. "What else can you do?"

"We can try talking to the ghosts, but they haven't exactly been chatty with me," I replied. "I think we need to focus on why they're fixated on Annie. They seem mildly interested in me, but ever since they found Annie it's as if they're obsessed with her. Why?"

"I guess I don't understand the question," Belinda said.

"Most ghosts fixate on adults because they can help them and they're less likely to be terrified," Marnie said. "At their heart, most ghosts are good because they're victims. You do get the occasional vengeful ghost, but they generally take the form of a poltergeist. We vanquish those instead of helping them pass over."

"So why would these ghosts be focused on Annie?" Belinda asked. "What can she possibly give them? She doesn't know how to help them pass over. From what I understand, they're not interested in passing over. They're more interested in getting her to join them."

"I think you're missing the point," Maggie interjected, taking me by surprise with her fortitude. "I haven't seen these ghosts, but it sounds as if they're fixating on the youngest member of the group for a reason."

"That's just what we were saying, Mom," Sam said gently. "We're trying to figure out the reason."

"I already know the reason," Maggie said, causing every head in the room to swivel in her direction. "The ghosts want Annie because she has the lightest aura. I already told you that. The ghosts live in a world of darkness, so they're drawn to the light.

"On a limited level they probably understand that they're dead," she continued. "They've been trapped where they are for so long, though, time has ceased to hold meaning. All they know is they saw a flash of light when Bay hit the tanker, so they followed her home.

"That light grew brighter when they saw Annie," she said. "They want Annie to come to them because they probably think she'll be able to keep the light burning forever. They don't understand that her light will dim if she does what they want."

"That actually makes a lot of sense," Aunt Tillie said, causing Maggie to beam. "You're smarter than you look. That's a relief."

Maggie's smile slipped. "I see you weren't exaggerating at all when you described her, Sam."

Sam shook his head. "Aunt Tillie needs no exaggeration."

"That's the way I roll," Aunt Tillie said. "I think Maggie is on to something. The ghosts are attracted to the light. They don't care how they get it. They simply want to keep it."

"So how do we get them to stop focusing on Annie?" Landon asked.

"We give them another light to focus on," Aunt Tillie answered. "It's simple."

It didn't appear simple to Landon, and when he shifted his eyes to me he was clearly confused. "Did she just explain something?"

I couldn't be sure, but I had a feeling I knew where she was going. "Maybe," I said after a beat. "We need to provide the ghosts with a new light and make them walk into it."

"You mean make them cross over, right?"

I nodded.

"Well, great," Landon said, mustering a minimal amount of fake enthusiasm. "How do we do that?"

Aunt Tillie's grin was mischievous. "I have an idea."

Thistle groaned. "And those are words no one ever wants to hear."

"Watch it, mouth," Aunt Tillie said. "You're already on my list. Do you want to be in the top spot?"

Nobody wanted that. "Okay," I said, forcing everyone's attention to me. "Where should we start?"

Aunt Tillie didn't appear bothered by the question. "With magic, of course."

Of course.

TWENTY-SEVEN

"Do you have any idea what you're looking for?"

I watched Clove and Thistle bustle around their shop shortly before noon, their eyes intent as they studied the shelves and collected ingredients.

"Aunt Tillie gave us a list," Clove answered, holding up a piece of paper but not looking in my direction.

"Yes, it's a delightful list," Thistle deadpanned. "It says to grab things like wolfsbane, dandelion root and nettle. We expected that. It also gives us little chores ... like stop kvetching and refrain from being an obnoxious mouth."

I bit my lip to keep from laughing at the murderous look on Thistle's face. That sounded exactly like Aunt Tillie. Somehow the knowledge lightened the mood. "I'm sure it will be okay," I said after a beat. "She knows what she's doing."

"Yes, but none of us have ever battled a group of ghosts before," Clove pointed out. "It's a mess. Sam feels responsible, but his mother seems to be having the time of her life. Is it wrong that I'm excited about that?"

"No," I said. "It would be wrong if you put Maggie having fun ahead of Annie's safety, but you're not. As for the tanker, well, it should be fine and full of fun stories once we get rid of the actual ghosts."

"I can't help but feel a little guilty about that," Thistle said, moving three plastic bags to the counter and fixing me with an odd look. "These ghosts have already been traumatized. They were obviously murdered. Now we're working against them to force them to cross over. Doesn't that feel somehow ... mean?"

She had a point. "It doesn't feel good, but what else are we supposed to do?"

"We could try talking to them."

"We could," I agreed. "I haven't ruled that out. I want a contingency plan in place for when we hit the tanker, though. Once we climb that ladder again – and I'm totally making Landon carry Aunt Tillie this time – I want it to be the last time we see them. We can't mess around with Annie's safety."

"No, we definitely can't do that," Thistle agreed, her expression thoughtful as she started tossing ingredients into a small box. "What did you think about Belinda this morning? She seemed to take the news about us being witches fairly well."

"She's apparently known for a long time. She's a great actress."

"Yeah, I was surprised she knew, yet ... I wasn't really surprised either. I don't know what to make of that."

I pursed my lips as I locked gazes with Thistle. She was rarely melancholy. She's moody as crap when she wants to be, don't get me wrong, but she seemed almost wistful and philosophical this afternoon.

"I think she didn't say anything because we didn't say anything," Clove offered, handing Thistle a stack of herbs. "I mean, think about it from her point of view. What if she was wrong? How do you accuse people of being witches?"

"Especially when they're your employers," I added. "She was in an untenable situation. I don't blame her for keeping quiet. I do blame me for hiding the information about the ghosts. She has every right to be angry about that."

"What were you supposed to say?" Thistle asked. "Were you

supposed to walk up to her and say, 'Hey, Belinda, sorry to bother you but there's a pack of ghosts haunting your daughter?' I'm guessing that wouldn't have gone over well."

"I think we had a bad situation all around," Clove said. "Dwelling on what we did wrong doesn't help matters. We need to focus on finishing this up right. That's the most important thing."

"Oh, that was almost poetic," I teased.

"Yes, that's what happens when you've got your nose stuck so far up your boyfriend's mother's bottom that you have nothing better to do than think up dumb things," Thistle said. "You become a poet."

"I'm going to make you eat dirt," Clove threatened, her calm demeanor slipping. She'd been nothing but serene in Maggie's presence over the past few days. It was nice to see shades of the real Clove come out to play.

"Oh, there she is," Thistle cooed, giggling when I clapped my hand over my mouth. "It's good to have the kvetch back."

"I'm definitely going to make you eat dirt," Clove grumbled, shaking her head as she turned back to the herb display. "We have everything but the eyebright."

"Crap, we're out of that," Thistle said, sobering as she moved toward Clove. "I forgot all about that. We don't even have any in the greenhouse. I looked the other day. There are plenty of pot sprouts disguised as mums if anyone is in the market, though."

"What is eyebright?" I asked, racking my brain. It sounded familiar, but mixing potions and spells had never really been one of my favorite activities.

"You basically use it to induce visions," Clove explained. "You're supposed to put it on your eyelids every day."

"And why do we need that?"

"Because Aunt Tillie thought it might be smart to make it so everyone can see the ghosts," Thistle answered. "She thought it would be less dangerous. These ghosts are working as a group. They're not technically poltergeists, but that doesn't mean they can't hurt us if they band together."

That was a very good point. "What should we do?" I asked,

glancing around. "Do you know any place where it's growing wild? I can pick it while you're getting the rest of the stuff ready."

"I don't," Clove said. "We had to order seeds online so we could grow it in the greenhouse in the first place."

"I actually do know where there is some," Thistle said, tapping her chin as she took on a far-off expression. "I don't know if it's in season, though. I haven't looked in months."

"Well, it can't hurt to try," I said. "Where is it?"

Thistle's expression shifted from thoughtful to impish. "Take a wild guess."

Oh, I didn't even know the answer and I already didn't like her happiness. This wouldn't be good.

"UGH, WHO plants witch herbs in a cemetery?" I complained, narrowing my eyes as I scanned the expansive plot in search of the grave Thistle told me to look for. According to my cousin, Aunt Tillie planted emergency herbs throughout the entire cemetery years ago – something I didn't know, but which came in handy now.

"Apparently someone who was thinking ahead," Maggie replied, her tone pleasant and teasing as she watched me glance between graves. "It obviously worked out in our favor."

Given the fact that ghosts kept showing up and threatening a small child to the point she was sneaking out of the house after dark, I wasn't sure how well things were working out in our favor. I decided to let that slide, though.

"Thank you for coming with me," I said, changing the topic. "Landon is with Chief Terry working on the arson investigation – apparently they managed to lift partial fingerprints from the containers we found last night – and Clove and Thistle are busy at the store. I'm not keen on being alone in a cemetery given our issues with ghosts."

"I'm happy to do it," Maggie said, her smile pretty. "You're not what I imagined, Bay. You're so much more than I expected. I ... don't know why I just told you that, but it's true. You're different."

I wasn't sure how to respond. "What do you mean?"

"When Sam mentioned he was going to visit the infamous Winchester witches, I told him it was a bad idea," Maggie explained. "He didn't seem to think that was the case, but your reputation precedes you. Well, actually, Aunt Tillie's reputation precedes her. In certain circles, people are warned about going near you. Do you know that?"

I shook my head. "I didn't know that, but it doesn't exactly surprise me. Aunt Tillie has worked long and hard to cultivate a reputation that terrifies everyone. She's good at it."

"She is," Maggie agreed, bobbing her head. "She's also the most loyal person I've ever seen. The way she backs all of you up is … well, it's wonderful."

I wasn't sure what she meant. "How does she back us up?"

"She takes up for you when you're not around," Maggie replied. "Your mothers are wonderful people, but they like to complain. Their favorite three targets are you, Clove and Thistle. When you're not around, your great-aunt argues on your behalf. When you are around she enjoys messing with you. Why do you think that is?"

I shrugged. "She says it keeps her young," I answered. "What do you mean she takes up for us, though? How does she do that?"

"Well, the other day your mother was complaining because she could see you and Landon making out in the back yard when you were supposed to be coming for breakfast," Maggie said. She didn't appear bothered in the least to be ratting out my mother. I liked that about her. "Your mother watched through the window, making a fuss about you guys doing it out in the open. Tillie ordered her to quit spying and leave you alone because you were happy. I thought it was kind of cute."

That didn't sound like the Aunt Tillie I knew at all. "The euphrasia is over here," I said, gesturing toward Uncle Calvin's grave. "Thank you for telling me that. I had no idea Aunt Tillie was such a softie."

"She doesn't want you to know," Maggie said. "She wants you to live in fear of her. That's just the persona she wears, though. It's not the person she is."

"Wow. Twice in one day," I intoned.

"What's twice in one day?"

"I'm hanging around potential poets," I teased, smiling as I knelt to snap off several of the plant's white blooms. "Can I ask you something?"

"Of course."

"You like Clove, right?" I asked, turning my eyes to Maggie to see how she would respond. "You don't dislike her, do you? She really wants you to like her."

"I adore Clove." Maggie seemed surprised by the question. "Does she think I don't like her?"

I shrugged. I honestly wasn't sure. "She was manic before you showed up," I said. "She's never met a boyfriend's mother before. She tends to be irritating when she overdoes things, and I was a little worried she overdid things where you were concerned."

"She's been nothing short of delightful," Maggie said. "I think she's a wonderful woman. I can't wait until Sam proposes and she's officially part of the family."

The words effortlessly rolled off Maggie's tongue, but they stunned me. "Propose? Is Sam going to propose?"

Maggie realized her mistake too late. "I ... you can't tell Clove! Sam asked me to bring his grandmother's ring. He seems excited to plan a big evening and everything."

"I won't tell her." My heart warmed at the realization that Clove was about to get everything she ever wanted. "I'm happy for both of them."

"Are you?" Maggie's expression was earnest. "My understanding is that you've been dating Landon longer. Don't you wish you were the one getting engaged first?"

That seemed like an odd question, but it was also fair. "Landon and I aren't Sam and Clove. We're from two very different worlds. Sam and Clove live in the same world. It's okay."

"I'm glad you're not the jealous type," Maggie said. "I wouldn't worry about you and Landon being from different worlds. You seem to fit each other quite well."

"We do. It's a work in progress, though. Sam and Clove seemed to fit right away."

"And yet you didn't want them together at first," Maggie mused. "Sam told me you were unhappy when they started dating."

Of course Sam would be the type to confide in his mother. "When Sam came to town we were worried because we didn't understand his motivation," I explained. "We got over it eventually. My problem with Sam and Clove's relationship when it started wasn't Sam. It was that Clove tried to hide it."

"Why do you think that is?"

"Because we didn't trust Sam," I answered. "I get the circular nature of her logic, but things were tense back then. We've worked everything out. Sam is a good man. I really like him. He's wonderful to Clove."

"I'm glad that Sam found his way to all of you," Maggie said, smiling as I straightened. "You're magical in more ways than one."

"Thank you."

Maggie and I fell into step together, the silence between us comfortable instead of draining. We were almost to the cemetery gate when a huffy Kelly Sheffield interrupted our serene walk as she barreled her way past us. I could hear her grumbling under her breath – something about busybodies and spies – as she stomped down the pathway.

"Is anything wrong?" I called out. I had no idea why I cared. It wasn't as if Kelly and I were going to be friends just because I voiced concern for her mental wellbeing.

"Mind your own business," Kelly barked. "I'm so sick of busybodies. You have no idea how sick of busybodies I am."

Since I lived with a bevy of busybodies, I could relate. That didn't mean I was willing to share horror stories with Kelly. "Okay. Well, have a nice day."

"Oh, blow it out your butt," Kelly shot back.

Maggie pressed her lips together to keep from laughing as we continued toward the parking lot. She seemed amused by Kelly's attitude. "Is she a friend of yours?"

"Never. I ... ." I narrowed my eyes when I caught sight of a second figure racing toward the cemetery. I recognized this one, too. The new visitor was shorter and older than Kelly, though. "Mrs. Little?"

"What are you doing here, Bay?" Mrs. Little barked. "Are you lying about alibis for Tillie again? Where is she? All my day needs to be complete is a visit from her."

Apparently Kelly Sheffield wasn't the only one having a rough day.

"Aunt Tillie is at the inn," I replied, keeping my voice even. "I didn't make up an alibi for her the day your shop caught fire. She was really with us. I am sorry for what happened. I know it's going to take a lot of work to get it up and running again."

"Oh, don't act as if you care," Mrs. Little said, making a face. "You don't care. You would be happier if the store burned completely to the ground and couldn't be rebuilt. I know you."

Apparently she didn't know me at all. "That's not true. I don't like anything that's bad for the town's business. We all rely on the tourist trade. That's why we need to bolster each other instead of being jerks."

"Well, you would know all about being a jerk," Mrs. Little challenged. "You learned from the best, right? You love your Aunt Tillie, and she's turned your entire family into monstrous clones."

I'd had just about enough of her attitude. "I do love Aunt Tillie," I agreed. "That doesn't mean I don't feel bad about what happened to you. We're running late and we'll get out of your way."

"That would be great," Mrs. Little snapped. "You can host your daily Tillie fan club meeting without me getting in the way."

Wow! She was really in a mood. "Aunt Tillie doesn't need a fan club. She has herself."

"Yes, well, one of these days Tillie is going to get the payback she deserves," Mrs. Little said. "You reap what you sow, Bay. That's in the Bible. Tillie will eventually reap what she's sown."

What was that supposed to mean? "I ... um ... okay."

"Ask yourself this, Bay: What has Tillie sown?" Mrs. Little challenged. She acted as if she had someplace else to be, yet she had no problem arguing the merits of Aunt Tillie's history as if she didn't have a care in the world.

"She's sown a family that loves her with irritated devotion," I answered without missing a beat. "She's a complicated hero, but that doesn't mean she's not a hero. I'm sorry you can't see that given everything that's happened over the past few weeks."

"And I'm sorry that you can't see what a manipulative beast she is," Mrs. Little said, shaking her head. "You'll figure it out eventually, though. You're a smart girl."

"Thank you ... I think."

Mrs. Little ignored my tone. "Now go on about your day, Bay. I have business." With those words Mrs. Little dismissed me and stalked further into the cemetery. She was only quiet for a moment. "Kelly! I'm nowhere near done talking to you. Where do you think you're going?"

I guess that answered that question. I would be running to hide in the cemetery if Mrs. Little was chasing me, too. I tried to work up a little sympathy for Kelly but failed. Apparently people really do reap what they sow. Kelly Sheffield was proof of that. If anyone deserved to put up with a complaining Mrs. Little, it was her. The older woman was crazy, but harmless.

I truly believed that and yet ... why did this entire situation feel so off?

TWENTY-EIGHT

"I don't see why we're not doing it now."

Patience is one of those virtues only some people get. It seems to skip wide swaths of Winchesters. Although most people think I'm one of the most patient people in my family. That's not saying much.

"We can't do it now," Landon said. Speaking of patience, I often think he has piles of it stored inside his expansive chest. How else could he put up with us? "It's still light out," he reminded me. "We're supposed to get to the heavy action after dark. Calm yourself."

As much as I admire Landon for his boundless patience, I also find him irksome when he won't engage in a good round of handwringing. "Calm myself?"

Landon smirked as he sipped his soda. We sat at a picnic table on the north side of the town square, everyone but our mothers agreeing to meet at the festival so we could patrol the location before heading to the tanker to conduct our séance. My mother and aunts thought it best to stay at the inn so they could watch Annie should a hole appear in the protection grid. I thought having more witches at the ready during the séance was a good idea, but I couldn't argue that leaving Annie to fend for herself was the right way to go.

"I can't calm you right now," Landon said. "I have to focus on work. You'll have to wait until we go to bed tonight for me to calm you. I promise to do it right when we have the time."

He's so full of himself sometimes. The problem is that he always backs it up. "Fine, but I expect a massage, too."

"Oh, I was talking about a massage," Landon deadpanned, his face full of faux innocence. "What were you talking about?"

"Ha, ha." I heaved out a sigh as I settled next to him. "We have hours to burn here before meeting at the tanker. What do you want to do?"

"I think that's a loaded question," Landon teased.

"You just said ... ."

"I was talking about giving you a massage," Landon said, cutting me off. "You have such a filthy mind, Bay. It's completely disgusting."

I pinched his side, causing him to bark out a laugh as he slipped his arm around my back and kissed my temple. "How are you feeling after last night?"

The quick shift in the conversation – from playful to serious – took me by surprise. "I'm okay. How are you?"

"I'm fine," Landon said. "I'm more worried about you. You take things to heart more often than you should. I've been worried about what Belinda said to you. It wasn't your fault. You couldn't have known what would happen."

I knew he was trying to make me feel better, but for once that goal was out of his reach. "Landon, I should've told Belinda right away that Annie wasn't making up stories," I said. "That's on me. I can't take it back, and Annie went through several harsh days of her mother calling her a liar."

"Belinda didn't call her a liar," Landon clarified. "Belinda didn't realize the truth and thought Annie was exaggerating."

"That's the same thing as calling her a liar."

"No, it's a nicer way of calling her a liar," Landon said. "Sweetie, I know you're worried about Annie. We all want to keep her safe. You were in a tough spot, though. Admitting the truth to Belinda was a risk. There was no way you could've known that she already knew you were witches."

"Yeah? I was talking about that with Clove and Thistle today. We think it was kind of stupid to believe she didn't catch on to the truth," I said. "Thistle said that she understands why Belinda didn't bring it up – and I do, too – because no one wants to be the person who calls their boss a witch.

"So much weird stuff goes on at that house, though," I continued. "I kind of forget because I'm used to the craziness. Aunt Tillie has started storms and cursed us into a fairy tale book since Belinda arrived. We've fought ghosts … and crazy people with guns … and other stuff. We should've told her the truth instead of letting it fester."

"I think that's a good rule of thumb no matter who you're dealing with, but in your case keeping your secret isn't just a matter of not hurting someone else's feelings," Landon countered. "You need to protect yourself above all else."

"We need to protect ourselves, but not above all else," I corrected. "Annie is more important than protecting ourselves."

"You fought for Annie and protected yourself at the same time," Landon said. "That's the most important thing to me." He tucked a strand of hair behind my ear. "I would be lost without you, so protecting yourself is very important. I need you to remember that even when the guilt eats at you."

"I could never forget that," I said, offering him a genuine smile and a soft kiss. "It's going to be okay. We're going to figure this out tonight. Have faith."

"Well, you're going to figure out your end tonight," Landon said. "I definitely have faith in that – mostly because Aunt Tillie refuses to lose and she's a force to be reckoned with. I don't know what I'm going to do about my end."

"The arsonist?"

Landon nodded. "I think we made a mistake collecting that box you found last night. It was a stroke of luck that you stumbled across it."

"No fingerprints?"

"We have fingerprints, but they're not on record," Landon replied. "Even if they were on record, we have no way of proving that the lighter fluid belongs to our culprit. It would give us someone to focus on, but that doesn't mean we could get a conviction."

"I think you're looking at this the wrong way," I said. "Because we found those supplies and you took them in, we probably saved someone's business – or maybe even someone's life."

"You think because we took the supplies the arsonist didn't have anything to set another fire," Landon mused, nodding his head. "That's an interesting thought. I hadn't really considered it."

"That's because you're a downer sometimes."

Landon widened his eyes. "Excuse me?"

"I'm just repeating something Aunt Tillie told me," I teased. "She says you're a downer because you can't help yourself from focusing on the negative. I think you mostly see the positive, but when you do find something to be negative about you do seem to dwell on it."

"Oh, really?" Landon sounded serious, but I could tell he was feeling playful. "What if I told you I wanted to dwell on you for the next few hours?"

"I would consider that a positive."

"That's what I thought." Landon pressed a lingering kiss to my mouth. I sank into it, basking in his warmth and the comfortable way his body seemed to meld to mine. I was so lost in what we were doing I initially missed the distinctive sound of someone clearing his throat. That didn't last long, because a second person added his vocal disdain to the mix, and when I shifted my eyes to the spot across the picnic table I found Chief Terry and Noah staring at us. Neither looked happy.

"I'm going to start carrying around a spray bottle full of water," Chief Terry announced, sitting across from us. "That way I can spray the crap out of Landon whenever I feel things are getting too hot."

"I'm fine with that," Landon said. "Bay looks good wet. Why do you think we take so many baths?"

Chief Terry was horrified. "You're a sick man."

"Yes, and Bay is going to check me for a fever later," Landon said, purposely ignoring Noah's steady gaze and focusing on Chief Terry. "Do you have anything?"

"We've been wandering around for two hours, but haven't seen anything out of the ordinary," Chief Terry said. "I'm not sure what we can do other than wait."

"I've been thinking the same thing," Landon said. "We have no leads or suspects. We have the fingerprints that led exactly nowhere. It feels as if we've been working nonstop, yet nothing has come of our efforts."

"You've been working nonstop?" Noah arched a challenging eyebrow. "As far as I can tell you spent three hours with us this afternoon. That's after you spent the morning doing something with Bay. You claimed it was for the case but never really explained what that something was. Then you took off early to meet Bay to investigate something else, and from what I can tell the only thing you've been investigating are her tonsils."

Well, that was fairly insulting. "I'll have you know that I no longer have tonsils," I said. "He was investigating my tongue."

Landon chuckled as he shook his head. "You're not helping, Bay."

"Oh, I didn't know that's what I was supposed to be doing," I said, rolling my eyes as I crossed my arms over my chest and channeled Aunt Tillie's attitude. Landon, Chief Terry and Noah continued talking about the case while I ignored them and studied the festival. It was packed for this time of the week, the good weather beckoning everyone to enjoy summer's last gasp, and for some reason I couldn't shake the feeling that whoever was responsible for setting the fires was close.

I didn't get a chance to dwell on it long because that's when Aunt Tillie made her appearance.

"Oh, holy hell," Landon gritted out when he caught sight of her. "I just ... what is on her legs?"

I rubbed my cheek as I studied Aunt Tillie, the necessity to laugh warring with the inclination to hide so no one could see us together. She'd apparently pulled out another pair of leggings to entertain the masses, and she wasn't lying about them getting progressively worse.

"Are those ... cupcakes?" Noah asked, dumbfounded. He was staring over his shoulder with his mouth gaping open. I couldn't really blame him for being taken aback. He hated Aunt Tillie with a passion, but that didn't mean he could look away.

"They appear to be cupcakes with gummy bears on top of them," I said, forcing myself to remain calm. "Oh, that one on her hip seems to have a gummy shark on top of it."

"That's not her hip, sweetie," Landon said.

"What is it?"

"Don't answer that," Chief Terry warned, turning his back on Aunt Tillie and staring at me. "I don't see a thing. I never saw her, so I don't have to deal with it. I'm focusing on you. How are you, sweetheart?"

He used to call me "sweetheart" all of the time when I was younger. He'd gotten out of the habit now that I was an adult, but I could tell Aunt Tillie's outfit had thrown him for a loop and he was grasping at anything to focus on so he wouldn't have to deal with the approaching horror.

"I'm good," I said, forcing a smile for his benefit. "Landon and I were just talking. Do you know it's been almost a year since we met? Doesn't that seem weird to you?"

Chief Terry shrugged. "No. It would seem weird to me if you weren't together. I've gotten used to seeing you as a couple, even though I fought it at the beginning."

"You fought it?" Noah asked, curious. "Why?"

"Because I've known Bay since she was a child, and when I met Landon all I knew was that he was undercover and full of himself," Chief Terry answered. "It took me a bit of time to realize that most of that swagger was manufactured."

"That's not true," Landon protested. "I really am that egotistical."

"No, you're not," Chief Terry said. "You want people to believe you're egotistical. In truth, you're a big softie – especially where Bay is concerned."

Landon slid his eyes to me. "Do you think I'm a big softie?"

"I think you're my hero."

"Oh, such a cute answer," Landon teased, poking my side. When he risked a glance in Noah's direction he found Aunt Tillie standing directly behind his young partner. She was making faces. Given her leggings and the over-sized sweatshirt – which appeared to have the neck missing and be inspired by *Flashdance* – the entire sight was somehow jarring. "Aunt Tillie, how are you this evening?"

"I'm ready to rock and roll," Aunt Tillie answered, smiling brightly when Noah jolted and swiveled so he could stare at her. "Hello, Agent Ten."

Noah swallowed hard. "What's Agent Ten? Is that like Agent 007? If so ... thank you."

"No, it's like ten, as in ten is your IQ," Aunt Tillie shot back. "I know that's probably being generous, but I'm a good person at heart."

"That's just what I was thinking," Landon said dryly, shaking his head. "Okay, I have to ask: What's with the leggings?"

"I'm starting a fashion trend," Aunt Tillie answered.

"And what would that be?"

"Leggings."

Landon blew out a sigh. "I saw that coming and I asked anyway," he said. "I have no one to blame but myself."

"That's certainly my motto," Aunt Tillie said.

"What are you even doing here?" I asked, narrowing my eyes. "I thought you were eating dinner at the inn before meeting us at ... the Dandridge." I switched course at the last second. I had no idea why I didn't want to mention the tanker, but for some reason the idea of letting Noah know what we had planned for the evening seemed a bad idea.

"I decided I didn't want to eat pork loin," Aunt Tillie said. "I thought I would show off my leggings to everyone at the festival instead."

That sounded suspicious. "Did you get in a fight with Mom about the leggings?"

"I did," Aunt Tillie confirmed. "She said she wouldn't feed me if I wore them and I said if she didn't feed me I was going to wear them to the festival. She thought I was bluffing. It turns out I wasn't bluffing."

I pressed my lips together to keep from laughing. "Well, at least you stuck to your guns," I said, following Aunt Tillie's gaze as she stared in Mrs. Little's direction. She seemed interested in her enemy's appearance even though she'd never admit it.

"I saw Mrs. Little today," I offered. "She was in the cemetery."

"What were you doing in the cemetery?" Noah asked.

"She was visiting the dead," Aunt Tillie replied, cuffing the back of Noah's head. "The adults are talking. We'll point at you if we want you to interject any of your wit and general obnoxious attitude into the conversation."

"Hey!" Noah was affronted. "You're not my boss."

"That's a pity," Aunt Tillie said. "I could whip you into shape in two weeks flat." She shifted her eyes to me. "What was Margaret doing in the cemetery?"

"She seemed to be chasing Kelly Sheffield," I replied. "Kelly came through in a huff, and she was angry and mean. I didn't think much of it because she's always angry and mean. Then Mrs. Little came in and said some mean things about you."

Aunt Tillie's eyes narrowed to dangerous slits. "What did she say about me?"

"That you reap what you sow and she thought you were due for some payback."

Aunt Tillie tilted her head to the side, considering. "I do love payback," she said after a beat. "Speaking of payback, how long do we have before we have to leave for our ... thing?"

"Three hours," Landon answered.

"What thing?" Noah asked.

Aunt Tillie ignored him. "I'm going to play a little game with Margaret, but I'll be ready to leave on time," she said. "Don't take off without me. I'm driving with you."

Landon made a face. "Why can't you drive yourself?"

"Because then you wouldn't be forced to see my leggings, and I enjoy torturing you with them," Aunt Tillie answered honestly. "I'll be ready to go in three hours. Don't forget me."

"We could never forget you," I said. "Just out of curiosity, though, what are you going to do to Mrs. Little?"

Aunt Tillie's smile was so wide it almost swallowed her entire face. "I'm going to show her my leggings up close and personal."

"That sounds like torture," Chief Terry said. "That right there must be the war crimes Tillie was talking about the other day."

All I could do was laugh. "Have fun," I said. "Meet us in the parking lot in three hours. Don't make us find you."

"Like we could miss her in those freaking leggings," Landon muttered.

"I heard that," Aunt Tillie barked. "You're on my list."

"I guess it's better than being close to your pants," Landon said. "I'm honestly never going to be able to eat a sausage link again. That's all I can think about after seeing those leggings."

"At least she doesn't remind you of bacon," I said, looking on the bright side of things.

"There is that."

TWENTY-NINE

"I'm sorry, you want me to do what now?"

Landon's expression was hilarious as his gaze bounced between Aunt Tillie and me. We stood on the dock next to the tanker shortly after dusk. I had to explain the issues with Aunt Tillie and the ladder twice before he responded. Apparently it still wasn't sinking in.

"She needs help getting up the ladder," I said, hoping that if I appealed to his macho side he would capitulate. "You're the strongest one here. You're ... the strongest man ever, in fact."

"Oh, don't stroke my ego," Landon complained, glaring at Aunt Tillie's leggings. "Bay, you know I love you, right?"

I had a feeling I knew exactly what he was about to say. "We need Aunt Tillie do this right," I reminded him.

"But ... ." Landon broke off, swearing under his breath as he stalked the small area in front of the tanker. I left him to pout while Sam rubbed his chin and stared at the side of the vessel.

"I really need to get the docking situation figured out for this thing," Sam mused. "I'm not going to have Landon around to carry up every senior citizen every weekend. I'll only be able to rely on that for six weeks at the most."

I pressed my lips together to keep from laughing as Landon scorched Sam with a hateful look.

"Keep it up," Landon warned. "I'll carry you up and throw you over the side if you're not careful."

"Wow," Clove said, stepping between the two men as if she worried they would suddenly start throwing punches. "Landon seems to have lost his sense of humor."

I wasn't remotely worried about Landon and Sam throwing down. Sam wasn't much of a fighter, and Landon preferred even odds when taking on someone else. "Would you have a sense of humor if you were him?" I challenged.

Clove shifted her eyes to Aunt Tillie's cupcake-covered legs. "You have a point."

Aunt Tillie seemed annoyed with the entire discussion. "I don't need help with the ladder," she snapped. "I'm fully capable of climbing up and down on my own. You act as if I'm ... old." She said the word "old" as if she really meant that I called her decrepit and near death.

"You are old," Thistle shot back, moving to my side. "I suppose you somehow managed to forget that Bay and I had to carry you down that ladder the other day, huh? Did you forget that little trip?"

"Of course I didn't," Aunt Tillie said. "It was the highlight of my week. The way you two grunted, groaned and complained about my leggings was something straight out of a comedy show ... and I'm talking about one of the good ones. I'm not talking about one of the bad ones like you see on television today. What you two did was *Three's Company* funny, not *Fresh Off the Boat* funny."

I ignored the dig and focused on Landon. "If you don't want to carry her up there ... um ... maybe we can do the séance down here." I wasn't serious, but I figured I needed to propel him to move faster and that was all I could think of given our limited timeframe. "That might work and save your back at the same time."

"Yes, because we all believe this is about you," Thistle said, earning a dark look from Landon. "What did I say?"

"Fine," Landon said, heaving out a sigh as he moved in Aunt Tillie's direction. "I'll carry her up the ladder. If my hands slide on that slippery legging fabric and touch something that will haunt me for life, though, I'm going to blame you."

I fought the urge to grin, somehow managing to keep my expression solemn. "That seems completely fair."

Landon locked gazes with me, something crackling between us. "Oh, don't placate me," he said finally, breaking the stare down. "This is totally going to bite."

"I think you should look at it in a different way," Marcus interjected, his eyes flashing as he watched Landon shift closer to Aunt Tillie. "The way it is now, we're basically saying that we think you're the strongest man here and you're the only one we trust with our precious cargo."

I had to hand it to Marcus. If he was attempting to drive Landon insane, he was doing a marvelous job of it.

"You're our hero, man," Marcus continued. "Way to take one for the team."

The look Landon blasted Marcus with was chilling. He opened his mouth to respond, but Thistle cut him off.

"I'm glad you feel that way, Marcus," Thistle said. "You need to go up right in front of Landon so you can help if Aunt Tillie starts slipping."

Marcus' face drained of color. "Excuse me?"

"Sam, you need to go right after Landon," Clove ordered. "We need to make sure Aunt Tillie makes it to the top, so we need her buffered. That means the three of you have to work together."

Landon puffed out his chest and flashed a smug grin as Sam and Marcus groaned in unison. "It's not so funny now, is it?"

"Oh, it's still funny," Marcus said. "You still have to do the bulk of the work."

"Going up," Thistle agreed. "We can't expect Landon to be responsible for the heavy lifting on both trips, though. Someone else will have to help her down."

"And down is worse," I added. "Trust me. I know."

Marcus' jaw tightened as he met my gaze. "You really know how to suck the fun out of a good torture party, don't you?"

"I learned from the best," I said, smiling at Aunt Tillie. "Let's get this started, shall we? I'm ready to put some ghosts to bed, and we can't do that until we get on board."

"I'm definitely ready," Aunt Tillie said, tossing the bag of spell ingredients in my direction and opening her arms so Landon could pick her up. "Giddyap, horsey!"

THAT WAS the worst thing that ever happened to me," Landon announced when we were on the tanker's deck. He kept rubbing his hands against the thighs of his jeans and glaring at me. "You're a terrible girlfriend for making me do that. You know that, right?"

I couldn't help but laugh at his outrage. "You'll live," I said, running my finger down his cheek. His hands slid over the leggings three times during the trip – each time landing someplace Landon refused to speak about – and by the time he hit the deck he was a shaking mess. "I'll make it up to you later."

Landon's expression softened as he regarded me. "We're going to need a bath when we get back to the guesthouse, so you'll have to make it up to me there."

"Done."

Landon pressed a quick kiss to my mouth before straightening. He hadn't bothered glancing around the tanker yet, and as his eyes took in everything the vessel had to offer he appeared surprised. "This thing is huge. How are we going to find the ghosts?"

"We're not going to find them," Aunt Tillie replied, snatching the bag of supplies from me. "We're going to bring them to us."

"Is that a good thing?" Sam asked nervously, wringing his hands as he stepped closer to Clove. "What if they get angry about us calling them as if they were dogs?"

"We're not calling them like dogs," Aunt Tillie clarified. "We're simply using magic to harness their souls and make them do what they don't want to do."

Sam's expression darkened. "Is that somehow better?"

"It'll be okay," Clove said, patting his hand. "I'm here to protect you."

That was fairly hilarious coming from the woman who believed Bigfoot would get her one day, but I let it slide. Apparently it was a turn-on for Sam, because he smacked a loud kiss against her lips.

"That sounds like the best thing to happen to me all day," Sam said, cupping the back of her head. "I love you."

Because Clove and Sam lived together I didn't get a chance to see them interact in a romantic way very often. Even before that happened, Sam was always leery of spending too much time with us. Seeing them together now made me realize what a good fit they were.

"What are you thinking?" Landon asked, moving up behind me and resting a hand on my shoulder. "Do you want to protect me from the ghosts, too?"

I snorted as I shook my head, lifting my eyes so they could lock with his. "I'll always protect you."

"Right back at you," Landon said, gracing me with a soft kiss before separating. "What should I do while you guys are doing this?"

"Just stand back," I replied, my mind turning to business as Thistle and Aunt Tillie created a circle with candles and prepared the baggies to use for our spell. "Er, wait. Where is the eyebright? That's for Marcus and Landon, right?"

Aunt Tillie nodded, distracted. "Sam can already see ghosts, so he shouldn't need it," she said. "Given how frisky these ghosts are, I don't want Marcus and Landon to be caught unaware should they attack."

Marcus swallowed hard. "The ghosts are going to attack? That sounds like a terrible reality show on the Syfy channel or something."

"I'm right there with you," Landon said. "I'd rather see what's coming than make up things in my mind. Where is this eyebright stuff?"

"I didn't have time to make a solution to use as drops, so you'll have to eat it," Aunt Tillie said, opening a package and handing a white bloom to Marcus before turning to Landon and doing the same. "It'll taste awful, but you need to suck it up."

Landon took the small flower and stared at it. "This won't kill me, right? It's not poisonous, is it?"

"It's fine," I said, resting my hand on his arm. "I promise."

"I believe you." Landon gave me another kiss before shoving the flower in his mouth and chewing. He made a series of disgusted faces until he swallowed it. "Well, that tasted like ... ass."

"You'll live," Aunt Tillie said. "Not everything can taste like bacon."

"Oh, that would be an awesome world to visit," Landon mused, taking on a dreamy expression. "You should write a fairy tale about a bacon world and curse us there for a day. I wouldn't complain at all. I might even thank you."

Aunt Tillie rolled her eyes. "I'm going to write a story about a cabbage world and send you there."

"Whatever floats your boat," Landon said, his eyes busy as he scanned the deck. "Is this eyebright stuff going to work? Can you see anything?"

"We haven't called for the ghosts to join us yet," Aunt Tillie reminded him. "There's nothing out there that we can see. Besides, from what I hear, you might not even need the eyebright. Did you really see the ghosts in the mirrors at the festival?"

Landon's mouth dropped open. "Who told you?"

"You saw ghosts?" Sam leaned forward, intrigued. "That's new, right?"

"Thistle had to tell you," I said, glaring at my cousin, who refused to make eye contact. "She's the only one I told."

"That's not fair," Clove complained. "Why didn't you tell me?"

"Because I didn't see you right away," I shot back. "Don't give me grief."

"I'm going to give you all grief if we don't get this train moving," Aunt Tillie said, drawing our attention to her. "It's time."

"Oh, she's using a creepy voice," Marcus complained. "I don't like that."

"Then come over here and dislike it with me," Landon suggested, grabbing Marcus' arm and pulling him away from the circle. His eyes landed on me before he could move too far away. "You be careful. I'll be extremely upset if something happens to you."

"Will you swear off other women forever and become a shell of your former self as you mourn me?" I teased, going for levity.

Landon didn't crack a smile. "I'll never get over it. And I don't like jokes about you possibly dying."

I stilled. "I'm sorry."

"Don't be sorry. Be safe."

I blew out a sigh as I turned to join Aunt Tillie, Clove and Thistle in the circle. Aunt Tillie made a clucking sound as she shook her head and glared at me. "What?"

"You're such a girl sometimes," Aunt Tillie complained. "You're worse than Clove when you want to be."

Clove was affronted. "I heard that."

"I wasn't whispering," Aunt Tillie shot back, grabbing my hand. "It's time to make our circle and call the spirits to us."

I clasped hands with Thistle and Aunt Tillie before shooting a reassuring look in Landon's direction. He looked tense as he watched us, but otherwise remained silent. Aunt Tillie lifted her head to the sky and began to chant.

The words weren't important. We didn't call to the four corners of the winds like we usually did, instead calling to the powers of the underworld to grant us strength. We overlapped our words, pleas for rest and conversation on the tips of everyone's tongues as the magic started to build.

I caught glimpses of magical wisps as they darted around us, myriad colors brightening the darkness as we created a new light to entice the spirits. The overlapping chants built to a crescendo as the sky split with lightning and thunder shook the deck.

"Did you do that?" Marcus asked, nervous.

That was a good question. I risked a glance at Aunt Tillie and found a puzzled look on her face.

"I don't think we did that," Thistle said, glancing around. "I ... do you hear that?"

I didn't at first, but once she said the words I recognized the tell-tale sounds of whispers on the wind. The sky picked that moment to open up. Rain pelted down on us and I could hear something in my head – it sounded like drums, which I instinctively knew was ridiculous. There's no other way to describe it, though.

"What's going on?" Sam yelled over the sound of the wind. "Is this what you expected to happen?"

"Not even close," Aunt Tillie said grimly, clenching her jaw as she stared at the far end of the deck.

I followed her gaze, my stomach constricting when I saw the streaks of light heading in our direction.

"What is that?" Landon asked, stepping toward me.

"It's the inhabitants of the ship," Aunt Tillie replied. "They're extremely ticked off."

"What do we do?" Marcus asked, terrified. "Should we run?"

"I think it's too late to go down the ladder," Sam said, racing toward the side of the tanker that faced away from the dock. "We need to jump."

"Are you crazy?" Clove barked, horrified. "We'll die."

"It's not that far down," Sam argued. "It might hurt a little bit, but we'll hardly die."

"What about Aunt Tillie?" Thistle asked. "She can't make it over the railing."

Landon already figured that out on his own. He scooped Aunt Tillie in his arms and raced toward the side of the tanker.

"Knock that off!" Aunt Tillie shrieked, smacking his shoulders. "It's undignified. I don't need to be carried like an infant."

"I don't have time to mess with you," Landon snapped, shifting her over the edge and meeting her gaze. "If you curse me for this, just remember that I'm trying to save your life."

Those were the last words he said before dropping Aunt Tillie over the side of the tanker. I heard a splash seconds later ... and then a string of curse words I hadn't heard leave her mouth since I was a teenager. I turned back toward the approaching ghosts – they were close enough now that I could see their eyes glowing red with fury – and sighed.

"What do you want?" I asked.

The ghosts didn't answer, and I was forced to turn away from them when Landon grabbed my arm.

"Come on, Bay," Landon ordered, pulling me in the direction of the railing. "We're leaving right now."

"But ... ."

Landon firmly shook his head. I could see Marcus and Sam helping Thistle and Clove over the railing. "We're going, sweetie," he said. "It's not safe here. I know you want to protect Annie, but we're going to have to think of a different way."

I merely nodded. Landon helped me climb over the rail and met my gaze before I took the plunge.

"I love you," Landon said. I didn't get a chance to respond, because he unclasped his hand from mine and shoved me before jumping after me.

I hit the water hard, the cold water stinging. I was momentarily confused as the dark underwater smacked against me, but somehow I managed to right myself and surface. I gasped for air and almost jumped out of my skin when Landon slipped his arm around my waist.

"Are you okay?"

I nodded as I gave him a hug. Then I remembered the rest of my family and turned to find everyone moving toward the dock. "Is everyone okay?"

"Other than our pride, we're fine," Thistle said, treading water near the dock ladder. "I don't think that's what Aunt Tillie had in mind when she decided to force them toward the light, do you?"

I shook my head and found Aunt Tillie's gaze. "Now what?"

"Don't worry," Aunt Tillie said. "I have an idea."

More frightening words were never spoken.

"Well, great," Landon muttered. "If I have to carry her up that ladder again, there's going to be a mutiny. I'm just warning you now."

"Oh, hey, I just realized I got out of carrying her down," Marcus mused, grinning. "Tonight must be my lucky night."

"I'm totally going to beat your ass when we get on dry land," Landon said. "You've been warned."

"And yet I still feel lucky."

THIRTY

"How do you feel?"

Landon was warm as he snuggled closer the next morning, pushing my hair from my face so he could study my features. I could already tell my bedhead was completely out of control. We took the bath Landon seemed eager for before the séance went to hell and then turned in with wet hair. His messy hair made him look handsome. I had a feeling I resembled something scraped off the bottom of your feet during a pedicure.

"I'm okay," I said, resting my cheek against his chest. "How are you?"

"I'm okay." Landon rubbed the back of my neck. He didn't seem to be in a hurry to get out of bed. "What happened last night was ... odd."

I snorted. "That's a nice way of putting it," I said, leaning my head back so I could look at his face. He seemed well rested and awake, but looks can be deceiving. "Did you sleep?"

"I slept hard," Landon answered. "I was out as soon as my head hit the pillow."

"Did you have nightmares?" I had no idea why I asked, because for some reason I knew he did.

"I had a few wild dreams," Landon replied. "One involved you and a coconut shell bikini."

"Landon ... ."

"I had a few nightmares, too," Landon conceded. "I kept seeing ghosts chasing you. There might've been some fire involved as well. Don't worry about it. I think our two cases are converging in my head. It's to be expected."

I wasn't so sure. "I'm sorry things went so wrong last night."

"That's not your fault. You couldn't have known."

"I'm still sorry," I offered. "You wouldn't have even been on the tanker if it wasn't for me."

"Bay, there are a lot of things I regret in life," Landon said. "I once shaved my hair into a mohawk, for example. That was not a smart move. I don't for a second regret going on that tanker with you."

"You had a mohawk?"

Landon grinned. "Why doesn't it surprise me that you latched onto that?"

"Do you have photos?" I pressed. "I would love to see what you looked like as a kid. I'll bet you were cute."

"I'll ask my mother to scan some in and email them to me," Landon said. "You have to show me photos of when you were a kid, too. That only seems fair."

"You saw me when I was a kid," I reminded him. "We were trapped in Aunt Tillie's memories. How could you forget that?"

"I'll never forget that, but I still want to see the photos," Landon said, stroking the back of my head. "Speaking of Aunt Tillie, what do you think she meant when she said she had another idea?"

"Nothing good."

"I already figured that out myself," Landon said. "She seemed surprised by what happened last night. I don't think she was expecting it."

"None of us were expecting it," I said. "We thought we would be drawing the spirits to us so we could talk. If everything went as planned, we would be able to help them move on. Instead, they went after us and we didn't even get a chance to talk to them."

"Maybe they can't talk," Landon suggested. "Maybe they're warped ghosts or something."

I chuckled, delighted. "I think all ghosts are warped in some form," I said. "If they were well-balanced they wouldn't remain behind. As for the rest, I think the power of living together has somehow corrupted them. I don't know how else to explain it."

"Well, we'll figure it out," Landon soothed, stroking my hair. "I think Aunt Tillie considers it a challenge to go after them."

I had a feeling he was right. "She's not going to take any prisoners when we face off with them again. She doesn't like being made a fool."

"That goes for both of us," Landon said. "I don't care what happens, though, I'm not carrying her up that ladder again. That was the worst climb ever."

I giggled. "Did your hands slip?"

"Into places I didn't know existed," Landon said, kissing my cheek. "So, how would you feel about a shower and a big breakfast? I have a feeling we're going to have a long day ahead of us."

"How about we cuddle for five more minutes and then take a shower?" I countered.

"Sold." Landon tightened his arms around me, seemingly content and happy. Then he spoke again. "Do you think there will be bacon for breakfast?"

I couldn't stop myself from groaning. "Seriously? Is there ever not bacon when you're here?"

"I keep thinking there will be a bacon shortage one day," Landon admitted. "Those will be dark times. It will be like the zombie apocalypse. I'm worried I'll lose my will to live if that happens."

"You're a strange man, Landon Michaels."

"And I love a strange woman," Landon said. "Get your cuddling in. I need bacon, woman."

"Yes, sir."

Landon smirked. "Okay, you can have an extra five minutes of cuddling for calling me sir."

"Do you find that a turn-on?"

"I find everything you do a turn-on."

"Oh, and for that you can have my serving of bacon, too," I said, laughing as he tickled me.

"I always knew we were the perfect couple."

"OH, GROSS," Aunt Tillie said, making a face as Landon and I walked through the back door of the inn shortly before breakfast. She sat in her usual spot on the couch in front of the television, a dour look on her face. "I think you guys have been sinning all morning, haven't you?"

Landon arched a challenging eyebrow. "Sinning? I don't really consider it that. Although … that somehow makes it dirtier and more appealing. Yes, Aunt Tillie, we've been sinning our tails off."

I snorted as Aunt Tillie made a horrified face. "Ignore him," I said. "We haven't been sinning. We slept in and then got ready for breakfast. That's all we've done this morning."

"I'm not stupid," Aunt Tillie said, getting to her feet. "I am hungry, though. Your mother said we couldn't eat until you guys showed up because we have a lot to discuss."

My mouth dropped open when I got a full gander at Aunt Tillie's wardrobe choice for the day. She was wearing leggings again – which shouldn't have been a surprise – but this pair was somehow worse than the rest combined. They featured a bevy of dragons swooping around castles, but the biggest dragon was strategically located in her crotch and appeared to be blowing fire in a specific spot.

"Aunt Tillie!" I was flabbergasted.

"I see my outfit has the exact effect I was looking for," Aunt Tillie said, puffing out her chest. "That's a good thing. I can't wait for your mother to see it."

That's a good thing? That was hardly a good thing. "Aunt Tillie, those leggings are obscene," I said. "That dragon is … ."

"Smiting his enemies," Aunt Tillie supplied. "That's exactly what I want him to do."

I risked a glance at Landon and found him to be just as mesmerized as me. "You need to stop staring at it," I whispered. "People will think you're a pervert."

"I'm pretty sure that memo has already been sent," Aunt Tillie said. She seemed delighted by our reactions, which meant my mother and aunts would melt down in terrible fashion.

"I can't look away," Landon muttered. "That dragon is staring at me. I think he wants to kill me."

"I think it wants to kill everyone," I said, grabbing his arm and dragging him toward the kitchen. "Don't look. Think of it as Medusa. If you stare too long, you'll turn to stone."

"Turning to stone would be preferable to seeing that." Landon let me lead him away, yet he kept staring as Aunt Tillie followed us. "Seriously ... turn me to stone."

"You can't eat bacon if you turn to stone," I pointed out.

"Huh. For once I found something that's stronger than the lure of bacon," Landon said. "I just ... I think I might pass out."

He wasn't the only one.

We found everyone else sitting around the dining room table. Annie was there, her hair pulled back in a ponytail, excitedly chatting with Marcus. Other than Maggie and Richard, the only people in attendance were friends and family. That was good, because we had a lot to discuss.

"How was your night?" Chief Terry asked Landon, grinning. "I heard you had to ... oh, holy hell!" Aunt Tillie stepped out from behind Landon, and Chief Terry caught sight of her leggings.

"That's what you get for making fun of me," Landon said. He was feigning being blasé, but I could tell he was still rattled by the sight of Aunt Tillie in her newest ensemble. "You were going to make jokes, and now you're scarred for life. I believe that's called karma."

"What is that?" Mom asked, her hand flying to her mouth. "Is that ...."

"It's Smaug," I said, smirking. "He's about to kill all of the townspeople to protect his ... cave of gold."

Landon barked out a laugh as Mom frowned.

"That is not funny, Bay!" Mom exploded. "That is not funny at all!"

Despite being traumatized, I couldn't help but find it a little bit funny. "She's your aunt."

"Where are the dwarves when you need them?" Thistle intoned, her face ashen as she stared at the dragon. "We need Bard. Someone get Bard."

"What are you talking about?" Clove asked, confused. "Why would singing help? I can sing if you think that will frighten away the dragons."

Clove's offer was enough to snap Thistle out of her reverie. "No one needs to hear you sing," Thistle snapped. "That's cruel and unusual punishment for everyone. I would much rather put up with the dragons than your singing."

"You're just jealous," Clove sniffed, crossing her arms over her chest.

"I think you have a lovely singing voice, honey," Sam said, patting her shoulder. "Now is not the time for song, though. Thistle was talking about Bard from *The Hobbit*. She wasn't asking for a bard."

"Oh." Clove wrinkled her nose. "Who is Bard? Bay and Thistle made me watch the movies, but I got really bored because there were a ton of hot guys but none of them took their shirts off."

Now it was my turn to make a face. "You're a disgrace to fantasy fans everywhere."

"I never said I was a fantasy fan."

"We're getting off track," Mom said, her voice strangled as she stared down Aunt Tillie. "Where did you get those leggings?"

"The internet." Aunt Tillie didn't seem bothered by Mom's attitude. In fact, she seemed to be enjoying it. That spoke volumes about Aunt Tillie's personality. Whatever war she'd been waging was won. I had no doubt about that. No one could look in the face of the dragon and not cede the war.

"You cannot wear those leggings," Mom snapped. "They're ... terrible."

"I think they're neat," Aunt Tillie said, a pretty smile on her face as she sat in her usual chair and reached for her napkin. "They weren't expensive either. I'm thinking of ordering more. They have some with big phallic snakes that I'm interested in."

"Don't even think about it," Mom seethed, extending a finger. "You'll be sorry if you do."

I had no idea who Mom was talking to because Aunt Tillie had already won and everybody knew it.

"Can someone pass the pancakes?" Aunt Tillie asked, purposely avoiding eye contact with Mom as she stared down the table. "I need the syrup, too."

"Apparently the dragons are ravenous," Landon muttered.

I shoved the bacon platter in his direction. "Eat up, hon. You're going to need the fuel if you expect to make it through the day with those dragons without passing out."

Mom sat slumped in her chair as Aunt Tillie focused on her breakfast. For a few blissful minutes the only sound filling the room was flatware clinking against plates. That all changed when Annie decided to speak.

"The ghosts are still around," she announced. "I saw them through the window last night."

"We know the ghosts are around," I said, forcing a smile. "We tried to talk to them last night, but ... well ... it didn't work out very well."

"You can say that again," Thistle said. "That water was cold and I think it stunned my ... dragon ... when we landed." She laughed hollowly at her own joke as Mom, Marnie and Twila glared at her. "Oh, that's funny! We're going to get so much mileage out of those dragons."

"We're never going to speak about the dragons again," Mom corrected. "Aunt Tillie is going to retire the dragons and we're going to burn them during the autumnal equinox."

"Oh, that sounds delightful," Aunt Tillie said. "You'll have to pry them off my cold, dead thighs, though."

Landon reached for another slice of bacon and kept his focus on his plate. "We need to talk about the bigger problem," he said. "Your plan clearly backfired last night. We can't go on that tanker a second time without being better prepared."

"My plan didn't backfire," Aunt Tillie argued. "Everything went exactly according to plan."

"We ended up in the lake," Thistle pointed out.

"It was cold and it hurt when we landed," Clove added.

"But it told us a lot about our enemy," Aunt Tillie said. "I know exactly what to do now."

"Oh, I'm almost afraid to ask," Landon said, pressing the heel of his hand to his forehead. "What are we going to do?"

"Our mistake was going to the ghosts and fighting them on their turf," Aunt Tillie explained. "That's where they're strongest, so of course they won when they had home field advantage."

"So what are you saying?" Thistle asked, ripping a slice of bacon in two, her expression thoughtful. "Do you want to bring them here so we'll have the advantage?"

"Yes."

"Absolutely not," Mom said, shaking her head. "Why would we call ghosts to this property? Annie is here. That can't be safe."

"The house is warded," Aunt Tillie reminded her. "Annie will be in the house and perfectly safe. We're not calling the ghosts to the house."

Mom's face was blank. "Then where?"

"The bluff," I answered, things coming together in my head. "Aunt Tillie wants to bring them to the spot where we're strongest."

"You're smarter than you look, Bay," Aunt Tillie said, nodding approvingly. "That's exactly what I want to do. If we perform the ritual here we can draw the ghosts to us and then help them cross over on the bluff. We'll draw a circle and open a door, so to speak."

"How will that be any different from what happened last night?" Landon challenged. "I mean … other than the fact that we won't have to jump into the lake to save ourselves, that is?"

"It will be different because we're the strongest witches in the land and our power base is that bluff," Aunt Tillie explained. "We have several generations of witches who were born and died here. Their power feeds us, just like the added power from the tanker fuels the ghosts."

"There's a reason the ghosts kept trying to get Annie to go to the tanker," I explained. "That's where they're most powerful. They thought they could control her there."

"We'll call the ghosts here and have a much easier time controlling them," Aunt Tillie said.

"What if that doesn't happen?" Landon wasn't quite ready to capitulate. "They surprised you last night. What if they surprise you again?"

"We can't deal with a problem until it's in front of us," Aunt Tillie explained. "We'll be better prepared this time."

"We'll also have more witches," I added. "By calling the ghosts to us, we can add Mom, Marnie and Twila to the mix."

Belinda balked. "What about Annie?"

"She's safe as long as she's inside the house," Thistle replied. "Marcus, Sam, Landon, Maggie and Richard will be inside with you to make sure nothing happens."

Landon immediately started shaking his head. "I'm going to be with Bay. Everyone else can stay inside the inn, but I'll be outside with you."

"What good will that do?" Thistle challenged. "You're not magical. You can't fight the ghosts if they attack."

"I don't care," Landon said. "I won't be away from Bay. That's a deal breaker for me."

"So we're agreed," Aunt Tillie said, resting her hands on the table. "At sunset tonight, we're going to take out the ghosts. Does anyone have any questions?"

Thistle raised her hand. "Are you going to scare the ghosts with the dragons?"

Aunt Tillie's smile was serene. "The dragons will be victorious on multiple battlefields today. I have no doubt of that."

Sadly, I knew from past experience that she was probably right. "Okay," I said. "We have a plan. Now we have to work it."

THIRTY-ONE

"I'm going to be haunted forever," Chief Terry said, leaning back in his desk chair and clasping his hands behind his head. "I'm not joking. I'm traumatized."

"I've been considering having my eyes removed," Landon said, playing with the cap of his water bottle as he sat across from Chief Terry.

After breakfast – which seemed to go on forever because Mom would not stop talking about the leggings – we didn't have anything to do with our morning, so Landon suggested going into town and working on the arson case. He offered to leave me at the inn – although I don't think his heart was in it – but I declined. Sitting at the inn with nothing to do but stare at dragons seemed an absolutely terrible way to spend a day.

"If you have your eyes removed, you'll never be able to see me again," I teased. "Won't that make you sad?"

Landon didn't immediately respond, instead looking me up and down. "You're the prettiest thing I've ever seen," he said after a few beats. "The dragons are the most horrible. Bay, they're fresh in my mind. I think they could consume me."

"I think they're trying to consume something else. I'm definitely going to have nightmares," Chief Terry complained. "Seriously, what is that woman thinking?"

"She's thinking that she wants to bully my mother and aunts into doing something they don't want to do," I supplied. "She's gotten away with torturing them for years, and she seems to enjoy putting together the wackiest outfits to force their hands. That's what she's doing now."

"Do you know what she wants?" Landon asked.

I shook my head. "Whatever it is must be big. She's pulling out the big guns ... er, dragons ... to get at them. She's wearing them down with very little effort. She told me the other day that the leggings got increasingly worse and she wasn't kidding. She also said this was merely payback because they were picking at her outfit choices, but I'm not sure I believe that. I think she definitely wants something."

"If I were Winnie, I'd pretend I didn't notice the dragons and let her wear whatever she wants," Chief Terry said. "Eventually she'll stop acting up if people don't give in to her."

"Yes, but people always give in to her," I pointed out. "She knows exactly what buttons to push."

"And dragons to slay," Landon added.

"You've got to let the dragons go," I said, grabbing his hand. "Your brain will explode if you keep thinking about them."

"It's worse than that, Bay," Landon said. "I'm afraid I'll never be able to touch you again because when I do ... I'll see dragons."

I bit the inside of my lip to keep from laughing. "Are you saying we're going to live a celibate life from here on out?"

"That sounds good to me," Chief Terry said dryly. "I think that's the way you should plot your future. Celibacy and twin beds are the way to go."

Landon made an exaggerated face as he rolled his eyes. "You're quite the ray of sunshine, aren't you?"

"I like to think of myself as a realist," Chief Terry said. "Speaking of that, last time I checked we came here to discuss how we should approach the arson case. Does anyone have any ideas?"

"I still think the culprit feels young," I insisted. "I know Noah thinks I'm an idiot for believing that, but I can't stop myself from feeling that way. I don't know how to explain it."

"You know the statistics, so I'm not going to bring those up again," Landon said. "Can you explain exactly why you believe it's a young person, though? I don't get it."

I held my hands palms-up and shrugged. "It's just a feeling I got when I was in the unicorn store," I explained. "Unicorns are juvenile, and for a moment I felt this weird sense of ... childish glee ... when looking at the smashed unicorns on the floor. Someone enjoyed ruining Mrs. Little's happy place. That's the first thing that popped into my head, and I still believe it today."

Landon pushed a strand of hair behind my ear, his expression thoughtful. "I'm not sure I can see that. I don't pretend to be psychic or anything ... ."

"I'm not psychic," I said hurriedly.

"No, but you get gut feelings that often turn out to be true," he said. "I'm not saying I believe one way or another, but I will always have faith in you and your intuition."

"Oh, you're so cute." I moved to climb from my chair so I could sit on Landon's lap, but Chief Terry stopped me with a firm shake of his head and I plopped back in my chair instead. "I'll show you how cute you are later."

Landon's smile was so wide it threatened to overshadow his handsome face. "I'm looking forward to that."

"Now I want to be blind because of the dragons and deaf because you two are so schmaltzy," Chief Terry intoned. "It's not a fun combination."

"You'll live," I said, refusing to feel sorry for him.

Landon dissolved into laughter, not stopping until the sound of a man clearing his throat by the open office door caught his attention. I glanced over my shoulder and swallowed my disdain when I saw Noah Glenn standing behind us. Great! He was the last person I wanted to see. This day really was going down the toilet quickly.

"Am I interrupting?" Noah asked.

"Of course not," Chief Terry lied.

"You're totally interrupting," I said. "But we're used to it."

Noah ignored me. "I'm here for the briefing."

Chief Terry's face went blank. "What briefing?"

"The one you said we would have today because you were too tired yesterday."

"Oh, that briefing," Chief Terry said, causing me to swallow my giggle as his lips twitched. "We were just discussing the case."

"You were discussing the case with a civilian present?" Noah's pointed gaze landed on me.

"Oh, knock it off," Landon snapped. "She's part of the team. She's not doing anything and she's certainly not hurting you. Why do you have so much attitude where she's concerned?"

"Because she's not a trained agent, yet you treat her better than me," Noah answered.

"She's not treated better than you," Landon protested.

"Yesterday you kissed her fifteen times when you thought no one was looking, rubbed her shoulders when she was at a crime scene and called her 'sweetie' eight times when we were going through old fire files."

Landon stilled. "You counted?"

"I did."

"I'm not sure what I should do with that information," Landon admitted. "Do you want me to kiss you and call you sweetie? If so, we're probably going to have to go to couples therapy or something, because I don't really see that happening."

Noah was scandalized. "That's not what I want."

"We're trying to help you here, son," Chief Terry interjected. "What is it that you want?"

"I want to be a professional and solve this case in a professional manner," Noah snapped. "Having a civilian present ... and holding the hand of the lead agent while we're supposed to be conducting a briefing ... is not professional."

I instinctively released Landon's hand and forced a smile as I stood. "You don't have to worry about me being professional," I said.

THE TROUBLE WITH WITCHES

"I'm going to take a step back and let the three of you be professional and stay out of your way."

"What? Why?" Landon did his best not to sound whiny ... and failed.

"Because Agent Glenn is right," I said. "You have a job to do. I do, too. In fact, I haven't checked in at the newspaper office in days. I'll do that while you chat about the arsonist."

"You don't have to leave," Landon offered.

"Definitely not," Chief Terry agreed.

"It's fine," I said. "You said yourself that my instincts don't back up the statistics. I can't fight the feeling that a young person did it. You guys don't think that's possible. I'm just getting in the way."

"Finally someone agrees with me," Noah muttered, sighing as he took my vacated seat.

"Fine," Landon said after a beat, his expression unreadable. "Do you want to meet up for lunch?"

I didn't miss Noah's exaggerated eye roll. "I'll have lunch with Clove and Thistle at Hypnotic. I'll see you for dinner."

"Just head straight out to the inn," Landon said, tossing me his keys. "You can take the Explorer since I drove. Chief Terry is having dinner with everyone so he can take me back."

I eyed the keys with wide eyes. "You're going to let me drive your vehicle?" That had never happened before.

Landon snickered. "You can drive anything of mine you want."

"Oh, I'm going to kick the crap out of you," Chief Terry complained.

"Just don't attach a plow to it and let Aunt Tillie take control," Landon said. "Other than that ... be safe. I'll see you in a few hours. Hopefully by the time we're together again we'll have some answers to share."

That would be a nice change of pace.

THE WHISTLER OFFICE was empty when I let myself in. It wasn't exactly surprising. Even though Brian Kelly owned the business, he spent very little time in his office unless he was trying to woo potential advertisers. Because Hemlock Cove's advertising base is pretty much static, there isn't much growth to capitalize on. That didn't sit well with Brian, but because I dislike him immensely, that isn't something I spend much time worrying about.

I unlocked my office door and sat in my chair as I waited for my computer to boot. I was lost in thought, the reality of how difficult tonight's séance would be and the evasive nature of the arsonist warring for top billing in my cluttered mind. I was so out of it I didn't notice Viola pop into view until she floated in the middle of my desk, giving me no choice but to focus on her.

"Good morning," I said, tamping down my irritation. I was used to ghosts in the newspaper office – Edith lived here for decades until she passed over a few weeks ago – but this was the first time since that day Viola had appeared at my place of business.

"Is it morning?" Viola glanced out the window. "I lose all track of time now that I'm dead. Is that normal?"

How was I supposed to know? "I've never been dead," I replied. "I don't know what's normal."

"So ... what are you doing?" Viola asked.

"I'm going to check on the layout options for this week's edition and read through the stringer copy that was emailed to me," I replied. "What are you doing?"

"Well, I was hanging around your cousins' store and bothering the one with the strange hair like you told me to do," Viola replied. "She kind of lost her temper and threatened to curse me into a vortex. I don't know if she can really do that, so I ran away."

I snorted despite my irritation. "That sounds just like Thistle," I said. "For the record, she can't do anything of the sort. You're fine, and you'll stay here as long as you want to stay here."

"But you still think I should move on, don't you?"

I shrugged. "That's really not my decision to make," I replied. "You know who killed you and why. You chose to stay anyway. That must mean you have a reason."

"I like the idea of haunting people."

For some reason, Viola's answer was so simple I could do nothing but smile. "I think Aunt Tillie might do the same thing when she goes," I said. "Granted, she has someone on the other side she wants to see, but she might hang around just to bug us for a bit. That's how she gets her jollies."

"Tillie is strong enough to bring the people she loves back to this side of the wall so they can haunt you guys together," Viola said.

"She is indeed," I agreed, picturing the dragon leggings and internally cringing. "So other than bugging Thistle, what have you been up to?"

"A little of this and a little of that," Viola answered. "Did you know that Margaret's unicorn store burned down?"

"I did. Someone threw a Molotov cocktail through the front window."

"Do you know who did it?"

I shook my head. "No, do you?"

"Well ...."

I wasn't expecting an answer, so Viola's response caught me off guard. "Do you know who did it?"

"I didn't see it happen, if that's what you're asking," Viola replied. "I have been watching Margaret, though. She seems a little ... deranged."

"What else is new?"

"Yes, but she seems even more deranged that usual," Viola said. "She thinks Tillie did it. I heard her talking to Agnes Newton over coffee this morning, and she was adamant Tillie did it. Then she started gossiping about someone having financial trouble and how she was going to lose her house, but then she went back to Tillie. She's obsessed with Tillie."

"I already know that," I said. "For the record, Aunt Tillie didn't do it. She was with Thistle and me when the incident happened."

"Oh, I know Tillie didn't do it," Viola said. "She would much rather take on Margaret in public and not cause any lasting damage that isn't psychological. Arson's not really her style."

"That's true," I said. There was something about Viola's demeanor that caused the hair on the back of my neck to rise. "Do you have a suspicion about who did it?"

Viola nodded, causing my stomach to flip. "I saw someone putting containers of lighter fluid – or maybe it was kerosene, I can't be sure – in the trunk of a car."

I leaned forward, intrigued. "Do you know who it is?"

"I don't know her name."

I stilled, surprised. "Her?" Landon had insisted that arsonists were almost always men.

"It's definitely a woman," Viola said. "My memory isn't great. I recognize the woman's face, but can't put a name to it. Things have been better with my leaky memory since I died – huh, I never thought I would say that – but I still can't put a name with her face."

"Do you know where she is now?"

Viola nodded again. "She's at the bakery."

"Then let's go," I said, grabbing my keys. "You can show me the car and then I'll turn over the information to Chief Terry."

"I don't have anything better to do with my day. Why not?"

"ARE YOU SURE?"

I stared at the older model Buick in the Gunderson Bakery parking lot and shook my head. This had to be a mistake.

"I'm sure," Viola said. "Whoever owns this car has a trunk full of lighter fluid."

I glanced around to make sure no one was looking in my direction. While I wasn't a child any longer, the idea of being caught talking to a ghost wasn't high on my to-do list. I also didn't want Kelly Sheffield to catch me staring at her car.

Kelly had always been a royal pain in the ass, immature to a fault, but I never pictured her as a firebug. She was clearly having problems with Mrs. Little. I witnessed that at the cemetery. That didn't explain why she would burn her own festival booth as well as Mrs. Little's store ... unless she was trying to throw off the cops.

"I don't understand," I admitted. "What does Kelly have to gain by setting fires? Are you sure there's lighter fluid in this car?"

"If you don't believe me, check," Viola instructed, rolling her eyes. "And people say I'm slow."

"I didn't say I didn't believe you," I said. "I can't check, though. The trunk is locked."

"She has a hidden key in a little container over the rear tire," Viola said, pointing toward the driver's side. "I saw her put it there before going to find you."

Well, that was convenient. It was also illegal for me to open Kelly's car. Of course, I was partially raised by Aunt Tillie. I wasn't always married to the idea of following the rules.

"You need to keep watch," I ordered, casting a furtive look around the parking lot before moving to get the key. "If you see someone come out ... ."

"I'll tell you," Viola finished.

I found the key exactly where Viola said I would, and I sucked in a breath when I slipped it into the lock. I lifted the trunk lid and frowned when I saw the three containers of lighter fluid sitting in a box.

"I told you." Viola was smug.

"I guess you did," I said, shaking my head as I reached to touch one of the containers. I thought better of it at the last second and snatched back my hand. "I still don't get it. Why would Kelly do this? Why would she set fires?"

"I have a better question," a chilling voice said from behind me. "What are you doing going through my trunk ... and who are you talking to?"

I recognized Kelly's voice before I could turn around. The gaze I shot Viola was murderous. "Really?"

Viola shrugged. "I forgot. By the way, she left the building and she's here."

"I never would've guessed." I squared my shoulders, readying myself to turn around. I didn't get a chance, because something heavy hit my shoulders and pitched me forward. I didn't lose consciousness and I fought my descent, but the trunk was huge and once my body weight toppled me over Kelly grabbed my legs. I was in too awkward of a position to fight and could do nothing as she tossed my legs over the side and slammed down the trunk lid, plunging me into claustrophobic darkness.

"Well this just sucks," Kelly complained from the outside. "What am I supposed to do now?"

That was an excellent question.

THIRTY-TWO

I screamed as I kicked against the trunk lid, but no help came. I heard Kelly muttering to herself as she got in the car and fired up the engine. I rolled to the side of the trunk as she sped out of the parking lot, but I had no way of knowing which direction she headed – or what she had planned.

Well, great. I was being held captive by a woman I had hated in high school and no one knew where I was. I moved my hand over my pocket and heaved a sigh when I felt my phone. I was relieved when I saw that I had service and immediately pressed Landon's name on my contact list. He picked up on the second ring.

"Do you miss me already?" His voice was low and seductive.

"I've been kidnapped!"

There was nothing but silence on the other end of the phone call, so much so that I thought I'd accidentally dropped the call.

"Landon?"

"That's not funny, Bay," Landon said after a beat. "That's not even remotely funny. Why would you say that?"

"Because I found out who the arsonist is. She caught me, and now I'm locked in her trunk." I knew I should be frightened – and part of me was – but I was more angry and disappointed in my stupidity than anything else.

"She?"

"Yes, it seems we were all wrong," I said. "Although … ." Something occurred to me. "I think I felt youthful glee at the unicorn store because the energy I associated with this person was tied up with my feelings of being young. That means I was technically right and you were wrong."

"I'm not messing around here," Landon snapped. "Have you really been kidnapped?"

I swallowed hard. "Yes."

"Where are you, sweetie?" Landon said, his voice cracking. "Tell me exactly what's going on."

"Viola came to see me at the newspaper. She said she saw someone with a bunch of lighter fluid in the trunk of her car, but couldn't put a name to the face," I explained. "She took me to the car and then told me where to find the hidden key, so I looked in the trunk."

"You looked in the trunk?" Landon exploded. "What is wrong with you?"

"Now isn't the time for that," I pleaded. "I've been kidnapped. Keep your eye on the ball."

"I'm going to kick the ball into your behind if you don't tell me where you are," Landon seethed.

"I don't know where I am," I said. "Kelly Sheffield caught me going through her trunk and hit me. I fell inside … er, well, kind of. She tossed my legs in and then locked me in here. Now she's driving, and I have no idea where she is."

"What kind of a car?"

"A really crappy old Buick," I replied. "Luckily, the trunk is big, so I'm not crying because I'm cramped or anything."

Landon lowered his voice. "Are you crying for another reason? Are you in pain?"

"I'm embarrassed and a little worried," I admitted. "I think … I think I should jump out of the trunk."

"You just said you were locked in the trunk." I could hear Chief

Terry asking questions in the background, but Landon shushed him. "How can you get out of the trunk?"

"I can cast a spell to unlatch it, but ... she's driving fast so I might hurt myself if I jump."

"Then don't jump!"

"What happens if she keeps driving for hundreds of miles?" I challenged. "What happens if she drives to the middle of nowhere and has a gun in the glove box or something? I don't see where I have a lot of choice."

"You could break your leg jumping from a moving car," Landon argued. "You could smash your head."

"That's better than a bullet to the head," I said. "The longer she drives, the worse my position is."

"No, you could let us find you," Landon countered. "Chief Terry is sending out an alert so everyone will be looking for the car. We'll find you."

"We both know there are hundreds of country roads out here," I said, fighting overtime to rein in my growing despair. "I need to take control of the situation."

"Bay ... ." I could picture Landon pinching the bridge of his nose as he held the phone to his ear, worry and dread overwhelming him. "Fine. If you're going to do it, you're going to have to turn off the phone and try to put it someplace safe when you jump."

"You're letting me do this?" I couldn't help but be amazed.

"I'm not letting you do anything," Landon replied. "I have faith you'll realize that I can't live without you and that you'll do your very best to survive this."

His words caused my stomach to flip. "I love you."

"Don't say your goodbyes," Landon gritted out. "You'll see me very soon."

"I know," I said, gathering my courage. "I'll call you as soon as I can."

"Just take care of yourself," Landon said. "Push up the trunk lid after you get it open. When Kelly realizes that you're making an escape, she'll hopefully slow down. That will be your chance. You need to hide instead of fighting. Do you understand?"

"Yes."

"Call me when you can, but don't risk yourself when you're doing it," Landon said. "And, Bay?"

"What?" I was near tears.

"I love you. Don't you dare die on me!"

I disconnected the call and slipped my phone into my bra. I couldn't think of a safer place. Then I blinked back tears and focused my attention on the trunk lid, muttering a spell Aunt Tillie taught me so that I could break into the pantry as a child. The trunk lid popped open and I sucked in a breath before shoving it up.

I could see the trees speeding by from my position and when I sat up, a blast of air struck me full in the face. The road behind us was empty, but I recognized where we were – Longham Drive. The road intersected with the road the inn was on, but that was more than a mile behind us.

Kelly must've noticed that the trunk was open, because the car began drastically slowing. She didn't hit the brakes so hard they locked – which was a blessing – and as the car began to coast I swallowed my fear and jumped toward the nearby ditch.

I hit the ground hard, the air momentarily knocked from my lungs. I rolled to my back and stared at the bright sun as Kelly's car screeched to a stop. I shifted my eyes and met Kelly's hateful glare as she opened the car door. I had no time and only one option. I pushed the pain out of my head and rolled to my knees before struggling to my feet. I gave Kelly one more glance and then bolted into the woods.

The Overlook was at least two miles away. I had no idea if I could stay ahead of Kelly long enough to reach my destination.

THE GOOD NEWS is that I know the area surrounding The Overlook better than most because I spent my childhood playing in the trees and my teenage years doing things I wasn't supposed to do and trying to hide it from my mother. I knew the woods better than anyone.

Kelly was still chasing me, and my hip ached from my jump, so I couldn't move very fast. I found a small hollowed out area on a hill and covered by branches, and slid into it as I waited for Kelly to either leave the area or give up and go home.

I kept one eye on Kelly as she looked behind trees and under bushes. She was a good five hundred feet away, so I pulled my phone out of my bra. It was warm from being pressed so close to my skin and seemed to be working. The first thing I did was turn it to silent so a text message or phone call wouldn't reveal my location. I probably should've done that before I jumped, but I was too nervous to think about it. I typed out a text to Landon.

I'm okay. I'm on the ground.

Landon started typing back immediately, asking where I was.

I'm about two miles from The Overlook. I'm hiding right now because my hip hurts and I don't think I can outrun Kelly. She's searching for me.

Landon texted back that they were on their way, but I knew the odds of him finding me were slim. They would find the car, but I couldn't remain where I was in the hollow. I would have to start moving, and that meant putting distance between Kelly and me. That also meant putting distance between Landon's rescue attempt and me.

I have to move toward the inn. I can't wait. I'll meet you there.

I studied the screen, willing Landon to write back one more time before I risked leaving my hiding spot. His response was simple: *I love you.* I swallowed the lump in my throat and crawled out from under the branches. I could see Kelly heading toward the road – hopefully looking for her car – so I turned in the opposite direction and kept my head low as I began to limp.

The Overlook wasn't too far. My family was there. Landon was on his way. Everything was going to be okay.

IT TOOK what felt like forever to meander my way to the family property. My hip pain progressively worsened and each step became agony, but I couldn't hide in the woods and wait for help to find me. That would leave me vulnerable should Kelly stumble across my location. I had a feeling I'd angered her to the point she'd kill me rather than negotiate, so I pushed forward.

When I finally neared the inn, I heaved out a sigh. I was on the east side of the property – still a decent hike to The Overlook, but much closer to the guesthouse. I figured if I could make it inside there, even if I was alone, I could lock the doors and call for backup.

I increased my pace, my limp becoming worse as I pushed through trees. I pulled up short when I saw movement through the foliage, my heart leaping as I worked overtime to tamp down my anxiety. The figure moving around the small clearing wasn't Kelly. It was someone I recognized ... and I'd never been so happy to see her in my entire life.

"Aunt Tillie!"

Aunt Tillie jerked her head up at the sound of my voice, narrowing her eyes as I limped in her direction. She seemed surprised by my appearance at our ritual location – I couldn't blame her – but she hurried to me when I stepped closer to the recognizable landmark. This was where we cast our biggest spells – and occasionally danced naked under the full moon – and it was the location of our planned séance for this evening. This was where we were strongest.

"What are you doing out here?" Aunt Tillie asked, confused. "If you've come to complain about the leggings ... ."

I made a disgusted face as I leaned over to catch my breath. "For the first time today, I totally don't care about your dragon invasion," I said, grimacing. "I'm being followed. Er, I think I'm being followed. I was definitely being followed a half hour ago, but now I'm not so sure."

"You're babbling," Aunt Tillie said, quickly losing interest as she turned back to whatever she was doing. Hey, what was she doing? It seemed to involve a circle and lighted candles. There was a pile of herbs in the middle of the circle. "I hate it when you babble. Get to the point."

So much for family sympathy. "Kelly Sheffield is the arsonist," I gritted out between gasps. "You remember her, right?"

"Yes, she was Lila's little goat minion," Aunt Tillie said, nodding.

"I once cursed her so every time she took a step she passed gas. It just happened to be during that parade when she was on the homecoming court. People thought she was sick or something. It was glorious."

I stilled, surprised. "You did that?"

"She was mean to you and got what she deserved," Aunt Tillie replied, her eyes busy on the ground. She'd moved a series of small rocks into a circle on the other side of the candles. I didn't think I could focus on two things at once given my pain. "But I can't take credit for thinking of the curse. That was all Thistle. She wanted to be even meaner, but I didn't think everyone would be keen on a bear attack in the middle of a parade."

"I didn't know you did that," I said. "I ... thank you."

"No thanks are necessary," Aunt Tillie said. "I fight evil every chance I get. That's what I do."

"Still ... thank you," I said. "She's the arsonist. Viola came to me at the newspaper office and she said she knew who it was, but couldn't remember the name. Her memory isn't great, but it's better than before she died."

"Viola always was a forgetful nuisance," Aunt Tillie said. "She was an annoying human. She's a downright dreadful ghost."

Given how angry I was with Edith at the end, I couldn't help but appreciate the newness of Viola. She may be a pain, but she was entertaining and didn't appear to be overtly hateful or racist. I considered that a step up in the ghost department.

"That's really not the point now," I said, rubbing my hip. "Kelly caught me looking in the trunk of her car. She hit from behind and dumped me in her trunk."

For the first time since I stumbled upon her, Aunt Tillie looked intrigued. "How did you get out of the trunk?"

"I cast a spell and she slowed down when she saw the trunk lid lifting," I answered. "Then I jumped into a ditch and started running in the woods. Landon knows I was running back to The Overlook. The bad news is that we're still a good distance from there. We should head back."

I moved to limp toward the inn, but stopped when Aunt Tillie shook her head.

"You don't want to go to the inn?" I asked, confused.

"I'm in the middle of something here," Aunt Tillie replied. "You should definitely go to the inn, though. You're in pain and your mother will dote on you. Once Landon sees you're alive he's going to turn into Prince Charming and fall all over himself to take care of you. You'll be okay."

Something wasn't right. "But ... ."

"I'm in the middle of something, Bay." Aunt Tillie was snippy and her eyes were busy as they hopped between candles. "You should definitely go to the inn. I'm staying here."

"I just told you Kelly is in the woods," I argued. "I have no idea if she's armed, but that doesn't mean she's not dangerous. If she's following me, she'll come through here."

"Kelly Sheffield is the least of my worries," Aunt Tillie said. "She's never been worth anyone's time, and that doesn't change now because she's suddenly decided to set fires and be a general loser of the first order.

"She's nothing, Bay," she continued. "She's nothing to you and she's definitely nothing to me. Ignore her. She's not a threat. She's ... well ... nothing."

I opened my mouth to argue, but snapped it shut when I heard the sound of approaching footsteps. When I shifted to the right I found Kelly walking through the trees I had scurried through moments before. This time she was armed, a tire iron clenched in her hand and a scowl on her face.

"I'm so glad you think I'm nothing," Kelly said, her anger apparent. "How about I show you just how much damage nothing can do, huh? How does that sound?"

This couldn't be good.

THIRTY-THREE

"Huh. I guess you weren't making up that story about being kidnapped and jumping out of a trunk, were you?"

Aunt Tillie was surprisingly blasé given the circumstances. She kept her hands on her hips as she stared at Kelly, finally making a clucking sound with her tongue and shaking her head.

Kelly didn't appear to appreciate Aunt Tillie's attitude. "What is that noise?"

"What noise?" Aunt Tillie asked, feigning confusion. "I didn't make a noise."

"You just made a noise," Kelly said, waving the tire iron. I had a sneaking suspicion she returned to her car to fetch a weapon before following me. That would explain why I managed to stay ahead of her despite my bum hip.

"I didn't make a noise," Aunt Tillie countered. "You're hearing things."

"No, you clucked like a chicken or something."

"That wasn't me."

"It was you!" Kelly was becoming increasingly shrill, which was making me increasingly uncomfortable.

"Kelly, why are you doing this?" I asked, hoping to appeal to whatever sanity she had left. I was afraid it wasn't much, but I had to try. "I don't understand why you'd set your own booth on fire."

"I did that for the insurance," Kelly replied, not missing a beat. She clearly didn't see any point in denying her actions given the fact that I already saw the lighter fluid in the trunk of her car. "I planned on turning in a big claim for things that weren't even in the fire. I need to make some quick money. But the booth didn't burn nearly as much as I thought it would, and you guys put out the fire, so I couldn't claim as much as I'd hoped."

"But ... why?"

Kelly shot me a "well, duh" look. "Because my husband left me! I need to pay the mortgage somehow."

Now that she mentioned it, I did hear something about that through Hemlock Cove's very busy gossip mill. I wasn't fond of Kelly to begin with, so I couldn't muster up much sympathy for her. That didn't mean I wished bad things upon her.

"You could've gotten a loan," I suggested. "The bank would've probably helped you. If it was just a short-term situation, I'm sure the bank would've tried to help."

"Except they wouldn't," Kelly said. "The bank didn't give a fig about my problems. They said I had bad credit. Like it's my fault they keep sending me credit cards."

That would explain the expensive shoes she always wore. "I ... don't know what to tell you," I said after a beat, keeping my eye on the tire iron as I shifted my weight off my bad hip. "Perhaps you should've reined in your spending."

"Perhaps you should shut your mouth," Kelly shot back. "Everything was going fine until you stuck your nose in my business and opened the trunk. Why did you do that?"

"Because I heard a rumor that you were the arsonist and I didn't believe it," I replied. "I couldn't figure out what your motive would be. Kelly, you know that many people saw exactly what was in your booth that day. If the insurance company is suspicious, they'll ask questions and then you won't get anything because they'll suspect fraud."

"She's not going to get anything from them anyway," Aunt Tillie pointed out, her eyes predatory as they flicked over Kelly. She clearly wasn't worried about our predicament. That was good because I didn't have the energy to fight off Kelly should she attack. Aunt Tillie could do the heavy lifting today. "Instead you're going to go to prison, Kelly. How does that sound as a nice tradeoff?"

I was happy to let Aunt Tillie do the major work in this takedown, but I had to wonder if poking the angry pink bear in her custom-made boots was a good idea. "Aunt Tillie ... ."

Aunt Tillie ignored me. "I get that you're not smart enough to realize how the world works and that you thought setting your own booth on fire and collecting a big payout from the insurance company would be good, but why did you go after Margaret? What was in it for you?"

That was a really good question. If my hip didn't hurt so much, I would've asked it myself. No, really.

"I went after Margaret because she told everyone at the senior center that I was living beyond my means, and I was embarrassed," Kelly said. "My mother asked me if what Margaret said was true. I lied, of course, but then I figured I might as well make Margaret pay. I thought if there were two fires the insurance company would pay out quicker."

Kelly sounded like a petulant teenager who felt as if the world owed her something. There was a certain entitlement in her voice. That was probably why I sensed the arsonist was younger. Kelly's emotions had somehow stunted during the development process. She'd never become a true adult.

"How did Mrs. Little even know about your situation?" I asked.

"I tried to buy my mother a unicorn for her birthday and my credit card was declined," Kelly supplied. "Margaret cut it up – she actually cut it up, can you believe that? – right in front of me. People don't cut up credit cards any longer. The company didn't tell her to do it. She did it on her own."

Sadly, that sounded exactly like the Mrs. Little I knew and ... well, is "loathed" too strong of a term? "That sucks, Kelly, but there were a lot of other ways to deal with your problem," I said, keeping my voice even. "You could've sold some of your shoes to pay your mortgage. You know, had a garage sale or something."

"I am not the type of woman who shops at a garage sale, let alone holds one of her own," Kelly snapped, horrified. "That's something poor people do because they have no other options."

Kelly clearly didn't have an understanding of her financial situation.

"You could get a job," Aunt Tillie suggested. Her voice was far snottier than mine. "That's what most people do when they need money."

"I have a job," Kelly said. "I sell love potions at festivals."

"Fake love potions," I muttered, earning a hateful glare from Kelly. What? That's an important distinction.

"That's still not a job," Aunt Tillie said. "A job is something you work at forty hours a week. Hemlock Cove may have a lot of festivals, but selling fake love potions at them is hardly full-time work."

"Oh, that's rich coming from you," Kelly snapped. "You don't do anything but cause trouble, from what I can tell. How do you make a living?"

"She's in her eighties," I argued. "She worked for a long time. She worked hard to make sure my mother and aunts were taken care of after my grandmother died. She's retired now."

"Thank you for taking up for me, Bay, but I'm hardly retired," Aunt Tillie scoffed. "I still make a fine living with my … side endeavors."

I pressed the heel of my hand to my forehead and gritted my teeth. Great. Now the conversation was going to meander into a direction that would benefit no one.

"What side endeavors?" Kelly seemed legitimately curious. "Is it something I could do to make extra money?"

"She's talking about her wine business," I supplied, leaving out the pot portion of Aunt Tillie's income. No one needed to discuss that now. "She's been honing her craft for a very long time. I'm sure she'd like an apprentice, though."

"I never thought of making wine," Kelly mused, scratching her cheek. "I'll bet the profit margin on that is high. What do you make a month?"

I turned my attention to Aunt Tillie. "What do you make a month?" She'd never owned up to any hard numbers as far as I knew. It was a family curiosity, though. She seemed to have plenty of money for leggings and combat helmets ... and a chainsaw no one knew about, for that matter. I still hadn't heard what she did with that chainsaw, by the way. Did I really want to know? Probably not. That would only increase my heartburn.

"That's hardly important." Aunt Tillie brushed away my question. "The point is that I work. I work hard even though I'm older. Notice I said older, not old, Bay. You seem to have missed the part where you need to work and make money so you can buy things. You simply want to buy things."

"That's the fun part," Kelly said, her face twisting. "Who wants to work? Working is for people who aren't pretty ... like Bay."

"Hey!" I had no idea why I was so offended. It's not as if Kelly's approval was important to me – and she was wielding a tire iron as a weapon, for crying out loud – but I can't stand that high school mentality. It's irksome.

"It's true," Kelly said. "You have to work because you can't find a man to take care of you. That FBI agent you're running around with clearly doesn't want to marry you and supply a good household to share. You have no choice."

"You have no idea what you're talking about," I seethed. "I don't want Landon to take care of me. I want to be self-sufficient. I'm glad I have Landon in my life, but I don't expect him to spend all of his money on me."

"Then you're doing it wrong," Kelly said. "He's hot, though. Once you're gone, do you think he'll keep coming around town? I'd like to nurse his broken heart. He'll certainly buy me what I want."

I narrowed my eyes. "Landon wouldn't touch you with Aunt Tillie's chainsaw."

"She's not wrong," Aunt Tillie interjected, her eyes narrowing as she focused on one of the candles in the circle. She seemed suddenly agitated as the smoke on the two nearest candles turned from black to purple. *What the heck is she doing out here?* "Landon loves only Bay. He'd never fall for the likes of you."

"Thank you, Aunt Tillie," I sniffed, brushing the dirt off the arm of my shirt. "I appreciate you saying that."

"She's only saying that to make you feel better," Kelly said. "She knows as well as I do that I'm prettier than you."

"You're no prettier than my hemorrhoids on treatment day," Aunt Tillie said. "Bay is beautiful inside and out, which is exactly why Landon loves her."

That was possibly the nicest thing Aunt Tillie had ever said about me. I was instantly suspicious. "Why do you keep staring at the candles?"

Aunt Tillie ignored my question. "Your problem is that you don't live in the real world, Kelly," she said. "You don't think you should have to work or pay for anything. You think that people should fall at your feet even though you have the personality of an inbred hooker in the middle of a train pull."

My mouth dropped open at the imagery. "How do you even know what that is?"

"We have HBO," Aunt Tillie replied simply. "Those shows have a lot of sex. I Google anything I don't understand."

Ugh. I'd hate to see her search history. "That's inappropriate."

"Does that really matter now?" Kelly snapped, annoyed. "Try focusing on me instead of each other. If you can do that, I would really appreciate it."

Aunt Tillie made an exaggerated face. "That's also your problem," she said. "You think the world revolves around you."

Kelly's face was blank. "It does."

"No, it doesn't," Aunt Tillie shot back. "The world revolves around the sun and we're part of the world. No one person – not even me – is the center of anything."

Oh, that must've been hard for her to admit. "You're growing as a person," I said, looking her up and down appraisingly. "I didn't know that was possible."

"Anything is possible, Bay," Aunt Tillie said, her eyes going wide as another two candles started passing purple smoke. "Speaking of that ...."

As if sensing something, Kelly risked a glance over her shoulder and frowned when she caught sight of the building clouds. "I didn't know it was supposed to storm."

"Did you do that?" I hissed, shifting closer to Aunt Tillie even though my hip vehemently protested the movement. I should've realized something big was happening when I found her in the ritual clearing. I was too caught up in outrunning Kelly to focus on exactly what she was doing, and I had a feeling that would turn out to be a terrible mistake. "What's happening?"

"You need to calm yourself," Aunt Tillie said, gripping my arm. "This isn't my fault. Remember that."

Remember that? "What isn't your fault?"

Aunt Tillie pressed her eyes shut as the sky, which was sunny and clear when I left Hemlock Cove in the trunk of a car, darkened to midnight hues. Oh, this couldn't be good.

"What is this?" Kelly asked, confused. "Is it a tornado? That would be great, by the way. Everyone will think the two of you died in the storm."

Kelly's simple statement drew my gaze back to the tire iron. She gripped it tightly, and her eyes had turned from annoyed to malevolent. She was ready to make her move. That appeared to be only one of our problems.

"Aunt Tillie, what did you do?" I asked, frustrated. I was frightened of the tire iron – mostly because I didn't think I could move fast enough to protect Aunt Tillie – but I was even more terrified of the storm. "Did you draw a circle and call the tanker ghosts here? Why are you doing this on your own? We were supposed to do it after dark."

"Yes, but I have a date with Kenneth after dark and I don't want to change my plans," Aunt Tillie said, crossing her arms over her chest. "I thought I could handle things on my own and ease everyone's burden."

I didn't believe that for a second. "Why really?"

"I don't want my date with Kenneth to consist of babysitting you lot," Aunt Tillie answered. "We want to have a nice picnic ... alone. I can't deal with the junior witch squad when I want to be the senior witch and go all the way."

"Omigod!" I was disgusted. "Did you just say what I think you said?"

"Stop being a prude, Bay," Aunt Tillie admonished. "It's very unattractive."

"I have no idea what you two are babbling about, but I love watching you melt down," Kelly interjected. "I don't want to be here when the big storm hits, so we're going to have to move this along. I'm sorry." She took a step in our direction, raising the tire iron. "If you have any last words for one another ... ."

"I have a last word for you." A warm male voice, one I recognized from every good dream I'd experienced over the past year, washed over the clearing and I jerked my head to the side as Chief Terry and Landon walked through the underbrush, both of them armed. "I believe the word is 'freeze.'"

The color washed from Kelly's face when she realized we weren't alone. "I ... what are you doing here?"

"I was about to ask you that question," Landon replied, his eyes focused on Kelly even as he worked his way toward me. "What are you doing on private property with a tire iron?"

"You don't understand," Kelly said, recovering from momentary shock. "They're trying to kill me. I'm simply trying to protect myself."

"Really?" Landon arched a dubious eyebrow. "Then why did you hit my girlfriend from behind, dump her in your trunk and stalk her through the woods?"

Kelly was beside herself. "I didn't do any of those things."

"You did all of those things!" Landon roared, the wind picking that moment to speed up as the final candle's smoke turned purple. "She texted me while it was happening. You took her. You were going to hurt her."

Kelly shot me a dirty look. "You texted him? That hardly seems fair."

And we were back to petulance. I couldn't focus on Kelly, given the purple smoke. I knew exactly what was about to happen. I read about it in one of Aunt Tillie's books when I was a teenager.

"You set a spirit snare, didn't you?"

Aunt Tillie shrugged. "I thought it was the best way to go," she replied. "Drawing the ghosts here and forcing them over through a magically created door is the only way I know to ensure that Annie will remain safe."

"What's a spirit snare?" Chief Terry asked, his eyes widening as the wind whipped around us. "Seriously, what is going on here? It was completely clear in town."

"Things are about to get ugly," I said, tentatively reaching out to grab Landon's hand. "We need to get out of the circle."

Landon didn't immediately respond to my words because he was focused on Kelly. His anger was palpable.

"Landon!"

"Kelly Sheffield, you're under arrest for arson, attempted murder, kidnapping ... and whatever other charges I can come up with when it's not storming," Landon said, holstering his gun and reaching for his cuffs. "Do you understand what I'm saying?"

Kelly was incredulous. "You can't arrest me. I'm ... pretty."

Landon wasn't swayed by her argument. "You're ugly," he said. "Only an ugly person would do any of the things you've done. Drop the tire iron and turn around."

I could hear a keening on the wind and when I turned to my right I saw glowing eyes – at least ten sets of them – flying toward us fast. The spirits were being drawn to the snare. We were out of time.

"Landon!" I slapped Landon's hand away when he moved to grab Kelly's arm. He widened his eyes, surprised, but I didn't give him a chance to respond. Instead I used my injured hip – pain screeching through me – and pushed him to the other side of the circle.

I shoved so hard Landon couldn't control both of our flailing bodies, and he tumbled to the ground. I grunted as I landed on top of him, the wind causing my hair to whip in a hundred different directions. Landon instinctively wrapped his arms around me.

"What is this, Bay?" He had to yell to be heard over the wind.

"Aunt Tillie decided to deal with the tanker ghosts herself," I said, pressing my forehead into the hollow of his neck.

"I don't know what that means."

The ghosts hit the circle with screams of protest, and I watched as Chief Terry shoved Aunt Tillie to the ground next to us. He didn't look panicked, his cop training kicking in, but he didn't look happy either.

"How long will this last?" Chief Terry shouted, using his arm to protect Aunt Tillie's head.

"Until they're all gone," I said, cringing when I heard Kelly scream. We'd left her in the circle. I knew doing that would probably end badly for her, but Landon was more important.

Landon pressed my face to his chest and wrapped his arms protectively around my shoulders as he stared at the whirling shapes in the circle. They were trapped and Kelly was somewhere in the middle ... her screams growing weaker.

"What happens now?" Landon asked.

"The spirits are either forced to move on or – if they fight the process – they remain until they burn away."

"That doesn't sound pleasant."

"It's not."

I forced my eyes from the protective shield Landon made with his arm and focused on Kelly's terrified eyes. The spirits swirled around her rigid body as her mouth opened in a scream that didn't quite vocalize. I widened my eyes when I saw a door appear in the middle of the circle. It looked like an ordinary house door, and when it opened I saw Edith standing in front of me.

She looked different, younger somehow. The severe bun was gone, and even though she wore one of the pencil skirts she favored, she somehow looked lighter when she locked gazes with me.

"It's almost over," Edith said, her eyes kind as traumatized ghosts began disappearing through the door. Only the captain and two cohorts – I was guessing they were the strongest ghosts in the bunch – remained. "You'll be safe."

"How do you know that?"

"Who are you talking to?" Landon asked, glancing around.

"It's Edith. Don't you see her?"

Landon shook his head. I guess that answered the question about whether or not he could see spirits on a regular basis. The mirrors tricked his mind and because the ghosts were strong they forced a situation that was unlikely to occur again.

"What is she doing?" Landon asked. "Is she trying to help the ghosts?"

"No. She's helping us. She's serving as a ferryman – er, ferrywoman."

"I don't know what that means."

"She's helping them cross over," I said, tears sliding down my cheeks. "She's doing the right thing."

Landon pressed a kiss to my forehead as he rolled on top of me, using his body to shield mine as he tried to protect me from the screams and vicious wind. "How long?"

"I'm not sure," I answered, shivering as Kelly managed one more scream before falling eerily silent. "Not long now."

"Bay, you were right," Edith called out as she reached for the captain. "I'm sorry for ... everything."

The apology warmed me. Perhaps she'd learned something after all. "Have a good ... afterlife."

Edith smiled as she wrestled the captain through the door. He fought her efforts, expending a huge wave of energy as she pushed him through the door. The energy wave rocketed through me, causing me to see everything I'd missed during the short flashes.

Then the door slammed shut and the storm dissipated.

It was over almost as soon as it had begun.

THIRTY-FOUR

"Bay?"

I could feel Landon shift on top of me as I attempted to put the cascading images into some form of context. When I finally opened my eyes after what felt like forever – I had no idea how much time had really passed – I found Landon's eyes focused on me as he cupped the back of my head.

"Bay?" His voice was barely a whisper.

"I'm okay." I forced a smile for his benefit because I knew he needed it. "I know what happened."

"Well, that's great," Landon said, his hands shaking as he pulled me in for a tight hug and buried his face in the hollow of my neck. "I don't really care about that right now, though. I just want you to be okay."

"I'm okay." I said the words even though I knew they sounded lame. "Landon?"

"Hmm."

"You're crushing me."

"Oh, sorry." Landon rolled so he wasn't on top of me but he didn't move his hands from my waist as he rubbed my back. We remained in that spot as Chief Terry checked on Kelly – she was dead in the circle – and Aunt Tillie pursed her lips and stared at the sky.

"We need to come up with a story here," Chief Terry said, moving closer to us and crouching beside me. He looked concerned as he pressed a hand to my forehead. I was cold and clammy, my hands shaking as Landon covered them with his own. "I don't think I can explain that Kelly Sheffield was killed by ghosts."

"How did she die?" I asked, my voice cracking.

"We won't know until the autopsy," Landon said, smoothing my hair.

"I was asking Aunt Tillie," I supplied, leaning my head against his chest and staring at my great-aunt. She didn't seem distressed by the afternoon's events. "When they conduct the autopsy, what will show?"

Aunt Tillie shrugged as she straightened. "My guess is that she died of fear, but that probably manifested as a heart attack or something. The autopsy will either turn up inconclusive or as natural causes."

"How can you know that?" Landon challenged. "Have you seen this before?"

Aunt Tillie shook her head. "No, but what else could it be?"

"I have no idea," Chief Terry answered. "That's why we need a story. Noah will be here any second, so get it together."

I realized he was putting himself on the line for me. He was trying to cover up what happened here because he didn't want any of the blowback landing on me. It made me love him even more, if that was even possible. It also made me feel guilty.

"You can't lie to Noah on my behalf," I protested. "You have to blame this – whatever it is – on me. That's the only way the two of you will be safe."

"Don't even try being a martyr," Landon chided, struggling to his feet. He slipped his arms around my legs and hoisted me up so he could carry me. "We'll tell Noah most of the truth, but we're fudging the end. It's not just for your sake. It's for ours, as well. No one is going to believe the truth, and the truth would open us up to scrutiny we might not be able to shoulder."

He had a point. Still .... "Landon, I don't want you to lie for me."

"Bay, I will do whatever it takes to protect you," Landon said. "Aunt Tillie, pick up all of these candles. They're not going to be part of the story. We're going to say that Kelly chased Bay through the woods – which really happened – and then you ran into each other here.

"We're going to say you were convening with nature. You're quirky, so people will believe it," he continued. "That's when Kelly found and threatened you. That's when a surprise storm blew through. You didn't actually see what happened to her because you were covering your faces."

"We showed up in the middle of the storm and did our best to protect you," Chief Terry added. "The story should be enough coming from us, but we'll play it by ear. Noah is a little gung-ho for my taste."

"When the storm passed, we found Kelly dead," Landon added, resting his forehead against my temple. "That's the story. All the witch and ghost stuff didn't happen. Do you understand?"

I mutely nodded.

"I wasn't talking to you, sweetie," Landon said, turning his pointed gaze to Aunt Tillie. "Do you understand?"

If Aunt Tillie was bothered by Landon's tone, she didn't show it. "Of course I understand," she said, bending over to grab her candles and giving Landon an aerial dragon show he wouldn't soon forget. "I'm not an idiot."

"You're definitely not an idiot," Landon grumbled. "You might just be the death of me, though."

Aunt Tillie's smile was impish. "What a way to go, huh?"

LANDON FOUND me sitting under a blanket in the library after dinner. We were separated most of the afternoon because Noah arrived with a bevy of questions and bluster. He insisted he be put in charge of the investigation thanks to Landon and Chief Terry's close ties to my family. Landon and Chief Terry didn't put up a fight. Either they were too tired or worried about him causing a fuss and drawing more attention than necessary to the incident. I couldn't be sure which.

By the time everything calmed down, though, Noah was satisfied that Kelly somehow died in the storm, and we were free to carry on with our lives. Er, well, at least for the time being.

"How are you feeling?" Landon asked, lifting my legs so he could slide under the blanket with me. He rested my knees over his lap and then slid his hand behind my back and tugged me closer. "Are you sure we shouldn't take you to emergency care to have your hip looked at?"

"It's just sore," I replied, weariness overtaking me as I leaned into him. "I'm sure I will be in pain tomorrow, but it will get better. You can act as my nurse until I'm a hundred percent again."

Landon snorted. "I will gladly take on that job," he said. "We should probably talk about you checking out Kelly Sheffield's trunk alone."

"How was I supposed to know she would do that in broad daylight?" I protested, my voice climbing an octave.

Landon smirked. "You weren't, but you still should've called me to be on the safe side. I have no intention of giving you grief about it because you're safe and here. I'm still surprised she grabbed you in the middle of the day like that."

"I think she felt like she could do it because she was such a mainstay around town that no one really saw her," I said. "I mean ... that's what I believe anyway. She kind of faded into the background, if you know what I mean."

"I don't." Landon tucked a strand of hair behind my ear. "I want you to tell me, though. I want to hear what you think."

I couldn't help but smile at his earnest expression. "Are you going to dote on me like this all night?"

Landon returned the smile. "Forever."

"Well, it's something Kelly said," I explained. "She kept demanding we focus on her, give all of our attention to her, and she harped on the fact that she was pretty. It was if she needed us to acknowledge that.

"No one seemed to notice her, though," I continued. "She was here, yet no one realized it. I think it had something to do with the fact that she refused to let go of her high school mentality. She thought her popularity while younger would give her a good life ... and it didn't work out that way.

"She talked as if we were still in high school and was unbelievably entitled," I continued. "I think that's why I had that niggling feeling about the arsonist being younger. She couldn't get out of high school, and that's where I recognized her aura from."

"I guess that means you technically beat Noah," Landon teased.

"I guess, but that's not important given everything that happened." I heard Annie giggling. She raced past the library door, Marcus on her heels, and she squealed when he caught her and hauled her up in his arms. "Annie seems better."

"The ghosts are gone," Landon said. "You never got a chance to tell me what happened. Noah showed up too soon."

I rubbed my cheek as I tried to escape his gaze. "I ... ."

"Bay, you can tell me anything," Landon said. "You can tell me as much or as little as you're comfortable with. If you're still processing ... ."

"I'm not still processing," I said. "It's not that. It's just ... it was all for greed. The Gray Harker crew was killed for greed."

"Were they carrying something?"

I shrugged. "Kind of," I replied. "The owner, who is long since dead, got an insurance payout for the crew and contents while the ship was missing. He was there the night they were attacked, though.

"He brought a bunch of men with him, and they killed the entire crew so they could get money," I continued. "It happened fast ... and there was a lot of screaming. It wasn't some tragedy on the lake ... or murder for love. He killed them and then had the other men take the bodies off the tanker in another boat. I'm not sure where their bodies were disposed of, but they were taken from the tanker and ... well ... then I guess they passed into legend. It was all for money."

"I know that upsets you, Bay, but we kind of figured that was the case," he reminded me. "There were only so many scenarios that made sense. Did you see what happened to all of them? Did the ghosts show you as they were ... being forced over?"

"They showed me." My voice hitched. "I don't want to talk about that. It was ... worse than any horror movie I've ever seen."

"You don't have to talk about it," Landon said, pulling me in for a hug.

We sat like that for a few minutes, comfortable in our silence and solitude. We didn't pull apart until Annie appeared in the doorway. I forced a smile for her benefit – it wasn't her fault that everything happened the way it did – and fixed her with an inquisitive look.

"Are you sad, Bay?" Annie asked, genuinely curious.

I shook my head. "I'm just tired."

"She's going to bed soon," Landon explained. "She needs her rest. I think you probably need your rest, too, don't you?"

Annie didn't look impressed with the suggestion. "Marcus is here. I'm not going to bed."

Landon smirked. "I guess that makes sense," he said. "You know you can sleep easy tonight, though, right? The ghosts are gone."

Annie nodded. "I felt them leave," she said after a beat. "They didn't want to go. For a second or something ... I think I felt happiness."

I understood what she was saying. I felt the same thing when I caught a glimpse of Edith opening the door. The happiness was overwhelming thanks to the fact that it came on the heels of such oppressive grief. "They're in a better place," I said, narrowing my eyes when I saw she was holding something. "What's that?"

Annie glanced at her hands and smiled. "I almost forgot," she said, stepping forward. "Aunt Tillie gave me a dreamcatcher to protect my dreams. She said it's powerful magic."

"It is," I said, smiling. "That looks like a good one."

"Oh, this isn't mine," Annie said. "Mine is in the dining room. This one is yours."

She handed the dreamcatcher to me, the smile never faltering from her lips. I was surprised by the gesture. "Aunt Tillie told you to give this to me?"

Annie bobbed her head. "She said that you'll need it to keep out the dreams tonight. She says it's charged and everything, and not to say she never gave you anything."

"We'll take it," Landon said, studying the catcher. "I'm going to tie this to Bay's head to make sure she's protected."

Annie giggled at the visual. "That would be silly," she admonished. "You're supposed to hang it over Bay's pillow."

"I'll do that, too," Landon said. "Thank you, Annie. This is a wonderful gift."

"That's just the way we do things in this house," Annie said, her expression serene. "We all give each other wonderful gifts."

"That's true," I said, warmth washing over me. Annie was so much more at ease that I didn't regret one moment of the day's angst. "We do love our gifts in this house, don't we?"

Annie nodded happily. "Sam has a big gift for Clove, too. Actually, it's kind of a small gift."

"What do you mean?"

"He has a big ring with a white stone," Annie said, lowering her voice.

"Why are you whispering?" Landon asked, glancing around.

"Because I told Aunt Tillie what I saw and she told me this was one of those times I shouldn't open my mouth," Annie answered. "She said those times are rare, but they happen."

"A big ring with a white stone?" I asked, leaning forward. That could only mean one thing. Apparently the proposal Maggie let slip was happening soon. "When did you see that?"

"I saw Sam in the lobby looking at it. He was talking to himself," Annie replied. "I told Aunt Tillie, and she said I shouldn't tell anyone."

"Well, good job," Landon teased, resting his hand on her head as he glanced at me. "I guess we both know what that means, huh?"

"It means Clove is going to finally get everything that she wants."

"What about you?" Landon asked. "What do you want?"

I smiled as I locked gazes with him. "I already have what I want."

"No, you have a beginning to what you want," Landon clarified. "You're going to get everything before it's all said and done. I promise."

I grinned as I tightened my grip on his hand. "What do you want?"

"Bacon and you."

"What else?"

"I'm a simple man, Bay," Landon said. "I really only want bacon and you."

"I think I can make both of those things happen," I teased.

"I know you can." Landon smacked a loud kiss against my mouth as Annie made disgusted gagging sounds. Finally he forced his attention from me to her. "If you don't like it, there's the door."

"Kissing is gross," Annie said, sliding her stocking-clad feet along the hardwood floor as she headed for the hallway. "You're gross for doing it all of the time."

"There's a simple solution to that," Landon said. "You don't have to watch."

"Oh, I'm done watching," Annie said, the corners of her mouth tipping up into a smile I recognized. "You're both on my list, though."

And just like that, another junior witch was born.

Printed in Great Britain
by Amazon